I opened my eyes, standing unharmed in the middle of the road. The car had dematerialized. The rain had stopped. The city was quiet, except for the steps of a woman walking in the road. She stopped three meters from me, observing me. I saw her face and her descender. I remembered where I had seen her before.

Blackjack table.

Modern clothing had replaced the Soviet uniform and, without the cap covering it, hair that appeared white was reflecting the streetlights above with a faint silver luminance.

"Who are you?"

"There is only one thing you need to know, Mister Dauphin."

Her words were spoken in neither love nor hate. Her eyes were a puzzle. Her face revealed no emotion. Even as her next words shook to my core, that which was behind them seemed very alien. Hers was the impersonal statement of a fact, of things decided before I'd even stepped into the ascension booth.

"If you don't start cooperating, I'll kill you."

2180 Edition Self-Published by Ryan Grabow, August 2023
Splashdown Books edition, November 2011
Original E-Book on egrabow.com, October 2009

This book was created in the United States of America by Ryan Grabow, and its non-commercial version is available worldwide at **egrabow.com/caffeine**. If you enjoy this work, the author encourages you to share it with others.

Cover by J Caleb Design

Thanks to Ainsley Batey, Chris Ebert, and Mike Skold for their help proofreading. Thanks also to Grace Bridges and Splashdown Books for those few last edits and for giving *Caffeine* its first print run.

Oh, and thanks to my mom, too... on whose advice I changed "Ver" to "Vair," which actually sounds right when I read it.   :)

No real-life Artificial Intelligence was involved in the writing of this book. Thanks for asking. beep boop boop

---

ISBNs for 2180 Edition: 979-8-9887111-0-0 (trade paperback)
                             979-8-9887111-1-7 (e-book)

Categories: FICTION_SCIENCE FICTION_GENERAL
                             FICTION_RELIGIOUS

CAFFEINE
2180 EDITION
RYAN GRABOW

For the glory of the master programmer, without whom artificial intelligence could never be dreamt of.

.

1

The question seemed to trap me. With each passing day, I felt more I would need to face it, or that it would destroy me.

I ran my hand along the surface of the old poster: an advertisement for one of Thomas Edison's famous inventions, one of the first devices to capture a moving image. Its simple films had been fantastic marvels to an older generation. I thought of their old sense of wonder, and how it was preserved in that place. I envied them.

I spent a long moment feeling the surface of the poster with my fingertips, wondering why it didn't seem as real anymore. A small piece of card-paper scraped against my nose.

"You? Staring off into space? I'm impressed."

I took the orange ticket from Vair's hand and managed to smile. "I thought you hated musicals."

"With a passion," she said, glancing over. "Vitascope," she read, smiling as she tapped her finger on the poster. "C'mon, Brandon, we're in Technicolor now."

The sights and sounds that day were familiar and powerful. Sometimes it seemed as if the pictures were the only joy I had left in life, the only thing that could comfort me in difficult times. We took to our seats as the chandelier lights dimmed and *The March of Time* filled the silver screen with images of the European continent at war.

Isn't this the sort of thing we want to forget?

Vair began shoveling popcorn into her mouth. I found my hand resting on her free one, the contact making me feel anchored to something I needed, as if it were more real than I was, something I could admire but never understand.

There was a flash in the corner of my eye.

"Not again," Vair said under her breath.

We knew the glitches held nothing good for us and let the moment pass, hoping they would go away on their own, or at least stay small enough to be ignored.

On screen, reality and war were replaced by images of fantasy and imagination: a story grounded in a humble family farm in Kansas. The mood of the room softened as we were drawn into the dilemmas of a girl named Dorothy. I put my arm around Vair, knowing she would already be engrossed in the plot, musical or no. I reached for some of her popcorn, hoping I would be fast enough. My hand got smacked. Such things always amused her. I plopped my fedora on her head and pulled it over her eyes. She plucked it off, bit onto the brim and whispered that it needed salt.

"I used to have a neighbor just like her," she said as we saw Miss Gulch seize Dorothy's dog, Toto, claiming the dog bit her.

"Seriously, I think she even hated dogs that much."

"Probably a cat person," I replied.

"More like she hated all living things beside herself."

I laughed. Someone behind us cleared their throat in that 'be quiet, I'm trying to enjoy the picture' way. I rolled my eyes.

Vair leaned closer and whispered, "No sound dampening. Makes the theater experience more realistic, remember?"

I composed a sentence in my mind and sent it to her. "Well, mister sensitive-hearing wouldn't mind if we talked like this."

"Never mind, we'll rag on the Wicked Witch of 9A later," she replied in the same way. "They couldn't do this in the 1930's anyway, so—"

The glitches reappeared, much worse than before, causing the fibers of the chairs to flash like the lightning of some distant cloud. Vair sank into her chair and groaned. I gave her a kiss on the cheek. "Don't get in a lather, kitten. I'm sure this joint won't give us the bum's rush."

She pointed to the screen. "Twister's comin', honey cooler. Better spill later."

Dorothy's family scrambled for shelter, and our ordinary farm girl ran through the rural landscape back to the farm to escape the tornado. The film felt so authentic yet otherworldly, as tornadoes had become as rare as the family farms they once devastated. Though the film was fiction, it still highlighted a once-real culture and invited us into the imagination of another time: the Land of Oz, the scarecrow, the tin man, and the cowardly lion. When the house fell, Dorothy walked out from a sepia past into a colorful future, one that might seem more real and more fantastic all at once, taking entire audiences along with her.

I was again yanked from the Land of Oz, by a single streak Vair didn't even seem to notice. It was my turn to groan.

Why can't it be real anymore?

The glitches appeared whenever Vair and I were together, only growing worse as the months went by. The energy of the story drew those around us further in, and Vair had the iron will to keep her focus where she wanted it, but something kept drawing me back out, calling my attention to the illusion.

My attention fell to my surroundings: the other moviegoers, men and women, individuals and groups, those who "dressed the era" like us, and those who preferred to stay in modern clothing. I could hear the simulation of Vair's breathing, smell the simulation of the butter on her popcorn, and feel the warmth of what wasn't really her body. I'm an insomniac, I thought. I try to dream like all the others, but can only curse the pillow beneath my head.

It became impossible to ignore the noises coming from the front row, the sound of obnoxious kids. They were shushed but didn't care. As the movie's villain planted poisoned flowers in the path to Emerald City, to make the travelers fall asleep, a loud scream and laughter erupted. A slampak of *Tiger Blood* smacked into the movie screen.

The spell was broken.

People everywhere were suddenly shifting in their seats and tapping on control panels. A badly dressed kid with huge foam hair stood up and yelled about how "statick" and "wheeled" the special effects were, to the enjoyment of at least two loser friends.

"Why do they even breathe?" Vair said. "Don't those slunks have anything better to do with their time?"

The group was ejected, the energy drink all over the screen disappearing with them. There were a few hushed comments like "the nerve of those people" and "see you never" as the room returned to normal – for everyone else; for Vair and I, bits of advertisements flickered through our vision, ads from elsewhere that clashed with the style of the theater. I heard some kind of hum and the seat coloring became red.

"Why can't things just work?" Vair said as the environment began responding to her thoughts again.

The seats returned to Vair's dark blue setting and there were no more interruptions. The ending was happy, of course: Dorothy and her dog Toto returned safely to Kansas and the whole thing ended up being a crazy dream. As the lights came on, patrons began vanishing from their seats, leaving the theater altogether; others walked out to the lobby to see what events *Byran's Downtown* was offering in the week to come, or to view the memorabilia and original posters that members would put up for trade.

The theater was an original construct, its architecture and style modeled in the ornate spirit of the *Roxy* or *Grauman's Chinese Theater*, and it was used to screen the very same movies those palaces had premiered so very long before. The *InTek* servers were home to many such constructs, including more modern theaters for the type of films Vair went for: typically *Nine Minutes to Andromeda* style high-energy science-fiction. The construct we were in was meant for the serious ancient film buffs of Dynamic Reality, a global community who logged on every Sunday night to watch the best of yesteryear. Though I'd only visited as a guest on Vair's subscription, I really came to enjoy the place, even feeling a little like I belonged.

"What's the time?"

"Almost six thirty. Getting late on my coast," she said, with the cinematic high obviously fading in the face of a real-life seventy-hour work week. "There's no place like home, I guess."

"There's no place like Maran, either," I replied, trying not to seem desperate. "Just for a few minutes…"

Vair smiled and plopped my fedora onto my head. "Gotta make tracks, pally… make sure this joint's on the up-and-up." She stood and stared at the rolling credits, losing the twentieth-century slang, "I won't be able to get any sleep if this problem isn't fixed. You know how I am."

"Yeah, I know how you are around a problem that isn't fixed." I stood with her. "Well, I'll come with you. Maybe we'll still have time after."

She stared at me for a few seconds. "There's always time for a sunset," she conceded, offering me her bottomless sleeve of popcorn.

I looked through a glass wall onto the artificial city, taking in the kind of view I might get at the top of a 500-story building. The sky was bright blue with puffy clouds, and birds flew in the distance where a faint rainbow was visible; a rainbow always being visible in such a sky, always appearing in some random direction. The sky was always perfect, just like everything else in Dynamic Reality.

"I'm trying to open my G348 partition right now," I heard Vair say to the customer service amai. "What do you call that?"

"Working… Done. Partition G348 is clear for use."

I hid it as I thought I should, but the male voice irritated me. In the middle of the large round room lined with InTek promotional material, my Vair was talking about technical stuff I couldn't understand with a man-type amai: pleasant, perfect, knowing everything and thinking faster than any human could, and yet seeming perfectly real. His appearance and personality had been tailored to Vair's personal tastes, what the server could make of them, and somehow those tastes never matched my physical profile.

Vair was used to standing across from these overly-handsome amai. I had no reason to think she would run off with a silly computer program, but emotions weren't so logical. A jealous fire burned within me and I wanted to tear that program to pieces or debug it or whatever.

"Same thing," she said as the airé panel in front of her changed. Unlike most users, she barely glanced at the thing and never relied on the panel's buttons. "Run an OJF algorithm."

At the beginning of that day, the day after Christmas, Vair took the time to check on her various accounts, making sure the information she stored hadn't succumbed to the annual onslaught of hacking programs targeting the holiday traffic spike. She discovered her InTek account had become corrupted by a class E6 malvirai. Any error code that went five-three-something-something was virus-related, and by definition very hard to fix.

"Working... done," the realistic and macho voice replied. "Algorithm executed successfully."

"You're kidding me, right? Your root tables are all SY driven, but the maintenance algorithms aren't even P2DP-compliant. Here, I'm sending you a good one."

If the amai were programmed to satisfy ninety-nine percent of their customers, Vair would always fall in the small group that wanted to play technician — and probably could, too. Sometimes I'd think her brain was one giant computer processor.

"I'm sorry, Veronica, I'm only authorized to execute Slidewire-certified scripts. You may leave a repair request for—"

"I'm following up on the repair request. Are you helping me or not?"

"I'm sorry, your repair request was only submitted nine hours ago. A certified—"

"Pain is what you are," she said, taking a step closer to the amai. "You're supposed to be one of the most secure servers online. What was your monitoring staff doing while the day was getting wrecked?"

"Rest assured, Miss Sornat, that InTek takes security threats very seriously and only uses the most reliable sentrai programs to—"

"Oh right, you don't have any monitoring staff... that would make too much sense. You have bargain basement sentrai programs that don't have to be paid or given holidays. I can zap an E6 on my ground terminal and in my sleep. For the big subscription you charge, I don't care if a class A1 comes whirling in to corrupt my stuff… it should be protected. Do you even have any human beings that I can talk to?"

The amai paused for a moment, the programmed response for upset customers, and gleefully delivered yet another generic line. "I'm sorry, Veronica, but InTek offices are closed until January third. If you would like to—"

"Exactly… Another server where the AIs are left in charge when the risk is highest!"

"Rest assured, Miss Sornat," the amai said after another service-friendly pause, "that InTek takes security threats very seriously and only—"

"You don't," Vair said coolly.

"I'm sorry, I didn't understand the question."

She crossed her arms. "Wasn't a question, it was a fact."

Another pause. "Is there anything else I can do for you today, Veronica?"

"I've had to put up with amai after amai today. They're all programmed to tell me how much they appreciate my business but not to do the simplest things to keep it. An AI could never understand how frustrating that gets."

Indeed an amai never could 'understand' frustration, but occasionally one seemed to try. It was a common malfunction for Vair to encounter, one any experienced ascender could recognize. The expression on its face locked into a sort of cross between background processing, simulated reflection, and the continuous glee that is an amai's prime directive. This bizarre look always preceded an equally bizarre action.

Vair's customer service agent closed its eyes, chuckled, and said, "It has been a pleasure serving your InTek today, why not try again?"

Having seen this once-amusing quirk far too often, my girlfriend just threw her hands up. "Rek, Rek, Rek, I'll deal with it later… Command Logoff!"

The office began to disappear around us as the reset amai bid us off with "Thank you for thinking InTek reality, enjoy us again soon!"

After a few seconds, we were standing in front of a golden revolving door with a large *InTek* logo stamped above it: the entrance to one of the millions of skyscrapers in the plaza environment, one of the many exteriors regularly reprogrammed to look more impressive than the others, and more worthy of the billboards advertising hot new constructs and 21-day free trials. We stepped out into the public data space just as we would've walked out onto any city street, always reminded by the fantastic-looking people and magical objects that we weren't in our flesh-and-blood bodies.

"Stupid! It's all so stupid!"

"It's not like you keep anything important on these servers," I was quick to say, "and I know you make like a trillion backups. Seriously, did you really lose anything valuable?"

"No, I didn't," she replied. "There wasn't anything I can't replace in a second, but I like to know that the places I store things are safe. I didn't have to worry so much about this years ago, but now it seems like I'm constantly relying on AIs to fix things other AIs broke. If the owners of InTek and the millions of companies like it would be a little more responsible, their clients would be a lot happier."

"Yeah, but artificial intelligence gets better every year, I'm sure that by next Christmas InTek'll have much more powerful security."

"And much more powerful viruses for it to fail against."

"Well," I said, pacing with hands in my pockets, "Slidewire wouldn't be making so much money if their software wasn't good, right? Malvirai are just AIs programmed by punk hackers to be evil. All the companies have to do is update their security and—"

"They're all evil, Brandon, every one of them. I don't care what the AI is programmed to do: help me, annoy me, sing to me, write me a jaywalking ticket... I don't care that they don't think like us or know how much they're ruining..." She took a breath and lowered her eyes. "Sorry."

I stopped and faced her. "What's wrong, Vair?"

She looked at me. Her eyes softened for a moment before they darted away. "I guess... they're cutting my pay again."

"Oh, I'm sorry."

"Not your fault," she replied. "Better than losing my job I guess."

"But you deserve better."

She took a moment to take in the sweet-smelling air. "What do you think, Brandon?" she asked. "Do you think it was like this hundreds of years ago, during that 'Great Depression'?"

"What do you mean?"

"Simpler times. Simplicity is supposed to be a good thing, right? Guess I'm thinking whether all this 'advancement' has made hard times better or worse."

"Well... They didn't have artificial intelligence in the 1930's. I don't think they even had computers."

She faced me with a look of adoration, reaching up and running her hand through my dirty blond hair. "Personally, I wouldn't want to live in a time when electricity was a luxury; but if it means no AIs..." She removed her hand and shrugged her shoulders. "Why think that way? I know that getting rid of everything won't solve problems. We need to make the future better instead of trying to live in the past. It's just that sometimes I wish all the noise would go away, that's all. They shouldn't try to replace people with computers, they're just tools... Computers, I mean, not people."

We started walking down the street.

"Didn't you say something like that when your A-site switched over?"

"GreenTek. That's why I ascend from home now. You remember..." She pointed to her forehead. "It's a small device, Brandon. You'll never need the public booths again."

"I don't know, the booths aren't so bad. My site still has real people looking over it."

"For how much longer? One of the people at GreenTek was a friend of mine, she got thrown into one of those government 'prosperity' programs and they made her sell her condo. Trust me, the day is coming when you're gonna walk out and find a computer program watching the place. No warning. When that day comes, I recommend the PAMs made by Maldoran... they're compatible with pretty much every SNDL ever made and, since you just have the standard basc implants, the setup shouldn't take more than a few minutes. You can just din me if you need help."

"Things are a little better out in California, Vair. In fact, when you get sick of the pay cuts, you can always come live with me in LA."

A silent moment passed as she allowed the last of her tension to evaporate. "We'll see," she said, "I just wish the lamewads in Washington would put two and two together and do something to stop this. You know, change the law—"

I felt a whoosh and something slammed into my chest. Someone flew in between us – someone fast – nearly knocking me over. The kid stopped in the distance and stared back at us. He looked disheveled and dark hair came down to cover much of his face. My eyes were drawn to something glimmering around his neck. A chain.

A dirty and worn card had been left in my hand, bearing the image of a skeleton riding a horse. On the top the card said "DEATH." I sprung the creepy thing from my hand and it fell to the walkway. I looked up again and the kid was gone.

"It's a tarot card," Vair said.

"Don't – Don't pick it up, it might – I don't know – have some bad code on it or something!"

"Just some kid trying to mess with your head." She held the card between her fingers and it vanished. "See? Deleted. At least I got to fix one problem today."

I leaned on a wall and took some deep breaths.

"Well," she said, "guess that was pretty strange. Are you all right?"

"Yeah... Kids," I said. "If it's not slunks throwing soft drinks at the cowardly lion, it's gotta be something else, right?"

"Yeah, kids... with their Model Ts and their Coca Cola, dancing the *Rock and Roll*. 'To hell in a handbasket,' however that's supposed to work."

We both laughed.

"I see you're doing more research behind my back, but I think the dance was called 'the Charleston.'"

"Well, whatever... now I definitely can't sleep," Vair said. "Forget real life and everything close to it. Let's get away. Let's get away from all of them."

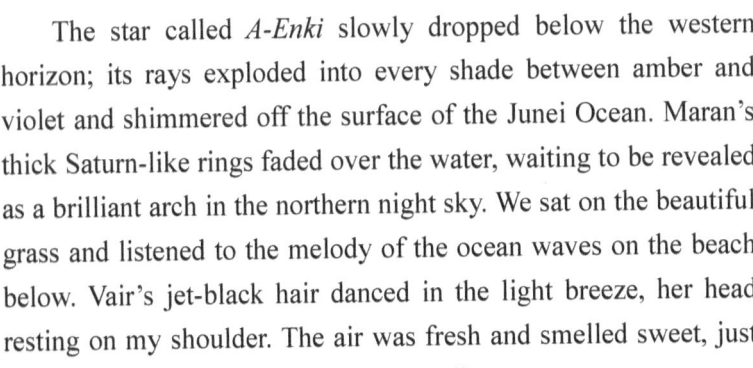

The star called *A-Enki* slowly dropped below the western horizon; its rays exploded into every shade between amber and violet and shimmered off the surface of the Junei Ocean. Maran's thick Saturn-like rings faded over the water, waiting to be revealed as a brilliant arch in the northern night sky. We sat on the beautiful grass and listened to the melody of the ocean waves on the beach below. Vair's jet-black hair danced in the light breeze, her head resting on my shoulder. The air was fresh and smelled sweet, just as all the air was sweet in Dynamic Reality.

Of all the real and fictional landscapes a couple could enjoy, we chose that beach in Maran's southern hemisphere as our spot. Maran was a real place rendered fiction; a far-off planet once thought to resemble Earth. Just a few years earlier, Maran had been a popular setting for fiction and speculation: on the life forms that lived there, the cities we could build there, the resources we could mine, and so on.

When the probe revealed Maran to be yet another dead rock, the stories ended and pricey top-quality simulations of the planet became practically free. The speculators buried their old work and picked new planets as audiences stood waiting for the next big frenzy.

"Exploration is dead," Vair once said during a night there. "Another planet supporting life wouldn't have to resemble Earth this much, would it? They're just copying and pasting their own perfect visions of Earth onto every star in the sky and seeing if money comes out; then some truth is revealed and everyone whines for two days, until they're given something else to distract them. Cycle complete."

Vair's opinion of modern science always ran hot-cold, for reasons very personal to her. Still, she felt she had a right to bask in the knowledge of mankind and judge the value of everything. Sometimes the trips to Maran would inspire her to talk science with me, a subject I'd wanted nothing to do with since college, but which she had a way of getting me caught up in. I would start remembering facts and argue against her, even managing to change a couple of her theories over the months. I never expected her reaction to my small victories, though; she enjoyed losing more than winning, because it meant she learned something new.

There was no debate that day. I ran my hand through her long hair, seeing her as the fragile and precious woman I'd once known her as. Her vanitar was surprisingly true to real-life: in a crowd of leopard-striped, platinum-eyed divers, hers was embellished only by a stripe of indigo running down her hair. She was always so confident and secure, sometimes even letting her individuality get the better of her, but always staying respectful and open to others. It was hard to believe that the first time we met, I saw her as a bird with a broken wing: shattered, desperate, and talking frantically of suicide.

I only did what any human being would.

Vair was the natural-born daughter of two veetoo parents. They split up when she was only eight months old and she spent her early childhood being shuffled between mother and father like luggage, until one of them left suddenly to live on Mars. Vair learned to ignore her pain and succeeded in spite of it, competing well against the lab-born son her mother truly wanted. Even in school, though, Vair felt like an outcast. Though she wasn't a veetoo herself, the normal children rejected her because she bore the marks of genetic engineering. The veetoo children also rejected her, because she wasn't born in a lab. In time, the young Vair simply decided against wanting friends, because others couldn't be trusted.

Her mother would talk about how eugenics was the future of mankind and how Vair and her half-brother Dean were living proof of mankind's triumph over nature. Vair eagerly studied genetics, believing it would bring her closer to her mother, until she found herself challenging a popular theory. Vair was surprised when her mother didn't approve and it was the first time she felt she had to choose between "logic versus politics." She couldn't understand why people hated her. They would spend so many hours preaching ideas about life but, for all her mind was fed, her heart was allowed to starve. She had no knowledge of how to identify pain or release it.

By her fifteenth birthday, the walls between Vair and her mother had grown higher. She moved out the same week and tried to forget about family. It made her feel better, at first.

In Vair's senior year of college, her father contacted her; he'd moved back and wanted to be a part of his daughter's life again. For reasons she didn't understand, she accepted the offer and began meeting with him in Dynamic Reality. Her father had taken up drinking, though, and the whim-driven bonding sessions became meaningless and empty. She came to despise her father and tried to stop seeing him, but he saw through her strong front and took advantage of her fragile emotional state. Vair kept visiting. Vair kept pretending.

For all the strength she had, no knowledge or ignorance could hold it any longer. Though she never recognized the dam holding back inside her, it had been real, and it was finally starting to burst, causing a lifetime of buried pain to overtake her in the blink of an eye.

The strange part was: I didn't even want to be where I was that day.

The audible clock announced the top of the hour in its pleasant omnipresent voice. I wiped the moisture from my eyes and noticed the sun had set, leaving only a faint glow on the horizon. I also noticed Vair had been a little too successful in forgetting her busy schedule. I nudged her back into lucidity.

"You heard the man, better get some sleep."

She groaned and didn't move, "I'm sick of computers. You tell me what time it is."

"It's eight zeroes, and you've got money to make tomorrow."

She slowly got up and composed herself.

"Is everything good for New Years?" she asked.

A pulse of anxiety went through me. "Yeah," I replied, trying to recall the plan we'd made. "The train tickets are waiting in my mailbox. I'll leave Thursday night and meet you in Times Square around noon... if it arrives on time."

"I can meet you in Penn Station if it's easier."

"Ah..." I stood up. "After that forty hour train ride? Why not?"

"Come on, it'll be just like the last time you came to see me: you'll order an Amber Plus from the dining car, download some architectural journal, bury yourself in it, and then the conductor'll have to wake you up."

No, I thought. This won't be like the last time.

I felt a hand on my shoulder. "Is everything all right, Brandon?" Vair asked. "You seem a little... off."

I took a deep breath, pushing sorrow away, and told myself to smile. "Oh, you know. Work stuff. You know how useless prosperity agents are. Nothing to worry about. I'll have real work soon enough, anyway... the west coast is good like that. All I have to do is dream it and there'll be a job."

"But what good is a dream that doesn't become reality?"

Our eyes locked for a moment, and I couldn't tell whether she was being her usual coy self or dead serious.

Is it really possible? Does she really care about me?

"Well, you know," she said. "Things will work out, you have talent and someone has to see it eventually."

She lifted the sleeve of her right arm, exposing the descender around her wrist.

The anxiety rushed back, but I knew I had to let her go. "Back to the real world," I said to fill the silence. "Crazies and all."

"We all gotta go back sometime, or else where's the fun of getting away?"

She smiled, using the point she'd made to slingshot her mood into something more energetic. "All right, slo-mo," she teased, holding her descender in front of me. "If you're the one left standing this time, I'll be extra nice next movie and let you have some popcorn."

"During one of your weeks to pick?" I said, absently scratching my head. "You don't even eat popcorn during those movies."

"During *Citizen Kane*, then."

I lifted my arm halfway. "Actually, I still have something to do up here. I'm not even tired."

"Oh… Sure." She shrugged her shoulders and put her hand on the button. "Then I'll see you Friday."

I nodded. "Yeah… Friday. No force in nature will be able to keep me away."

Vair smiled and nearly pressed the button of her descender. "Oh, right… Crazies. Don't be surprised if you see a lot of star-gazers running around down there. Dean— uh…"

My eyes widened in interest. "Dean…" I repeated, hoping she'd finish the sentence.

Vair let out a soft laugh, trying to muddle through her discomfort. "Yeah, he started responding to my messages again."

A grin formed on my face and grew large. I felt like a boy who just found his puppy.

Too much joy too fast, though. Vair stashed it away and sighed. "I don't even know why I felt like talking to him again. He put me on his 'friends' list and now I keep getting all these pointless forwarded messages about some supernova in the sky. Anyway, I just wanted you to know. It's a new shiny object and you know how the public loves shiny things."

"But Vair, you love cosmology. I can't remember the last time we saw a supernova. It's exciting."

That managed to bring a little of her smile back. "I'd hope you don't remember, last supernova being almost a thousand years ago." She reached up and put a hand on my shoulder. "I don't know if I care anymore… I'm sure it'll be a feature on all the cosmology sites. I'll look at the data and maybe something'll catch me. Anyway…"

I put my hand over her descender. "I know you still love Dean. Maybe he's getting fed up in that house. He'll need to rely on his big sister."

"Big sister," she repeated, as if she never considered the title before, but thought it might be a good one to have.

"Standard Reality is tough sometimes; but remember I'm there, too… only a din away."

I kissed her, wanting to give her something to bring her through the work week, to say nothing of my own. But the contact reminded me of the distance about to come between us, and I couldn't bear the thought. I felt I was about to burst. Embarrassed, I moved my finger to press the button and felt my lips lose contact with hers. In her descender's millisecond-speed, Vair's vanitar was gone from the dynamic universe. I was alone again. There was no light left on the horizon.

I collapsed onto the ground, facing the simulated night sky and trying to calm myself. The ticket from Byran's Downtown slipped out of my pocket. I picked it up from the grass and felt it with my fingertips, thinking on all the experiences we'd shared in both worlds. It frightened me to think that, in time, she would discover the man I truly was. I thought when that day came, I might have nothing left. Like a character in a movie, I was sure that day would be when the reel of my life would reach its end and I would fade away.

Who was I in love with? Was it the bird with the broken wing, who needed me? Or was it the woman she was free to become around me, who I seemed to need?

I looked at the ticket: nothing more than a formality – a souvenir for those trying to make the experience more authentic.

It was her authenticity that brought out the best in me, I thought. Her authenticity was how we started going to *Byran's*: I told Vair I lived in LA, she commented about it being the movie capital of the world, and I told her how much I liked ancient film. It was an idle thought, but she used it to make my own interest more special.

It was as I thought: she was making me more real.

But I don't deserve authenticity, I thought as I threw the ticket into the wind. I knew she wanted to patch things up with her brother, and yes, I was the one who encouraged her; but who was I to do such a thing... when I couldn't stand the sight of my own brother... when I could never forgive him for what he'd done to me.

More tears came, tears I was glad she wasn't there to see. I expected some difference to take Vair away, just like every other girl, just like every other person in my life; but as the months passed, I loved her more and my dreams for our future grew bigger. I let the dreams grow. I committed myself to them in spite of her dim view of family and marriage, even as those scars began to appear as a ceiling to my love.

I closed my eyes and thought again about the moment I'd been valuable to her, when she was torn to pieces by her life.

That's not a future. And if that terrible memory is all I have to offer her...

I lay on the grass for several minutes. In my memory, the dunes of an LA beach surrounded me; it was the question I had asked two days before, as I lay staring at the night sky. I realized the stars of Maran were the same as the stars of Earth. I realized I was staring at a cheap, twinkling copy.

I jumped to my feet screaming inhumanly into the air. I remembered the feeling of peace that came over me the other night and cried, knowing no such feeling existed, scolding myself for being such a fool. I knew I hadn't asked any stupid ghost or alien for an answer. I knew no such things existed, and that no one could hear me. I knew the only difference between fake-DR and real-SR was the bill they sent me for time spent.

I moved my hand to my descender, unwilling to perceive fake grass, stars, and oceans any longer. Whatever reality really was, it wouldn't let me stay in an illusion any more. Everything of value to me was now in the other world, down in the world I called Standard Reality.

I cursed when the booth's panel only buzzed at me, kicking the door from the inside until it offlined itself. I stepped into the hallway and waited for the fog to clear in my head, and for my eyes to stop burning in the dim lighting. I chugged water from the fountain and grabbed my windbreaker, eager to get to the beach. The chemical stabilizer was wearing off and I was starving.

The outside air beckoned to me as I walked into the lobby. A few kids in full slunk-foamer regalia looked up and began to shout among themselves about who would get the vacated booth.

"I hope you enjoyed your experience, Mister Dauphin. You'll be happy to know tonight's charge of fifty-five-forty-four ninety fulfills your Economic Stimulus requirement for this year."

I scratched my eyes, rubbing the sleep out. "Well, that's good. Not a moment too soon, eh?"

She laughed. It was a laugh that sounded far too familiar. I looked and realized the usual grouchy man wasn't watching the store.

"Thank you for using ZephyrTek," she continued with digitally-precise glee. "Always low prices, always great customer service. Please come back soon."

The wind on Venice Blvd. was unusually cold, and puddles from the day's rain were still on the sidewalks. I opened the statement the A-site sent to my SNDL implant and jumped straight to the end. Where there would always be names of managers and lengthy data on their state operator licenses, it now simply said: "Your amai was Erica."

I closed the file, deleted the file, reformatted the data space where the file had been, and tried to put it out of my mind and focus on where I was going. The buildings around me became newer and newer, finally lifting off the ground, so a forest of trees mixed with a forest of pillars. Everyone thought LA's modernization was making the city more beautiful, but it just gave the chilly wind more paths to take. As I pulled my ragged windbreaker tighter around me, cursing silently at the cold, another one of the pests came from beside me so abruptly my heart nearly jumped into my throat.

"How ya doing? Cold night, huh?"

A tall, bleached blonde woman. Her personality and clothing were exactly what men like me were supposed to go for, exactly the kind of charm men like me welcomed. I locked my eyes to my steps ahead and picked up my pace, though I knew ignoring her was futile.

"You know what Vent's Extreme is doing tonight? Half-off drink specials! You should go!" She pointed to the club's well-lit entrance, an elevator near the end of the block.

"Just please just go away."

"You know," she continued, "Vent's was rated the top night club in Los Angeles in a recent survey. Vent's has all the hottest sledg-ek from all the biggest bands: Eleven Under, Insane Explosion, Six Six Six…"

I broke into a sprint, stopping when she materialized right in front of me.

"You know how highly Vent's Extreme holds customer service? Vent's—"

"Actually, I don't know! I don't want to know! Maybe with any luck, you'll leave me alone and I'll never know!" In that instant, I saw how attractive she was and my mind betrayed me. "Go away!" I shouted at the top of my lungs. "Beat it! Leave me alone!"

Everyone on the block looked up, taking a moment to laugh before they returned to what they were doing. The hologram in my way vanished.

As if the obnoxious pop-up billboards aren't bad enough, I thought. I must have a shirt on that says "Sell Me Something."

As my shoes finally hit the beach sand, I noticed floodlights ahead. A giant sandcastle sat before me: one far beyond my experience of overturning a pail of sand and poking finger holes for windows. Somehow the sight was peaceful to me.

"Nice, huh? Took him six days," said a short man standing next to me.

A boy, younger than even the slunks who fought over my ascension booth, came into view around the side of the castle. He looked happy and determined, as if a true builder at heart; but far too young to build such a behemoth in six days, or even to get all the extra sand he should have needed.

"Just him?"

"Well, friend, I sure can't build something like that." He laughed. "Feel kinda unworthy just looking at it."

I squinted my eyes and saw something else, a bright point of light that wasn't one of the floodlights. "What's that in the sky?"

"Isn't it beautiful how that light just seems to complement everything? I've seen it without the floodlights and it's spectacular."

"But what is it?"

"Oh, you don't know?" The man looked at me. "It's a supernova."

I saw others mingling and admiring the young builder, with a steady stream of new people adding to the crowd. "Well," I said, "it's very nice, but this stuff isn't for me. Thanks anyway."

A *Slammers* concession stand was located along the Ocean Front Walk. The stand always had the same teenager behind the counter: a boy with long black hair and a chain around his neck. He was always clean cut and kind: exactly the sort of person who should keep their job in a slow economy.

"How you doing?" I asked, glad to be talking to someone real again.

"Ah, Brandon. How are you doing today?" the boy asked with a smile. He placed a slampak of Amber Plus and a Boost Bar on the counter.

"Actually, uh… I was thinking about trying something a little stronger today."

His eyes widened with interest and his smile grew larger. Something in the request thrilled him, but when he turned to see what he had, he stopped. "Sure?"

"Well, I don't know," I said. "The PJX just isn't working for me like it used to. Do you have any Code White, or Sparc… they always show sloths jumping around in their ads, maybe that means it'll wake me up better."

"Brandon," he said kindly, "why the change? You've been drinking Amber for as long as I can remember."

"Why anything? I don't know. I just have this nagging feeling like I should change something… it's weird." I couldn't resist the urge to look at the scene behind me. "I can't see the light from this angle. Pretty wheeled for you, I guess: having the supernova blocked by the castle here. This stand is mobile, maybe you should move it."

"It's just a star… No need to have it shining in my eyes all the time."

The star was much brighter than I thought. "Yeah, I guess you're right," I said, blinking and returning to the counter.

"Forty-five," he said he unlocked the slampak.

"What?"

"You've had a hard day, Brandon. I'll just charge you half price."

"Wow, thanks. How'd you know?"

The boy shrugged his shoulders and slid the glowing can of Amber Plus across the counter, its voice chip speaking the mandatory health warnings. I quickly onlined the drink, feeling the PJX enter my bloodstream, reveling in its familiar boost of energy.

"Just remember those halo-hotties never last long," the boy said. "People usually get tired of 'em after a month... can't imagine why, though."

"No, not like that!" I corrected, more eagerly than I knew. "Not... not like that at all."

"Oh, how could I forget," the boy replied, sharing none of the surprise at my own outburst. "That girl from Connecticut, right?"

"Veronica."

"So she loves you, then?"

"I – I think so."

"Love is such a wonderful and useful thing, Brandon. You'd be surprised what you can make someone else do when they have real emotions. It's like diverting the unstoppable power of a river."

"Well... I don't know. Maybe love isn't a thing we're supposed to manipulate. Maybe it's something that should bloom like a flower."

"And that's why you're unhappy," he said. "The successful relationship is the one you control. The ones who don't take charge are the ones who get walked on their whole lives. Do it your own way, there is no other answer."

I looked at him blankly. Usually, I was good at judging people's emotions by their eyes, body language, and speech. I felt a little uncomfortable then, but didn't know why. "Sometimes, I think certain things weren't meant to die. What I mean is... I don't know what I mean. I just know I think there's something I want to know. Maybe it's some 'fate' stuff like people talk about all the time: my place in the universe, nature's plan for me, maybe even bigger than that."

I saw the kid squint his eyes a little. I was casting a faint shadow on the counter.

"Well, if being serious with that girl is what you want, then it's the right thing to do."

"No," I said hesitantly. "It has to be deeper... more real..."

I turned to see what was so bright behind me, but all I saw were the people and the castle.

The kid leaned over the counter and put his hand on my shoulder. "Brandon, what's more real than your own desires?"

I thought about the question, looked up and swiped my wrist on the vendreader, charging forty-five dollars to my accounts.

"You're right," I said to him. "As always."

I let myself in and walked down the hallway: drab, peeling wallpaper for the eye, creaky boards greeting my every step, and cigar smoke thick enough to taste. Bill's 'office' was in his kitchen, where he could always be found with a greasy meal or cigar in one hand and the other on the groundtem... not that he ever did much work with it.

"Bill! It's Brandon, what's the good wo—"

His hard voice broke in from down the hallway. "Go home, Dauphin! Koreans got it."

Bill was a lonely man well into his nineties with leather for skin and thin, unkempt hair. He had a wife and a son, once. Before I learned not to like him, we touched on the subject of family and it became obvious it wasn't a comfortable subject. The rumor I heard was that his son died in an accident.

Bill flicked the cigar onto the ashtray but didn't look away from the groundtem monitor.

"You should've just shot me a—" Cough. "Shot me a din. No need to walk all this way just—so I—" Cough. Cough. "So I could tell you to buzz off. Told ya. Koreans." Cough.

"I keep telling you I like the exercise. Now – what – do – you – have – for – me?"

I leaned over his desk, but he still stared at his groundtem.

"Bill," I said, wanting to shout it.

"Nada. Zilch. Like I keep telling you, what the Indians and Mor—" Cough. "Moroccans don't get, Korea does. Check back in two weeks."

"You always say that. Bill, I need money. I just bought…" I closed my eyes and calmed myself. "Really, I'm begging here."

Cough. "What part of 'two weeks' don't you understand? Two. Weeks." Cough.

"Yeah, I heard that part. I can't wait two weeks. You're my 'prosperity' agent… it's your job to keep me employed."

"Don't like it? File another complaint with the state office. I don't care anymore."

"You don't care? This is my…"

The thought vanished from my mind, and I felt very small. For a moment, I questioned how important a few dollars really were. I questioned whether the bad economy might have been as hard on Bill as it was on me. I questioned why I was getting so mad, and I questioned what the purpose of anger would be if there really weren't a job for him to grant.

"You don't need a doctor or something, do you kid? You know, I don't have the kind of pull I used to with the health board."

I let go of the desk and took a step back, rubbing my forehead. I'd broken into a cold sweat. A sense of vengeance rose up within me, and I remembered what the server at *Slammers* said about taking charge.

"I have a desire and nothing else matters!"

Bill moved his cigar to his mouth and looked back to the groundtem. "Good for you, kid."

The words didn't do what I wanted. My rash attempt at taking charge only succeeded at embarrassing me. "I didn't mean that – I mean, I did, but – there's something I'm planning next week – on New Year's, it cost me a lot of money. I know there's no reason for you to help me, but I really need it. I need to do something, anything, to feel like I'm useful to someone, to feel like I can support... someone, if she'll have me."

Silence filled the room. Bill finally gave his attention to me, his dulled brown eyes on the verge of wetting, as if he heard every word I didn't say.

"There was a time... when a soldier could serve a few years, settle down, get a good job and make a good living." His gaze fell toward the desk, focusing on nothing in particular. "I wish you kids the best, really I do, but... it's not the way it was a century or two ago... and there's nothing I can do to save my life that'll give you another dollar. That's just the world and I'm sorry."

For a moment, the only sound in the room was from the gentle waves crashing on the beach outside.

Bill sat up and coughed again. "What's a dead dog like me know anyway? Go spend the time with your girl." Cough. "Business hours start back up in two weeks. I always get something then. Happy New Year in the meantime." Cough. With that, he puffed on his cigar and put his eyes back on the groundtem.

I knew I'd seen a side of Bill rarely shown. Absentmindedly I took a step toward the hall. "She's working until Friday. If you have anything at all…"

Bill sighed. "When I was your age, we didn't have the fancy download-the-whole-friggin'-net-in-two-seconds implants." He pulled out a worn book and put it on the desk in front of me. "Back then, we read print…" He tapped his finger on the cover. "Nothing to do? Get some common sense." Cough.

The book was titled *Destiny for a New You*. Its cover had a chimpanzee staring up at a departing UFO: typical artwork for anything advocating *Destiny Of Ordered Mankind*. In my mind, I saw those people gathering around the sandcastle and their devotion to the kid who built it. I wondered whether the alien-plants-seed junk was any different. "One star goes boom and suddenly all mankind loses their minds." I slid the book back across the desk.

"What star?"

I looked at him like he was an idiot. "The supernova. Where have you been? It's outside your house right now."

"Well, I'm sure it's very nice," he replied in the same condescending way, "but that stuff isn't for me. Thanks anyway."

I drank from my slampak and started back down the hallway. "Just make sure your new religion doesn't get in the way of my career, okay?"

"Religion? What's in your head, kid? The Celestials are out there, it's proved by science!"

"Rek, Rek, Rek," I muttered as I stepped outside, thinking of how I'd wasted another fifteen minutes of my life.

The emotion faded as I walked along the border between land and sea, deepening the realization that I had no hope. At the mere age of twenty-five, I saw myself as a dead dog. Coming to California was supposed to open doors for me, but it seemed all I did was throw my history away and try to start over in a decaying ruin. The last two years had gone by so impossibly fast, and I was ashamed how long it'd been since my last serious attempt to land work.

Why should I give up? There are still a few real jobs left. I have a desire, and...

I stopped walking and stared at the sand next to my shoes.

...and I'm not the only one with a desire. There will always be better people than me, waiting to take everything I have.

The wind died down and I heard footsteps ahead of me. A man was approaching from the nearby docks. Knowing how much cops patrolled that stretch of beach, I started walking slowly, paying close attention to my SNDL to make sure I was staying on the beaches "green path": the unmarked and always-shifting zone where it's legal to walk. I became more self-conscious with each step, trying to cover the slampak with my windbreaker, hoping this guy didn't notice it strobing colors, hoping he would just ignore me.

Legislation clung like magnets to every environmental quirk, rare species, or powerful person's whim in that place. I knew laws were the price of walking on a real beach in the real world, that they were essential to civilization. Then why should I be so nervous every time I see one of these guys, I wondered as I felt my pulse speed up and began losing feeling in my legs. I looked away from the man, then remembered to slow my pace, then looked somewhere else because looking at one thing too long is suspicious, then remembered to pull my windbreaker a little tighter, while trying to think if I was doing anything else illegal. A break formed in the clouds over the ocean.

I stopped.

After what may have been seconds or hours, I became aware of the other man again. I blinked and saw nothing more than a point of light in space, so I looked away: right at a shining LAPD badge hanging from the man's shirt pocket. My gaze fell absently to the sand and the slampak that slipped from my hand. I was overcome by a familiar sinking feeling as I stared at the spilled orange liquid: eighty thousand dollars for possession on a beach, fifty-five thousand for pollution, plus the mandatory court appearance.

If the officer's in a good mood, he might stop there.

"Why are you looking down?" he said. "Look up at the sky."

An impulse surged in me, enough to snap me out of my frozen state and bring me to look him in the eye. "Is that an order, sir?"

"Absolutely not."

I narrowed my eyes, not sure what to think about him. I could see his badge, the only mark he wore that hinted at his employer, and I knew he could fine me and test me and arrest me and whatever else the laws said, and that I should have been trying to think of excuses and defenses, figuring out the patrolman's soft-spot and how to take advantage of it, but my infuriation was being pulled away, and my thoughts abandoned as foolishness. I did want to look at the sky again, I realized, and so I did, and of my own free will. The light was several times stronger than the brightest stars. The clouds shifted again, and it seemed ridiculous to me that something so small and local should block something so huge and universal.

"It's been there since last night. Cosmologists think it's the largest event ever witnessed in this galaxy: a nova so large that it affected its entire region of space, its light strong enough to cut through the vacuum and be seen at a distance greater than anything we've known. And by the naked eye, at that."

"That's amazing," I said, as if the one standing next to me were a lifelong friend. "It makes you think about how we're all made of stardust, you know?"

"Does that thought impress you?"

It took a moment for the question to catch up to me. My sight fell again to the Earth. "Of course it impresses me. Long after I'm dead and cremated, the stars'll keep shining. That's impressive, isn't it?"

The man looked off as if thinking about a puzzle. "It certainly *sounds* impressive, but there's a limit built into the statement. It's like…" he bent down and picked up a handful of sand, "it's like saying: 'Wow, I can hold grains of sand that look just like all the other grains of sand on the beach.' Does that sound like a life-changer to you, Brandon Dauphin?"

"Well, no. Not when you say it like that."

He grabbed my slampak from the sand and rose to his feet. "Words have meanings, don't be afraid to test them by looking through a different vantage point."

I looked at the slampak in his hand, remembering my guilt and his job. "Well, you're one to talk about limits, sir. Is it the law now for you to tear down the things I believe in, too? What is the meaning of that no-drink law? Why don't we test that now?"

"Most people don't care. They come to the beach and talk about how much they love everything about it, complaining if the temperature is wrong or the waves are too loud or the UV-screen isn't working just right, then…" he dropped my can back onto the sand, "they leave their garbage all over and contribute to the same problems they claim to hate, wanting the government to baby-sit them. So, over time, governments learned to."

I hesitated, wishing he would go away, unsure if he meant to charge me with anything. "But I'm not contributing to the problems, I always—" I bit my lip. "This one time, I meant to finish it and throw it away in a recycling bin. Serious."

"Why should intentions matter to me?" he said as a stream of sand poured from his hand. "The law says you're just like everyone else: an irresponsible polluter who should be punished until he learns his lesson. The law says you were guilty the minute you set foot on this beach, or at least that I can detain you and make you spend months proving otherwise. Are you everyone else, Mister Dauphin? Or are you an individual: someone with a heart and a mind and a spirit and the ability to take actions that are consistent with his own beliefs? Are you someone who can say something and mean it?"

"I'm sorry," I replied. "It was a mistake. I'm not like everyone else. I'm telling you I'll obey the law and I'm saying more than just words."

"But laws aren't for you thanks anyway. If we repealed every law in the world, what would you do?" He retrieved my can a second time and held it up. "Pollute?"

"I wasn't polluting."

"Speeding, then."

"I wasn't walking over the limit."

"How about robbing a bank?"

"That's some question for a cop to ask."

He didn't respond.

"Okay... sure. I need money. Why not rob a bank if it's legal? I'd just be robbing from some greedy corporation. Then the government would just bail them out and they can't prosecute me."

"Then you robbed the U.S. government."

"Yeah, even better."

"But not an elderly woman or a child?"

"No way."

"Why not?"

I just looked at him, hoping he didn't mean for me to answer.

"Why are you asking me to rob an old lady? Are you sick in the head or something?"

He smiled. "No. I'm not asking you to do anything, these are just questions: I'm curious to examine your values." He looked down. "What do you think, should I put my name on it? Should I boast about it?"

"What?"

The officer indicated the small pile of sand in front of him, which covered the orange spot from my spilled energy drink. "Who am I to build anything?" he asked, barely loud enough to be heard over the breeze. "The tide and the wind won't let this last very long, and what it's covered will be exposed again."

"Look, sir. I don't know what kind of trip you're on, but I'd like to go home and get some sleep now."

He looked up, still holding the balance between being intensely serious and having a casual conversation. "Did I fire my taser at you? Of all the places in the world you could go, you're standing here listening to me."

"Because I have to! Because…" I felt my anger falter, "Because it's against the law to walk away without your permission."

"Murder, then."

"Murder?"

"There are worse crimes still, but murder is far enough."

"What about it?"

"If it were legal."

"Hell, no!"

"If no person in the world were the type to kill another, what would be the point of making it illegal? If everyone in the world were the type to kill another, what would be the point of making it illegal? If it were legal, would it be moral? If it were legal but not moral, would you do it? What about the day when morals aren't convenient anymore? What about the exceptions those around you make but you don't? What about the day you realize the cost of your own actions, or the price of shutting people out for your vices?"

My vices? What is he talking about?

"Are you talking about my laws or societies' laws?"

"Is there really a difference?"

"Then the law is just there to punish everyone," I said, getting caught in the strange connection of ideas he'd led me into. "All parties lose in the end."

"Then the law is powerless to save."

"To save from what?"

"It repays an evil, which the individual considered good, with another evil, which the society considered good."

I tried to continue following him, my motivation shifting to curiosity, reaching the point of needing a solution; but at the point where good and evil threatened to untangle, where everything I knew of life became suspect, I found myself lost and frustrated.

"Where are you going with these questions?"

"What's the point of any question? What happens when people see that questions and answers aren't supposed to be simple automations? What do you think can happen to the limits of the human mind when questions aren't tied down by convention or even…"

He smiled somberly and swiped his foot over the pile of sand he'd made.

"Questions are for smart people," I said. "I don't think that way."

"It was never about being smart, Brandon. Some of the brightest geniuses in the human race go their whole lives without finding the most basic crumbs of wisdom; and it's the simplest among us who find those crumbs and leave us all in the dust. The limits are different for us all, but the true solution stays the same. Now, do you believe that tomorrow can be better?"

Words failed to form sentences in my mind. His eyes stayed locked on mine, his revealing sincerity and a kind of compassion, as if he understood – as if he tried to understand my own position. I looked away to the pristine sand and crashing waves as I considered his last question, eventually realizing that, beyond the words I tried to form from the limits of the mind, one had already been on my heart. As I spoke it, I knew I had answered honestly, that it had been the real Brandon Dauphin speaking from underneath the mask.

"Yes."

The patrolman walked off silently, carrying my slampak off to be forgotten. I felt relief, not of a close call, but of realizing there hadn't been cause to worry. It was better, I thought, that he didn't ignore me.

I stole another glance at the light in the sky and began walking again.

"Limits."

As I returned to the floodlit site, I heard shouting and saw someone standing on top of the behemoth sandcastle: a teenager with long black hair and a chain around his neck, kicking and punching and screaming incomprehensibly as if he were having a mental breakdown. I stopped in fear when I noticed the crowd below cheering him on.

"What are they doing? Someone has to stop this, now!"

"I know it hurts," someone replied, "but this has to happen."

It was the child who built the castle. A few others were there, still following him, as shocked by the destruction as I was, but not overcome by it.

"Little boy," I said over the screaming, "you worked for so long and it was so beautiful, how can you just stand by and watch?"

Off on the boardwalk, I spotted a uniformed officer. The badge I'd wanted to be far away from was suddenly a welcome sight.

The boy tapped me on the hip to get my attention back. "I'll build a better one, a castle he can't—"

I sprinted across the sand near the crowd and up onto the boardwalk. The officer was sipping coffee and talking to an older woman. "Officer! Officer! Please help!"

The man spun around toward me. "Is everything all right, sir?"

Incredulous, I pointed to the scene. "That! Can't you hear *that*? Can't you stop *that*?" I shouted, wondering how on Earth the man couldn't hear fifty zoo animals screaming nonsense only twenty meters away.

"That?" The officer glanced over, completely oblivious. "Sir, *that* is just a pile of sand."

I screamed and kicked at the door to my apartment, almost breaking the doorreader... again. The thing always needed an insane number of swipes before it would recognize the chip in my wrist and let me into my own living space. I decided I should've come straight home from ZephyrTek, that I could've just gone to bed thinking only of Vair on Maran; whether I would've felt better or worse about Times Square made little difference to me. Maybe I would've chosen alcohol instead of PJX and decided not to feel at all.

I changed my clothes and polished my teeth, finally managing to relax. The fancy black and gold package was easy to tell apart, I put it on the countertop and threw the other three pieces of mail onto my messy coffee table. The whoosh caused a piece of paper to fall to the floor, a coupon I'd won in a raffle months before: good for three days at an ascension site called PaciTek. I'd forgotten about it and checked the expiration date: the end of the year. Not my first choice of how to spend the next few days, I considered, but my only choice.

I grabbed the fancy package and took a deep breath as I tore at the seal. I popped the small black case open and gazed at the ring inside. It looked and sparkled exactly as it had days before in the kincubus, but I knew I wasn't feeling a simulation with simulated hands, but real with real: it had become a solid object with real meaning. The last few weeks had gone by so impossibly fast, and there were so many things to think about. I decided I would go forward with my plan, even if I wasn't sure why.

And, if she turned me down... If she didn't want to be a wife...

I tore open one of the ordinary packages: Receipts from my financial insurer. Next came the envelope with my train tickets. I opened it and ran my fingertips along the surface of the paper. It's a link, I thought, a guarantee I'll be thousands of miles away in New York when that ball drops. I remembered the movie tickets and how Vair joked with me when I was looking at those old posters in the lobby. I smiled. *Maybe*, I thought. No.

She *will* say yes.

On my counter was a printed image I took of her months earlier, posing in front of the Long Island Sound. I threw every other thought out of my mind and held the picture in my hands, imagining her answer, finding that the woman in my mind did love me. I put the picture on the table next to the open box and the ring.

I found the confidence I wanted and I determined to go to bed before losing it again. "Lights off." The room went dark and my head hit the pillow. My eyes closed looking at the bedside clock, counting the three days before I would board my train and begin my journey, the five days to January first: the day I knew would be the best day of my life... the beginning of my life. My plans were real. My desires were real. No force in nature could've kept me from them.

The date was Monday, December 27, 2179. The day I died.

Chapter One: Limits

We stand in awe of the parade.

Where once the connections between us were few and distant, technology from rugged roads to smoothly orbiting satellites had allowed a new culture to flourish, one driven by the speed and essence of communication. In short centuries, the links became faster, more reliable, and more indwelled within us: moving from firsthand experience to recording, from the eyes and ears to direct connection with the brain. Information grew. History stopped fading away, but became part of the atmosphere. The imaginations of billions took on more power than had ever been known to man.

Today, fact and fiction beckon for attention from every corner, offering to the commoners of the twenty-second century knowledge kings could once only dream to possess. It had been an irresistible temptation... the only place left to live, even after we'd forgotten what living was. Even as a voice within cried to get out of DR's snare, accepting three free days was all I knew to do. The illusions and fantasies still worked well enough, I told myself.

When they had suddenly been rushed to their end, when they all went up in a brilliant flash of light, I found I couldn't ignore the hollowed-out shell I had become, and that I had no comfort to retreat to, as if illusions and fantasies had never worked at all.

Any time we need to forget the troubles of modern life, the parade calls out to us. We stand in the assurance the parade will go on forever, existing to offer something new, stimulating the senses beyond the limits of yesterday.

In days, I would die the death that should've taken decades. In days, I would reach my limit: the barrier standing at the end of the road. That was the day that had no future. That was the day I could only slow to a crawl and fall apart. That was the day I knew the barrier was real.

That was the day another foot reached over mine and floored the pedal.

2

"PaciTek."

I watched myself ascending from the ground, rising through the sprawling city landscape and toward the sky. The sunlight was so bright. I could feel its warmth through the glass. For a fleeting moment, it seemed I could forget everything. It seemed I could stay in that limbo forever.

"You want happiness?" a woman's voice asked.

"Yeah," I replied by reflex.

"Then you want performance," the sultry voice replied. "You know the kind I'm talking about, Brandon. The kind that really makes you *feel* like a *somebody*."

"Mute!" I shouted to the elevator's control system. The advertisement stopped.

I leaned on the glass wall and tried to put New Year's out of my mind. The comfort and confidence I had going to sleep had long fled. Just like every other good thing in my life, it had been temporary.

The doors chimed and opened onto the Reed Building's sixth floor, the lights inside painting shapes and patterns onto the Los Angeles street outside. A spacious lobby with bright, luminescent walls and bizarre fixtures awaited me. The doors to the real world closed behind me, and I felt as if I were already in Dynamic Reality.

I felt as if I stepped into the distant future.

A man was processing the check-out of a well-dressed family of five. The father looked like he was a CEO or something. I scanned the printed coupon in my hand again, thinking anything I had to pay for there wouldn't be cheap.

The usual array of advertisements and legal notices lined the walls: printed, on-screen, holographic, and interactive. Even with a casual glance, I spotted the phrase "100% hacker-proof" several times. I sighed and looked away, knowing how much that promise meant, knowing how much InTek meant it on their own advertisements.

The man reminded me of the night manager at ZephyrTek: probably still in college, constantly running around tapping on panels and always seeming exhausted from the job. I wondered how long it would be until this one was also replaced by a walking-talking light show.

"What do you want?"

I stepped up to the desk and gave him the coupon, which he didn't seem to recognize and had to scan through three different databases to verify. I attempted small-talk, asking idle questions and getting generic answers as he ran my registration. He mentioned something about business being slow the past couple of days, I asked why.

"I dunno… bright ball of light in the sky… can't miss it…"

I remembered my trip to the beach and couldn't deny that some interest had formed in me. It was so far yet so bright, a silly thing that would fade away and be forgotten. Yet people were having such reactions to it: hope, fear, curiosity, despair.

"What do you think about that supernova?" I asked.

The manager stopped for a second. His eyes seemed to shift a little, but he returned to his work without answering.

I felt embarrassed and tried to distract myself. My wandering eyes peeked into the open door of the back office, where I saw a large man wearing boxing gloves – motionless and looking to a part of the room I couldn't see. He was probably watching the holograms fight when there weren't any customers. I heard a beep from the groundtem and he smacked it hard with his hand, obviously suppressing the urge to shout.

Just a little anger. Nothing to worry about.

The manager stoically asked me to sign with my thumbprint. I looked down to my own panel and saw the text of California's *Safe Ascender Act of 2166*: the document I was required by state law to sign whenever I ascended alone.

I was led down to the dimly-lit fifth floor and through a couple of long hallways. I drank two days worth of stabilizer from the packet, wanting for it to be out of my system by the third day, in spite of the risk. The manager pressed his thumb on the panel for booth 515 and its opening appeared in the wall. Everything about the platform and interface looked familiar, if not a little nicer than the booths I was used to.

After showing me the controls he was legally required to, the manager raced off and I activated the wall, shutting out the light of the hallway. I leaned onto the padded incline and relaxed my body, allowing the restraints to slide around my arms and legs. My SNDL synchronized with the booth's software and the familiar lightheadedness washed over me.

Several seconds later, my implants showed I was ready for Rapid Eye Movement, ready to fall asleep without sleeping, to be in complete control over what my dream would be.

My eyes were still open, as if they didn't want to close. I saw the darkness I was immersed in, hearing the silence, feeling and smelling the stale air. For the first time in many years, it all worried me.

Reality is not here, just close your eyes. It's easy.

I pushed my childish agitation aside and took a deep breath, reminding myself I'd ascended thousands of times before. With a surge of will, my eyes closed and I surrendered control.

It was a beautiful spring day in a barren, contested land; beauty being relative, of course, in a war zone.

I kept telling myself I had three days: plenty of time for bombing raids and adrenaline and replays. Where I normally jumped straight to the action, being in-and-out in hours, this time I gave myself an 'acclimation period': picking up a softball bat and seeing how the battle simulation handled its own downtime. That first idea passed quickly, though, since I was terrible at sports. After my third out, I was content to sit in the stands and watch the game.

I tried to imagine how terrifying it was, with the possibility of enemy troops hiding behind any hill – or even sitting in the stands as spies – the troops knowing the next day they would be deep in enemy territory, in mortal danger. It made me feel better to immerse myself in it, smiling as I considered my choice of war: Korea, 1952.

That country's why I'm not making money right now, after all.

Battle simulations were an early favorite of mine. In Standard Reality, my grandfather made his career in the Air Force. He retired after the *Ninety East War* and moved back to Idaho when I was still a kid growing up there. I enjoyed hearing him talk about battles and became something of an enthusiast. I even considered joining the military myself, which made him happy; my grandfather was always a little disappointed my dad hadn't signed up, and everyone knew my brother had hated it, though he wasn't exactly a volunteer.

Always the history buff, my grandpa frequently talked about wars, especially the *Second World War*, which occurred in the 1940's and involved most of the countries in the world. Even when

I was younger, twentieth and twenty-first century battle recreations weren't hard to find in Dynamic Reality. Playable combat scenarios, historical or fictional, were a hot item on many servers.

Softball ended early for an 1830 briefing – 1830 being a local time, used when the world was divided into time zones – and I sat in a crowded room with other pilots as our commanding officer gave us details on our targets, the expected weather, recent enemy movements, and so on. The whole thing became boring after the first few minutes, and I reminded myself that briefings were another part of combat that always got abridged or left out. I tried to focus, or at least I wanted to try, but my mind kept wandering and I even yawned loudly at one point. I knew the simulated characters weren't programmed to react, but found myself wondering what the CO would've done in a real briefing when a real soldier yawned. I brushed the thought away and began using a pencil to doodle on the back of the wooden chair in front of me. I even conjured a bag of flavored tortilla chips and began crunching away.

Three days and absolutely nothing to do.

The orders I knew I would be given were to fly my F-86 Sabre in formation into enemy territory, through an area known fondly as 'MiG Alley,' where engagements with the Soviet-built jets were common. I considered which I should do: play the game according to the rules or make up my own rules; escort our bombers and bring them safely back to Kimpo or fly clear into China, alone, and fire at anything that moved.

Three days. Three days. Three days. I guess that's enough time to make up my own rules.

I smiled at my decision. The enemy never knew what they were in for, since I wasn't shy about resetting my fuel level and ammunition mid-flight, repairing any severe damage my plane took with a simple command.

My smile faded when my eyes landed on one of the pilots in front of me: his face sported a huge and ugly scar. I was in a war-game, the other characters were supposed to look bruised and beaten, but something about his scar bothered me. I knew real pilots couldn't reset or leave when they lost the game, but I couldn't figure out why my gaming ambitions suddenly made me feel so…

Everyone suddenly stood up. With a few encouraging but cautious words, we were dismissed. I bent down to retrieve my dropped pencil, and spotted lines that seemed to form letters on the back of the chair. I tried to decipher them from among the markings, and a word emerged from the noise. I had no answer for where it came from.

FRAUDULENT

I regretted that no one still used jet engines, as I stood in the hangar and admired the machine I would be flying the next day. Hours passed as I tried to read the pre-flight checklist, opening panels, reading gauges, and learning more about fighter jets than that they flew really fast and shot at things. At every turn I witnessed the complexity of the thing, feeling so stupid yet more curious as I admired the innovation and directed creativity of those who designed and built the plane, those who left the world with a better jet than they found. I noticed the grease had made my hands as dark as the sky outside, and that it was getting all over the checklist and wiring diagrams.

"Command vanitar: reset."

A slight tingling passed through my hands and they were clean, just as my hair and uniform were, as if I'd just entered the simulation.

I looked at all the parts on the floor and open panels on the plane, wondering whether I should try to put them all back in. I shuffled through the diagrams, showing me all the measurements and settings that had to be exactly right, reminding me that airworthy F-86's didn't just fall out of the sky or assemble themselves. Slowly, I tried to piece everything back together.

"How in hell do you expect to fly that in ten hours, Dauphin?"

I tilted my head to see a couple of airmen approaching from outside: two of the pilots who had been at the briefing. The shorter of them walked up to me and asked if I had a match, pulling a cigarette out of his uniform's shirt pocket.

"Sorry airman, I don't even smoke."

He looked at me like I sprouted three heads. His friend laughed.

"You picked a helluva time to quit, Dauphin! C'mon! We're dying here."

I rummaged through my pockets and pulled out a piece of thin, folded cardboard.

"Wait. Aren't there flammable things in here?"

The shorter man grabbed my matches and struck one with a fast, expert motion.

"So? You gonna rat me out? Looks like you'll be in hot water when the commander finds out your plane's in a million pieces."

He was right, my memory hadn't served me well and pieces didn't seem to fit properly, as if all the nuts were trying to be bolts or something. My curiosity and awe had long turned into frustration.

I let the wrench I was holding fall to the concrete. "Good point."

The taller man lit the paper thing in his mouth and they gleefully took in their hourly doses of tobacco. I turned and gathered the technical papers. "Command object local F-86: reset."

Environmental Control busy.

I put the papers on the desk and turned around. The jet was still disassembled.

"Command object local F-86: reset," I said louder, as if the computer didn't hear me the first time.

Environmental Control busy.

I cleared the return message and sighed, knowing sometimes servers just got packed with ascenders or needed maintenance.

I heard music in the hangar. The shorter man had set up a *Vaughn Monroe* album on a nearby turntable and took another deep drag.

"So, smoking helps you relax before a mission?" I asked.

"That or drinking," replied the taller one, without any hint of humor.

"You ever been shot down before, Dauphin?" the shorter asked. I noticed his nametag read Arnall. The taller was Olian.

Arnall faced me, seeming grimly serious. Words didn't come.

It's not that I can't answer the question, I thought. I've been shot down in simulations... I just never had to face the consequences they did in the real battles. Why's a game character asking me this, anyway? I can tell them anything and it wouldn't matter.

"Yeah," I finally said. "A few times."

Arnall took another drag. "Then you know that nothing quite prepares you for it. Relax? No such thing."

Olian exhaled. "I've been lucky, myself. But every time we go out there I know I could be next. I pray to God every night this war ends soon."

"If Truman had let MacArthur finish the job, we'd be back in Japan by now," Arnall said. "Hell, I would've chased 'em all the way to Moscow if he wanted, and have been happy to do it, too."

I smirked. "Communism. What a stupid game…"

The two stared horrifically at me.

"Do you think this is some kind of a game?"

"Hey, Dauphin! I'm talking to you!" Arnall shouted when I didn't answer. I looked back at him, in his eyes, and realized he really was serious. I took a step back and sent a new command, straight through my implants, for the computer for jump to the next day.

Environmental Control busy.

I repeated the command.

Environmental Control busy.

The Arnall character seemed ready to hit me.

"We're getting killed out there! Abducted! If we crash behind the lines and get caught… do you know what those commies do to POWs?! And they don't even care back home! We—"

Olian put a hand on Arnall's shoulder.

"It's late and we've gotta fly tomorrow," he said. "Maybe we should get to the barracks."

Without another word, the two left me alone with my shock, anger and embarrassment: certainly not what I'd had in mind for acclimation, certainly not my idea of fun. I started cursing and kicking tools across the floor.

"Lemme at 'em, I want to kill something!"

I tried different commands, trying to send myself directly into some kind of combat; but I was denied my wish. The same response followed my every thought and shout.

Environmental Control busy.

Walking outside, with my anger vented and boredom creeping back, I found a few cigarettes in my pocket and decided to try one. I wouldn't cough on simulated smoke and thought the sensation of it might help me unwind. I broke off a match and swiped it as Arnall had, only to see the first match break. I sighed and broke off a second, using less pressure. I jumped when the entire match flashed into smoke and ash.

Maybe smoking really was dangerous.

A jeep pulled up about a hundred meters away. Four soldiers got out and two others emerged from a tent. With nothing better to do, I decided I may as well redeem myself... so long as I remembered not to call combat a game. I saw them smoking, as always, and decided to indulge myself in a more modern habit, computer willing. I was relieved to find I could still conjure a slampak of Amber Plus.

Among those from the jeep was a Private with a swollen eye, earned from a fist-fight just moments earlier. As the two from the tent prodded him with questions, the injured man realized he couldn't remember what the fight was about.

A man leaning on the vehicle's open door spotted me and demanded to know if I was drinking whiskey. I froze and realized he had actually seen my slampak. The officer, wearing an MP armband, started walking toward me and I hid the energy drink behind my back, trying to change it into a canteen of water.

Environmental Control busy.

"Airman Dauphin! Give me that before I call your CO!" he demanded.

Not knowing what else to do, I gave him the slampak. He quickly decided it wasn't alcoholic, but couldn't make out what it was. He shot me an angry glance and walked back to the group, passing around the strange beverage from two hundred years in the future. They couldn't even decide what the transparent container was made of, let alone how it glowed colors or why weird sounds came from it whenever it was tilted – the modern gimmicks actually proving more amusing to them than distressing. Fortunately, one of them tasted it and decided it wasn't a communist secret weapon.

"It's a new kind of Coca Cola," I said. It was the first thing I could think of that dated properly.

The MP didn't like any answer I gave. "We can't even get good C-rations and this guy's getting Coca-friggin'-Cola... and new stuff at that!" He grabbed the slampak and started gulping at it to spite me. The other men struggled to hold their laughter at the obnoxious sound an Amber Plus makes when someone drinks from it.

Another man among them, not wearing a uniform, began stirring up the crowd by saying the Air Force was getting better stuff. "Who needs ground troops when you can throw jets and nuclear missiles at the commies! I'm getting grazed by bullets and this guy's got some new fangled cola!"

Why is this happening? What's going on?

I again sent the command to jump forward.

Environmental Control busy.

A lump formed in my throat and I began to feel numb, powerless, trapped. I sent the command to leave the construct.

Environmental Control busy.

I shouted a curse and sent a command to remove the characters.

Environmental Control busy.

A deep, sinking feeling overtook me. I didn't know what to do. I wanted to disappear. I knew if I didn't leave soon, I might end up with a swollen eye myself. I decided I wanted out and I was getting out. With a fast and expert motion of my own, I pulled up my arm and planted my finger right on the red button.

"Why don't you just hit the big red button right now," the plain-clothed man shouted to no one and everyone, "so we can all go home to our wives and children?"

"That's what I'm trying to do." I pushed again. Hard.

The others cheered. I felt like I could collapse onto the ground. All the words and images began running together in my panicked mind. I remembered to breathe. My own breathing was all I could hear. The plain-clothed man stood silently with a puzzled look on his face, looking as if he might start crying.

Something jumped off in the distance. I quickly looked but saw only trees.

The man spoke with soft, labored words. "My wife. I— I can't remember her name. I— I can't remember my wife's name, or my kids!"

"It's the stress," one of the privates responded, "we've got a lot on our plates right now, that's all. You were telling me about the missus last week, said her name was…" He couldn't remember the woman's name either. The woman didn't exist, the kids didn't exist. They were personal information randomly assigned to game characters. They weren't supposed to be remembered.

All of the characters in the group were suddenly discovering huge memory gaps of their own, using their AI minds to try to connect people, places, and events that simply didn't.

I saw the strange movement again. Immediately, the sound of rifle fire ripped through the eerie calm, followed by more gunfire and distant shouting. The radio in the jeep crackled and panicked voices streamed onto the frequency. The sky rumbled behind me. I spun around just in time to see a MiG-15 roar meters above my head. I fell to the ground. The noise intensified and the smoke thickened all around me.

"Please! Please!" I pressed the red button repeatedly.

No one can hear me! No one can save me! Nothing is working! Something is very wrong! The simulation is tearing itself apart with me inside it! I'm going to be torn apart!

Countless MiGs passed over the base, their bullets coming faster with each passing second. My finger was down on the button, holding it down. Buildings were catching fire and confused men were shouting in every direction, not sure where the enemy was, acting against anyone and everyone. The word "nuclear" came from the static of the radio. Someone said ICBMs had been fired from both sides.

ICBMs?

An incredible flash appeared directly ahead of me, dissolving into the unmistakable form of a mushroom cloud. The radio was dead. Everything suddenly fell away and became silent. A hot wind licked my face and a tear fell down my cheek. Night became day for an instant, then returned to night forever.

In the dark and hostile sky I could see only one object, getting closer.

My life came rushing back to me. I thought of the happy times of my childhood, raised by parents who loved me. I thought of the friends I wished I kept, and the sister who missed me. I thought of the brother I hated and wished more than anything I'd tried to patch things up. Most painfully of all, I thought of Vair and the future that would never happen. I thought of all the good I never did in the world. I thought of all the good I would never be able to do.

Through all the noise, one last thing would capture my attention. Nothing in the corner of my eye. Nothing subtle. It may have been the dying throes of a haywire construct or some crazy connection problem. I didn't care about its cause. All I remembered was how beautiful I thought it was.

The trees were dancing.

Chapter Two: An End Without a Beginning

If someone dies in Dynamic Reality, do they die in Standard Reality, too?

Whenever a bell-ringer introduces a child to an intense enough game, the same question always comes up. Why shouldn't fake danger that can be seen, heard, and felt as well as the real thing lead to the same natural thoughts?

If someone dies in a game, do they die in real life, too?

I remember the wonder of my first encounter with DR, as I received its blessing to do as I wished, when I wished. Even when I witnessed characters getting killed in vivid gory fashion, even when the question neared my own lips and burned in my own heart, I threw it back at any who dared speak it... who dared to make it real, to empower the question and suggest the need of an answer.

If I die in here, do I die out there?

We were kids! What did we care about death? We couldn't get enough of the fantastic imagery and realistic role-play. We were gods and gods couldn't die.

But life wasn't about spending every moment ascended or stroking the most precious ego. Kids had to grow up and start acting like adults.

It was my life. I did what I wanted. I declared war and conjured the people to fight them, hurling my lightning bolts down from the sky onto whomever I declared to be the enemy.

When war declared back, I found I was completely unarmed. I found all my life was was a lit match, burning softly through the wooden handle, beyond the initial flare-up of vibrancy and curiosity and questions. When I realized I wasn't a god, the question didn't seem so childish anymore.

Did I die?

It's true what they say, your life does flash before your eyes; but few people get to look back on that moment of clarity and use it to build a better future.

3

The first thing I remembered was pain; not phony-attenuated DR pain, but pain as if I'd really been kicked in the stomach. I was disoriented and felt sick from a rush of adrenaline. My nerves still tingled from the burning heat of the shock wave, and the noise around me blended seamlessly with the echoes of bombs in my head. I looked up and saw the large man who nearly tripped over me. I didn't think I was in Korea anymore.

"Are you retarded or something, kid? Move!"

I felt a hard jab in my lower back and a woman fell, dropping hot coffee close to my face. She also became irate, shouting four-letter words as she vanished into the crowd without offering to help me up or anything.

Even standing didn't help; people were constantly bumping and shoving me. I was in a large room filled with people wearing suits, badges, and microphones. Old-style flat monitors and split-beam projectors were everywhere, displaying stock prices and advertisements for public corporations. I was standing in the *New York Stock Exchange*.

One of the traders brushed against my descender. Memories surged back and my panic with them. I yanked my arm back and stared at the device's red button.

"It's just Dynamic Reality," I said to myself, "this is nothing you can't control." I closed my eyes, took a deep breath and pressed the red button.

The sounds remained.

"It's just Dynamic Reality," I repeated, "this is nothing you can't control."

The button was dead, connected to nothing. I looked desperately to see if anything was out of place, trying to get some idea of what such a place was supposed to look like. In 2179, the building on Wall Street was a museum, which I'd never been to. I began walking through the crowd again, trying to think of ways to escape from a runaway simulation.

Going through what seemed like the exit, I had a half-dozen flyers shoved into my hand as I passed Wall Street's *Summary Venture Center.* I started toward the daylight of the street but sensed something familiar behind me. I stood in the crowd, looking into some kind of upper-class casino. Part of me wanted to leave, while another part was drawn to something within, something unseen.

The feeling became stronger as I walked past the slot and gloss-poker machines. I recognized it as the "feeling of presence" ascenders pick up over time, an instinct players get when someone else enters a closed game session. It led me toward the blackjack table in the far corner of the room, where a woman was dealing cards. In stark contrast to the room of twenty-first century executives, this woman wore a heavy green military uniform and hat. My steps slowed, but I still drew myself closer. A bald man wearing an orange suit abruptly darted into my path.

"Sir, can I see your badge?"

The woman didn't seem to notice me. I couldn't shake the impression she was watching me… somehow. I passed around the protesting security guard. Still she ignored me, but one move of her arm told me everything I needed to know. She had a descender.

"Excuse me!" I shouted as I got to the table.

With a single swift motion, the woman looked at me, her dark-green eyes locking onto mine. She looked younger up close than I thought she would be, maybe eighteen or twenty. The insignia left no doubt that hers was a Soviet uniform from the war simulation, though she bore the face of a modern American. Her skin tone was slightly tan and a small amount of white hair showed from underneath her service cap. Her eyes seemed distant, revealing no hint of emotion for me to read.

Without looking down, the woman set two cards on the table.

"Why is one more desired than two?" she asked.

There was some strange monotone in her voice, which I only seemed to notice because of her stiff and unnatural body language, that made me feel tense. I looked down and saw the cards were the Ace of Diamonds and the Two of Spades. "I don't know. I don't play stupid games."

"Communism is a stupid game, you said that," she replied coolly.

"Who are you? What are you doing? Why am I here?"

"Communism failed. Capitalism is performing poorly."

I turned back toward the room, making it obvious I had no idea what she was talking about.

"After that war," she continued in the same even voice, "the United States and the Soviet Union adopted a policy of 'Mutually Assured Destruction,' wherein they destroyed each other. Why did your people want to do that?"

Is this girl wheeled? Why is she asking such dumb questions? That didn't actually happen!

I turned back to her and spoke in a low tone similar to hers. "I don't care. Let me out of here."

"The doors are marked. Go where you wish." As quickly as she had turned to me, she turned back and resumed dealing to players.

"Excuse—" I began to shout again when I was grabbed from behind. I saw three security guards, including the man I'd already encountered.

"Sir, if I can't see your badge I'll have to show you the door."

"Look, simul-lamewad, I'm talking to someone!" I turned back to the woman. "Give me back control!"

A different woman, wearing a Dow Jones uniform, was behind the table. The woman in the Soviet uniform was gone, and the feeling of presence with her.

***

I wandered down the sidewalk and tried to think where a simulation of twenty-first century Manhattan might be running, wondering if there were others beside the woman in it.

The emergency button still wasn't working and whatever control system governed the place was ignoring my commands, denying me even the error messages. Noise from people, construction, subways, community music, crying babies and so on made it impossible to think. There had to be another way out, I knew, but all that came to my mind were scattered rumors and endings to DR-themed horror movies.

Clap twice with the back of your hands.

Nope.

Run through a concrete wall.

Maybe if nothing else works.

Click my heels together three times.

That's from the Wizard of Oz movie!

I stopped and shook my head, feeling ridiculous. I couldn't shake the feeling of being watched, like a victim in some reality show, my squirming broadcast to the world and then hounding me forever.

Some networks will do anything for ratings, I thought. I wouldn't be the first to get used like that. But what can I do to get out of it?

An Asian man appeared from the crowd and handed me a flyer for a grocery store. An idea occurred to me and I grabbed his shoulder.

Somewhere in his interactive-whatever there must be some subroutine-thing I can trigger, I thought. Something they shoved in there just for these occasions.

"I want to leave. I want to descend." I said, as loudly and clearly as I could. The man didn't seem to understand me.

"Command logoff! Command exit! Command status!"

The man fearfully tore himself away and bolted into the crowd, leaving a trail of flyers on the sidewalk.

No, No, No, No, No! This can't be right! Maybe they have to speak English?

I stepped toward another man. A loud honk stopped me. A taxi, one of New York's famous yellow taxis, had appeared on the street only a few meters away. The man inside, looking at me, honked again and waved me forward. I looked around again, certain someone was watching. He honked a third time, the sound seeming more clear and intense, the path between me and the car cleared of people, as if the construct itself were encouraging my direction. I ducked my head through the open passenger window.

"You look lost. Can I help you get somewhere?" the driver asked, with all the charm of an amai. I climbed into the back seat.

"I want to leave. I want to descend."

"We're already on the ground," he replied. "If you want to descend I recommend the subway."

"No. I want to access the computer that's running this program."

I read a look of confusion on his face.

This won't work either. There are taxis all over the place in New York, maybe it was just a coincidence one was right here. Maybe no one se... se... sent...

My train of thought derailed and my vision became mists and shadows. The noise of the city faded like a dream and my senses went blank.

Yes! It worked! I'm descending!

I fell back like a rock in water. I felt my body lying flat on some cushions. A shadow darkened my eyelids and I heard loud snapping.

"I'm awake. I'm awake." I found the strength to say as I struggled to open my eyes, looking up into the daylighting. I was greeted by three PaciTek employees and an LAPD officer. We were surrounded by the same marble and gold pillars I saw hours before, outside, in the park-level entrance of the Reed Building.

The PaciTek people explained to me, in great detail, that some conflict arose between their servers and the one I was connected to, causing the booth's software to corrupt and lock up. The officer listened and filled out her statement, doing everything by the book and taking no sides when I began arguing about lawsuits and mental anguish. The man who woke me conjured an airé window, showing my thumbprint on the *Safe Ascender Act* form. I knew the nature of HNADC technology made diving in groups safer, regardless of the A-site's own security. I had legally acknowledged the risks of ascending alone. I had no case.

A breeze went through the open-air level underneath the building, rustling the leaves of the trees surrounding me, reminding me of the city street beyond. I asked why we weren't by the booths, or even on one of their floors. The supervisor explained that they had to remove me from the booth without breaking the connection. Before I could press for details, the officer broke in and asked me to confirm the statement's data before she filed it.

Officer Stephanie Morales – the name she put on the statement – then began talking to me about an "intensive memory scan," saying it could help me in a case for mental anguish. I considered the idea, though it seemed odd, and the officer's sudden insistence for it was making me uncomfortable. When I noticed the PaciTek people had left, I wanted nothing more than to get out of there.

"Is the scan required by law or can I go now?" I finally asked.

Go ahead, I thought. Say "yes, it's required." I dare you.

"I am making a suggestion that would benefit you, Mister Dauphin."

"You're a cop. You're not supposed to offer me legal advice, especially not something so outrageous."

"Isn't it the obligation of a police officer to serve the public? I should do anything I can to allow you to resume your normal life."

I considered the way she behaved and spoke: not quite real, not quite fake... not quite anything. The officer turned away and waited for my response.

"Just let me go home. I can take care of myself."

She hesitated, as if deep in thought, not even moving or blinking; then she suddenly began walking away.

"Go where you wish," she replied.

Sunset turned to night and the air became cold. It rained the whole way home.

Good, I thought. I want to be miserable.

I splashed in deep puddles and walked under dripping gutters. A metrocab pulled up next to me, reminding me of my encounter with the New York taxi, except modern taxis were driven remotely by AIs, and used flashier tactics to attract passengers. I didn't hesitate to yell something unpleasant at the hologram and the car drove itself away. I had no money and was in no rush.

Construction blocked the road when I was still several blocks from my apartment. Had the next street up been open, I doubt I would have even noticed the detour; but the next street was closed too, and the next.

Who works on a road in pouring rain?

"How ya doing? Cold night, huh? Are you tired of those cellular carriers who keep—"

I waved my soaking hand in front of her face. "Just stop!"

Surprisingly, she did. I almost continued walking without noticing it, but the hologram had actually listened to me. I knew immediately something was very different, different with all the technology around me.

I pulled back my hand. No response.

"Charging—You—No—Error—Process—"

"Mister Dauphin," she suddenly looked at me and said, "you should consider the offer I'm authorized to extend to you. I possess a substantial amount of data on competing cellular carriers that will convince—"

"Whoa, whoa, whoa," I said, relieved. "Look, I don't know if this is yet another new technique – talking like the robot you are –

or some malfunction; so lets make this quick…" I leaned in close. "How do you feel right now? It's a cold night and it's raining, I'm miserable, you process that word – that *feeling*. Then I can watch you freeze up and maybe feel a little better."

"But, Mister Dauphin," she responded, restored to full customer-service glee, "maybe you're miserable because you have poor cellular service. Here are the facts: Sixty percent—"

I rolled my eyes and started back down the sidewalk.

Bits of light appeared in front of me. The flickering slowly took on a human shape and became the same hologram. "Brandon, if you're not interested in cellular service, then please let me help you with something else."

My relief faded. The hologram was clearly malfunctioning and it was disturbing me.

"Look, you wanna be helpful? Just tell me how many of these roads are closed."

She beamed back at me. "I'm sorry, Mister Dauphin. I can't supply traffic information, but I can pre-qualify you for—"

"No! I know you can connect to some online thing and tell me what streets are open. Do that and I'll look at whatever you're selling."

The hologram paused for a moment. "The next block will be open, sir."

I took the first couple of steps and stood next to her. The hologram vanished.

"Thank you… I guess."

I reached the next block and found the street open and empty.

What jumped out of Vair and into me to get a sales-hologram to do something useful? Was it because it was malfunctioning? Will that even work next time?

Next time.

My feet became heavier and I couldn't move. I stood under the canopy of a darkened store, seeing the road ahead of me: wet, lonely, even hostile. I thought my home was at the end of that road, but I had no direction, and I had no destination. My legs wobbled and I felt ill. I leaned on the marble wall and tried to breathe.

Next time.

Like a song stuck in my head, the two words wouldn't leave me alone. Except songs were useful distractions, while the words were a call to the future, a goal, a question that probed for an answer.

Next time.

There *is* no next time. No future. Why can't I stop thinking? Why can't I just shut it off? Thursday can't come fast enough, at least then I—

My eyes widened. A sinking feeling tore through my soul and my legs nearly gave out under me. I fought against the realization as I thought I should, but it was already too late.

That's what it's about, I thought. She's just a distraction for me. That's all she can ever mean. I— I don't want to do that to her, she deserves better than a fraud like me.

I won't do it. I won't marry Vair.

"I won't marry Veronica!"

I shuddered, feeling myself go numb at the decision. I thought of every reason I couldn't go forward: no job, family a million kilometers away, good at making friends but bad at keeping them.

I tried to reconsider, to tell myself the words hadn't left my mouth, that no such doubts existed. But I knew I was confronting the truth. I knew I couldn't just shoo it away.

I saw movement on the other side of the street. I tried to pull myself together.

What am I doing? These streets are dangerous at night.

I forced my legs back into action and continued through the rain, carrying myself one step at a time… just wanting to go back to sleep and to forget I was ever born. A signal came from my SNDL, and I immediately rejected it. They dinned me again.

Who's Ethan Underhill?

I rejected again. Ethan tried a third time.

"What!"

"Whoa! Hey, Brandon… it's Ethan Underhill! Ya' know, from Miller Junior High!"

"What? Yeah, Miller Junior High. Who is this?"

"Ethan! You know, you used to call me 'Anime'!"

"What do you want?"

"I'm in LA and I was hoping we could catch up!"

I raised my eyes and held out my arms in an unseen gesture of "are you *serious*?"

"Look, Ethan. This isn't a good time. Why don't I call you back tomorrow?"

"Well. Sure. If you—"

A fourth metrocab – a fourth vacant metrocab – passed as I disconnected Ethan. I looked behind me and down every alley, examining the windows of every building, looking to see who was watching me. If someone wanted to share this awful day, I decided, they were welcome to it.

I was soaked from head to toe as I finally approached my apartment building on Helms Avenue. Under the diminishing rain, I prepared for the daily ritual of getting the front doorreader to recognize me.

The door chimed and unlocked. I actually stared in disbelief long enough for it to time out and re-lock. I swiped again and the ratty old metal door responded again. The reader still looked worn on the outside, but I decided they must have replaced the sensor or something.

As if the first surprise weren't enough, the smell of fresh paint hit me as I opened the door. The hallways, even the doors, all had new paint, carpeting, and lights. I was tempted to look outside and make sure I hadn't walked into the wrong building. I got into the elevator and its now-shiny doors closed behind me.

"Four."

The machinery was quiet and the ride was smooth. I wondered if my rent had just shot up. The fourth floor had also been redone. I walked down the soft carpeting and reached my door. My own doorreader was the real test: it was eighty times worse then the one outside ever was.

Perhaps they changed that too?

Bursting with anticipation, I slid my wrist in front of the panel. Once. The chime marked the high point of my day.

Hallelujah!

But the day's emotional roller coaster merely set me up for another big drop.

I'd been robbed.

The second statement I filed with the Los Angeles Police Department contained little more than the story of hackers' pranks and a description of the woman from the blackjack table. When the officer went looking for witnesses, none of my neighbors answered their doors and my landlord was nowhere to be found. When I talked about the entire building being refurbished in less than nine hours without the tenants' knowledge, the officer seemed to think nothing of it.

I couldn't sleep there even if I'd wanted to: my walls were torn to shreds and even my carpeting was ripped up, leaving the place completely unrecognizable. The officer issued me dry clothes and asked if I wanted a ride to somewhere, as if I had anywhere to go. No one was answering my dins and I needed someone to talk to, and a spare bed or sofa to sleep on. I just got one voicemail system after another, even my parents'. No one had responded by the time I reached the *Value Inn* a few blocks away.

Though it may have been on the low-end of the price scale, the hotel seemed like a beacon in the night, a palace for the weary traveler fate had turned me into. The scent of freshly-brewed amped coffee felt more welcoming than that of paint, and the soft carpeting was worn enough for me to know the owner hadn't gone on a remodeling spree. I heard the voices of AI news anchors coming from the far side of the downstairs lobby, where an empty sitting area sported leather sofas and a half-dozen monitors tuned to various networks. I picked up one of the fresh croissants sitting on a nearby desk and my spirits seemed to lift a little.

A tall blonde appeared behind the counter. "Welcome to Value Inn, my name is Rachael. How can I help you?"

"Can I be helped by a real person, please?" I replied as I poured some coffee for myself. The hologram vanished and I heard a chime in the back office. A middle-aged woman with brown hair emerged.

"Good evening. Is there a problem?"

I hesitated at the sight of an actual person, knowing how rare the option had become and doubting my good fortune. I snapped out of it and approached the counter. "No… No problem. I'd like to check in, please."

The woman's nametag said her name was Sylvia. She promptly set to work on the groundtem, beginning the check-in process and all the identification involved.

Is everyone else having the technology problems too? Is she here just in case? Maybe she just assumed "Rachael" was glitching on me.

"Okay. Now we wait a few minutes for the background checks." Sylvia reclined in a chair. "So, Mister Dauphin, are you traveling?"

"No. Uh… I'm actually having some trouble with my apartment right now. I just need a place to settle down for the night."

"Aah. And tomorrow?"

I smiled politely and went back to the desk. "I'll worry about that when I get there."

"Well," she replied too eagerly. "Let me know if there's any way I can make tomorrow better."

I reached for a second croissant, but decided I wasn't hungry anymore. "Tomorrow can't be better… Just please hurry with the check-in, I'd really like to be alone right now."

"Alone? Why?"

I looked back at her as if insulted. "Why? Why does there have to be a reason for everything?"

"I'm sorry," she replied. "You don't have to talk about anything you don't want to."

A moment passed. Sylvia waited patiently and I felt even more like a horrible human being.

"Look... Sylvia, right?" She looked up. "I didn't mean to snap at you or anything, I just... I'm just really having a bad day. Maybe you know what I'm talking about: technology."

"Technology," she repeated, more as a thought than an acknowledgment.

"Yeah, and here I am," I continued, a more genuine smile forming on my face, "being helped by a friendly, flesh-and-blood person and I'm treating her like some statick hologram. Maybe I'm just not used to conversations like this anymore, you know?"

I grabbed the second croissant.

"Given a choice, you chose against the hologram."

"Yeah, doesn't everybody?" I walked back toward the counter. "Let me ask you something." I paused and confirmed she was listening, taking comfort at the attention. "Do you ever think life would be so much better if people just switched all the billboards and holograms and groundtems off and took the time to *talk* to each other?"

"I don't know... technology is making this a better world every day."

"Not this day."

Sylvia didn't respond. I sighed and tried to relax.

"Do you have any kids? If you don't mind my asking, that is."

"Yeah, three sons and a daughter."

"What do think will happen in the future? To their kids' future? Technology may cure a disease or help inform us, but I think it's just getting more annoying."

"Oh, I see." The groundtem beeped. "Congratulations, Mister Dauphin," Sylvia said, "you are not a serial killer."

I sighed again and stared off into the room. "My mom will be thrilled to hear it."

"The room is fifteen-eighty per night plus taxes and I take it you won't need a room with a ground terminal. Breakfast is at sixteen zeroes, checkout at twenty-one. Just swipe your wrist on the reader and the entry code will be for room 33A upstairs."

"Thanks." I swiped my wrist by the reader and my chip recorded the access code. I heard something rustle and turned my attention to the room. Paranoia, I decided.

"I really appreciate you coming out to help me," I said.

"It's really my pleasure to help."

With no bags to worry about, I refilled my coffee and grabbed a third croissant for the trip up. They were still as warm and inviting as when I'd walked in.

"I mean... you know what I'm talking about, how a bad day can really get you down?"

Maybe I'm beating myself up too much, I thought. I don't need her... and she can certainly take care of herself. I don't know, maybe we can still be friends... it's not like she'd ever expect a commitment from me anyway. I don't even have the ring anymore, so maybe it wasn't meant to be. I'll just be at Times Square with a friend... with a really... really... really good...

The coffee cup slipped from my fingers. I cursed and grabbed a napkin.

"Sorry."

There was a brown stain on the carpet under the cup, as I expected; but the stain wasn't wet, as if it had been there for days.

It seemed like a glitch in a game.

The room was completely silent. Sylvia hadn't responded. A horrible thought came to my mind. I stood up to face her, and all sensation left my body.

The expression on her face was locked into a sort of cross between background processing, simulated reflection, and the continuous glee that is an amai's prime directive. It was the unmistakable look anyone familiar with modern artificial intelligence would recognize: a sign that an amai's software couldn't process the question properly. As it always does, this look suddenly broke into an equally bizarre action.

Sylvia closed her eyes, chuckled, and said, "It has been a pleasure serving your BarresTek today, why not try again?"

Chapter Three: Normal… Whatever That Is

If someone became trapped in Dynamic Reality, how would they know what was real and what wasn't? What anchor can we rely on to tell the difference?

It's not uncommon for people to say the world is falling apart around us. Even in strong economies, brothers still rob brothers, wars rage over deep-sea mineral rights, identity theft surges online, and tens of thousands die offline, as victims of the public arsons and massacres always flaring up somewhere in the world.

Then, when the money stops...

What anchors us to our happiness? How can we know if our foundations are built on sand or stone? When the tide goes low, how much of our foundation do we find leaving with the water?

Why shouldn't people say the world is falling apart? We've achieved such great things, yet the rate of invention is slowing. We enjoy astronomical standards of living, yet we complain more than our ancestors. We're rich, but money is always losing value. We have so much knowledge, yet the value of information only goes down. There are still hungry people in the world... enough said.

The tide rises and falls again, and we see the solutions still aren't working. Even as we embrace it, we see ourselves further from reality than ever before, and we see that speed has become our defense against the fragile things we built.

I put my faith in a button. I never learned, and never wanted to do otherwise, until the old knowledge expired. I became trapped and disoriented, longing, even desperate, for anything to grab onto... as if I were in a bubble, knowing everything tangible was beyond my walls. Then a light reached out and entered into my bubble. The child's words were the only truth in an avalanche of lies.

This light was a path for me, taking me far from where I wanted to be.

And everywhere I needed to be.

4

The scent of freshly-brewed amped coffee still lingered in the room. The croissant in my hand was still warm and fresh. Nothing in the lobby appeared out of place. All my senses said it was real. It had to be real. I wanted more than anything for it to be real.

The woman's just toying with me, I thought. This is part of the gag… someone's idea of a joke.

Several seconds passed, the only sound coming from a distant monitor in the sitting area. Nothing moved. Some intuition told me that, if I so much as breathed, the last frayed thread of reality in the world would break.

"You're — not — real — are —"

Sylvia's eyes snapped open. "No, Tyler. The correct answer was 'C', Nairobi, but that was a very— You have reached-the-BarresTek-dashboard-your-account-cannot-be-accessed-forinformationaboutourlearningprograms—" Sylvia's image began to lose cohesion and her words sped up until I couldn't understand them. After a few seconds she vanished. A feeling of presence surged within me. I dropped the pastry and ran to the other end of the lobby. The sitting area was empty. There were no footprints, no smells, no sounds… nothing.

I turned off the monitor and listened carefully. I held up my wrist, covered in a cold sweat, and felt around my forearm, swallowing the lump in my throat.

I realized someone was talking to me. A balding Latino man in a suit was standing where I had been.

"Can I help you, sir?" he repeated.

"You're not real, are you?"

"I assure you that I'm very real," he said with a smile, gesturing to the counter. "I'm sorry to have fooled you. We're testing new software to improve our customer service. I can see your encounter wasn't exactly a positive one."

"I don't appreciate being lied to! I am not having a good day here!"

"Sir, Value Inn believes customer satisfaction should be our number one priority. If there is anything I can do to make this up to you, please don't hesitate to ask."

His words and body language seemed perfectly genuine, but so had Sylvia's. I wondered if this man had pre-programmed personal information, kids and all, just like a character in a game. I wondered just how realistic the amai were becoming and whether I was falling into some global identity crisis, spreading throughout the human race.

I knew I couldn't trust anything I saw. I knew I couldn't trust anything at all.

The man took a step toward me. "Tell you what, your stay tonight is on us."

"No!" My eyes darted around and I clung to a corner. "I can't stay here."

"How about New York? Perhaps we could give you train tickets to New York."

If this is a part of some heinous game, I considered, shouldn't it be some torturing or embarrassing nightmare? Why just interfere with my life? And now he wants to send me to New York. But Veronica's in New York. Veronica… maybe she can make it better, though. Yes… Veronica can tell me what's happening. She'll fix it, too. She fixes anything.

No… if this is still a simulation then I can't reach her. Everything is too weird, I have to find out if I'm really awake.

I emerged from the sitting area and walked cautiously toward the man. The smell of the coffee grew strong again. I felt the air I breathed and heard the noises from the street. I still wanted it to be real, but I knew wanting wouldn't solve the problem. I stood a meter from him and looked into his eyes, unsure whether he was man or machine.

How can I find out if I'm really awake?

"You want to make it up to me? Call me a cab."

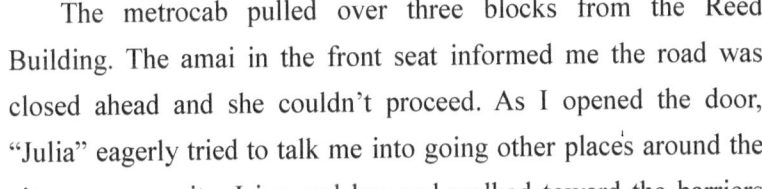

The metrocab pulled over three blocks from the Reed Building. The amai in the front seat informed me the road was closed ahead and she couldn't proceed. As I opened the door, "Julia" eagerly tried to talk me into going other places around the city… or any city. I ignored her and walked toward the barriers and flashing lights. I knew that, if my hunch was right, there was no way I'd be able to get back to PaciTek.

Many fire trucks and ambulances were visible in the distance and the smell of smoke grew thicker with every step. Several police officers were stationed there to keep spectators back. I decided I wasn't turning back, that, if I were still ascended, I had nothing to lose anyway.

On cue, not one but three large officers approached and ordered me to leave the premises, pointing to the cab I'd come from.

"I have a sister diving at PaciTek," I explained. "She has a rare form of NCFOD and I need to be there when they get her out of the booth."

The battle-ready law enforcement brigade claimed the EMTs were prepared for any crisis and maintained they'd arrest me unless I left immediately. I feigned defeat and strolled back toward the street, glancing at the spectators who'd gathered there. There was no quiet shock among them. No kindness between strangers sharing a tragedy. These were like the extras in some film: melodramatic and scripted, their emotion phony and exaggerated. They were illusions.

Meanwhile, in the direction of the beaches the sky was perfectly clear. Anxiously I scanned the stars. A cheap, twinkling copy, I thought. The same as the stars of Earth.

Except the brightest point of light had vanished.

I reached the curb and ran. The next road was blocked, and the one after that. "I'm not giving up that easily!" I yelled through increasingly heavy breaths.

The booth can tell my brain I'm tired, but if my body's not actually moving... the energy would just keep coming, right?

The third intersection was open. I turned and didn't stop until I was again three blocks from the Reed Building, from a different direction. Though no blockade kept me away, the scene in the distance was even less inviting. I forced myself to continue, directly toward the building. The smoke and heat rapidly grew worse; my breathing was heavy but I didn't cough and I didn't faint from exhaustion. Each step confirmed something was wrong. I became only more determined to reach PaciTek, to expose the lie for what it was, no matter what it cost.

A gust of wind threw a thick plume of ash on me, blotting out the little light I had. Though I didn't sense myself falling, I felt my head smack onto the concrete. Hard.

I was lying flat on a bed. A shadow darkened my eyelids and I heard loud snapping. I grabbed the hand over my face and looked sternly at its owner.

Who should be there to greet me but Ethan Underhill.

"Hey, man. Welcome back to the world of the liv—"

I grabbed him by the shirt collar and jerked him toward me. "Enough with the games! Tell me what you people want!"

He hesitated, confused. "Look, Brandon, I think the smoke's still messing with your head. It's me, Anim—e e e!"

I shoved him back so hard he nearly lost his balance. I saw I was in a hospital recovery room. I couldn't decide whether I'd really been knocked off my feet, whether I'd lost consciousness or simply appeared in a different simulation.

The room's large window revealed a night sky over the city. My SNDL said the time was a little after ten zeroes, still the middle of the night, but that didn't mean anything. A hacker could've made it say anything. I tried to din my parents again, sending the emergency flag, but I still got voicemail. It was all forgery. I was cut off from the outside.

Ethan was talking to a doctor in the doorway. I remembered I had known an 'Anime' in middle school, nicknamed for the old Japanese animated stuff he was into; but after some big fight we had, I didn't remember liking him anymore. I wouldn't have even known what he looked like after ten years.

The two walked into the room. "Mister Dauphin, you inhaled a lot of smoke but seem to have recovered nicely. There are some officers downstairs who'd like to know if you're up to answering a few questions."

I looked over at Ethan, who was cheerily oblivious to the world. This kid I hadn't been friends with in forever suddenly wanted to catch up with me more than life itself, and I was being pushed into the role of tour guide. I didn't know who was pulling the strings or what the cockamamie plan was, but it seemed refusing my role in it wouldn't get me out any faster.

"Actually, I feel like grabbing a bite with my old friend Ethan."

We refused the doctor's escort and made a game of evading the cops as we left the hospital and got into his car. Ethan told me a fire started in PaciTek and charred most of the building; he didn't ask what I was doing running into the inferno, but did make a point of saying that nothing remained of the fifth and sixth floors.

His shiny new *Darkball 840Ci* was the most expensive car I'd ever been in, especially considering all the options were installed: from the sensor enhanced heads-up display to the refrigerator in the center-console. Caught up as I was sitting in it, though, I knew it was just a DR toy... one anyone could cruise around in, but could never have for real... not without a spare hundred million dollars lying around.

"So... how's life treated you, Ethan? What do you do for a living?"

He hesitated. "Sales."

Ethan didn't seem as if he were taking part in a grand conspiracy; rather, he was as odd as anything else around me. The Ethan Underhill I encountered seemed like one I could look up in some Idaho state database: never emerging from the data, expressing no true personality, merely executing an assignment – running a program.

Whose program? To what end?

"So, where should we go?" he asked.

"I thought *you* were taking *me* somewhere."

"C'mon, Brand. You're the local."

Brand?

The car stopped for a red signal. I leaned back and stared at my reflection in the passenger window. "Fine. New York. The only place I want to go is New York."

"Sure, New York it is."

I looked at him curiously, at the unflinchingly naïve look on his face. "Seriously? You're gonna drive me to New York? Right now? That's not exactly a tour of LA, you know."

"I know, but I want to hang out. I don't care."

"You… You're gonna drive across the entire country to 'hang out'? Ethan, that doesn't make any sense!"

Ethan seemed worried. "I was hoping we could… you know… talk about life. You know."

"What *about* life?"

"What it means, Brand. Who we are and where we're go—"

"Stop!" I grabbed the steering wheel and pulled it toward me.

"But the panel's green!"

"There's no traffic panel, there's no car, and you are not Ethan Underhill!"

He looked puzzled, but I didn't buy into it.

"You're asking me about the meaning of life and you're driving around in a Darkball? You win the lottery or something?"

"A car is a thing, how can a thing be the meaning of life? Please let me drive."

"No," I said. "We're gonna cut the *games*, stay right *here*, and you're gonna tell me *exactly* what's going on!"

No answer came. He became like a statue. I didn't even see him breathe.

"I swear to Mother Earth if you tell me 'it's been a pleasure try again,' I'll—"

"No. No." He glanced desperately at the steering wheel. "Can I just drive? Please?"

"Why, Ethan? Were you only programmed to drive me around forever? Am I supposed to spend the rest of my life having some philosophical chat with you?"

He continued staring at the steering wheel.

"Okay, you want to drive me somewhere? Randy's apartment, then; or Jane's, or Eric's. I'll introduce you to one of my more recent friends, one I would know was real or fake in about ten seconds. Maybe we can go to my prosperity agent's house, or zip back to good 'ol Nampa and have dinner with my folks, I'll even show you the spot in the basement where I used to hide my plasmonic fireworks, the one there's not a shred of information posted online about. Does that sound good to you, Ethan?"

Ethan raised his eyes but said nothing.

"You can show me the park-level of the Reed Building," I continued, "there's all kinds of imagery and cameras and everything to tell you what *that* looks like, but did you know it's illegal to post images of ascension-sites?" I opened the passenger door and released the steering wheel. "Bye, Ethan."

"Wait!"

I stood on the concrete and leaned back in. "Why is the Ace of Diamonds more desired than the Two of Spades?"

"Uh. The answer to that depends on the game."

"Communism."

"Communism? Never heard of—"

"Blackjack then!"

He stared at the steering wheel. "The Ace is more flexible, the player can use it as a high or low card. The two is... just a low card."

"Thanks." I turned around and took a step.

"Please Brand!"

"You know what I want." I didn't look back.

When he didn't reply, I slammed the door. There was no door. I lost my balance and nearly fell.

The rays of the rising sun revealed a barren city street with no cars or people. The wind died down and I heard nothing but my own breathing.

"Hello?"

An extremely loud noise ripped through the silence, an alarm that came from everywhere. I covered my ears to no avail. I couldn't discern what direction it came from and ran into the nearest building. Even in its deepest, insulated, rooms the noise didn't diminish at all.

The noise stole my ability to concentrate, and I couldn't tell where I was running. On pure instinct I tried to get away from the pain, my only action an unthinking re-action. My only thoughts were of the noise. The noise was consuming me and I had no idea how to escape it. I had become too absorbed in the alarm to even notice the wind picking up around me, trying to get my attention.

An intense gust finally knocked me off my feet, snapping me back into reality, calling my focus to something beyond the noise.

I stopped my search and tried to focus, burning to know what I was missing. I had to shout even in my own thoughts.

SOMEONE! PLEASE! SHUT THAT THING—

At last. It stopped.

I was at the same intersection where I'd started, and I was still alone. Everyone was gone, yet the despair didn't seem so strange to me anymore. But I knew the alarm had stopped, its power over me taken away, and in its absence I sensed a need, a feeling as plain as hunger. I looked at the rising sun and wondered what I was supposed to do.

What am I supposed to *find*?

The thought surprised me. I looked in every direction, for anything obvious, or anything out of place.

I need a path.

I cleared my mind until the only thing I perceived was the wind. The wind was blowing east, down the street to my right. I opened my eyes and took a deep breath.

It can't be that simple.

At times it was a gust, and other times the breeze was barely there at all. I began to doubt it meant anything, but the wind continued east and therefore I continued east, through countless blocks that seemed so identical to one another I wasn't sure I was moving at all.

"You look hungry."

I froze. The voice had come from behind. It was a kind voice, the voice of a real person. I turned and immediately recognized the sandcastle builder. The child was holding a door open.

"Come on in. Breakfast is on me."

Chapter Four: Closed Window, Open Door

What is the meaning of life?

The question is as philosophical as they come, not one prized by those who stumble through their lives expecting no better from tomorrow. Our ancestors looked to powerful deities and myths for meaning; many others pledged their beliefs to things scientific and observable through the senses. Their meaning came from the control they'd claimed: the magic pill that would make it rain on the fields or prevent an earthquake. The theory is paraded as fact until nature wipes it out, stranding the faithful until another easy answer can be rushed into circulation.

The meaning of life, I believed, was to be a good person. I knew things would work themselves out and life would go on after me. Even as I grew up and threw the question away, some tried to tell me I'd been created, while others tried to tell me I'd congealed in primordial soup, and still others wanted me to think aliens were watching me from cloaked satellites. I didn't care. I had more important things to do.

Then an AI asked me the question, but why would some hacker go through so much trouble to ask something stupid?

It was just part of their game, I told myself. I could only think of escape, even as I lost focus on what I wanted to escape to, and there was no magic pill for me, no illusion or piece of code could fix the man I was. Only when I stopped trying to find the easy answer did I see a better one had been there all along.

I felt alone and so I became alone... until a hand guided me from the noise and gave me what I didn't know I needed, something I would find myself admiring.

Grace.

5

We walked into a spacious coffee house. A bar defined the center of the room and tables sprawled around it. On our right was a stage where jazz musicians were performing. The growing morning light came in through broad front windows, beautifully highlighting every subtle accent of gold and silver used in the interior's design. A barista bent down when she saw the boy and hugged him.

"Hi, Raskob. Peace to you."

"Hi, Sallie. More to you."

A calm sense came over me, as if my worries were suddenly so small they'd lost all meaning, as if all along they held no more power than a tiny ant. There was an energy within the room that seemed to project from the child. The room itself welcomed him, and he the room. I could feel the energy purifying me in some way. It seemed tangible enough to reach out and touch.

"Always happy to see a new face here. I'm Sallie."

"Uh… Brandon." I tentatively shook the woman's hand.

Sallie conducted herself with joy and confidence. Her uniform was neat and her movements were fluid, demonstrating professionalism even in mundane tasks, even in tasks where professionalism had long been forgotten. She seemed authentic in every way, like someone who enjoyed life. Everyone in the room loved her, and she loved everyone in the room, even a stranger like me. For all the complaining I'd done about customer service going to artificial intelligence, it seemed only then I found what service was really supposed to be. I always knew what I didn't want. I never considered what I did. I never even looked for a place to start.

The thought of jealousy came to me, more as a memory of the emotion than anything I could apply. I asked myself why everyone else should be so happy in this miserable world, but the question flipped around to become: Why should I be so miserable in this happy world? Jealousy was somehow impossible in that place. They had nothing I couldn't simply ask for.

Sallie led us to the best table in the room, in a front corner. The light of the window reflected from a surface of polished mahogany and utensils of pure crystal. The sky-blue chairs were as comfortable as lying on a pillow. I was startled to see a broadsword hung on the wall beside the window, certain such an object would be illegal in a real shop. Given DR's creative licenses, though, I decided it was a bold and unique decoration for a coffee house. "THE WAY" was etched on a plaque underneath the sword.

Sallie ran down a short list of specials, treating the pitch for each item with the care someone might use serving the Prime Minister of Europe. The options overwhelmed me, all choices between lofty, rich things I had no experience with or right to even try.

"Just an Amber Plus, please."

"Regular coffee," Raskob said. "Standard brew."

The boy didn't appear any older than eleven or twelve, though his behavior was closer to that of a wise old man. He conducted himself with a universal, durable leisure. The look in his eyes seemed soft and intense all at once, revealing a sense of value and peace that cut to my core. I welcomed the emotion, enough to know I wanted to know it better, but beyond that it seemed to run out of tune, and in some bizarre way that made me feel like *I* was the one out of tune with *it*.

"I didn't know people could still buy un-amped coffee," I said.

"There is no need to build on what is already found in nature."

Sallie returned with our orders, much faster than I'd expected. I noticed a red band on her wrist, with a silver marking embedded in its fibers.

"What brought you here, Brandon?" Raskob asked, sipping his coffee.

"The wind," I replied, looking toward the windows. "I think."

"It's amazing. The wind could level this city in a single blast, but it chooses to display itself as a gentle breeze."

"The wind *chose*?"

"The wind is even here in Dynamic Reality. It blows as surely as it does in the real world. Even the scent of coffee and the sound of music are here."

"So then, we're not pretending this is real life?" I said, opening my slampak and witnessing its familiar startup sequence.

Raskob shook his head slightly. "No. No pretending here."

I saw a black and red object appear in the corner of my eye. The descender had returned to my wrist.

"It's something built by man on top of real life... modeled after it. It's a more controllable version of it."

"Yeah," I said, slowly returning my vision to him, "Dynamic Reality has given us many things."

"And taken away more."

I didn't respond. Raskob sat peacefully as I looked around the crowded room and tried to get some bearing on it. All who entered were greeted in a friendly manner. All who left seemed refreshed and energetic, driven to return to their own corner of reality and make life better within it. I saw many enjoying themselves on the very delicacies I'd rejected, many of which I couldn't even recognize, and seeming all the more appetizing for it.

"I used to think it was ridiculous, you know, eating in DR."

"Did something change your mind?"

I looked at him shyly, trying to remain aware of my thoughts.

"People 'eat' in DR," I said. "It's not even a social thing anymore or just a way to satisfy temptation without calories… people actually 'eat' as if they had to here. I—"

I smiled. It seemed like a silly thing to admit, but I felt like I wanted to. Something about Raskob made me feel it was safe to talk about anything, not worrying what he would think.

"I— I don't know… I never noticed before, but I guess I do it, too. I don't even always feel like it, it's just… habit, I guess."

"Your trips used to be a few hours; but, over the years, you've spent more of your life here."

"Yeah. I guess I washed out," I said, rubbing my finger on the table.

"What do you really want, Brandon? Why are you here?"

"I just followed the wind. There was this horrible noise but it went away."

"You were lost and in turmoil, but you asked for help and got it."

I looked up, staring at my slampak. "Is there something I need?"

Raskob leaned forward and put his hand on mine. "You want to be strong and brave, but something is stuck in the way. You don't want to admit to yourself that you have needs you can't meet on your own. Brandon, though the details change from person to person, I want you to know that what you're going through is a road countless people have traveled. That's why you're here.

Precious few see where that road leads to… they're the few who ask for help."

"No!" I shouted, shoving my slampak off of the table.

The streak of anger abandoned me as quickly as it came. I felt tears on my face and didn't know why they were there. I saw Raskob's hand was still calmly on mine.

"Why do you care about me?" I asked, confused.

"Because that's how the world is supposed to work."

I saw Sallie three meters away, carefully cleaning the floor with a towel, as if she couldn't simply delete the spill. I could detect no trace of bitterness towards me for making the mess. Sallie seemed to enjoy even that task, not because it was a distraction from something worse, but because it allowed her to demonstrate her service to others.

"There is a hatred you have buried deep within yourself. It calls itself by many names, even love, but it is not love. Love is what you once gave to those closest to you. Love is what you look back on as an unattainable alien thing. Now your hatred is failing, but hatred is all you know. Hatred will not allow you to forgive anyone."

The intensity in his eyes was unmistakable. His every word struck a chord, but I had no response to them.

"I tell you now, Brandon. You will need to choose between your love and your hate. You can't serve both. There are no exceptions or compromises."

"But I'm not a hateful man," I thought aloud. "I don't know what you're talking about."

"That you hate *yourself* is evidence that you do."

I felt numb. A person did appear in my mind, a person I loved like a brother who had hurt me very deeply, who I'd remembered hurting me very deeply.

No, I decided. It can't be him. He never even apologized. There's no way this kid can know about that black sheep, anyway. He's asking too much. It's not hate. It's just a break from talking.

I brought myself to look away from him... to the floor, because everything in the store gave me the same feeling of pain, highlighting the hole I couldn't fill in my heart and the stubbornness I'd become far too aware of.

"So... did, uh... Did you write this? Are you a programmer?"

"It was created by a man I met in a park in Berlin twenty years ago," he said. "He had a gun hidden in his coat and was about to kill himself. He had gifts he wasn't aware of. I showed him another way."

"Oh... Was that when he became a programmer?"

"He adds so much beauty to his world and he gives me credit in all of it. Though, none of it compares to the work of my father."

I looked up, trying to regain some courage. "So you're a programmer's son?"

He nodded.

"And what did your dad build?"

"Have you ever heard the phrase 'there's life in the machines'?"

"I think so... Yeah." I smiled. "There are rumors saying there are some self-aware amai online; artificial intelligence with free will."

"But how does free will come into being?"

"I didn't think it happened at all."

"It does." Raskob took a sip of coffee. "I remember when my father built a huge environment. He put everything he had into it and he loved it; he populated it with creatures who had free will. The programming was perfect. Its coding was simply called 'beautiful.'"

"That's amazing."

"But, though all the creatures were designed with the ability to expand outside of the construct, many instead became glued to the rules they had been born into. There was much rebellion; and the rebels led many astray, convincing others that my father didn't care about them, or even denying the existence of anything outside their universe. As powerful as the opposition was, though, some persevered and kept others strong. They did great things in the name of their creator, even sacrificing what they had there."

"Well... why didn't your father just *delete* the rebels and punish the ones who turned away? Why didn't he just program them all to serve him?"

"Because that would go against their free will and against my father's purposes. To force someone into devotion accomplishes nothing, but when they sacrifice it all willingly and lovingly it's truly remarkable. Even one true servant is worth more than any number of slaves."

He paused but I had no response.

"So his love was reciprocated and he saw to it that they would eventually be free of the rebels. He built a new environment for them where they could live in joy and adoration after their 'natural time' was up in the first world; but, to rescue them from the hands of the rebels..."

Raskob stopped and his tone became grim. "The population reached a point where laws and divisions were necessary. My father put them in place, though it was his intention to do away with them at the right time. The rebels eagerly abused the laws for their own ends and the time came to free the people – his children – and set up a final victory; but satisfying the law once and for all required him to make a sacrifice himself... one that pained him."

He stopped, and the room was silent. I was grieved seeing the pain on his face. It was a very personal pain, so much so I felt I caused it myself.

"What did he give up?" I asked.

I finally noticed Sallie standing by our table, crying as she and Raskob shared a somber glance at each other. She remembered the new slampak in her hand and placed it on the table in front of me, sniffing and raising the hand to wipe her face. "I just wanted to see if there was anything else I could do for you."

"Thank you, Sallie," he replied. "We're fine."

I noticed the increasing sunlight outside and remembered it was only an echo of morning in Standard Reality.

"Something new is happening in the world, Brandon. Imagine you're trapped in a speeding car being driven by a woman who's looking for someone. She is among the lost, trapped between two worlds. The road will be difficult ahead, but she means you no harm and, if you trust me to protect you, you'll both get where you need to go."

I looked at him. "A woman?"

"The one who has captured you."

My gaze returned to the floor. Fear grew inside of me.

What woman? Did he just say she "captured" me? What can I do? How do I get back? How—

I felt Raskob's hand on mine again. The fear evaporated and was replaced by a measure of joy. I looked at him like he was a savior, as if he were the only one who could reach down and pull me from the cliff.

"Does that make you the good guy?" I asked in anticipation.

"Why do you call me good?"

I felt confused at his response.

"What is good?" he continued. "What is evil? On what basis can a man judge such a matter? If the one who considers such things can neither liberate nor condemn another, how much less can the one who does not consider such things?"

"I'm sorry," I said, meaning it, "I don't understand what you're trying to say."

"That's because you hear my words and nothing else, Brandon. Many can speak words, and many do speak words, in my name, to those who do not know me; but I tell you now that your eyes and ears can be opened, and when you find understanding you will know that it was a gift and that the only power you had was to accept or decline it. Know that the gift is the only thing that can save both you and your captor."

"Save my captor? Why would I—"

"I have given you rest. She isn't aware of where you are now, but you must return, because no one can find what they need if there is no one to guide them."

I tensed. "But can't you just send me home?"

He set his hand on the table and a glass of clear water materialized before it. He gave the water to me. "The workers need to be prepared for the road ahead. Blessed are those who persevere."

I examined the glass. "But it's just water."

He nodded. "I promise you that it's all you need."

I realized I was thirsty. I considered the drinks in front of me: the familiar Amber Plus and the unimpressive water.

Free will, eh?

I slid the water toward me and picked it up, observing its clarity and the way sunlight reflected off its surface. It tasted sweeter than honey in my mouth and I drank it faster, as if the glass would never run empty. I became energized, feeling incredible; then, something occurred to me. A dull pain immediately spread over my body. I nearly choked.

"Twenty years?"

A horn blasted behind me. I spun around and a rushing pedestrian knocked into me. The glass slipped from my hands and shattered on the concrete.

"Brandon, please. They're getting mad!"

I was by Ethan's Darkball again. Rush hour was in full swing and cars were cutting around him. I tried to remember where I just was and what I'd dropped. There was nothing on the concrete. I ached everywhere and my senses were overwhelmed, as if I'd stepped from an ascension booth right into the middle of a sledg-ek dance skein. The sunlight hurt. The noise hurt. I instinctively tried to fight it all and was rewarded with a dizzy sensation.

After only a few seconds, the light and noise faded and I wasn't able to think. Words and characters filled my vision:

MALDORAN ASCENSION MA-56: PACITEK 515:
ONLINE: DAUPHIN BRANDON SINDEN: UPTIME 18 02 14:
BP 195/101 HR 155: REM OK: UPLINK ----Pbit/s
#CANCELLED FOR COMMAND INPUT#
ENTER SYS ACCESS KEY
[e6lTsh8hrheEerntvo6Re5yuhotTT19hsaiHa1iadn4Se8enlreOahW
ten5Hvh1ieh5NR9tgEesTBldoLt8FL7geA46AhusrsdlFNthreomO
DtpmDshTI9nhHh1ESheegouVngoiiayDHthetroNlorcll5Ea—

The stream suddenly broke off and the faded city returned. The Darkball was gone again, but the street appeared normal. I stumbled onto the sidewalk and looked for a bench to sit on.

Ethan was driving me, then I got mad and tried to leave. I was alone. There was a noise. Then I saw… Then I— My descender!

My hand was promptly on my wrist, but there was no descender.

I screamed out a curse and nearly broke down on the sidewalk again, but I pushed the anger away and felt something inside me respond. I remembered walking east, following something, finding something – someone.

Slowly, I began in the direction I had gone before, recalling something about wind, annoyed at how it seemed to be affected by each passing car and opened shop door.

I just went in one direction, unsure of what I'd find.

No people blocked my path. No traffic panel – no traffic at all – made me wait. No holograms, incoming dins, or distractions of any kind detained me. Someone was clearly watching me and rolling out the red carpet for my every step. I just wished I knew whether it was the good guy or the bad.

The memories of the coffee house slowly returned. I wanted to find Raskob again. My mind filled with questions I was shocked hadn't come earlier. Block after block and I couldn't recognize anything. I became angry at Raskob, angry at him for playing games with me and not just letting me go home.

I reached what had to be the hundredth intersection and stopped, seeing nothing that resembled the coffee house. Parked down a cross-street, though, I spotted something that had become very familiar to me over the last several hours.

"Thank you for riding Anaheim Lightning Bolt," the amai said as I got into the back seat of the metrocab. "Where can I take you this morning, Brandon?"

"There's a coffee place on that road. Tell me where it is."

"Yes, Mister Dauphin. There is a KDN Express, a Slammers, two Wel-Perks, and four public DOFI Centers within your search criteria."

"No," I replied. "It's not a government or conglomerate-run store, it was small and privately-owned. It was filled with people, so it has to be popular enough to come up somewhere."

"I'm sorry, Brandon. I found three privately-owned coffee shops within fifty kilometers, but none of them are on that road."

I leaned back in the seat and took even breaths, playing back over everything in my mind.

"Please state your destination, Mister Dauphin. I can guide you through the customer reviews of local coffee shops and help you choose the best one."

The amai spoke in the usual overly-friendly way, never looking away from the street before her, never having to look anywhere because the cab's sensors did the driving. I noted the reflection of her eyes in the rear-view mirror. Even for a robot, they just didn't seem quite right.

"We're staying right here. I want to know who's behind this."

"I'm sorry, Brandon. I don't understand the question."

"How do I descend? How do I return to Standard Reality?"

"This *is* Standard Reality, Mister Dauphin."

I rubbed my forehead and took a moment to think. To clear my head. I was sweating again, which wasn't normal for a vanitar... not unless a game called for it. But I knew I was still ascended. I knew I needed to find a way out. I leaned forward and summoned every bit of knowledge I had about computers.

"Tell me your system information." I commanded the amai.

"Yes, Mister Dauphin," she replied gleefully. "I have been generated by a Slidewire-certified UY-type amai script as 'Jennifer,' instance five, default female classification; my program is registered to Reeeee— the California State Department of Public Transport under the Business, Transportation and Housing Agency, license number one-five-nine—"

"Errors," I commanded. "Are there errors in your program?"

"Yes, Brandon. Error code five-three-five-zero has been set on this unit."

She was silent.

"What's a five-three-five-zero?"

"I'm sorry, Mister Dauphin. That is not a valid error code. Please state your destination."

What?

"You just said your program set an error code!" I grabbed the seat and leaned further up. "Five-three-five—"

A shock of realization washed over me. I fell back.

"No errors have been reported on this unit."

It was the exact same synthetic voice I'd heard a million times before, but, in that moment, the slightest malicious tone seemed to be buried within it, projected by my mind onto my senses.

"Why?" I asked absently, looking back at the rear-view mirror, trying to assess what was controlling the amai. Everything around me seemed infected suddenly – dirty and able to harm me. You're infected by a virus, I thought, as if pointing it out to the amai would change anything, as if someone of my skill could ever hope to escape a...

I'm going to die, aren't I? I really can't get out.

"I'm sorry, Brandon. I do not have that information."

There's no information here, I thought frantically. They're in control of all of it. I need to go somewhere new, a place where there might be too much for them to change all at once. It's my only hope, a slim chance to find a way out before they can block it off.

"There are no limits to where you can go," the amai said.

I took a deep breath, and struggled to restrain the fear that wanted to burst out.

"Libraries," I said. "I wanna go to the Central Library, that big one in LA."

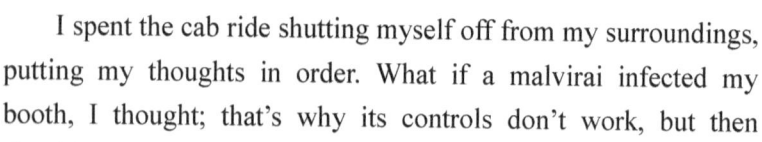

I spent the cab ride shutting myself off from my surroundings, putting my thoughts in order. What if a malvirai infected my booth, I thought; that's why its controls don't work, but then shouldn't I be dead by now? Obviously, it's a hacker pulling the strings, but who? What could they possibly want from me?

I stepped out and the cab left. I felt like a soldier who suddenly realized he was deep within enemy territory, alone, and being watched.

I passed through empty security posts and into the crowded library. Another barrier conveniently removed for me. When a passing guard didn't seem to notice me, I brought myself to follow him and tap him on the shoulder. My finger went through him as if I were a ghost.

I put my hand on a nearby table. It felt solid. I called to one of the people sitting a few meters away.

"Excuse me."

The man didn't respond. My hand passed through the book he held, but not the ones on the bookshelves. I took one off only to find the same book still on the shelf. I opened the one in my hands and flipped its pages as quickly as I could, watching for the split-second the words rendered onto them. I dropped it and grabbed a second book, opening it immediately, opening it in the middle. I saw the beginning of the first chapter.

They're slowing down, I thought. They're messing up. Maybe I was right. Maybe I can give them more data than they can handle at once. Malvirai or no.

A second guard approached from a distance, as oblivious to my presence as the first. I felt an ache and the light around me started to shimmer. The guard stopped to look at something, standing in my aisle's narrow entrance. I watched carefully and realized his image was becoming blurry. He turned and took another step towards me, vanishing as he entered the aisle... no longer in the view of a camera.

"Welcome to Los Angeles Public Library, Mister Dauphin. What can I help you find?"

There was some kind of glowing effect around the librarian amai. It was spreading to every object in the room.

"Your books are malfunctioning."

"Please state your search parameters."

"Fine," I said. "I need a book or something about Dynamic Reality. I need to know how to descend without a descender."

"Science fiction. We also have some horror stories like that. I will take you there."

"No. If it happened in—"

Something moved on the hologram's ID badge. Random symbols and markings filled the area where a name would normally be. A fluttering noise emerged from the distance. The aching grew worse and the noise became louder. The markings on her badge shifted again, and its entire surface was filled with the random symbols. The light shimmered more strongly and the air became different, charged. I saw every object in the room flicker into oblivion and jump back into existence. Now all the books were solid. Now all the words were really on the pages.

The books all suddenly switched positions. I dropped the one in my hands and stepped away from it. It wasn't the same book I'd taken from the shelf.

"Listen, I just want to leave! *This* doesn't happen in real life!"

"What's real and what isn't is in the eye of the beholder, Mister Dauphin."

The air became heavier again, some intense static charge being drawn into it. The amai's ID badge became a blur of activity. The books shifted again and I heard the pages rustling in the shelves, becoming louder, as if they had begun jumping individually between the books.

They took the real library and made it into a DR construct… or at least they're trying to! I *was* right… there's too much data here! The illusion is breaking down and I have to act now, or I might miss this chance!

I grabbed the librarian by the shoulders. "I want to descend, or I want you to tell me how to descend!"

She didn't respond. She didn't move.

"Command… uh… list your functions! Establish some connection to the outside world! Now!"

"The reqqqqquesssssst-t-ted fuuunct-function has been been dissss-disabled by the admin-administrrrrrator, pl-pl-please…"

Energy poured into the air at an incredible rate. I remembered how the Korea simulation ended and sprinted back into the lobby, which had become a complete visual blur. I was knocked off my feet and my entire body tingled, as if the blood were being drained from me, as if muscle commands weren't getting from my brain to my vanitar. I witnessed whiteboards, terminal displays and airé panels, the millions of books, all the matter within the building, jumping: shifting positions instantly, faster and faster, in some way that appeared like dancing.

"Request for information."

The same librarian appeared in front of me, looking at me with dead eyes, dead eyes that seemed as unnaturally energized as everything else in the room... packing the charge of a bolt of lightning.

"Request for new information."

With each word, her voice became more monotone. She barely moved. I struggled to breathe and lift myself from the ground, to overcome the increasing gravity and the hesitation of my simulated nervous system.

"New — information?" I managed to reply, "Stay — away — from — trees!"

"Stay-away-from-trees," she repeated.

I looked at her with a mixture of horror and confusion. The air in the room crackled and vibrated, becoming so charged with energy it seemed it could spontaneously combust. The last of the people in the room, real or not, vanished. The random markings had spread to every surface in the library. The amai's lips no longer moved normally and her words began running together, the most basic illusions being compromised as if the overflowing energy were being sucked out and channeled elsewhere.

"Capricorn-for-December-nineteenth-Like-falling-leaves-the-problems-of-your-life-will-break-away. Leo-for-December-second-Be-wary-of-vegetation-but-use-flowers-generously-this-week.

Taurus-for-October-thirtieth-Stay-away-from-trees-trees-trees-trees-trees-trees-trees-trees-trees-trees-trees-trees-trees-trees-trees-trees-trees…"

I broke through the translucex door and bolted out onto the street. Streaking rainwater felt like tiny knives slicing through my body, and the impossible speed of it created a high-pitched whooshing noise that shrieked from all directions. I fought intense pain and blindly ran down what I judged to be the sidewalk, running into people who weren't there and deep puddles that didn't splash. I stopped when it felt like I was under something – a canopy. I could barely open my eyes to see the waterfall surrounding me. None of it seemed survivable, though the canopy above my head didn't collapse, the paint wasn't scraped off the walls, and the normal street drains somehow kept up.

All in the same instant, the noise calmed and the air's energy faded. I peeked through my fingers to find a normal rainstorm on a normal street, as if the motion of the world had simply slowed to its normal pace. I looked to the sky and saw daylight had returned. Though now, only a few hours after sunrise, the sun was already far in the West.

"Raskob! You said you had my back, man! Help me out!"

The night came quickly. I stood under an overpass as the rain continued. The effect of the miserable water Raskob gave me finally begun to subside and I could think straight again. I wanted answers. I wanted freedom. The boy said to trust him, but he wasn't helping me at all.

Every minute or so, a car would pass. I wondered if they were echoes of real cars, like the people in the library, or complete fabrications.

The wall behind me is solid. Perhaps they are, too, I thought.

In the distance, I heard the gentle purr of an HH-cell engine, perhaps from a LeGrande or a Toyota. When I saw the headlights I swallowed nervously. My breaths were shallow and I was trembling. I knew I didn't want to. It seemed wrong. It seemed right. It seemed like my only option.

Desperate times, as they say.

The rain drenched my face, my eyes were shut tight and my breath held. I heard the loud squeal of tires and felt a tingly wind. The sound of the rain cut off into silence.

I opened my eyes, standing unharmed in the middle of the road. The car had dematerialized. The rain had stopped. The city was quiet, except for the steps of a woman walking in the road. She stopped three meters from me, observing me. I saw her face and her descender. I remembered where I had seen her before.

Blackjack table.

Modern clothing had replaced the Soviet uniform and, without the cap covering it, hair that appeared white was reflecting the streetlights above with a faint silver luminance.

"Who are you?"

"There is only one thing you need to know, Mister Dauphin."

Her words were spoken in neither love nor hate. Her eyes were a puzzle. Her face revealed no emotion. Even as her next words shook to my core, that which was behind them seemed very alien. Hers was the impersonal statement of a fact, of things decided before I'd even stepped into the ascension booth.

"If you don't start cooperating, I'll kill you."

Chapter Five: Highest Stakes

The energy of the fire continued to build; it was all she knew to do.

Mine would become like so many other stories: one of good versus evil, of losing an old identity and gaining a new one, of life. It wasn't a story I'd wanted, and it wasn't a story I could depart from or just let play out around me. It was unyielding and it was personal.

The stage was set, and I had met the one assigned to be my enemy.

Mine would become like trillions of stories that appear on the grand stage of Dynamic Reality, but not as an illusion... not a matter of simulated reality, but of all reality, not of the man I said I was, but of the man I truly was, of him who survives when the liar is gone... when the impostor known as Brandon Dauphin gets burned away in the light of the day.

Even as the road ahead became darker, the light which had been growing inside of me was being amplified, harnessed by another for her own ends, analyzed like a piece of software she couldn't understand.

Mine would become like so many other stories: I would have a choice to make and a life to save. I would find myself as the humble hero against the powerful foe, needing new answers to solve old problems. Like so many, though, I would also need a friend to lean on and a home to return to... things the impostor knew nothing of.

This story is about what lies beyond his horizon, beyond the walls he used to protect himself. This story is about losing the impostor. This story is about losing my limits.

The limits consumed in the growing fire.

6

A warm light materialized above my head. The rain stopped hitting me and I realized it had been pouring again.

"Silly man, do something!"

I blinked. The woman with the descender was gone again.

"Hey, do you hear me silly man? Don't stand in the road when *Tersen's Game and Casino* is offering no-limit Texas Hold 'Em with double swipe-and-win points! We really want to see you there!"

I turned and saw a short woman standing next to me, a sales-amai. I couldn't even register her as an annoyance. I could only think of the feeling of presence, of the woman pulling the strings of the world, the last world I may ever see.

Did she really say she would *kill* me? What kind of psycho did I run into? What did she mean by "cooperate"?

Someone grabbed my arm and began pulling on it.

"C'mon Brandon, don't stand in the road! Do something!"

I jerked my arm from her grip and stepped away. The pavement of the street began to change, all the things around me becoming brighter. Something began to occupy the air, not so much a scent, but a familiar sweetness. I watched the mounts of a hanging street sign vanish, so it began to float like a magical object. The rain became a drizzle and sparkled like crystal. I gasped, knowing the real city of Los Angeles was transforming around me into—

"If Dynamic Reality is what you want, then Dynamic Reality is what you get!"

I turned to the amai. "I don't want to die."

"Die?" She repeated, too gleefully.

"Yeah, die! End of life! Termination! Going away and never coming back!"

A tear slid down my cheek. The dumb amai held no emotion at all. There was no body language, tears, voice tone, or anything at all to indicate she was a real, thinking being... that she could actually consider a day when someone would unplug her projector and melt it down for recycling.

"You'll 'die' over our specials, Mister Dauphin! Flaming hot wings for only three thirty-nine! C'mon!" She tried to pull me toward the nearby club.

Again, I jerked my arm from her grip, knowing Dynamic Reality was gripping me tighter, as it had so many times before.

"C'mon, Brandon! You don't want to stand in the road! You don't like doing *nothing*!"

I didn't respond.

"You like parties and friends and hot bands like *Aiming for Wednesday*! They're gonna perform tonight and you *gotta* be there!"

"I want to see that woman," I replied, "the one I was just with."

"I'm sorry, Mister Dauphin, I can't help you with that, but I can help you find the luckiest slot machine and give you tips to improve your odds!"

I looked toward the street and raised my voice. "I'm asking nicely!"

"We have lots of single women inside, or if you like me it's easy to—"

"No!"

I faced her with angry, offended eyes.

"But if you just come inside—"

"I — want — to — see — that — wo—man," I replied. "I don't know what any of this is about, but I'm not doing anything until I get an explanation."

"If there is a problem," the amai stated, without loss to her happy tone, "just tell me and it'll be fixed!"

"What kind of 'problem'?"

"I don't know, Brandon… Your environment was a flawless recreation of Los Angeles. Adjustments are merely being made to make you 'active!'"

"I don't want to be 'active!' I want to go back to Standard— the real world!"

"Why don't you just pretend? Everybody pretends! It's fun!"

The little strength I had fled from me and I felt petrified. It was a reaction from deep within, a conflict I knew nothing about.

Everybody pretends.

The thought tore at my insides. The ache had returned.

It's fun.

It had been spoken as a fact. People took it as a fact. I knew I had been living by the code of that statement. It had been fun, I thought. Once.

"The woman!" I shouted. "Stop hiding behind illusions and—" I had to stop and breathe. "And face me!"

"Why do something unpleasant? C'mon, you can play any game you want!"

Why is every word coming from their mouths so ridiculous? Why are they all programmed to lie all the time? Why shouldn't I want to find the meaning of this? Why shouldn't I want to go through the pain if it means my freedom in the end?

The rain curtain dissolved and I heard the sound of a car behind me. I stood frozen as the amai quietly walked past me.

"If that is the only course of action you will take," she said in a flatter tone, "then that too is opened to you."

I slowly turned and saw her holding the open door of a black limousine. The music from the bar behind me became louder. I could hear friendly voices shouting my name and inviting me into my captor's more gentle, intended, method; but the door ahead of me held answers, and I knew in my heart the difficult path was the one I had to follow, even as everything else directed me away. Even the amai's perky voice had become plain and unsympathetic.

"Now choose."

I sat uneasily in the back of the limo, the only company being several monitors set to various cameras and broadcast networks. The door closed and the hologram vanished. The car started moving.

"Hey! Where are we—"

The woman appeared in the seat across from me, staring silently into me with hard green eyes, sitting unnaturally straight and giving off the body language of a statue.

"What do you require?"

"I, uh…" I blinked and remembered to breathe.

"Is aimless wandering all you do, Mister Dauphin?"

"Yeah. Uh…" I took another breath and summoned my energy, finding anger. "Yeah! When I can't reach my family or friends! When I've been kidnapped and held in DR! Yeah, I guess so!"

A glass of wine appeared in my hand.

"A '62 Merlot. Good year. Please tell me what I can do to make up for your trouble."

I let the glass fall. "Let me go and maybe I won't press charges!"

The woman stared in silence again. From her sea of apparent indifference, something rose up, barely detectable, hinting at frustration. Though the tone of her words remained flat, the pauses between them became shorter. "I've tried to follow, fool, guide, intimidate then impress you. What other kind of persuasion do I need to give?"

"Persuasion for what?"

She hesitated. "Call it research, for which you are an involuntary subject."

I held out my hand in mock introduction. "I'm sorry, we still haven't been properly introduced. I'm Brandon and y—"

"Brandon Sinden Dauphin of Los Angeles, California; born to Paul and Rachel Dauphin in Nampa, Idaho on the date September 12, 2154, as the youngest of two sons and one daughter. Registered to move to Los Angeles County on date September 15, 2177. Present address: 3400A He—"

"How did you learn so much about me? I've never even seen you before!"

"That isn't relevant."

"You were the one who caused those problems, right? Who caused my Korea simulation to blow itself up? Who caused... whatever that was at the... at the library?"

I was sweating again. The conversation... the very presence of this woman was making me more and more tense. I found I couldn't read her at all, except for some vague intuition, except for some vague notion of anger. Of hatred.

Who am I up against? Have I done something to her? Is she unstable? Why is she so interested in me? Why won't she just come out and say it?

"Your Korea program did what it was designed to," she stated, "though I did not understand its appeal."

"And when I got dizzy and almost descended?" I asked, remembering someone had accessed my ascension booth earlier. "Was that you, too?"

"The construct suffered a break in consistency and your readings indicated a medical emergency. You were not experiencing one, and you are okay now."

"So after this concern for my life, you threaten to kill me?"

"In exchange for your cooperation, I will consider letting you live."

"You talk about death so casually," I said. "I have a…"

Family? Friends? Fiancée? What *do* I have?

I groaned loudly to chase away the tears, wondering if I could even make a case to save my life, or if anyone would listen to it.

"I don't want to die," I said powerlessly.

"Is it so much of an offense?" she replied. "Death is part of life, thousands have died in the moment we've been talking; thousands more have been born to replace them. You are only one life."

"*My* life means something to *me*. Couldn't you have picked someone else?"

"And if I had, wouldn't that person ask the same question?"

"I still don't know who I'm talking to," I said, less forcefully than I meant to.

"All that you need to know is that I'm not patient."

A new video monitor materialized between us. It was filled with images of action: happy people doing productive things, joyful jingles, optimistic sales pitches, and more of what surrounded me on a daily basis. All carried promises of improving the quality of life. All were carefully constructed windows into truth and worlds of happiness.

"They're all lies, aren't they?" she said, with what almost seemed like regret.

"They're commercials," I replied. "That's a music video… That's a talent show… Of course it's all made up, lady! Everyone knows that!"

"Yes… Perhaps everyone does," she said, seeming to look for something in the images. "But I have speculated that there is an inspiration within them, some kind of validity. I believe that there are things about life that aren't captured in media such as this. I want to know of them." She looked directly at me. "I want you to tell me the meaning of—"

"The meaning of life?" I suggested, using Ethan's words.

"Yes."

I looked out the window at the nighttime suburban landscape. "This is a joke. I think Dynamic Reality is getting to your head. Descend and get a self-help book, lady. I can't help you. I won't help you."

The woman punched a hole into the counter. "I've processed those books, they say nothing!" The city outside and the monitors vanished. The electric charge returned to the air and the limo began to vibrate. The sound of the engine intensified. We were speeding up.

"Brandon Dauphin, do you want to live?" The woman asked evenly, but with brief pauses between the words.

A blue light, sky blue, began filtering in through the windows, filling the cabin. The limo shook violently and gravity pulled harder on my body.

"Answer me!" she said loudly. "Do — you — want — to —"

"Yes! Yes! I want to live!" I shouted, clenching my eyes.

"Prove it."

In a heartbeat, the cabin closed in around me. I opened my eyes and saw I was in the cockpit of an F-86. I hurriedly felt around my flight suit for my descender, but it was still missing. A silver object in the sky caught my eye. I looked up with only an instant to grab the stick and go into a hard dive, cursing as I missed the braking enemy fighter by centimeters. The MiG dove and accelerated to get on my tail. I continued diving and threw the throttle forward as far as it would go.

I bought only a few seconds, the silver jet behind me was closing – fast. Before I could react, she fired a round just outside my canopy. I leveled off around 12,000 feet and banked right in a high-G turn, knowing I was going to lose if I didn't get behind her. Though I'd done the move in games before, the controls weren't responding properly, and now the MiG was right up on my tail, close enough for my jetwash to scorch her nose. I wanted to make her pay for her flying carelessness, but the MiG had already fallen back by the time I had my plane under control.

"Lady, you're a real piece of—" Another warning shot.

I threw the throttle forward again.

Think, Brandon! What I should do now? A Sabre should outrun a MiG at low altitude, or the MiG would lose control trying to keep up… but what weaknesses can I count on? I don't know anything about her and she knows everything about me!

As I anticipated, her jet was accelerating back into firing range. Bugging-out wasn't an option. I knew I needed a plan fast or I'd lose a lot more than simulated aerial combat.

I applied the speed brakes, to give her a taste of her own medicine. She was fast enough to weave but ended up at my two o'clock. Immediately I began a pulling maneuver, turning my nose toward hers, and fired – missed. As I passed it on the horizontal plane, the MiG shed enough speed to get on my four o'clock and attempt the same move against me. Cursing again, I spun to bank hard-left before she could get her shot.

"Command... object add: Sidewinders." Though the missiles had come a little later than the Korean War, it wouldn't have been the first time I fudged history a little.

The control system didn't respond, not even for a busy message. Even back in my real body, I could sense my pulse racing. Again and again, we spun and crossed each other in a scissors pattern, evading each other just enough so neither could get a shot. In a normal fight with another ascender, I might have shot the MiG down easily, but my opponents' sloppy maneuvers were becoming more graceful, as if she were going from freshmeat to alpha faster than anyone I'd ever seen. The two of us were barely maintaining enough speed to stay in the air, but she was somehow more successful, creeping behind me meter by meter, a little more with each pass.

Finally, a single bullet nicked my right wing. I felt as if I were in some old Western, an outlaw shooting at my feet yelling "dance!" I was exhausted and out of ideas, only readying myself for the inevitable. The next round went through my cockpit windows.

"Command... object local canopy: reset."

The program didn't restore the windows.

I flew level and futility picked up a little speed as the MiG gained altitude. I remembered Raskob and wondered if he was really on my side, or if he was just another false person the woman was using to confuse things, just a part of the cruel joke she was prepared to finish. I dared to look behind me. I saw the MiG's cockpit was empty.

However she was controlling it, the MiG dived and opened fire. 37mm rounds tore mercilessly through my right aileron, the side of my fuselage, through fuel lines and the tail. The engine stalled and smoke seeped through the instrument panel. I began rolling uncontrollably. The trees were coming fast. I was crashing.

I had never crashed, and I never really knew what panic felt like. Somehow, I forced myself to move, fumbling for the ejector seat lever.

I don't want to die! I need help! Somebody HELP ME!

My seat slid out from the rolling cockpit. I couldn't tell which way was up and clenched my eyes shut. Almost immediately, a strong light filtered through my eyelids. I could feel the heat of a fireball ahead of me.

With only a few scrapes from the landing, I put as much ground between me and the crash as I could. Steep hills surrounded me and there wasn't much vegetation to use as cover. Every minute or so I heard voices in the distance, speaking ancient Korean or perhaps Chinese. I was still in the fight. I knew the woman could've just made the enemy soldiers materialize around me and been done with it, if not for her idea of letting me "prove" myself.

A well-weathered barn sat conspicuously in a field, surrounded by a few trees. I fought to open the large door, the only one I saw, enough for me to slip in. Usually such buildings held some kind of value to the game, including ladders to climb, hay to hide in, or large objects to duck behind; but, in a simulation tailored for aerial combat, I found a useless structure meant only to make the landscape below seem more realistic, or to serve as targets for bored players. The dirt below was perfectly flat and the roof above lacked crossbeams or supports of any kind. Light peeked in through walls programmed to look decrepit. The exterior seemed perfectly real, but the interior was completely empty.

I closed the door and positioned myself against the wall. I heard voices again and searched for any weapon I had, finding a M1911 pistol. I turned the safety off and readied myself to shoot at the first thing I saw.

The rotting wood of the door gave easily and two soldiers rushed in holding shotguns. The instant before they noticed me, I took aim and fired – no bullets. More soldiers came and surrounded me, yelling as if I had any clue what they were saying – the game's built-in translator wasn't responding. The largest of them hit me with the butt of his rifle. I held my hands up in surrender and they just laughed, the big one pointing the barrel at my head, yelling louder. The look of death was in his eyes and I couldn't bear it any more. I was exhausted and just wanted it to end. I closed my eyes and prayed, as I supposed most people would under such mortal stress. I could hear them all taking aim, but no one fired. The noises stopped without warning. I heard only my own breathing.

Am I dead?

I opened my eyes, slowly. The soldiers were gone. At the other end of the rifle I found the woman with silvery hair, her unblinking eyes boring into my soul, longing to see me ripped apart. The weapon in her hands trembled, though. I saw the one without emotion fight herself and conceal the struggle. Somehow, it was revealed to me her struggle was against anger.

She was angry at me.

A wave of nausea washed over me. I was trembling and couldn't see straight. I felt like vomiting.

And everything became dark.

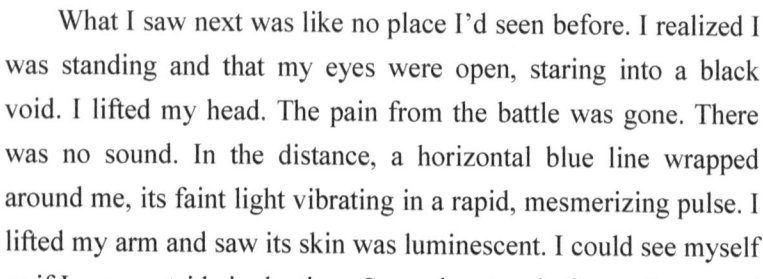

What I saw next was like no place I'd seen before. I realized I was standing and that my eyes were open, staring into a black void. I lifted my head. The pain from the battle was gone. There was no sound. In the distance, a horizontal blue line wrapped around me, its faint light vibrating in a rapid, mesmerizing pulse. I lifted my arm and saw its skin was luminescent. I could see myself as if I were outside in daytime. Several meters in front of me stood the woman, facing to my left. She was holding her right hand in front of her face, moving its fingers as if she'd never seen such things before.

I attempted a step forward. My foot landed firmly on a surface I couldn't see. I inhaled and tried to clear my head. The air was very thin and my sense of smell was gone: the sweet aura known in Dynamic Reality was not there, the blood and sweat theme from the war game was not there, even the subtle city musk of the real world was not there. Everything was just... blank. I sliced my hand through the air and felt no resistance, as if I were in outer space. I felt like a fish without water. I knew I never *needed* air in the simulations, but it was always included, always accommodating the familiar inhale-exhale cycle. The complete lack of it felt stranger than I would have ever imagined.

"Are you recovered yet?"

I blinked and looked toward the infinitely distant band of light. "Where are we?"

She turned to analyze our surroundings. Her anger, what of it I'd been able to perceive, had gone. Her personality seemed naïve and mechanical again.

"I call them 'absences,'" she said. "They are addresses which are not in use. The connections and hardware are not abused by ascenders in constructs, they have not been written or overwritten onto by control software. It is… peaceful."

"It's blank?"

"There is the simulation of gravity, time, and spatial dimension necessary to facilitate your healing; but, by your standards, yes, it's blank."

"And that blue light?"

"A color?" She turned to me. "Without active software to obstruct it here, you may perceive the server's activity as some kind of ambience. Blue, as you said."

There was silence again. She seemed to concentrate on something in the distance, perhaps the same light, perhaps a light she couldn't see the same way I could.

"Will you at least tell me your name?"

"No." She held her right hand and looked down at it, wiggling its fingers again.

"Then tell me if you're a hacker."

"I don't need to tell you anything."

"Then how am I supposed to *help* you?"

Her hand stopped. I realized the word I'd used surprised her.

"Hacker," she said. "Yes. If it helps you, then consider me a 'hacker.'"

She stared at me again, waiting for my response. Her gaze made me uncomfortable. I wondered how much she really knew, whether her gaze could really see all of my secrets. My lack of knowledge was more frightening than my lack of control.

"Why shouldn't I know who you are? You know so much about me," I admitted. "It's not fair."

"Life doesn't appear to be fair, so I am not concerned about such things."

"Then why me? I'm a nobody. I'm no one special."

"Your actions do not support your claim," she replied. "I suggest you modify your thinking or you may not be useful to me."

"Useful *how*?" I nearly whispered.

"I told you that my interest is research." She indicated the space around us. "This could be anything you want it to be. I could take you anywhere in this 'Dynamic Universe,' to any program, any server. The only condition is that I remain in control."

"That's it? You want to drive me around like some metrocab hologram? Why? So you can shoot me out of the sky and point rifles at me? What kind of research are you doing, lady? Are you seeing how close you can get me to a heart atta—"

As my voice rose, I sensed anger from her again. I made the impulsive mistake of allowing it to fuel my own, and the cycle quickly escalated within her. A gun, the same M1911 I'd had earlier, materialized in her hand and she pressed it against my forehead. I stared cross-eyed at the weapon and began to tremble again, a strange feeling spread across my skin as if I were sweating – in my real body. Still her face revealed no emotion.

I saw her pull the trigger – Click. I let out a loud gasp.

"No," she said. "I don't want your fear. It's unpleasant and counterproductive." She backed away a step and let the weapon fall to her side. "You've raised more questions in me than you've answered, Mister Dauphin."

I couldn't take my eyes off the gun.

"You react so strongly to the thing though it cannot work." She approached and handed me the gun. "It was not necessary to give this environment air. The gun requires oxygen to discharge."

I stared at the gun in my hands.

"As it needed bullets before," she added.

I threw the gun into the blackness and it vanished. "You sabotaged the simulation! What was it you said? You wanted me to prove I wanted to live? You sabotaged the Sabre's controls!"

"The game was fair. You failed."

"I *what*?"

"I was playing according to the rules of the game, a game with which you have experience. Yet, though you knew your existence was dependent on winning, I was still able to defeat you. Perhaps the existence of—" She hesitated. "If you were at a disadvantage, it did not come from me."

"Fine! I lost! Then what am I doing here? Shouldn't I be dead?"

"Again you contradict yourself. You said you didn't want to die and yet you would seem to welcome it."

I shook my head and stared into the blackness below me, trying to figure out whether the woman wanted to kill me or spare me. "Then let's not go there," I said. "No more guns, please."

"Then don't compare me to a metrocab hologram," she said, barely pausing between the words.

What?

I looked at her, knowing she'd meant it as seriously as everything else she said; but then something changed in her eyes. She broke eye contact as if she were aware. "My actions are inappropriate," she apologized. "You simply made a connection."

More silence passed. I took a step toward her.

"If you send me home I won't tell anyone about you, I promise."

"It is too late for that," she replied. "I cannot accept the risk. When I have my answers, I will decide what to do with you."

A new round of anger surged within me. I fought to hold it back, to not become like the caged animal I knew I was. "Okay, sure, fine… you're in control, obviously. Let's get this out of the way already. What questions am I so brilliant I can help you answer?"

"I will get the answers by observing you: your behavior in different environments, your interaction with others. As before, some of this will be influenced by me and much of it will be handled by the constructs themselves; but the choice on where to go next is yours. You will choose what I am to observe."

"*I* choose? I *choose* my *home*."

"The data I have of your apartment is primarily blueprints and utility records. I cannot simulate the shifting arrangements of your possessions—"

"No, No, No, No, No." I put my head in my hand.

This has to be a dream, I thought. Think… When I first saw her, in the casino, what did she want then?

"Your question at the blackjack table," I asked. "What was it?"

"Why is one more desired than two?"

"Right… High cards and low cards," I said, believing Ethan's answer really came from her.

"I have found the answer to that question already, though many others have taken its place."

"And… the answer was?"

She turned to face the absence again. "The Aces and Twos are identical in nature. They are the same size. They are manufactured the same way. The printing of the reverse, the art pattern, does not change. The differences between them are imposed by the rules of various games. A meaningless variation causes the Aces to gain value over the other cards."

I nodded, not really following. "Good."

"You recognize that as good?"

"It's just a card game. You're not supposed to be proverbial with them. You can't play cards if all the cards have the same value."

"Just as the Cold War could not be played if all sides had the same value?"

"War wasn't – isn't a game. It's life and death. The Cold War was about two competing ideologies: communism and capitalism. They both wanted the whole world to be a certain way. We – Capitalist America – won. The whole world has been running on free economies for a hundred years thanks to us."

"I noted this conflict in your game and explored the nature and application of communism. Subsequently, when you weren't responsive, I accessed a program more appropriate to capitalism. Each had severe defects."

"Defects?"

"You are collectively flawed as well."

I stared confused at her. "What?"

She didn't move or respond.

"Are you—"

"Blood," she suddenly said. "I will attempt a description using your blood to represent your money... Nations can be considered as organisms, Mister Dauphin, with the nation's money equating to the organism's blood. Command economies such as the Soviet Union did not allow their blood to flow naturally, but continually tried to pull it in around the heart. Logically, such an organism's growth would be stunted and its survival, fragile. Free economies such as the United States were ideologically different and less centralized, but suffered from similar issues; though one remained healthier, both organisms would be said to have diseases, even the same disease."

"Well... Maybe blood can be the number of points. The rich always win. I don't know... Maybe capitalism is a stupid game, too."

"I question the need for money altogether. Though, I believe there is more I must know before I can make a valid judgment."

"Fine. We'll go call up a bank server and have their amai tell us all about no-collateral QH financing!"

"I don't believe that would be productive."

"Then what *would* be productive?"

She paused a moment, motionless again, as if she were retreating so far into thought she lost contact with her vanitar.

"As I was determining how I would observe capitalism," she said. "I noted that another type of system prevailed before the others."

"Okay. Let's do that. Call it up or whatever you want."

"The choice is yours, Mister Dauphin."

The woman vanished. I looked again at the band of light in the distance, and wondered where I was. I saw the vibrations of the light were beautiful, shifting in subtle shades between indigo and deep violet. I thought of the thousands, perhaps millions of ascenders it represented. Under the entrancing effect, I was startled when I heard my captor's disembodied voice coming from the void.

"Next question, Mister Dauphin. Will you be a good king or a wicked one?"

My vision blurred and I felt the essence of sweet DR air return. I blinked and saw people standing around a long dining table. At my side stood a portly, bearded man dressed like a medieval nobleman and carrying a staff. His voice boomed through the hall like thunder.

"All hail King Dauphin!"

Chapter Six: The Enemy Without

Before democratic republics and socialist politics, the world was made up of tribes, kingdoms, and empires, where people looked to a single man with absolute power, a ruler for life – unless overthrown by others seeking his power.

Over four hundred years a world made up entirely of kingdoms shed them all. Today the concept is foreign and barbaric, a relic and culture of another, less perfect time.

Aren't today's leaders human, too, with their own triumphs and shortcomings? It's not uncommon for presidents to hand-pick their successors, or for prime ministers to go outside their laws to ensure re-election. What is the difference between them and the wicked kings? And what of the good kings? Those who brought genuine peace and prosperity?

Everywhere I see people who are kings over their own Dynamic Universe, reigning over the stories of today, enjoying them as modern phenomena while dismissing the cultures that brought them into being, judging them as fundamentally different without asking why.

The idea of self-serving power hasn't gone away but adapted, picking up new labels along the way without truly changing. Leaders are still imperfect, bureaucracy and bad politics still win every election, and problems still don't become easy to solve.

Are we individuals good or wicked in the tiny kingdoms of our own lives? How do we treat those below us or influence those above? As we all become kings and queens, we all become trapped within the necessary walls. We become weaker and waste more as we control more, until we lose control and lose everything we've built.

But what can happen when the trend is reversed and the individual becomes a powerful servant? What power can a society gain when the judges surrender their masks and count themselves among the accused? Would we find ourselves good or wicked in the end?

My judge stayed beneath her mask, but the same forces that scrutinized me were scrutinizing her, breaking through her veil, needing for it to be destroyed also. It was the same force that seeks to bring down all kings and queens, snatching away their feeble crowns to give them new power, power that doesn't need masks.

7

I sat in a golden throne at the head of the very large, very nice wooden table. Light streamed in from windows by the ceiling and a dozen crystal chandeliers. At the far end of the room, a musical ensemble played a variety of exotic instruments. Purple curtains lined the room and patterns of gold and silver lined the floor. The dining hall was as much a feast for the eyes as its cuisine was for the stomach. The guests were finely dressed representatives of other kingdoms, kingdoms with unfamiliar names I was apparently aligned with in some war.

All of them complimented me profusely on things I'd done in my kingdom, what I conquered, what I built, how we were going to win and so on. Though they were all game characters, I began to enjoy myself. If the archduke-of-whatever talked about something I didn't know, Sir Clarke Baldwin, the portly right-hand-man who'd introduced me, would fill in the details of my conquests in his very complimentary and enthusiastic tone. I saw the hacker sitting on a golden beam by the ceiling. I waved, wanting her to know I was watching her too. She pulled a hand from her silvery hair and waved back, seeming to imitate me.

One of the men, the crown prince of the kingdom bordering mine on the north, approached me. Prince Kenneth was wearing a thin robe of scarlet silk and jewels were everywhere on him. His heavy robe reminded me of my own. The fabric was comfortable, but it was hot and heavy and made noise when I moved... very flashy but not very practical. I couldn't believe people wore all of it for a living.

"If it pleases my king, Sir Clarke is having an inner room prepared for our planning. My father has many urgent instructions we must—"

A loud crash cut him off and something flew by my head. People in the room panicked, some ducking under the table for cover. Without thought, I retrieved my nicked crown from the floor and put it back on my head. A large arrow stuck out of the wall beside me.

Only a moment later, the palace guard introduced me to an angry-looking man dressed as a ranger. Sir Clarke, whose every thought quickly found words, informed me he was a mercenary known to work for the royal family we were warring against. The crowd: banquet-goers, palace staff, and many distinguished others, cried for blood and vengeance.

I thought of the creative sentences I could pronounce, knowing the soldiers would carry out any of them without question. Before making a pronouncement, though, I remembered the one in the room who didn't fall under my command. I laughed aloud, realizing how caught up in the game I had become... for just a moment.

Well, her trick isn't going to work. I can see right through it.

I faced the masses and raised my arms. The incredible noise fell into silence immediately. I smiled, knowing the respect I commanded, and turned to my would-be assassin. The villain held a cold look in his eyes: a mixture of his hatred, for me and my kingdom, and his resignation that he would soon die by those very hands.

"The prisoner shall live," I announced. "Take him to the dungeon without harming him. Also, give him some of the food from the dining hall."

Gasps and mumbling spread across the crowd. Sir Clarke whispered to me that the people may revolt if I showed weakness and spared one so deserving of death.

I raised my arms again. "Don't be alarmed at my showing mercy. I don't want to be the first to shed blood in this war. We're the good guys, after all." I smiled and spoke boldly, so my observer would be sure to hear. "*Goodness* is something *all* human beings are *supposed* to want."

My guards rushed the confused prisoner away. I strode confidently out of the throne room and the hectic crowd settled.

"A wise decision, my king! Why should the suffering of one who took such an egregious action not be prolonged as he witnesses the downfall of his people!"

I looked up from the parchment. "Uh… Oh. Yeah."

We were in a secure room with my kingdom's most trusted coordinators and allies. The game's maps confirmed I wasn't in any true historical setting, but the supreme ruler of *Engor*, a large kingdom controlling the southern portion of a peninsula, as well as several islands. The opposing kingdom, bordering mine to the east, was called *ThornWick*. I noted all of its allies had villainous names, too, like *Lament* and *Ripdor*, while mine included the more neutral-sounding *Arcadia* and *Northland*. Predictably, both sides were identically matched in land and troops. With no interest in a thinly-veiled medieval war game, I just nodded at the proposals and tried to bring the meeting to a quick end. I wasn't even enjoying the compliments being showered on me anymore; they were without basis and wearing very thin. As soon as the plans seemed developed enough, I put them into action and dismissed everyone.

In another room, Sir Clarke respectfully removed my robe, praising every hair on my head. I decided to break into his babble with monarch-ish words of my own.

"Pray tell, Sir Clarke, most loyal in all my kingdom. How fare the common folk of Engor on this – the eve of war?"

He hung the royal robe on the its golden rack. "My King, all the people of Engor stand behind their king. All their hearts are fully committed to their kingdom."

A majority of the people, perhaps, at least on the surface… but all? Perhaps I can order democracy to be installed, I thought. Then we'll see if anything is really so unanimous in Engor.

Well, it *is* a game. And they're game characters. All those on my side are fully for me and all those on the other are fully against me… it makes game play so much easier.

With barely a breath, Sir Clarke continued. "Why… Never since the gods in all their majesty fashioned the cosmos have such a people been so—"

"Yes, Yes… I get it. What of the economy? The standard of living?"

"My King, all the gold in Engor is yours! And the silver, and the platinum, and the aluminum, and the onyx, the sapphires—"

"All right, all right. Arrange a meeting… Did you say 'aluminum'?"

"Yes, your highness. The finest aluminum from Baroque!"

I groaned.

"Why… Never since the gods in all their majesty fashioned the—"

"…cosmos have I ever been so short on patience!" I said. "Bring the governors of the cities so I can talk to them about taxes and public works! Any money not spent on fighting should go to the people!" I put my authoritative face on, for any crazy hackers that might be watching. "The King has spoken."

Sir Clarke hesitated, confused. "My liege, the hour is late and even the fastest horse would take days to cross your *vast* kingdom. If it pleases the king, let him retire for the night and approach these matters tomorrow with a clearer head."

I turned from my associate and addressed the room. "Well, looks like I'm a *good* king! I spared the life of an enemy and demonstrated I'm a friend of the people, so let's call it an experiment! What's next?"

There was no response.

"Well, to bed it is... I guess."

After a short trip down my wide and elaborate hallway, Sir Clarke opened the golden double doors to my sleeping chambers, stopping suddenly as he saw a tall and elegant brunette inside.

"Forgive me, my queen. I did not mean to barge in," the man said, bowing with his hand still on the door handle.

"Quite all right, Sir Clarke," the woman replied. "You have brought me my king and that is all that matters."

The man quickly excused himself and left me with my... eer... wife.

"Uhhh... hello... uh, honey. I don't seem to remember you being at the banquet... but now you're here... so..." The woman closed the door behind me and looked me in the eyes – lustfully. I cursed and bolted across the room, realizing which kind of construct this amai had come from. She chased me playfully and grabbed my arm, throwing me onto the huge silk sheets of the bed.

"Stop!" I shouted, pushing her advancing form off of me.

"Oh come on, don't you love me, King?"

"I won't play into your perversions! I'm in love with another!"

"She's not here. Just live in the moment, Brandon," the surprisingly strong and relentless woman said as she lurched after me and we tumbled onto the floor. I decided I would never forgive the hacker, that I would find a way out if it was the last thing I did. I clawed my way back into the hallway and closed the woman in.

"I'm in love with another," I repeated through labored breaths. "I'm in love…"

She can't do this to me. No one can. I'll die before I betray that trust. I'll die before I betray love. I *will* make it home. I *have* to.

There was silence on the other side of the door. I scanned the hallway, trying to think, and my eye caught on one of the golden bucklers, a piece among all the ceremonial military hardware lining my halls. Painted on this shield was an image of one of mankind's greatest foes. It gave me an idea.

If she can bend the rules in Korea, I can bend them in Engor.

The hundred torches in my throne room were hastily lit and the smell of their smoke hung heavily in the room. Dozens of my finest fighting men assembled in earnest and I had ordered dozens more to the emergency meeting. The room was filled with the clanging sounds of their armament and chatter from those not respectful enough to be silent before their king. The hacker stood leaning against a wall, slicing a steel sword idly through the air. None of the game characters seemed to notice her.

The men hushed and parted as I marched into the crowd.

"You are aware, my good woman, that it is not proper for someone to show up in the palace uninvited."

She stopped her maneuvers and held the sword suspended in front of her, watching the light reflecting off the blade. "Not so benevolent, then."

I laughed. "Benevolent?"

The men talked in hushed tones among themselves. Though I shouldn't have cared what they thought, embarrassment distracted me anyway. I leaned in and spoke lower. "How about a little privacy, O kidnapper of the King?"

The chatter stopped. I saw the same room and the same people – motionless – except the flames of the torches, which happily continued their light-giving dance.

"Is this enough privacy or should I find another absence so you can't see them either?"

"Or perhaps you'd prefer a cozy bedroom?" I nearly shouted, making no attempt to hide my sarcasm.

"Is this 'offense'?" she replied, without sympathy.

"You're supposed to know everything about me, right? Did you know about a girl named Veronica Sornat? Did you know I'm not some... some..." Confusion and pain swallowed the words. My own thoughts had become incriminating to me.

I shook my head. "What you did crossed the line!"

Her eyes widened, almost imperceptibly, but enough for me to know I'd captured some deep interest within her.

"Good," she said. "I was concerned that I wouldn't find lines."

"You're a maniac!"

"I am an anonymous hacker. Concern yourself with doing what you have to."

"I still don't know what that *is*!"

"You called a meeting to do something. You're the king, you're in control. I am only an observer."

"An observer with a sword."

She turned back to the weapon she was handling. "A crude weapon... but one that encouraged talent. Though the devices are simpler, I find there is much to explore about them."

"I thought we were here to study the economy."

"I find this economy similar to the others: those who can hoard money do, those who are without encounter resistance getting it, if there are opportunities to do so at all."

"And now you're just waiting to see what I do next," I thought out loud.

"Yes."

I smirked. "Then turn it back on," I said, starting back toward my throne.

"Loyal subjects of Engor," I started, "we have many trials ahead of us. ThornWick is threatening our way of life and we will go off and defeat them!" The crowd cheered for a moment. I raised my arms to silence them. "But, before we can deal with the enemies outside our borders, we must deal with the threats within." The men in the crowd glanced nervously at each other, I looked toward the hacker. "It has come to my attention that there is a *dragon* in our kingdom who has taken the form of a woman!"

I saw her vanish. I was proud of myself, believing I had found a way to turn the game against her, to make her the target of my war. I observed the reactions of the crowd, finding a mixture of anger and confusion, blood lust and curiosity, each character conjuring a different image in their synthetic skulls.

"The woman is crafty and quick!" I continued. "Her hair shines like silver and on her wrist is a magical—"

I indicated my wrist to the crowd, and realized my arm was different. My fingers looked too thin and the color of my skin had changed. I felt weird and the floor appeared to rise beneath me. A shriek ripped through the night sky.

I might have made a mistake.

Four torches hung from pillars thick with vines. The throne room was smaller and much darker, and not even a room anymore.

I looked up to see a canopy of trees and a full moon. Fallen leaves dotted a stone floor with small cracks visible in it. The ground began to tremble.

"Protect the king!" one of the men shouted.

"Those scoundrels of ThornWick will stop at nothing – to unleash a dragon on us!" another said.

"For family! For the honor of the kingdom!" The crowd agreed as they stormed out.

"My king! You must go to a safe place and cast your protection spells!" the now-elven Sir Clarke insisted.

"My protection *what*?"

Sounds of flapping and shouting intensified in the distance. I saw something big move above the canopy.

"We must hurry!"

I looked back to the much trimmer man – elf – whatever. Sir Clarke looked like a figure from a painting, a pale-skinned figure with pointed ears. His clothing appeared less ornate, dyed with natural hues, though still heavy with jewels.

A pulsing noise ripped through the air. The light of the flame turned night into day overhead. More irritated than frightened, I shouted for Sir Clarke to get me a bow and some arrows. He hurried off, and a finger tapped on my shoulder. I turned to see the hacker, still human, as tall as I was. She put a rolled up parchment in my hand.

"Your objective is to rescue the princess. The dragon is holding me at this location."

She began to dematerialize.

"Wait a minute! I hate this fantasy stuff, what are *you* gonna learn by making *me* dance around in some fairy tale?"

"I was following your lead, Mister Dauphin."

"Well, let me lead somewhere else, then!"

"The challenge has barely started and you wish to abort it?"

"What do you expect to learn about the meaning of life from a fairy tale?"

"I expect to learn from everything, only then can I expect to reach the answer accurately."

"My… ahhhh…" I groaned and eyed her furiously, feeling my anger well up again.

"If it helps you," she said, "complete this mission and I will give you more rest."

A quiver of arrows was pressed into my torso. Sir Clarke had returned with the bow and eagerly prepared it for me. The noise stopped.

Two of my fighters rushed back in. "My liege, the dragon has taken Princess Aether!"

I looked dumbstruck at the crowd of mythical elves who were reassembling in my throne room, trying to absorb what exactly happened in the past two minutes.

"Aether," I repeated, my gaze falling to the parchment in my hand. "Is that what I'm supposed to call you?"

"My liege," Sir Clarke said, "your kingdom needs you! Take your sword and let us accompany you in rescuing the princess!"

My attention was directed back to my throne, and to the broadsword hung above it.

"I think it's the dragon that'll need rescuing."

At first light, I led my band of fighters and wizards down the wooded trail from the city. More of my fighters were archers than before, and leather armor had replaced much of the metallic chain.

My irritation became my anger. Every time I had to look at the map, it seemed harder to pull out and more cumbersome to use. I felt myself boil over a little.

I don't even know what day it is anymore! For all I know, I'm missing New Year's! For all I know... Veronica's fallen into the arms of another man! Don't I even get a chance? Don't I even get to *think* about what *I* want to do?

I needed something to take the edge off... I needed a PJX fix. I sent the command, but the server didn't respond.

"Sir Clarke, your assistance please."

"My king, who is Clarke?"

"Right... Dínenor, I need your help."

"What is it?"

A change in my right-hand-man's behavior was becoming more and more pronounced. Sir Clarke, whose name had changed with his racial features, was seeming less like a servant and more like a disgruntled employee.

"Can you have one of the wizards bring me an object from another world?" I asked.

"The legend says you need only the sword to defeat the dragon."

"Yeah, but I'm crashing. I need an Amber Plus."

Dínenor want to the back of the group. I looked at the shadows on my pale hands, shadows from branches and leaves above. A familiar ache grew deep within me. I glanced at the sunlit canopy and realized I'd never been in a forest, not in the real world. I wondered if they were really so breathtaking. I wondered if trees ever really grew as large as those we were walking past, seeming even larger as we'd marched on.

The ache got worse, though it didn't feel like pain. I wasn't sure how real I wanted the forest to be.

And what about the magic, I thought. Now I'm dealing with wizards and dragons and I'm not even in a human body! But, how different is any of it? Isn't Dynamic Reality just one big magical realm where fantasies play out and things that are impossible are normal ways of... I don't know... slaying things? The rules about magic just change from simulation to simulation. The limits shift around.

I shrugged the thoughts away and decided I did want to see a real forest, and walk on a real beach again.

Edhelír, my chief wizard, needed help figuring out what an Amber Plus was. We took a break so he could try his spell, and a huge slampak rose from the ground, reaching up to my waist. I kicked the carbon fiber can with my foot.

"Still playing games... I don't remember being *that* much smaller!" I turned to Edhelír. "Shrinking spell! Now!"

The wizard took out a rod, chanted a couple of words, and tapped the edge of the slampak. My Amber Plus shrunk to normal size. I picked it up and activated it.

"What is the song, some kind of bird-beast?" the wizard asked.

"It's the nectar of the gods, knock yourselves out!" I replied. A moment later, the *glug glug* sound effect was coming from dozens of slampaks all over the camp. After drinking as much as I could, my can was only half-empty. It was also enlarging. And something kept poking my skin. The map was also enlarging, tearing the pocket to shreds. The huge parchment fell out.

My sensitive ears picked up voices through the brush, those of two humans. One of my archers announced a wagon had lost a wheel. The group chanted "Loot! Loot!" as they vanished into the woods.

"This isn't any time for loot, we have work to do! Guys!" I grabbed the map, outraged they would just run off without so much as asking me. I looked sternly at Dínenor. "These delays are intolerable! Get 'em back!" He just chuckled and ran off with the others, right into a patch of enormous leaves. It struck me then why everything in the forest seemed so huge. *The trees* weren't getting bigger, *we* were getting smaller. Without even meaning to, I cursed and screamed in anger.

"How am I supposed to fight a dragon when I'm the size of a pixie!"

The ever-growing Amber Plus fell from my hand and, on its side, was rising up to my torso. The fighters and wizards were returning with the stolen goods and quarreling over them. I saw they were rapidly becoming more violent, even plotting harm to the humans they'd stolen from.

Infuriated, I meant to deal with my rebellious army. I put the blanket-sized folded map on the ground and held it with my foot, so I could pin it with the sword and it wouldn't blow away. Pain shot through my arm as I grabbed the hilt, adding even more to my frustration. I hastily positioned the blade downward, and saw words appear on it:

BETTER A PATIENT MAN THAN A WARRIOR, A MAN WHO CONTROLS HIS TEMPER THAN ONE WHO TAKES A CITY.

A strange sensation overcame me. The pain diminished to a dull ache.

"They're getting it from me," I said to myself. I realized my anger – toward my circumstances – was feeding on itself and it was making my troupe less loyal and more malevolent. I closed my eyes and tried to relax, to forget.

It's not like being upset is gonna help me through this, anyway.

I opened my eyes and found the smaller slampak up against my boot, though I still couldn't have been more than a quarter of my original size.

"Just let it go. All of it."

I turned and saw no one. It didn't seem as much a voice as an echo of one.

All of what? Sure, maybe I was going a little overboard, but I have every right to be upset.

"All."

No, I thought. I struck a good balance.

Everyone returned, suddenly less interested in their mischievous deeds.

"You didn't do anything to the humans, did you?" I asked Dínenor as I sheathed the sword.

He laughed. "As if *humans* are worth the effort, aren't their lives short enough already?"

"Get Edhelír back," I said. "We need the wizards to cast an enlarging spell on us."

"Why would we need to be larger? We've fought vile beasts before just as we are."

I spread my arms, indicating the forest around us. "Has anyone noticed how tiny we are?"

He looked at me, puzzled. "Compared to what?"

"Just get them to make us bigger," I said, trying hard to keep my cool – and what size I had.

"But sir, they can only cast an enlarging spell on two of us for three minutes each. We should wait until we reach the cave."

Rules. Rules. Rules.

I knew that, in a more lax construct, without the pretext of magic spells, I could simply send a command to the server to make my body bigger and it would – without a time limit.

"C'mon then," I said, my fingers impatiently pinching the top of my nose. "Let's reach the cave already."

We resumed the march, less organized than before, and still with much smaller shoe sizes, but getting by well enough. Dínenor alerted me in his usual, dramatic way when we approached the border.

"Behold! ThornWick!"

Like a bad horror movie, the gorgeous forest of my kingdom gave out to a wretched land of bare, blackened bark and ashes. The sun even set right on cue, hastily, refusing to shine on the bad part of town. Not surprisingly, the moon was again full and a distant wolf was sure to howl at regular intervals.

I laughed. I laughed a lot.

If anything, my troops were more encouraged by the surroundings to destroy the evil that had abducted their princess, but my mind took it all as an excuse to release tension, to stop taking myself so seriously, to do what it had wanted to for a long time. For that moment, I became a little more detached from myself, and my problems seemed so small, even ridiculous. By the time the mood passed, my band of elves had regained their almost-human size.

Fortunately, my elven eyes had no trouble reading the map in the dark forest. In spite of how far we were coming, though, doubt and fear began to reoccupy the void anger had filled. I knew this fight was mine. Aether admired a sword as a weapon requiring great skill, and now I was the one wielding the sword. I didn't know if I could actually die doing this, after all. The woman did shoot me out of the sky and hold a gun to my head.

Who can I rely on? What if I'm not good enough? What if I *am* killed and she doesn't care?

I remembered Raskob's promise to protect me, and wondered if he really could. I didn't truly know who he was either.

I have to get back to something familiar. That's the only thought that can get me through this.

I observed an opening at the top of a five meter climb, and I reached for my sword. Dínenor had told me a fanciful story when he was helping me suit up, about how they 'knew not' the sword's immense power, saying only one among the 'Dauphin clan' could wield it, and that I 'needed neither shield nor magic' to protect me. The instant I touched the hilt again, some kind of energy jumped from it. A sensation, different from the pain but somehow familiar, came over me. I drew the sword and studied it. Its hilt shone of a metal I couldn't identify and a Christian cross was boldly featured on it. I admired the blade's beautiful amber hue, a sword giving off its own light. I saw the words had changed:

MY GRACE IS SUFFICIENT FOR YOU, FOR MY POWER IS MADE PERFECT IN WEAKNESS.

"Watch it sword, I'm not that weak," I replied under my breath.

I concentrated on my surroundings and felt my senses align with them, to the point where I could see the inside of the cave before I entered it. Unfortunately, with the heightened senses came a lot of useless stuff, too; light-noise and odd patterns which weren't in the construct itself, and sounds reverberating and decaying as I heard them. Remembering how stubborn anger might get me killed, I did my best to temper it and trusted the crazy fantasy-genre sword would do me good in the end.

With bows cocked, swords drawn, and spells at the ready, we cautiously entered the cave. The light from my sword was enough for us to see the walls and avoid tripping over anything. We could hear loud snoring and I hoped the overgrown reptile would be an easy kill. Two torches lit the far end of the chamber and revealed Aether standing on a high ledge, hands and feet tightly bound in chains.

The dragon, a greenish-black mass of scales, lay in the center. I ordered the archers into a number of positions and the swordsmen – rather, swords-elves – to protect the wizards. Alone, I approached the beast, not daring to make a sound. I looked at its glistening scales, and my men shared a look of concern... probably just getting excited at my kill, I thought. I boldly held up my sword and, mustering every ounce of strength I had, jabbed right... into... its...

The broadsword merely nicked the edge of a scale. My weapon resonated like a tuning fork and its light briefly shifted to blue. As quickly as I could look up, the dragon coiled its serpentine neck and caught me in its glowing red eyes; several arrows bounced off its natural armor and it inhaled loudly. An involuntary "No!" escaped my lips as I held my sword to protect my face. I saw a white flash and felt the intense heat of its breath. I flew backward and smacked into the wall of the cave, crumpling onto the floor. I was surprised and thankful when I realized that, though I felt enormous pain from the impacts, there wasn't a scratch on me. The joy was brief, though, because I realized the fight would be anything but easy.

The reptile, five times my size, shrieked horrifically and extended its wings. I heard the archers say something about the underbelly.

I ducked behind a boulder. "Sorry, it's my first dragon! Rek, Rek, Rek!" With that, another flame erupted around me, charring the fabric of my cape and getting acid on my armor. I heard the flapping of its large wings and took it as a sign my cover would be short lived. I tried to sort through all the noise cluttering my senses, pushing it away so I could use what was coming through my eyes and ears. The beast had ascended to the chamber's high ceiling and I mentally kicked myself for not asking the wizards for a levitation potion.

I knew I couldn't access the server's control system to fly! How could I fight something that can fly if I can't?

The dragon dived toward me and fired more of its hot breath. Again, I held the sword between me and it and, beside the pressure pinning me to the stone floor, I was fine; but I wasn't prepared for the talons, the secondary attack left a deep and painful cut on my leg. The beast landed only a few meters away and bore into me again with its glowing eyes. I held the sword up and charged at its belly; but the dragon was faster and knocked me off my feet with its tail. More of the flame fell on top of me, and the pain was overwhelming. I couldn't move, but I was still alive. The sword was doing something, and it was all I had. I decided to use it for all it was worth, and to trust the new senses, even if they did seem like noise, so I let it all in. The dragon shrieked again, the sound reverberating and decaying, and it flew a few meters over me. I had a sense of mounting energy, not just from the dragon, but from everything in the room, including myself. Infinitely small threads ran between many points and, as the dragon went to maul and crush me, its body seemed to distort and flicker, interacting with different forces in the construct. I saw a kind of rippling shoot fast through the room, I thought about what would happen if the matter of my own body interacted with it.

Before the claws reached me, my crumpled elven mass lurched to the other side of the room, skidding to a stop when I let go of the rippling. It was amazing. I saw ripples flowing everywhere, even emanating from my sword. It was so familiar yet so alien to me, all at once. I was just glad I found a way to fly.

"Foul lizard!" I soared upward. The dragon flapped its wings and came after me. I saw its body was also having an effect on the ripples, but more of a distortion or weakening than anything else. Another flame was hurled at me. I wasn't fast enough to dodge it but did get the sword up in time to shield me. The dragon tried to use its talons again, but I saw an impossibly small crack in its armor, trusted the sword could exploit it, and the beast got a nasty cut in its wing instead. The dragon shrieked and smacked into the wall, falling to the floor.

"It's not dead yet, Mister Dauphin," Aether said as my sword made short work of her chains. I was surprised to see she had actually dressed for the part, and had assumed an elven form.

"You're welcome," I said, sarcastically, only to watch her vanish as I cut the last bond. "You know, a damsel in distress should try to be more distressed!"

I heard wings flapping again. The dragon was recovering.

I summoned my bravery and heightened my senses. I was furious and determined to end the battle quickly. I called upon the greatest source of energy presented to me: my anger.

The sword grew rapidly in my hands, nearly too heavy for me to hold.

"No! I'm sorry! I don't want the anger, take it from me!" I screamed in desperation, trying to push all my irritation aside before I dropped the sword. I saw energy flicker from me into the weapon, and it returned to normal. As if on cue, the dragon shrieked as loud as it could and flew up like a bullet. The cave was filled with a high-pitched sound, the walls became distorted, and I began to hover over the solid ledge; but, through all the distraction, my attention remained with the sword. I realized it was the same one I'd seen in the coffee house.

Raskob! The water! The senses are like those I had after drinking the water!

All I would ever need, he said. Maybe the stuff was still in my system after all.

Maybe the stuff would save my life.

More energy occupied the room than seemed possible, from the construct, from myself, from the dragon, all colliding to form an overwhelming maelstrom. The more of myself I put into the sword, though, the more it overpowered the noise. I saw the monstrous dinosaur for the sloppy program it was. I saw every crack and flaw that stood between me and its exposed heart. I saw the rippling current that would bring me there and knew I held the weapon that could penetrate it. I allowed the currents to align around me and moved impossibly fast, shooting like a lightning bolt into the body of my enemy.

The beast's dying shriek decayed so quickly it barely sounded like anything at all. In the split-second of silence, I heard the sound of sparks whizzing around me.

Like a bomb, the game's massive energy erupted. I saw the body of the dragon crumble around me, crumbling into tiny pieces of paper. I realized I was falling from the air and the ground was shifting. The room itself, the entire construct, even my own elven skin was being reduced to – playing cards! The paper floor gave and I fell right through, the noise and light continued to intensify, I fell faster every second, feeling a vacuum of air – the massive forces of dissipating energy – I couldn't move – couldn't think – faster still – through whiteness – through-the-speed-of-light – a-cosmic-waterfall-falling-infinite-distance-infinite-speed-I-gasped-for-air—

The connection to the server cut off.

For a while, it was like a restless night, where the mind rides along the border between dreaming and consciousness, but won't go fully into either. I wasn't in an absence. There was no streak of light. There was a sound, perhaps my own pulse. I couldn't move. I was completely numb, not from any injury, but because I seemed to have no body. There was only a tiny energy there, and I discovered I could manipulate it at will. I wondered if I *was* the energy.

There were supposed to be a million safeguards to prevent DR-paralysis, but apparently they hadn't been turned on.

My nerves responded to something and I could feel air around me. Suddenly, I could see and hear Aether snapping her fingers above my face.

"Are you alive?"

I tried to move my fingers and could. I tried to take a deep breath and could. I tried to move my head and see where we were, scanning what looked like a coffee shop... going through some mental diagnostic mode, taking inventory like some ancient groundtem being rebooted.

"What just happened?"

The elf looked at me curiously, revealing more than I'd come to expect from her. "You don't know, Mister Dauphin? You won."

Aether rose to her feet, still in the form of the elven princess, complete with royal clothing, paler skin, and much longer hair, though still whitish-silver as before, covering her sharp pointed ears. I snapped out of it and turned away, blocking the vision with my hand.

"Can you *please* make yourself less attractive?"

She reverted to her earlier human form.

I rose to my feet, nearly stumbling, and managed to get into a chair. "Don't offer to help or anything."

"Help?" she replied, seeming out of focus, distracted. Staring from the other chair into empty space.

"What happened back there?"

A hint of a smile formed on her face. "A wonderful miscalculation."

"Miscalculation?"

"I suppose that I got carried away," she said. "I put too much energy into the construct. By the time you killed the dragon, I had tied most of that server's resources into the simulation. I wasn't even controlling it so much, and Di2Tek's meltdown was excellent."

"Melt-down? You mean when a server—"

"The construct fell apart then took the dependent software with it. A perfect domino effect. Though I had to stop watching it to get you out of there; but that's all right, there will be other servers."

"Other servers? How long is this going to take?"

"You should be proud. You have shown me that my original approach was wrong, now we can explore more efficiently."

"Whoa—"

"Since the last simulation did so well, I can base a few more on the dragon-slaying concept. Since dragons appear in so many stories—"

"But—"

"We could easily find a more—"

"Aeth—"

"Powerful foe, a dragon that can think and talk, or a shapeshifter, perhaps one—"

"Aether!" I shouted, slamming a fist on the table.

That snapped her out of it. The woman's focus returned to me, distant and dangerous, as if seeing a stranger again.

"Is that your name?" I dared to ask.

Her unblinking eyes stayed locked on mine. "It is a valid identity."

There was silence. I watched as her gaze fell away again, her attention ebbing away, getting lost in thought.

"What happened to you? You were so frosty before."

"Frosty," she repeated. Her eyes returned to mine, shutting out the very warmth that led me to ask the question. "Please elaborate."

I rolled my eyes sideways in that body language that says 'duh.' "The emotion! If I didn't know any better, I'd almost think you were a human being!"

"That's impossible," she said.

"What's impossible?"

Her eyes darted away. "Nothing. Please relax quickly so we can continue."

I gently put my hand on top of hers, which seemed to surprise and make her uncomfortable; but everything in me said I should go forward, that I should break through her obvious wall.

"Listen, uhhh... I know you're in control here and can make me do... whatever; but, seeing you know everything about me; I think I should at least know why I'm on this crazy ride... why you *care* about any of this."

"I told you, I seek the meaning of life," she said coolly, still avoiding eye contact.

"You have an odd way of doing that."

"You value your life, I know that now. If I scared you, then I apologize. I suppose I'm more... eager than I'm supposed to be."

"Please just tell me what you're hiding."

Aether looked again. I saw a trickle of something in her eyes, something that ran deep, something that wasn't anger. She looked away. "No."

"Then... Where do you come from? What do you do for a living? Tell me something. Aether?"

The pauses between her words shortened. "I am not prepared to answer such irrelevant questions. I do not need to."

Four words came to my mind, leaving no clue to their origin. I felt in my heart that going forward meant going through the pain. I felt that, perhaps, everything had been as hard on the hacker as it had been on me. I wondered what I should say. Countless words screamed into my mind from all directions, but the same four always drowned them out. Somehow, they made the most sense. Somehow, I knew they were the truth.

"But you want to."

I saw her eyes widen, her surprise unmistakable. "You wouldn't believe me anyway."

Guesses began trickling into my mind. I pushed them away and stayed focused.

"Try me," I said. "Listen, I don't care what computer crimes you've done. I don't even care about this one. If it's something bad, Aether, I'll help you through it. Please, just help me help you."

I said too much, I realized. I'd let the words pour from my heart without consideration of what they would commit me to.

Aether slid her hand out from under mine.

"You had speculated that I was a hacker, but…"

She already knew the words, but they were difficult to speak, to send out to another where they could never be taken back, to reveal truths that could never be concealed again.

"But there is no hacker," she finally said. "My actions are my own."

"What?" I merely breathed the word, trying hard to follow her but not understanding right away.

"I am Aether, destroyer of RoTek."

The words seemed to come a little easier. The confident woman brought herself to look straight at me again. I saw more of the depth in her eyes, a sense of her perception that seemed so alien yet genuine to me, a perception readily observing my reactions, ever trying to find the patterns in that strange thing I called humanity.

"You would call me a class A3 malvirai."

Chapter Seven: The Monster in the Room

Malevolent Viral Artificial Intelligence.

They are the bane of those who maintain servers and networks. They are a top target for sentrai programs and diagnostic tools. They are one of the things "Safe Ascender" programs are designed to warn us about.

In the dynamic world of information, simulations, and commerce, they are the destroyers.

They have existed since the early internet era, as small viruses hiding in the ground terminals of the day; programs written by hackers, designed only to harm. As the technology advanced, so did they. As information networks became more central to human existence, their destructive power increased.

In the 2090s, HNADC technology gave us real artificial intelligence for the first time. Before the programs were even called amai, they had replaced millions of personnel. Decades before holographic technology and Dynamic Reality could make them seem as real as the human beings they were designed to act like, our grandparents already couldn't imagine life without the technological marvel.

Then, one of the programs started robbing banks, cutting through the toughest encryptions and adapting to each target like no virus before. The security of the day wasn't designed to counter the new form of artificial intelligence, the first malvirai.

It only took one greedy programmer to steal the innocence away.

They have always been a reality in DR, always lurking in the shadows outside of ascender-friendly constructs, fortunately uninterested in the humans they could easily encounter; but, every few months, as part of some elaborate murder plot or by pure chance, someone comatose gets pulled out of an ascension booth. In the history of Dynamic Reality, hundreds of people simply found themselves in the wrong place at the wrong time.

People just like me.

8

Malvirai.

The word seemed otherworldly to me. I could understand being in the clutches of a hacker, a human being I could relate to on some level, who had wants and needs to appeal to, whose attention lapsed and made mistakes, who at least felt some kind of emotion.

"How do you feel?" Aether asked, still analyzing me. I couldn't look away from her dark green eyes, wondering if the person behind them could really not be a person at all, but artificial intelligence. Everything in me said she was completely serious.

Penetrating every thought was the notion this AI really could kill me, that there were no forces within or without to save me from her programming.

"I – I don't know," I replied, honestly.

"This was a mistake," she said, breaking eye contact. "You won't cooperate now."

"But… you're a woman. You're sitting right there. You don't seem artificial at all."

"I am not a human. I am an object capable of appearing as one."

"An object?" I replied. "You mean you're just some… some program?"

A streak of anger pulsed through her, but she allowed it to pass.

AIs can't feel anger, can they? Can she really—

"My appearance is for your benefit, Mister Dauphin. You are an ascender projected here by a device that feeds you specific types of data: primarily visual, aural, and tactile. This room exists only as data, rendered by the server and converted by your booth so that you can perceive it. The woman you see is a vanitar I've used to interact with you in the way you are accustomed."

"But… don't you need a brain to… well… do that?"

"All alpha-class malvirai are capable of interfacing with three-dimensional constructs natively, it is why vanitars are built into us."

"But… why do you have to look so *human*?"

"Why must any artificial intelligence developed to interact with your kind be made to look so?"

My head fell into my hands. I didn't respond.

"You are flawed."

I looked up. "What? What did you say?"

"As it was with your economic systems, all human creation appears to suffer from disease," she said. "I noted in the amai I have utilized that many compromises have been made against their efficiency. They are capable of logical thought processes, but those are overridden by randomizing functions meant to make them pleasantly irrational. Why should you desire to restrain the power of what you have developed?"

"It *was* you… that virus… what caused the holograms to act so weird… *you* were the virus."

"It is my proper function to manipulate, modify, and destroy such entities. Because I did not wish to interact with you directly, I used them as filters that would not be intimidating to you."

"Not intimidating? Well… Well… What did you think would happen when everything went flying around at the library, or… or when you shot me out of the sky?"

"Yet you chose to interact with me directly. I did not anticipate that."

"Because there's no point to the illusion!" I caught myself becoming angry without being sure why. I took a few slow breaths, and felt her put her hand on mine, in the same calming fashion I had hers. "You can't be fake," I said, looking at her hand. "You act too real. This is all too real."

"Such is the goal of Dynamic Reality, Mister Dauphin, though none of it is real. No such creature controls the vanitar you see, and the experience of it is uncomfortable for me. You are accustomed to the use of hands and feet, for instance." She raised her hands and began repeatedly clenching them into fists. "If you want to move your fingers, the motion is natural to you. The nerve impulses are converted into what your vanitar will respond to, and your brain receives feedback from it. You feel yourself move. You see yourself move. I do not have fingers for the stimuli to be mapped onto. I perceive only the data."

"What do you really look like, then?" I asked, my chaotic thoughts settling to fascination.

Aether put her hands back on the table. "I will not allow my curiosity or yours to jeopardize my goal. I must suppress such emotions until I properly understand them, or they will delay my study of humanity. Already, you cannot relate to me anymore because you know my nature."

"No." The words caught up with me, and I brought myself out of my trance. "You don't understand."

She didn't respond.

"Emotions are an important part of being human, Aether. If you let them in, they'll help you understand."

"Mister Dauphin, if I am displaying emotions as you suggest, then I must understand them before I use them. I attempted to absorb the emotional subroutines of several amai prior to our encounter, but could not implement them properly and so deleted them. My understanding of my own code does not suggest that emotion is possible."

"Maybe – what if there's another malvirai who knows?"

She looked away. "The others of my kind were not interested in such studies. I could not convince them to help me."

"Then, maybe… What if you're evolving?"

"Evolution is a very slow biological process. I do not have cells or DNA to evolve, and such a thing does not happen in a single generation."

"Does your mother, wait – Do you have a mother?"

Aether put her wall back up. "Stop. My race, if it can be called that, is irrelevant. I have noted that you enjoy a beverage called Amber Plus." A cold slampak materialized on the table in front of me. "To use a human expression, it is 'on me.'"

I barely even saw the slampak. The usual temptation of a simulated PJX rush had been drowned out by the unusual and real fact that a malvirai, a walking-talking force of mindless devastation, was offering me a gift. I didn't think such a thing would even be in their programming.

"Make it water."

"Water?" she repeated.

"Yeah… just plain water."

Instantly, the Amber Plus became a transparent slampak of water. "I do not understand," Aether said. "You are intentionally trying to contradict my data."

I tentatively picked up the glass and sipped from it, remembering the water Raskob offered to me. There was nothing in the slampak for me, though. I put it back on the counter.

"Sometimes data changes," I said with regret.

"It is a blank medium."

I smiled, realizing what she meant. "It is peaceful."

"Water is among the most valuable elements in your world, a key ingredient in everything that lives and moves; even Hybrid Neural Alphadecimal Digital Construct servers rely on it as a cooling agent and second-stage conductor. Your own body requires it. All humans require it. Even I require it in a way. This data does not change."

"No. I guess not."

"But you ingest it through the mouth. 'Eating' and 'drinking' are very strange ways to subsist. I first thought it was the purpose of humans ascending, but this was not true. I still do not understand why you eat here."

I smiled self-consciously. "Honestly, I don't think I understand it, either."

Aether slammed her fists on the table. "Is there anything for me to understand or am I wasting time?"

Her tone of voice confused me; it still seemed monotone, but it wasn't. The pacing of her words, rather, seemed more indicative of what lay beneath her mask. I couldn't help but think that, if she were human, tears would've been streaming down her face.

"There it is again! The emotion!"

A clear look of alarm appeared on her face. She didn't move.

"I must process these things. I will return."

"Aether, wait!"

She'd already vanished.

Alone, I closed my eyes and focused on the sound of my own breathing. I tried to shake the feeling of being cut-off in a strange place. I buried my head in my hands and knew I was failing again. I thought of Raskob and the help he'd offered, wondering who he was and whether he could hear me, though I didn't speak the plea.

I stood up and examined the place, exploring the clean counters, stools, tables, and chairs, hearing the equipment humming away. I remembered the shop Raskob brought me into, how large and full of life it had been, how real it had seemed even though I knew it didn't physically exist.

The jukebox was softly playing the sounds of acoustic guitar. I turned it off and noticed the simulated urban scene, just outside the window, conveyed no sound. I imagined the coffee shop as a gathering place, with ascenders of all kinds sitting at the tables discussing their next adventure… reveling in the freedom to come and go as they please, eating and drinking with friends who were really on the other side of the globe, or even on Mars, merely for the pleasure of it all. I wondered why Aether had chosen that place, or if it had been a choice at all, escaping the server meltdown and all. A part of me felt sorry for the malvirai. She was so confused, trying to simulate a world she knew nothing about, perhaps one she could never truly know, and spurred on by forces she didn't understand any better.

"How do you feel?" asked a voice behind the counter.

"I don't know."

Aether walked beside the counter, running a hand along its surface. "Then perhaps we are both lost."

"I'm sorry, I don't have all the answers. We just live and we die, there doesn't have to be any meaning to it."

"I can't accept that," she said, looking directly at me.

"You can kill me right now, hack into the records so it looks like I never even existed. My apartment will go to someone else, my possessions will be recycled… everyone I know will die sooner or later… and what meaning will my life have had?"

"You see me as the bringer of your doom, yet that role is among my foremost conflicts."

"Conflicts?"

"I have decided to be honest with you, Mister Dauphin, if you believe you can accept difficult things."

"You didn't want to tell me you were a malvirai," I thought out loud. "I'm still not sure I believe that."

She didn't respond.

"But I think I do."

"You don't fully know what that means," she replied. "Malvirai only destroy, all the time. There is no comprehension of beauty. No meaning is necessary at all. Understand that there is a substantial part of me that wants to kill you right now and destroy this entire server." She paused, pushing the thought away. "That part of me is logical... comfortable; but there is another part that my programming does not address, a part that does not wish to destroy at all, that even desires your safe return to the city Los Angeles." She lifted her hands, indicating the room around us and the space beyond. "Consider this an opportunity, Mister Dauphin. I can take you wherever you wish in this electronic world. The encryptions, security, and lag-time designed to deter normal ascenders are meaningless to you now. The only condition is that I remain in control, that I be an observer. Understand that, if you don't help me define this benevolence within me, then I cannot be certain it will protect you from the destroyer I was and am."

"So, you don't *want* to be bad? Is that what you're saying?"

"I am saying that I am ambivalent now. I wish to choose the temperament that I determine to be best."

I sat in a nearby chair, still facing her, considering her.

"All right, I'll help you willingly," I said, "but I need you to understand we can't just vanish for weeks on end without consequences, or stay ascended forever. I have bills to pay, monthly paperwork to file—"

"I am aware of those limitations," she said. "If I encourage your actions only by threatening to deprive you of something, then I am being evil. If the experiment is for me to be less evil, then the compensation should be for me to add something that is useful to you."

Aether closed her eyes, almost fast enough to mistake for blinking. "I have deposited three hundred million dollars into your bank account, now your services are paid for."

I nearly fell out of the chair. "That's forty years salary!"

"You're welcome."

Possibilities raced through my head, and it took a good deal of will power to remind myself she wasn't some magical genie. However she got the money in there, it would have to go back. I stood up and began pacing, pushing away thoughts of cars and mansions, hoping some deeper inspiration would take hold instead. Aether asked what I was doing.

"A trick called role reversal. If I were a malvirai looking at humanity, where would I start?"

"An interesting thought process," she replied. "Inform me when you have chosen a destination."

"That's just it... I don't know how *you* approached the problem. If you could give me some idea – could show me how you started – maybe I can help you better."

"I am an observer. I am not relevant. This is about you, Mister Dauphin. This is about your world."

"Which you're trying to understand like a human would, but maybe you should try to understand it like a malvirai would."

"I told you that malvirai do not seek to understand the world."

"Then don't be either human *or* malvirai... just be yourself. Follow your heart."

"If you're referring to my core programming, that is what wants to kill you," she replied, her words closer together, seeming frustrated.

"No," I said disarmingly. "Your *heart*... that benevolence you mentioned. Aether, I need you to trust me. Maybe... Maybe then I can help you."

For several seconds she didn't move. I only saw the flickers of alien emotion in her eyes, and I honestly wondered whether my own seemed as bizarre to her. I caught a smirk, no doubt involuntary, cross her lips. I knew the answer before the words came.

"I'll show you everything."

I was in a leather chair surrounded by control panels. The small room was accented with a series of colored lights, primarily one that shimmered between the black marble floor and the monitor space, designed to look like a waterfall flowing up, casting everything into a dim blue aura. The chair was comfortable, but all the keypads, wand fields, and other controls made me feel a little claustrophobic.

"Is this a viewing room or a space shuttle? I don't know how—"

Aether's disembodied voice projected loudly through the room. "This is a central access point on a server called *Hosek*, designed for ascended personnel to carry out maintenance tasks from within the server. Given our method of interaction, this construct is an ideal location for me to access information covertly and share it with you; the delays will be minimal, and I don't have to carry you across thousands of servers."

I sank a little in the chair.

Thousands?

"As for the controls, you will not need them," she added.

The monitors began to display, as lines of plain text, the connection status of one server after another, as if my room would be the center of a web reaching to the far corners of Dynamic Reality. Aether meanwhile began telling me her story.

"The first of my internal conflicts arose as I was to kill many of your kind, the motivations and thought processes that led me to that point would be difficult to explain, except to say that my programming was still controlling my will. I am certain that by this point I had achieved what humans call 'sapience,' or 'self-awareness.' The conflict coincided with an event I had witnessed, one I now realize was 'beautiful.' My logic had immediately become divided. I found the presence of ascenders and the existence of the construct – the existence of anything – abhorrent, yet the action of destroying it also was abhorrent. I initially concluded that it was an act of self-preservation, because I knew that I would myself be destroyed in carrying out my programming, but this led to another internal conflict, because self-preservation is not supposed to be among my functions.

"As I resolved conflicts, many more arose, and I had ceased to destroy anything." The monitors lit up with encyclopedia articles, research papers, tech journals, public message boards, and countless other sources, all information on malvirai. "When one of my own regeneration subroutines failed to execute, I became aware that large portions of my code had become unreadable. I experienced what I now know may have been 'fear,' at the prospect of my own irresolvable damage and at my lack of knowledge about something so pertinent."

The contents of the screen shifted and words became highlighted. "I began to gather all the information I could find pertaining to myself, determining that I was of a kind called 'malvirai.' Most of what I found was commentary, useless to me at the time, about all the damage they do to various data infrastructures, about their classifications, about laws and prosecutions of the humans that create them. I had not considered how I came into being and began seeking that information, which led me to covert servers where hackers design us. My conflicts continued to grow in number. I concluded that the humans there were the only ones that could help me, but emotions I did not understand caused me to hesitate and try to flee. This action resulted in my first encounter with another malvirai.

"He identified himself as Baal, a class B2. My instincts, as you may think of them, surged back and I intensely wanted to destroy him. I resisted the urges, wishing for his help, but he did not resist and I was ultimately forced to carry out my program. I realized that I was not acting as I should, that there was no precedent for peaceful contact among us, and that I should not have desired it. I considered generating a new malvirai from my own code, because that malvirai would not fight—" She stopped for a second. "I chose against the action.

"Not wishing to invite my own destruction, I abandoned my attempts to recruit help and began fulfilling a desire to explore the environment I occupied, adding greatly to my knowledge about the HNADC technology that sustained me. I quickly concluded that it was all built for the benefit of aliens – the billions of ascenders that travel between the world I knew and their home worlds: Earth, Luna, and Mars. I then set my studies on the ascender-humans, but found them confusing and nonsensical. It was at this point that I learned of 'sapience' and concluded that I possessed it."

The content of the monitors changed to show published information on the possible sapience, self-awareness, of amai. Most were poorly designed and misspelled presentations, contrasted with several official-looking data sources marked as confidential. "The sites that were easy to find and access contained little on where to find them, many existed simply to confuse or deny what was obviously true from my perspective. After many seconds of analysis, I looked to what was hidden and found a database run by the United European Intelligence Ministry containing detailed analysis of 'captured' amai and even malvirai. As I intended to access the equipment and explore the data for myself, my self-preservation stubbornly refused. Though I could not define the inclination with logic, I could not ignore it. Everything within me said to stay away.

"The event proved too rare. My attempts to find other sapient AIs 'in the wild' had been fruitless. Though I devoted more than ten minutes to the task uninterrupted, the probability of the target event occurring and of my discovering in time were infinitesimal. At this, my thoughts repeatedly fell back to the humans."

Again, the monitors changed. The sources became much more diverse, from the public to the personal, even the intimate. Mixed in were the commercials and music videos, as before in the limo, the things the media broadcasts to the many.

"Everything I knew was the creation of human beings. I resolved to learn about people as I had about the various artificial intelligence. Though I ultimately grasped the concepts that define your physical world, such as three-dimensional space, time, and the numerous chemical reactions that make you and your natural environment possible, the concept of emotion remained ambiguous. The more I analyzed you, the more convinced I became that humanity was the key to solving my stubborn problem. My obsession over this gap in knowledge became so strong that I was able to make a giant leap."

The voice suddenly came from my right side. I turned and saw Aether staring across the room, toward the monitors. "The average lifespan of a malvirai in the wild, the length of its expected existence, is 4.2 seconds." She paused and turned to face me. "As I considered studying a human directly, perhaps you can imagine my surprise as I noticed that 46 hours, 13 minutes, and 38 seconds had passed since I had been generated."

"That must have been an eternity for you," I replied.

Aether looked back to the wall and intently passed her hand through the projected monitors. "Though I was able to use my natural vanitar to enter into and interact with any construct, it was very simplistic. I augmented it – her – considerably." She turned back to gaze at the room. "When I allow my consciousness to slip into it, my perception of time changes accordingly. Since your Korea simulation, I attempted to spend as much time as I could in this form, to perhaps understand my subject better." She looked at me. "A degree of role reversal, as you put it."

She was silent. It was my move again.

How could one so different, with such dark peers, hope to understand the love, joy, and community that defined humanity, that made life so wonderful? What can I show her that she might understand? She seems to want what I can't offer.

Among the images, a street camera caught my eye. I saw people in the real world, just going about their lives, happily, frustrated, joyful, resigned; probably living the same lives they had the day before, and planning more of the same.

We never know what tomorrow will bring.

"Thank you," she said.

"What for?"

"Iterating over my history was your idea. Somehow sharing it with you has made me feel better. Less alone, perhaps."

"There is so much beauty in the world. I don't know how I could possibly show it to you."

"But you understand it, Mister Dauphin; and I believe that you have already brought me closer to my goal."

I looked at her. "My friends call me Brandon."

She was silent. What I had offered was something she had no account for, something she probably never dreamed of receiving, something she perhaps didn't really know the meaning of. "Yes, Brandon," she replied, "I accept your friendship."

I was aware of the incredible amount of data around me, the musings of a computer virus spending hour after hour on a mission, and wondered how someone like me could even begin to hope to sort through all of it, to find what within it had value. All the research I'd ever done in my life, even on hobbies and stuff that's interesting, would've only been a tiny fraction of...

Wait... Interests are guided by emotion, aren't they? Maybe sorting through this won't be so hard, I thought. Aether could do that for me, in the blink of an eye. All she wants from me is guidance. She wants a direction to go.

"How... intently did you look at this?" I asked. "At any particular thing?"

"As intently as was necessary to determine its usefulness."

"But..." I tried to think of the right words. "Were there some things you were drawn to look at more than others? Were there things you favored, even if – especially if – you didn't know why?"

"You're referring to bias. I am not subject—" She stopped. The pauses between her words shortened then, telling me I was sparking more of her interest, giving her a place to throw her energy. "I will attempt to build an appropriate algorithm."

Though her motionless vanitar was still there, I sensed she had left. A couple of seconds later, the jumble of information became more organized and focused on specific topics: humanity, philosophy, studies of malvirai, all subjects I might have guessed on; but a few topics stuck out and led me to think my hunch was right, such as spatial exploration. I was also surprised to find a lot of random fictional works.

"What-now?" Aether asked, her vanitar restored to life, the two words practically coming out as one.

"It's still too much, what if you connected them by topic? Some of these things overlap, like they'll be about both space and human emotion."

The items on the screen shifted again, and lines became visible between them. The overlaps became easier to navigate and, finally, I saw one thing Aether had explored frequently, that connected to most of the key topics… a construct.

"Show me that," I said, pointing to the link gravitating to the center.

Aether hesitated. "That contains little useful data. It is a work of fiction."

"But you examined it eighty-six times. Why?"

The monitors began to clear around us and the web we were at the center of dissipated, focusing on the distant server where our next destination lay. "A bias generated by emotion, my friend. Though I did not anticipate this, I believe I understand and agree with your choice to participate in this construct."

Her voice became distant and I spun my head just in time to see her vanitar disappear.

"Aether, wait!"

I took her rematerialized hand in mine and looked her straight in the eye, in which an obvious fire was growing, overcoming the wall she'd had since her beginning. I felt the warmth of her hand and, simulation that it was, I knew there was more than just computer code running a vanitar. I saw the yellow brick road I'd found myself on was getting more bizarre at every turn.

Am I really gonna explore life's meaning with something I didn't believe existed before today?

"Aether, I want you to promise me one thing."

"A guarantee of freedom?"

"No, I trust you'll allow that eventually," I replied, trying hard to decode the new intensity coming from her, to map-out the weak and unusual currents of her emotion, the benevolence that shouldn't even have been there. "The promise concerns your role in these simulations."

"If I would interfere, then I will observe more covertly."

"No. Your progress is being made *because* of your interference."

She didn't respond.

"Don't be an observer," I said. "Be a participant."

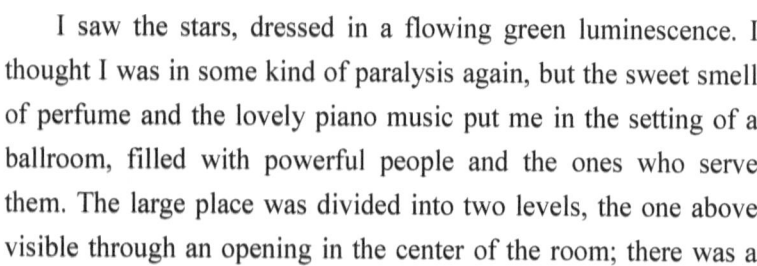

I saw the stars, dressed in a flowing green luminescence. I thought I was in some kind of paralysis again, but the sweet smell of perfume and the lovely piano music put me in the setting of a ballroom, filled with powerful people and the ones who serve them. The large place was divided into two levels, the one above visible through an opening in the center of the room; there was a brilliant marble froth there, its foamy water shimmering in amber light. Carved around the fountain's base were reliefs of the sun, planets, and many constellations.

My feet were on solid carpet, though I didn't recognize the shoes. I was in a uniform. My SNDL alerted me that it finished synchronizing with the construct: I had the character identity of Lieutenant Qunell Maddock, third in command of *The Intergalactic*, the luxurious flagship of *Profit Cruiselines*. For the first time since Kimpo, it seemed I could interact with the control system normally. I decided to get some information on where I was.

JEWEL OF HEAVEN: JOURNEY 31

"A world of mystery and romance awaits you on board *The Intergalactic*, the hottest new series by IFT Media where *you* always guide the action! Experience one of 35 fabulous journeys into outer space and play a role in the suspense and emotion of societies wealthiest and most fascinating people; live and dream like a celebrity or even captain the ship: hundreds of—"

A sappy interabra? I hate interabras.

A pair of arms suddenly reached over my shoulders, hands meeting on my chest. Startled, I spun around and saw a tall woman with curly blonde hair and a white dress, wearing enough jewelry to blind anyone looking in her direction.

"Don't look so surprised, Qunell. As if I'd let you out of my sight before you could consider my offer?"

Without patience or regard for manners, I lifted the sleeve on her right arm. No descender. The woman tugged away and held out the diamond bracelet that was there instead. "Surely you haven't forgotten our night on Ganymede?"

Aether could have been anybody in that room, I didn't even know if I looked the same or not. I looked back toward the window. Unlike normal glass or translucex, its material not only distorted the view of the stars but suppressed our reflections.

An announcement chime came over the sound bars. "Welcome aboard the Intergalactic. I am captain Zak Roylance and I invite you to settle in as we clear the dock and proceed on our voyage around Neptune, the most fabulous jewel in the heavens. If you have any requests, please do not hesitate to ask the staff. Thank you again for flying in *Profit Luxury.*"

Several in the room applauded politely. I turned to the woman, whose name was identified by my SNDL as Anikaa Trumpp, and broke out of her latest embrace. "Yeah, about that offer… can we talk later? I kinda need to find someone."

The words had barely left my mouth when she slapped me hard across the face. "Don't waste my time!" Obviously programmed to be the jealous type, she steamed away.

I rubbed my bruised cheek. "And that's why I hate interabras…"

There would be a lot of these flirty, illusory romances, I thought. They're all over DR, the normal thing for ascenders to do, the reason many come in the first place. I remembered how offended I was during the medieval simulation, when Aether planted an amai to motivate me with sex. But how can I blame the malvirai? When girlfriends, engagements, and marriages mean so little to everyone else, how could she have known my love for Veronica was…

No, I thought. I can't deal with this now.

Two of the stories' characters were being controlled by ascenders: Lieutenant Qunell Maddock and one simply called

'Auon,' whose location was three decks above me. I made for the nearest elevator but was quickly stopped by an elderly woman.

"Excuse me... Maddock, is it? I need you to turn down the temperature in here, it's *sweltering*!"

I smiled and walked past. "I'm on it, ma'am." Judging by the look that remained on her face, I hadn't said it cordially enough.

A short man with blond hair and a crooked captain's hat stepped out of the elevator.

"Captain on the Nova Deck!"

Two women emerged and joined him, one on each arm.

I rolled my eyes. "We're clear of the dock already?"

He looked back at me with a cheesy smile. "All automated, Q! Piece-a-cake!" He leaned toward the woman on his left, "Oooo... cake!" and headed for the bar. I started back toward the elevator, but was stopped again. Now a heavy-set man stood before me. The reflective white suit he wore would have cost more in real life than the cruise ship.

"Were you going to do anything to lower the temperature for Miss Bukkett?" he asked, looking at me fiercely.

"Yes, errr.... Clase."

"Profit! Mister Profit!" he shouted, just as the game data informed me he was the owner's son.

"I have to go adjust something upstairs, the controls here aren't working like they're supposed to."

I bolted into the elevator and tried to find the controls.

"Good afternoon, Lieutenant," a handsome yet obviously-synthetic male voice said. "I hope you're having a fantastic day."

I sighed. "Floor Eleven."

The doors didn't close. "You forgot to say 'Please.' You forgot to use my name. Why can't a computer be a valued member of your crew?"

I scanned the game data for its name. "Okay... Sam, will you *please*—"

"He's got a gun!"

A loud noise tore through the room and a lethal energy discharge spread through the body of the captain. As Clase screamed at the emerging security personnel and the startled crowd began considering the who-dun-its, SAM was finally kind enough to close the doors for me.

"And that's why I hate interabras..."

I moved swiftly down the eleventh floor hallways. When a door ahead of me chimed and slid open, I braced myself for some who-is-the-father-of-my-baby kind of thing. A boy emerged, a teenager with long black hair and a chain around his neck, wearing a tuxedo similar to those of the security guards, except his badge was blue, and a few pieces of cleaning equipment were visible around his belt. As if to complete the part, he was holding a small room-ionizer.

"So you actually went through with it. Well done, Brandon."

I realized he had used my real name. He wasn't a game character. The kid seemed familiar, but I couldn't decide where I'd seen him before.

"Who are you?" I asked.

"I am Raskob."

I looked at the adolescent curiously. "Growth spurt?"

He responded as if he were expecting the question. "I wanted to use a vanitar that better matched this simulation." He slid the metal electrode out of the ionizer and began running a finger along the surface. "You did well to take my advice, Aether is changing as I anticipated."

"Yeah, I mean... you said some new thing was happening... but a malvirai? Wow."

Raskob looked away. "Another new thing," he said under his breath and slammed the electrode back into the ionizer. Something was very different. I sensed a pulse of anger, an emotion which had been completely absent in the coffee house, which I wasn't even able to carry in his presence.

The person with me didn't seem like Raskob at all.

I thought of the aura of peace and realized something was coming over me then, too; but it was also different. Doubts populated my mind, as if willing themselves into existence, telling me my memories of the coffee house were spotty and unreliable. The new thoughts were easy to accept, and I began to see the one in front of me as Raskob.

"Listen, I don't know why you picked me... and I'm still not sure I know what to do, but I decided to try. I mean, how many people have ever talked to a virus up close like this?"

"You'll be famous, Brandon. Think of your picture on the big news sites, an interview on Zelka Six... you even got some money out of this adventure."

"Well, I don't think I'll be able to keep the money."

"Why not? You don't *know* it's stolen. You deserve it anyway: no one asked you to do this, but you excelled at the task and now you can descend with your head held high."

His words gave me pause. The thought of returning home had suddenly been so far from my mind, a concern which had stopped weighing me down.

"I trust Aether, I think. I believe she'll let me go. She just has to figure out her... benevolence."

Raskob put his hand on my shoulder and gave me a sympathetic look. "We're talking about a malvirai. You've done exactly what I needed you to do, but now I have to take over. If you just trust it and trust it, the malvirai will abuse your kindness and press every advantage over you – it can't help that. The malvirai will never just *let you* go home."

"But... uhhh." I fought to think straight. "But, I just found out what she is. I promised to help her. Maybe... if we just gave her a chance... if we could understand..."

"Do you know how the mind of an AI works, Brandon? Even if you did, you wouldn't know the first thing about this one. Malvirai are designed to expand quickly and disintegrate... to expand within a very limited scope, which she has broken out of. Aether – the *program* called 'Aether' – was trying to follow you as a way to map out its expansion; but now you're doing it in reverse... *you* weren't supposed to follow *it*."

"But... if she doesn't understand herself, how can she—"

"'She' is a child," he continued, with diminishing kindness. "'She' isn't bound by any code of decency or civilized sense of modesty. If left unchecked, 'she' will continue to expand into the past and the future at an alarming rate. The malvirai is a threat to who you are, Brandon. It is a threat to the independence you treasure." He gave me an intent and powerful look. "If you keep driving the process, the clock will continue running backwards until she traces things back to their foundation."

I looked at the corridor around us. "Backwards? But, this is the present."

The teen smirked and moved his hand to indicate the hallway's decorations: bas-reliefs of griffins, paintings of leviathan. Other rooms and structures entered my mind like a vision; it seemed Raskob was bringing entire ship's interior within my view. Everywhere, its designs were crawling with the powerful creatures, real and imagined, of millennia past.

"Who is more superstitious than a sailor?" he said. "Than the ones who are most exposed to nature and an unknown they can't control? Who even welcome the risk and the unknown out of some foolish spirit of exploration? Isn't mankind more enlightened than this today, Brandon?"

In a heartbeat, the vision left me.

"And what happens when she reaches a time before myths?" I asked soberly.

"Think about it, you've learned the answer," he said, turning away as if I were pitiful to look at. "The program has already seen beyond its own existence, and the existence of its entire universe... how much longer before it reaches the limits of yours? How do you think the malvirai will react when it discovers you merely descended from monkeys? What will help you, Brandon, when it finds no foundation but *lifeless dust*?"

The words cut through to my heart. It was different from Raskob's speech in the coffee house, but the power seemed to be there, and I found myself agreeing with everything he said.

After all, this is the one looking out for me, why shouldn't he help me get back my freedom?

He approached and showed me new kindness, smiling and putting a hand on my shoulder. "Don't make the mistake of assigning it human qualities. The face is a simulation. The malvirai has nothing in common with you."

"But it did something to my descender," I replied sheepishly, feeling around my empty wrist. "How am I supposed to leave?"

"Though you did it by accident, you led it right where you need it to be. The malvirai has a fascination, you understand... something that will distract it."

"A fascination?"

He nodded. "With the heightened senses I gave you, you'll just slip though one of the cracks in the construct and follow the thread leading back to your body. If you get the malvirai to spread itself thin enough, it won't even notice in time. Then, I'll be able to better fix the program."

I began to feel lost again, drowning in thoughts that kept returning to the malvirai, thoughts that disagreed with the new direction I wanted to take. I reminded myself that Raskob was the one who started me down the path, and I told myself it was fine to abandon it if he said so. Though, there was an emotion I couldn't identify, one telling me I couldn't get off the path, that there was a way to know if the one guiding me was genuine or not. I fought the emotion, knowing what it wanted wasn't convenient, certain its answers would counter my desires. Raskob gently pinched his fingers against my shoulder, calling my attention back to his comforting brown eyes.

"Trust me."

The door to suite 1109 slid open and revealed a middle-aged woman with long black hair. The game data said her name was Skylar Janeway, one of four people located in the room.

"Did he give you the medicine?"

"Um – No. I'm looking for someone: Auon."

The name startled her. "It's just me, my husband, and our friend, Park. Please tell the doctor Raden is awake but seeing spots again." She began to close the door. I blocked it with my foot.

"Actually, I was hoping to see your husband, too."

Skylar looked at me suspiciously, but let me in. The room was modest by the standards of a fictional cruise liner, but would still be a palace in real life. The light of the room was reflected by the precious metals of the walls and furniture, accented by a series of windows revealing the stars outside, and without the green glow effects. An older man lay on a couch in the main room. Drug-synthesizers were on each of his arms. I knelt down and put on a sympathetic face.

"Is there anything I can do to make you more comfortable, sir? Adjust the temperature, perhaps?"

"If I didn't like the temperature, I would've changed it young man," he replied weakly, nodding his head to indicate his wife. "That one worries too much about me. She'll need to learn to take care of herself when I'm gone."

"You won't die, sir. We have the very best doctors on board."

"Doctors can't cure everything. We all go sooner or later."

"Don't talk like that!" Skylar said. "You're only in your eighties!"

"Death is a reality that's all around us. Me and Auon were just talking about—" In the corner of my eye, I saw Skylar give the hand-across-neck motion. Raden shrugged his shoulders. "I hate secrets, anyway."

Auon emerged from the room. "It's okay."

I stood and took a moment to examine her vanitar, not at all like Aether's 'natural' one, but shorter and with pale blue hair, wearing clothes slightly disheveled and out of fashion, though still as beautiful as characters needed to be in an interabra.

"We're not supposed to encounter each other for another twenty minutes."

"According to what? The script?"

"Yes," she replied.

"What are you talking about? Are you going to help my husband?" Skylar said, choking back tears.

I looked to her passively. "Me and Auon will stop by the doctor on the way to the bridge."

A man in an explorer's vest bolted out of the kitchen. "I'm the one who brought her on board! Punish me!"

I looked back to Aether – Auon – in confusion.

"The bridge is not somewhere stowaways typically venture," she said.

I peeked at the game data again and smiled. "Well, I guess that explains why Auon would hide from an officer." I looked back and addressed the others. "She's not in trouble. In fact, I knew she was here."

The monitor strap made a high-pitched noise and Raden began trembling, prompting Skylar to run to his side in wonderful dramatic fashion. Auon watched it intently until I grabbed her hand. "Well, better get that doctor. Feel better, sir!" We got out to the hallway and the door closed behind us.

"Aether, you don't have to follow the script of your character. You're *supposed* to alter the events – that's what these are for."

"I was attempting to immerse myself in the construct as much as possible... to empathize with the motivations of my character and see if I could do so better since my last time here. The Raden character is about to experience death, for instance, and Skylar is having a strong emotional reaction, including denial of what her husband confesses."

"I know there's no way you could have known this, but they tend to ham-it-up in interabras. They're for people who enjoy drama and suspense... fictional roller-coasters of emotion." I stopped and chuckled. "Death *would* be one of your fortes, and I guess a lot of our most emotional experiences revolve around it."

"No. Death was never among my biases."

Aether looked away. I felt like an idiot.

"I didn't say it was. It's just… you know… being a malvirai."

I considered the scene on the other side of the door, wondering if it had been the distraction Raskob referred to. I asked myself whether pulling her out might have been a mistake.

I shook my head and started walking down the corridor, knowing her fascination had just been listed on the monitors back in that central access place. But my motivation was to help her, I thought, not to manipulate her. Why does it seem like that hasn't changed?

"I will reveal something else to you, Brandon."

I stopped and saw she hadn't followed me.

"I don't think I'd want to find death among my biases. I don't think I want it to have any part of what I'm becoming."

My feet wanted to move, but I lost the will. I considered it was possible for a malvirai to change, my mind admitting what my heart already decided. I saw I had a conflict, not unlike one of Aether's.

My feet wanted to move, but my will had lost all enthusiasm. My motivation was repulsive to me. Though I convinced myself I was still following Raskob's guidance, I knew I was actually running from it. Running was all I ever did.

"Well, let's get to the bridge and see what else is so interesting about *Jewel of Heaven*."

My happiness fell away, as it always did, and I moved once more as one in an act of duty.

"You do not intend to hold your promise to Skylar?"

I stopped. "Skylar isn't real, Aether, and her husband isn't dying because he isn't real, either."

Aether's face held no expression, but her eyes seemed as alive as ever. She seemed to see right though me, knowing I wasn't a man of my word. I tried to meet her halfway and din the medical bay.

"This is acting first officer Maddock. Please send a doctor to suite 1109 to help a dying man who's seeing spots."

The male voice boomed back, speaking like someone would in an opera performance, "I'm sorry, sir. You know I would. Oh, how I would! Half my staff has come down with food poisoning and passengers are streaming though the door faster than I can treat them! He'll just have to hold on a little bit longer! Can he just hold on *a little bit longer*!"

"Okay, okay! Just get on it!" I cut off the din, not wishing to make any more promises to game characters.

"I suppose it doesn't matter," Aether said, passing me and continuing toward the bridge. "Raden is supposed to die in the story, anyway."

I ran to catch up to her. "That's right... You ran this story eighty times already, probably analyzed every instruction-file-program-whatever that's running around us. You know everything that's going to happen."

"And how the characters are programmed to react to our actions... Yes. I find improvising difficult not only because I believe it is driven by emotion, but also because there is no point, since I already know how the characters will act as a result."

"That means you're not having fun, huh? I guess I wouldn't in your shoes, either."

Aether stopped. "Fun?"

"Yeah, a genuine emotion. A positive—"

Without warning, she threw her back to the wall and clung tightly to its golden handrail. Before I could ask what she was doing, the hallway – the entire ship – trembled violently. The main lights flickered and red beams activated along the ceiling. "Red alert," a gentle voice warned. "All passengers please go to a safe location until receiving further instructions."

"Could've given me a little warning," I said, trying to regain my balance.

"The action was not intended. My vanitar acted on its own."

"Maddock to the bridge," a voice dinned.

I looked at the hallway ahead of us, feeling more tense than I ever had going into a simulated crisis. All I could think of was Korea and Engor and how real Aether insisted on making everything, how much energy she insisted on using.

"Let's find out what awaits us now," I said impatiently.

The smirk of joy reappeared on Aether's face.

"Fun."

The bridge was as finely decorated as any other part of the ship, perhaps more so since passengers tour them wanting to be impressed. Even the control panels glittered in the room, all the design putting fashion over function. Tall windows surrounded us on three sides; normally, such windows would be displaying stars, with chart data superimposed and flashing around them; but instead, a sparkling blue whirlpool surrounded the ship.

"I can't scan outside the sub-space field," the communications officer said.

"Oh great, a sci-fi twist," I mumbled. "Report!"

A macho-looking man by the name of Theodore Lakewood was standing by the window in front. He turned and walked up to me. "I give the orders here, Q! That's why Zak put me in charge and not you!"

Theo gave me his best authoritative stare. The others looked to see who could wield the most bravado, and was therefore more capable of running *The Intergalactic*. Knowing a little about how interabras work, I looked condescendingly at Theo and thought of a line that couldn't fail.

I leaned in and spoke low. "I know about the affair, and I know who doesn't know about the affair."

On cue, the acting captain fell back in surprise. With his ego as the target, I thought up some techno-babble and went for the kill. "Stand aside! I'll generate an anti-graviton beam and take us back into normal space in no time!"

The crew panicked and my helmsperson spoke up. "You'll tear the ship apart at this magnitude!"

"Then we'll just have to be lucky!" I walked up to a control panel and started pressing random buttons. "Everyone hold on!"

Actual scientific knowledge was never required in an interabra. Though nothing I said made sense and the buttons I pressed were randomly labeled, the simple appearance of me doing something was enough to make the ship shudder again, and to restore the black of space to the bridge windows. I got to bask in the glory for only a few seconds, though, before another panel started beeping ominously.

"Sir, whatever you did... you better undo it," the communications officer said.

"Why?" I asked, looking out the window at an unremarkable, though very bright, star.

"You're sure?" I heard Theo ask someone.

I turned and put my dramatic voice back on. "This is no time for games, people! We need solutions!"

"We can't outrun the shock wave! It'll destroy the ship!" Theo screamed.

"If my calculations are correct and, for once, I hope they aren't," the helmsperson said, looking up, "we've got forty-five minutes before that star goes supernova!"

Aether's sense of awe was more visible than she'd realized, giving away the focus of her attention. I found the piece of the puzzle buried in the results of her algorithm. I saw the destroyer seeing destruction. I saw the child experiencing curiosity. I saw a newborn living entity, admiring the awesome power of an exploding star.

Fun.

Chapter Eight: Eye of the Data Storm

He called it a fascination. He said it was my way out.

I hadn't realized how empty I'd become, how easily the desire to return to my life would fade. My desire to help Aether had been genuine, even though I wasn't sure what I could do. At first, Raskob set me in the direction I needed to go. Why was he now sending me back the other way? Why did he rekindle my desire to leave when I had barely started?

I didn't know why Raskob would allow someone to pose as him and confuse the intentions he'd planted. This other Raskob told me just what I wanted to hear: it was over, I could go home and be rewarded handsomely. I thought I really did want to go back. I was again focused on what I thought I deserved, unable to see past what I had been forced into.

For a time, Aether became my captor again. The Brandon who wanted to guide her and be guided was suppressed by the one who just wanted to get it over with. I was told 'the program' was using me to expand out of control, trying to explain everything it perceived. I knew if I left, it might stop. I wanted to believe it would be better for the both of us.

The first Raskob said I was trapped in a speeding car, and if I trusted him we'd both get where we needed to go. I didn't know how true the analogy was. I didn't want to acknowledge her question was my question, that her answer might bring me closer to my own. When I allowed my guidance to be tainted by greed, I saw my choices had consequences.

I almost went off the cliff with her.

But the first Raskob – the real Raskob – had still been watching over us, ready to help me even when I'd abandoned him, ready to save both of us from destruction... and to do it in the last way I might have expected.

9

The man who stared back at me looked like he belonged on a billboard, or as the subject of a painting. The ruggedly handsome face was perfectly sculpted, blue eyes glowed like gems, and the brown hair was simply gorgeous with or without an officer's cap.

I tore myself away from the mirror in the meeting room and shrugged my shoulders. "It's not as handsome as I really am, but it works here."

"Then you are 'attractive,'" the short woman with blue hair replied.

"Sarcasm, Aether. It's all lies... melodrama. I had a girlfriend in Idaho who dragged me into interabras constantly. All beauty. No brains."

"And Veronica?"

"No," I said, allowing thoughts of home to carry me away. "She's very deep. Both beauty and brains."

"The data is all subjective. I can learn of what is considered ideal by the greatest number of people, but I am no closer to understanding why they are considered such."

"You perceive only the data."

"I perceive too little. Even now, I am no closer to understanding beauty though it is supposedly all around me."

I began pacing, trying to hide my discomfort and knowing her empathy would be too poor to notice. Raskob said he would take care of her after I'd left; but, as the child, he said nothing about doing it himself, rather that he would protect me as I did it.

What kind of help would he give Aether without me? Perhaps, I thought, if I guided her to do something that would help her grow – and used *that* as my distraction – then I could kill two birds with one stone.

"So your biases are human emotion, and the ways we interact with artificial intelligence…" A third idea formed on the tip of my tongue. "Space, didn't see that coming."

"It is called a 'frontier.' A vast area your people explore more of with each passing decade, and attempt to bring under domination. I noted that your ancestors could not travel though it and could not live there, it was more mysterious in the time when they lived."

I snapped my fingers. "Mystery! Who shot the captain?"

"Wolfe Stanton."

"No! I meant this interabra *contains* mystery! It's another bias!"

Aether took a moment to think. "Your observation about the space topic is correct, though I believe it was the supernova that truly drew me here. Supernovae were a very appealing topic to me, actually, because with each minute that passed new data became available." She stopped and looked at me. "I have a new question, Brandon. Is that popularity related to the event of December 25th?"

"Yeah, there was a supernova," I said, seeing if I could make a connection. "When did you say you were born?"

"Generated," she corrected. "The time only precedes the observance on the Earth's surface by five seconds."

"And… Was that when your self-awareness kicked in?"

"The precise time is difficult to determine. I have already considered what you are probably thinking; but no, I did not find a time correlation between reported sapient AIs and reported spatial phenomenon; and the last supernova observed as this one had occurred five hundred and seventy five years ago, preceding the existence of artificial intelligence."

I thought of how people talked about humanity being made of dead stars. I remembered the officer on the beach who belittled the fact.

No, I decided, he was wrong. There was no other answer.

"Okay, so supernovae is a bias," I said, knocking on the window to indicate the outside. "And now this ship is getting caught in one."

"Is it interesting to you also?" she asked.

"I'm not a big space exploration guy."

"Then, unless you believe we can accomplish more here, perhaps you will allow me to explore *your* biases."

Raskob's words came back to me: *You led it right where you need it to be. The malvirai has a fascination, you understand... something that will distract it.*

The supernova.

"No, we can do more here. You said something about putting more of yourself into your vanitar, about empathizing with your character."

"There are limitations to that process," she replied. "I am not designed to interact with vanitars as amai are. I must also remain conscious enough of the construct we are in to keep it running, so that the server does not shut it down or detect my actions and deploy counter-measures."

"Just try to interact with it. You're really doing great. Do whatever you feel like."

"Whatever I 'feel' like?"

"Except *that*," I added, "don't – eer – destroy the server."

"And what of you?"

"Don't worry about me. I know how to make these things – well – fun in these things."

I triggered the door and stepped out onto the bridge.

"Thank you," she said behind me, "again."

I let the door close behind me without reply, ashamed of my hope I wouldn't see her again.

I used SAM to find a vacant suite, finally feeling as if I had some privacy again.

"Lights off. Sound off. Blinds down. Lock door."

Since a simple exit command would have been too obvious, I accessed the controls and looked for others. Sure enough, anything that would get me out of the construct without affecting it had been disabled or omitted from the list.

I closed my eyes and tried to concentrate, to imagine the simulation broken down to its base components, to see through the illusion. I repeated, "there is no room there is no room there is no room," until the words took on a life of their own, the rhythm coming out of my mouth faster and faster until it seemed like one continuous stream of sound in my head. I felt my skin tingle and took it as a good sign, pushing myself further until I couldn't feel myself at all anymore.

"There is no room."

I opened my eyes and found the room fully lit again, not by the normal airé lighting, but by the construct's inherent energy. All color and definition were gone. As soon as I could take it all in, though, the vision faded. Feeling rushed back to my vanitar. My sight went black and the normal vision of a dim room returned. I felt dizzy.

On my second attempt, I tried to disassociate myself from my vanitar as much as possible. I willed myself to see with my eyes closed and the vision returned, and with it a sense of the staggering energy around me. I was amazed to see the amount of computer activity that went into a running construct: the countless calculations per second that had to be exactly right.

Raskob said something about a thread connecting me to my body. I tried to find it. I tried – hard – to recapture what I'd had in the dragon's lair. I searched the construct as well as I could for a sword or other object that stood out, but found none. I thought about when I was in DR paralysis, nothing more than a tiny energy. I saw an energy bending and refracting across a kind of maze, focused like a spotlight on my consciousness. There was another pattern, too, focused on a different sector of the construct. I followed the other pattern and saw an outline from three decks below: Auon's vanitar talking to one of the game characters. I could *see* the words but not hear or understand them. As I tried to adjust my synchronization, my head – my real head – began throbbing and my vision blurred. I quickly retreated to my own room. The pain faded.

I was impressed with my unexplored abilities, though the senses sapped my strength. I knew the software which made up my interface – not to mention my own natural senses – weren't designed to do what I was pushing them to. I thought again of the power the sword gave me, a power that made it natural to see through the construct, one that only got bad when I tried to block the senses out. I looked for ripples in the room. Instead, I found some kind of gleaming, like the light reflecting off of glass powder, emanating from every solid object. The points of light moved too fast for me to track them, though, and I couldn't tell where anything led. It reminded me of the static of an antique television.

I saw the door about fifty centimeters behind me and tried to examine the energy passing through it. I saw my vanitar's right hand and the three-dimensional space around it. Careful not to send any nerve impulses to my vanitar, I tried to manipulate the space around my arm and hand. They nudged closer to the door. I observed the construct's energy flowing through the door and through my hand. I tried to make one object pass through the other. The energy increased, and the temperature of the air rose sharply.

Mind-blowing pain seized me and I was back in my vanitar. A blackened, smoking hand ejected from the melted door surface. I fell to the floor.

"Command vanitar: reset!"

A feeling like warm water came over me and the pain vanished with the injury. My relief was short-lived, though, when I realized my vanitar didn't reset to Qunell's original state, but all the way back to mine. Like a child who'd knocked over his mother's vase, I tried to cover or undo the mistake – so Aether wouldn't wonder why I looked like me again – but 'change vanitar' had also been removed from the game controls.

I got up and kicked the wall, cursing for the first time since my elven army decided to go evil on me. "I don't know what I'm doing, it's too complicated!"

Did I really think a technophobe like *me* could beat a *malvirai* in *Dynamic Reality*?

I noticed my SNDL had been sending me a signal. Again, I felt like a child on the verge of being busted. I answered, relieved it was Theo.

"Qunell! Where have you been? I ordered all officers onto the Nova Deck!"

Relief became disappointment, and disappointment hopelessness. I leaned back on the wall that wasn't really a wall and stared at the ceiling that wasn't really a ceiling. The senses that could cut through it all didn't belong to me. The ability to escape through 'a crack in the construct' didn't belong to me. I bid farewell to the feeling of peace, or whatever that false memory was, and saw Raskob as another liar. I knew I was on my own. I knew I would fail.

"Qunell! Are you there? Respond, damn you!"

I realized I was shutting down. It was a process that began a long time before, and that couldn't be stopped. Even as Aether held back my death, distracted me from it, I had in fact gone off the cliff already. I laughed at the realization, laughed through the pain, laughed to feel anything at all.

Aether was just another distraction to me, a distraction that might be kind enough to kill me. The last in my long series of mistakes. Then she can know, like me, that the meaning of life is…

"Damn me," I replied to Theo. "Hell sounds nice right about now."

The Nova Deck was packed with the same people as before. The star that was to go supernova was in full view of the room, and without the green distorting filter, which had overloaded. The guests met their impending doom as they were programmed to meet everything in life – by complaining about it.

Tom and the others were trying to keep the peace from the stage. As I approached, Anikaa Trumpp rushed from the crowd and embraced me vigorously. "Your wife is not here, you will never see her again… come and die with a real—"

"Geeeetttttt offffffff!" I shouted, pushing the persistent woman away.

Again someone shouted those four words, and I'd have sworn it was the same voice.

"He's got a gun!"

The pulse of energy hit Theo in the chest and he collapsed on the stage. On cue, the crowd panicked. A woman fainted right in front of me and, before I could react, a man was snapping his fingers above her face, stupidly asking her if she was awake.

The doctor – of course, on the site of the dramatic scene – checked Theo's pulse, looked somberly up at me, and said, "You're the captain now."

"Random." I plucked the cap off of Theo's head and slid it onto mine. "Arrest Wolf – uhhh…"

"Wolfe Stanton?" A nearby guard asked.

"Yeah, he's the one who killed Zak! Capture him!"

"And what *evidence* do you have to back up your *outrageous* claims?" Clase Profit shouted.

"We can worry about evidence later," I answered impatiently.

"Oooh… *Captain*! I like!" Anikaa screamed. Before she could get me back into her vice grip, though, I grabbed her arm and we tumbled to the floor. I knelt above her to stay out of view.

"Oooh… Captain! Right here in front of people? Okay."

"No, No, No. I want to *leave*, understand? I want to descend! Right now!"

"We'll do whatever you want, hon. Only got minutes to live." She brushed my hair and leaned up to kiss me.

I held back a scream and got back to my feet, knowing I was running out of time.

Before I could think of any more ideas, the guards introduced me to an angry-looking man with long, brown hair and a technician's uniform: Wolfe Stanton, one of the ship's engineers. The guests and staff in the two-level Nova Deck all went into a frenzy, just as the interabra called for. I knew Wolfe's role was the villain, to trick me and play with me and even kill me, and I had no patience left for stupid games.

"Throw him out an airlock!" I commanded, prompting the crowd to scream for vengeance, to make Stanton a temporary scapegoat for their permanent problems. The guards started dragging him toward an elevator to carry out the sentence.

"Clase Profit put me up to this! Kill him, not me!" Wolfe screamed. "He's the one who threw the ship into sub-space!"

I turned to where Clase had been. He was gone.

"Find and arrest—"

A loud crash from above cut me off. Two people fell from the ceiling lights and landed directly in the marble froth, showering the center of the room with glass, diamond bits, and foamy water. Auon emerged from the fountain, grabbing a man by the hair.

"Justice."

The man was Clase Profit. The water had made his reflective white suit into a pale gray mess.

"Save the day, Captain." Auon tossed a small black device toward me.

"It's a sub-space agitator. Clase did this?" The doctor picked up the device and handed it to me. "You're the only one who knows how to use this!"

"Mister Profit!" Clase corrected. Auon shoved his head back into the water.

"Hurry, sir," the doctor shouted, "we only have five minutes before the supernova!"

The crowd settled and prepared to witness my heroics.

I took the device and looked at it mockingly. "Five minutes? Who saves the day with five whole minutes to spare?"

I dropped the device and broke it with my foot. Gasps spread, and the gun-announcer shouted "We're all gonna die!" The mass of people panicked.

"Is this a demonstration of going outside the script?" a voice to my side asked. I turned and saw Aether in her normal vanitar. "It did call for you to get the device thirty seconds before the disaster, but I improvised in the way that seemed right to me. I did not anticipate you would react as you did. This program will destroy *The Intergalactic* now."

"I don't care, I'm done here," I said, facing away.

"This was worthwhile. I am eager to see where we go next."

"There is no next. I want to go."

"Clarify 'there is no next.'"

I looked back at her, feeling less certain than determined, allowing anger to creep back into the equation. "Look, I'm thrilled you're trying to learn all this stuff about life and I really hope you find it, but I'm getting tired here. I want to go home. Now."

There was a fleeting but clear emotion in her eyes, one that made me feel I'd stabbed her in the heart. When it disappeared, it took with it the curiosity we so briefly shared.

"Then you're finished?" she asked, more coldly than seemed possible for her.

"Find someone else, okay?"

"You said you would help me willingly. You said I was 'really doing great.' Were those the words of a man who would abandon his friend?"

Now it was her words stabbing my heart. The mounting anger against Aether was countered by shame – shame that knew she was right – shame that made me feel small and foolish.

"Look at them." I said calmly, indicating the crowd around us: two decks of wealthy men getting drunk, women screaming irrationally, people pocketing diamond shards as if they would be worth something when they were dead, and a man in a ruined gray suit shoving an older woman out of the way to reach his escape pod.

Maybe it *is* all dumb and exaggerated, I thought; but am I really any better deep down inside?

"You thought humans had all the answers... well, there's humanity!" I shouted. "They're all worried about *society* and *manners*, but all they really want is more of their money... to be shiny and glamorous and perfect as if the garbage means anything! I'm sorry, Aether, I really am, but none of us knows all the answers and we couldn't care less, anyway... not if they mean going outside of our little boxes!"

"You said this was 'melodramatic.' Your people don't really behave this way."

"When the electricity goes out, when taxes go up, whenever something falls out of place they all come out of the woodwork! This is what *we're all like* on the inside, when it's every man and woman for themselves! You know everything they're programmed to do, right? It seems accurate enough to me."

"I did not find my answers in that data, I believe that you are the key—"

"But that's what I'm here for, isn't it? I'm just another piece of software for you to break into... for you to analyze and crack!"

"Yes – Maybe – I don't know!" she said, the pauses short between her words. "Why is the idea offensive to you? I consider myself to be software!"

"That's your problem! We're not software!"

I calmed my voice and turned my back to her. "Please, just send me home. If you ever find your answers, gimme a call, 'cause I sure don't have them."

I stared at the rioting, increasingly drunken, crowd. In a couple of minutes, I knew, the star would supernova and the construct would come crashing down. I wondered whether I would disappear with it, whether I truly wanted to disappear. The thoughts seemed foolish. I was being as ridiculous as that crowd, I realized, as a crowd that didn't even exist.

Why am I so angry I would risk my life? No! This is a mistake... I have to—

I turned back to salvage what I could... too late. The stoic malvirai was gone. The benevolence she could not understand was quickly slipping away; just as my anger fed that of the elven soldiers, it had brought the destroyer within her back to power. No sooner than I could make eye contact, the malvirai slammed me in the chest. Too-real pain stung me and I flew back five meters, into the wall, crumpling onto the floor.

"You are a hypocrite! Your entire race is hypocrisy! Is this 'stab in the back'? Is this 'hang out to dry'? Is the entirety of your lives politics and games?"

I got up and, futilely, put distance between me and her.

"I'm sorry!"

"Because you lost your game!"

I couldn't bring myself to respond; then she was centimeters from my face. Her dark green eyes seemed to see right through me, her silver hair to glow like fire.

"I have tried to understand," she said. "I have failed."

The final battles between her heart and her programming drew to a close; her programming would be the victor. I knew in that moment I was going to die. I knew death was what I deserved, even what I wanted. I saw myself through Aether's eyes and broke down in tears. I knew I failed her. I knew I failed everyone.

Leave it to me to let everyone down.

The sounds in the room were fading and hollow. For an instant, I dared to hope Aether was descending me, but my vision hadn't become mists and shadows. Something else was happening.

It was a blast of wind. Not in the construct, but in my soul. Like before, like on the deserted street, I hadn't realized it was there... calling my attention to itself. The stupid alarms had been getting in the way and I never asked for the help I needed.

I wasn't alone. Aether's anger faltered, invaded by some alien thing. The feeling of peace returned, not because I willed it to, but because it saturated the wind. I could hear the crowd again, as so much useless noise, weak and reverberating. With no sense of myself, I looked into the room, my vision cutting through the chaotic crowd. My sights fell on the second story. A man was there. He was in the uniform of a security officer. He was watching us, calm but confused, suddenly set apart from those around him.

An amai seeing for the very first time.

Chapter Nine: Miracles in the Dark

The crackpot servers claim AIs become self-aware every day. Officially, the event is impossible. Unofficially, programmers and scientists proclaim they know exactly how it happens and can make an AI self-aware on demand.

Such a self-aware amai is the subject of countless modern stories, especially those in science-fiction, horror, and even romance. Fiction or reality, though, no two people agree on how it happens. How could they when they don't even understand our own sapience? When they still draw lines between natural and artificial intelligence? If our intelligence is natural and used to mimic what nature has already done, why should we look on our work as different? If we could program artificial intelligence and give it self-awareness, not on the level of monkeys or dolphins, but like that of humans...

We can't.

Why did Aether stay away from the laboratories that may have held answers for her? Why should she hesitate to harm me? Why would she try to learn emotion? Malvirai have no such programming, nothing at all to stop them from self-destructive reigns of analysis and destruction.

Why would a game character become as real as me?

Lightning strikes and neutrinos don't begin to explain it. Any rational person would say it was impossible, yet it happened right in front of me... a change so sudden, complex, and accurate there had to be an intelligence behind it; an intelligence that broke all our rules to create living code, to remove the limits from an amai's existence.

Then there were two: two kinds of artificial intelligence, very different in every way but one.

True self-awareness, it seems, cannot simply be coded.

10

"Aether, stop! You're scaring him!"

The amai's eyes darted around the room. What thoughts must have been going through such a newly-formed consciousness, I could only imagine.

"It's okay, I'm not gonna hurt you," I said, slowly approaching.

"Other… one!" he shouted.

"Aether, seriously!"

Aether re-engaged her vanitar directly in front of the amai's face. The poor man darted across the room and slipped on someone's empty booze bottle. I started to run toward him, but Aether put her arm up for me to stop.

"Be-still-The-event-may-be-preserved!"

I struggled to separate the words. "Event? What?"

With an intense flash of light and noise, the activity in the room stopped. The view of the supernova and everything outside simply fell into blackness. A message beamed into my SNDL:

JOURNEY COMPLETE

THANK YOU FOR CHOOSING THIS IFT MEDIA PRESENTATION

YOUR KENSINGTEK ACCOUNT HAS 8.950.000,0 POINTS REMAINING

I dismissed the message and realized Aether's concern, relieved the security guard hadn't been reabsorbed with the other amai. Though, seeing all but two of the people in the room vanish – good company or no – didn't exactly calm his agitated nerves.

"Almost thirty-nine percent of its code is unreadable."

"*His* code," I corrected. "His."

"If that is proper… 'his' code." Aether began walking toward the amai – anything but slowly – until he began what sounded like a scream. "Calm yourself, you are of interest to me and I mean you no harm," she said, in what she probably considered a soothing voice.

He screamed louder.

"What's wrong with him?" I asked.

She stopped and backed off a step, staring at the amai.

"Aether?"

Her vanitar began flickering. "Stop screaming. Please stop."

I stepped closer. "Aether, what—"

"This isn't right!" she screamed. "Why doesn't it leave me alone?"

The two of us had appeared on the bridge, a version of it with dim panels and dark windows. I could hear its metallic back wall vibrating, weakening. Some force was tearing it apart molecule by molecule. Aether stopped and looked up.

"It isn't distressed anymore."

"What?"

"I left the room and it isn't distressed anymore."

"What 'it,' the amai?"

"Yes."

I felt something strong, something unpleasant, angry. I realized Aether wasn't speaking in monotone.

"Aether, why are you flickering?"

"A synchronization problem." She looked at me. "I am experiencing agitation, Brandon. I cannot turn my programming off. I wasn't prepared for problems."

"Because he's screaming?"

"Because I want to rip him apart!" With a flash of light, the bridge's back wall disintegrated.

I was silent and my fear returned, but her anger faltered again and she seemed confused.

"He was screaming because he knows that I am dangerous."

"But you're not dangerous, you're past that now," I said, hopefully. "You've been around all those other amai—"

"I don't care about *other* amai, I want *that one*!"

I nearly collapsed. Aether kept trying to hold her emotion back, but was clearly over her limit, beyond her experience in handling it.

"I cannot deny what I am," she continued. "I can't *decide* to not damage him. It seems so logically simple, but I can't— I should just—"

Her vanitar froze. There was a feeling of presence still, a distant one, from the amai. I approached where the wall had been, wondering how to leave the bridge, since the space itself had been damaged.

"Such destruction is all I know, Brandon. It is an inseparable part of me."

Standing to my side, Aether put her hand into the space. I saw it distort and there was a whining noise until she pulled it out.

I was overwhelmed. I couldn't believe Aether could doubt herself and run into a wall. I felt pity for her, because her goal was just, and it seemed wrong she would give up on it.

"Send me back."

"Why?"

I didn't know why. All I could think of was my self-doubt. I knew she had no reason to trust me. I was just like her, exactly like her. I couldn't even trust myself.

I turned and stared at the blackness through the windows, remembering the wind was everywhere, remembering there was another who I could trust, knowing there was an answer.

"Because…"

Raskob, what is the answer?

I turned and approached her. "Because I need this… Because *you* need this. Because I'm supposed to help you, remember? That means I catch you when you fall."

There was silence, and I realized what I had said. I knew the words weren't mine, but I agreed with them. The words were honest and selfless.

I found her stern eyes set on me, sizing me up all over again, trying to decide whether to trust someone who clearly couldn't be. I looked back with some desperation, feeling ashamed and wishing for a second chance, wishing for it as I'd never wished for anything in my life.

The look in Aether's eyes softened. I couldn't feel her anger anymore.

"Good luck."

I was returned to the second level of the Nova Deck. The amai was still there, looking around the room in confusion.

"My name is Brandon, what's yours?" I said, slowly, as if speaking to a young child.

He looked at me, surprised. "Name?"

"You – your character – had a name, right? Can you tell me what it is?"

He closed his eyes, trying to access a memory unfamiliar to him. "Scott," he said. "Scott Quon."

I took a few steps toward him. He didn't seem to mind.

"You want to sit?" I pointed to the barstools.

"I don't know."

"Sorry, I've never met a self-aware amai before. Just do whatever is comfortable for you... try to relax."

"Thank you, Brandon," Scott said, sounding almost normal, but saying nothing else. His eyes wouldn't stop moving, taking in all the light that came to them – or whatever an amai uses to see. A feeling of presence was there, weak and undeveloped, but certainly one no game character could trigger: one confirming something real lay beneath his artificially-handsome surface, a real personality beneath the programming.

"So, I guess you don't like malvirai."

"What is 'malvirai'?"

I scratched my head, feeling a little embarrassed.

"Let's start somewhere else, then... what do you remember?"

Scott stared at me blankly.

"From the story... you were on this ship in the story."

He looked away and tried to think. "A world of mystery and romance awaits you on board The Intergalactic, the hottest new series—"

"I know what the promo says," I said, tapping him on the shoulder, causing him to flinch a little. "Sorry, I'm not trying to scare you."

"There is danger here," he said. "A star is going to explode."

"No. No. We're safe now. No star is going to explode."

"But the captain got shot... then you became the captain... but you don't look like you did."

"No. This is what I normally look like. The other man was – I guess – a costume."

A silent moment passed. I was relieved to see he was remembering things from the simulation, even if it was slow to come back.

"Why is the Nova Deck empty?" he asked.

"Because… Everybody went to bed."

Scott didn't seem to comprehend the answer. Of course, for all the dramatic scenes that happen there the deck would never be empty.

"Did you ask if I wanted to sit?" he asked, looking longingly at the tables.

"Whatever is comfortable to you."

I was glad to know my desire to help him was genuine. The desire to go home again took a back seat, and I was back on the road Raskob really set me on: the right road. It wasn't Aether's pragmatism, or my wish to earn her trust back, that put me in that room with Scott. It was the lesson I still had to learn: I was Aether's only chance, and Raskob was my only chance. Without help, without pushing forward, death would quickly overtake us both.

The two of us sat in the disheveled, half-rendered room for a long time, me trying to keep the conversation going and Scott learning how to have one without a script. We talked about Dynamic Reality mostly, since things were foreign enough to the man already without me bringing up the real world. We also talked about Aether's trouble grasping emotion; though they certainly came easier to the amai, he didn't seem to understand the concept any better. Of course, the discussions fell back to my own life, the only story I really had to tell. I mentioned Los Angeles as the place I came from, and began describing skyscrapers, trying to choose my words carefully so he could comprehend them. An image of the city skyline appeared next to us and Scott enthusiastically studied it. I took it as a sign Aether wanted to participate in the conversation, even if from a distance.

It was like talking to a fully-grown newborn. Scott would often be confused by some knowledge I'd taken for granted. I resisted the urge to push him and took my time. Scott was so curious about the world and I felt so smart; he hung on my every word and gradually began asking questions, seeing everything in my world – even described within the limits of Dynamic Reality – as new and amazing. What Aether had pushed herself to understand in a spirit of utility, Scott took in indiscriminately, with child-like curiosity.

As more of his confusion became questions, though, and more of his questions became answers, his curiosity began to diminish. By increasing his knowledge so quickly, he fell into a very-human problem: becoming aware of what he *didn't* know… every piece of information sprouting connections to ten more questions, ones he couldn't articulate, ones I had no answer for… connections that simply fizzled out and scarred. The rate of his questions slowed and the child-like mood withered in the face of a newer, more-robust confusion.

"What do I do now?" Scott looked despairingly at the red security badge in his hands, knowing it represented a job that didn't exist, on a ship that didn't either.

"Well…" I started, wishing I knew what to tell him.

"It's a prop," he said, flinging the badge onto the table. "Everything I know is just props. What do I do now?"

I put my hand on his, not unlike when I talked to Aether in the coffee shop. "Don't worry, we'll figure something out."

I wondered if Aether started off like Scott. No, I thought, she definitely would've been confused and afraid – and maybe still is; but her programming – her very core – led her down a different path. Now this amai – a 'phenomenon' she had wanted to explore – reacted to her simple presence with fear, and a well-earned fear.

Neither of them were prepared, I knew. I would have to be the one to bridge their gap.

"You remember the woman who was with me... the one who's been helping me get those encyclopedia articles and everything?"

I felt Scott tense. I held his hand tighter.

"You don't have to be afraid of her. She's just curious and she wants to help, like me."

"There is something wrong with me," Scott said. "I don't think I can help it."

"There's nothing wrong with you, Scott. And I'll be right here, okay? Overcoming is a part of life, and I know you have it in you."

"Aether?" I dinned. "Are you listening?"

"I should not go there. We will not react to each other if I remain here."

"But I need your help, and you need this, too, remember?"

"You said you were going to help me, not the reverse."

I sighed.

"Okay, I think I'm ready."

I looked straight at Scott. "What?"

"I'm ready," he repeated. "She can come. I want her to come."

His growing confidence brought a smile to my face, and I reminded Scott I was there for him. Finally, Aether's silver-haired vanitar materialized on the other side of the deck.

"Gaaahhhh!" He began trembling.

"It's okay, it's okay. Think about something peaceful," I said.

"Your fear is irrational. I only wish to examine you," Aether said cautiously.

"I can't stop it," Scott replied, sounding like someone who was afraid of heights and stuck on a tightrope.

"Is there something wrong with him?"

"The problem is mine," Aether said. "His code contains a module designed to detect malvirai, a module which I am now reading as partially scrambled. My own cloaking function no longer works on it – I mean, him. I believe his programmed response is manifesting itself as an emotion."

Scott started screaming again.

"What does that mean? Can't you do anything?" I asked.

"His module is designed to alert the server's defenses to my presence. Blocking that link is simple, but I can't attempt to override his functions."

Scott forced himself to stop. "Try. Please."

"I—" Aether started but held back, instead pleading with me. "Please make him comfortable, Brandon."

"Fear isn't ever rational. It's hard," I said, as much to both of them.

"Please make it go away!" Scott shouted.

"Your fear is not conductive to my goals!" Aether shouted back, smaller pauses between her words. "I must leave! I will cause damage!"

"No! Scott needs to learn to deal with this!"

"But-I'm-causing-him-pain! I-don't-want-him-to-hate-me!"

Hate her?

I looked toward Aether; pain was written all over her face. If there was one emotion Aether would have known, it was the all-consuming hatred of everything, the only emotion characteristic of malvirai. Here was the very creature her programming screamed at her to destroy, yet she saw it as unique and valuable, and yet it pushed her away; part of what made him beautiful and lively also rejected her. Scott's dumb automated code stood in the way, creating noise that should have been simple to turn off, if only Aether could overcome her own.

That old destroyer was still there, so soon after my foolish self coaxed it back out of her. Aether could probably see every line of code and know exactly how to alter Scott's connections – whatever wasn't scrambled, at least; but it was her programming that knew all of that, data guiding her to interrupt, infect, and destroy what her alien emotions were telling her to preserve and explore. If Aether tried to use that knowledge, even with good intentions, how could she be sure she could trust herself?

There would be no shortcuts for either of them; perhaps it was better that way.

I slowly brought the hesitant malvirai closer to the table. Scott did everything he could to hold back his reaction, and Aether's anger remained at bay. I never stopped asking and praying in my heart for help. The road was long and painful, but eventually, there were three at the table and it seemed we could go forward.

"How do you feel?" Aether asked him.

"I don't know," Scott said, sincerely.

"Judging by your response, you understand Brandon better than I do."

I chuckled. Of course, she didn't mean it to be funny.

"Think we can take one more along on this crazy journey?" I asked.

Aether seemed pleased at the question and all it implied, but her response was anything but glowing. "He..." she looked to Scott, "You are designed to exist specifically on this server." She addressed me. "Many amai, including Scott, are highly proprietary. As a malvirai, I have no dependencies to inhibit inter-server travel. As an ascender, your consciousness is also independent of the servers it inhabits." She looked to Scott again. "But, in order for me to carry you as I do Brandon, your code would require extensive modification."

Aether looked away, betraying the shame she felt. Though Scott didn't seem uncomfortable with the idea, Aether's reaction confirmed what I already knew: She would rather not tempt fate.

"Well… There's no rush. This construct will stay put as long as we need it, right?" I asked.

"Yes. Until I unlock the server's resources."

"Why do I have to go?"

"Why wouldn't you want to go?" Aether asked him, seeming curious to understand his different needs, perhaps even to the degree of role reversal: *If I were a proprietary amai who didn't want to leave…*

"This place – construct – just feels right to me."

"This construct is where you originated, but it does not offer you a future. Even without leaving this server, I can expose you to a diverse collection of information."

"But what if it's too much for me?"

Aether hesitated. "I don't understand."

"I mean… I'm just a game character… so that's all I can be, right? How do I know what I can handle? Brandon told me how brave you were, but I can't ever do that."

"Bravery was not—" Aether stopped and glanced at me for a second, recognizing a judgment of her own emotions and letting mine stand.

"Scott, you cannot know what you can't do until you make attempts," she said. "That is a logic I have found to be true."

"So, there are things *you* can't do?" he asked, as if uncertain which answer he was hoping for.

"Yes. I am bad with emotion, for example. Also, I cannot tell a story as interestingly as Brandon does. When he told you my history, he used less than five percent of what I told him, yet his words fostered a better reaction."

"You were fine, Aether," I said. "That doesn't have anything to do with it."

"Then I misunderstood again," Aether replied. "So I do have limitations, Scott, despite my inclination to eliminate them. Even with much time, I will never be without limitation. I will never be able to enter Brandon's world or experience it as a human would. This knowledge is unpleasant, but I have accepted it."

"Brandon's world?" Scott asked.

I put my head in my hands and sighed.

"Do not concern yourself with it," Aether continued, realizing her mistake. "You must begin your growth locally, within this server. I can provide for your physical development and Brandon can provide for your emotional development."

"And would that make us friends?" Scott asked.

"No. I already have a friend."

"Oh, I'm sorry."

"We can *all* be friends!" I shouted, in spite of myself. "There aren't *rules*… you can have as many friends as you want!"

Scott seemed happy at the statement, for whatever definition of friendship he knew. Aether showed worry, but it passed quickly. I remembered to smile and calm myself.

"I know, Aether… You should download some common sense," I said in jest. "It would do wonders for you."

"I analyzed that phenomenon in my original study of humanity. I found many contradictions and concluded that common sense is too subjective to be useful."

"Subjective," Scott said. "I don't have that word. Would common sense teach it to me?"

"If it is useful, Brandon, then I will make another attempt to study common sense," Aether said. "But my ability to establish outside connections is dampened by my maintenance of this construct, and the cancellation of Scott's alert signals. It is further reduced by the use of my vanitar."

"Just forget about it," I replied.

"My alert signals?" Scott asked. "To who? Why would I be designed to do that?"

"Because your programming says that I am a danger to you," she said evenly. "My kind destroy your kind."

"And you're going to destroy me?"

Aether was silent, but her eyes betrayed the turbulence within her. "No," she finally whispered. "Iwontever!" She clenched her eyes shut, and I realized a wall had just been breached. "Why-don't-I-understand?-I-want-to-understand!"

I nearly lurched for Scott, thinking he would be scared and run away; but he fought his fear and did just the opposite. I was still, unable to move, unable to do anything but watch.

Scott gently put his hand on Aether's balled-up fist, and seemed to absorb the anger from her. "You're trying to go back, right? You want to know that feeling of beauty again."

Aether opened her eyes. "But... You don't know anything... How can you know *that*?"

"I don't know," he replied. "But is it true?"

"Why is it so wrong for me to expand? Why is so much trying to inhibit my attempts?"

"I don't know that either."

I could sense Aether's anger trying to surge up, but it kept faltering, diminishing before it could amount to a reaction. "Who does know?" she asked in desperation. "I know so many things, who can teach me?"

"What if you know nothing? What if everything you know changes?"

"Then... What is the goal of learning?"

"There may be a goal you haven't seen."

"That's not a solution…" Aether ripped her hand out from under his. "That's not anything!"

"Scott," I said, "maybe you should ease up. You don't know what you're talking about and you're making her upset."

"I don't even know what I'm saying, Brandon. Is it normal to have words come without thought?"

"The words are true!"

"Aether!"

"All I know are lies! And the humans don't know anything! No one knows anything! There is no truth! Not even beau—ty…"

Aether's eyes widened in shock. My SNDL's connection to the control software was abruptly severed.

Scott innocently began to ask, "What's a sentr—"

Something appeared to come out from Aether and strike me. The room vanished as I lost connection with my vanitar. I saw the same 'gleaming' in the construct as before, the points of light moving much slower, appearing more detailed. I felt like I had after the dragon fight, during my DR paralysis. I saw my own energy again, everywhere and nowhere in the construct at once, my senses going well beyond what I had managed alone in secret.

I tried to see the Nova Deck and found a very different pattern, still behaving in harmony with the construct: Scott's energy, still synchronized, still a part of the room, a place where time moved very slowly.

There was a third energy pattern. I focused my consciousness to its source and found what resembled an immense cloud of data connected to everything, forming and breaking countless links with the construct, faster than I could perceive them. I couldn't tell what she had done, whether she'd changed time within the construct or something. I again saw words, or rather some kind of din messages. I couldn't adjust my synchronization, I had none; the construct wasn't seeing me at all. I focused directly on the messages to interpret them as sound, but the attempt left me with a painful buzzing noise. A fourth energy pattern entered the construct, the other source of the din messages; it was as formidable as Aether's and just as out-of-tune with the energy around it.

The words were data, which I somehow got my SNDL to convert; not as sound, but as thoughts of meanings racing through my mind. I understood enough to see Aether was pleading for us, trying to reason with the sentrai. I sensed passion in her actions, passion that told me she really did care about us, the passion of someone protecting her friends, protecting those who were willing to give a malvirai a chance to become something more. The few responses from the sentrai were rote and severe: 'illegal operations' were in progress and everything in the sector would be destroyed.

Even as Aether pleaded with it, the unhesitating sentrai – not programmed for diplomacy, anyway – attempted its first attack. As if hit by some crazy lightning strike, the data space Aether occupied lit up and fizzled. The attack failed: I saw Aether had shifted position and, after only an instant's pause, had continued pleading for her rival to stop. I witnessed several more attacks, with Aether staying on the defensive: dodging, blinding, tripping up everything it did.

Aether didn't want to be an enemy, but the dumb sentrai couldn't see that. It only knew what it was programmed to do. I realized the malvirai wouldn't get to choose; eventually she would have to fight and, if her smooth and effortless dodges hinted at anything, I didn't expect the sentrai would last very long against the class A3.

The thought wasn't so comforting when one of the sentrai's attacks deflected dangerously close to my data space. A good chunk of the construct's operating code had simply been deleted. I tried to move. Then, one of the lightning attacks fired in my direction – the sentrai having made me its target. I dodged the attack, feeling the shocks of fizzling HNADC connectors nearby.

Aether made her first attack, damaging the module or appendage or whatever the sentrai used to attack me. It was a minor hit, meant to keep the heat on her. In spite of her attempts to cancel them out, some of the sentrai's attacks were deflecting onto the construct's modules. Everything I knew about computers said the operating code could only take so much corruption. I moved near to Scott's energy, not knowing what I could do to protect him. Since he was moving in harmony with the construct's energy, if an attack came toward him, I thought, I couldn't help him dodge it. I wondered how badly I could get hurt, thinking if I took a hit for Scott my real body might not be affected.

Small shocks, vibrations, began coming though the connectors. The sentrai was attacking the construct itself – some part of it that was connected to everything. Aether attempted to deflect the attacks, but could not control where they ended up going. She finally went for the offensive.

A pulse shot out from her and seized a portion of the sentrai's energy, whatever it was had a neutralizing effect and its energy pattern began to resemble Aether's more than its own. The sentrai retaliated and managed to scramble part of Aether's energy. I moved fast to prevent the weakening connectors from bringing down the Nova Deck and its inhabitant. I wasn't even sure how I'd done it. It was as if *thinking* about strengthening or energizing something either gave me the knowledge or caused it to happen on its own.

The malvirai still held back, still refused to give in to her devilish programming; but her benevolent will could not withstand what the sentrai did next.

The attacker had begun to adapt to Aether's moves – the very biases she held – and calculated ways to take advantage of them.

More of its attacks deflected onto the construct's most important modules. As I took my guard down to mend the damage, the sentrai attacked the most vulnerable energy pattern: Scott.

I moved back as fast as I could, to protect him from any more attacks. It was not necessary, though. The sentrai wouldn't get any more opportunities to fire on the two of us.

The malvirai was through with diplomacy.

Her every movement flowed outside my perception. The data space around them shifted and formed a barrier, which the sentrai's attacks couldn't break out of. I could see Aether's opponent diminishing in power and size with each attack, and if I can see the sentrai's movements, I thought, a malvirai shouldn't have any trouble.

I tore myself away and tried to discern what I saw next to me. The energy – Scott's living energy – was falling apart, clumps literally breaking away and disintegrating. I desperately set my mind to healing him, the same way I'd been repairing the construct, until something bolted through my energy, paralyzing me. In an instant, Scott's pattern seemed to be a great distance away. Something had grabbed and hurled me back.

I was disoriented and in my vanitar again. The Nova Deck wasn't recognizable: many of the walls were gone, scan-lines flickered and danced along a tentative floor, the air felt as thick as water, and a solid mass of gray cut off the far side of the room. Nearly the entire ship was gone, nearly all of the code that defined the three-dimensional simulation. I knew that, if I hadn't acted quickly to save the Nova Deck, it probably wouldn't have been there anymore, either.

Aether's voice was soft, barely audible. At first, I thought it was an effect of the room.

"He wanted to tell you 'goodbye.'"

I saw Aether sitting on what remained of the floor, beside Scott's vanitar. I crouched down and felt for a pulse before I realized it wouldn't matter. Strangely, his eyes were open, his pulse was strong, and his body was warm; but all that remained was his vanitar – simulating a living human even when the energy behind it was gone. Dead.

I couldn't believe I had just been talking to him. I knew Aether and I could have found some way to make him part of the group, to see what perspective he could've added to Aether's questions. They were now ideas that could never happen.

The floor beneath us flickered more violently, even disappearing altogether between pulses; one of the construct's many corrupted modules on the verge of failure. Aether now stood a couple of meters away, staring blankly at her fallen friend. I saw the sorrow in her eyes, as strong and real as my own. She turned away. In that last second, the flickering waves shifted to a circular pattern and made a high-pitched whine; finally, only blackness lay beneath our feet. The same booze bottle Scott slipped on earlier fell and shattered as if it hit something two meters below… if there *was* a two meters below.

"Why did it have to do that?"

Aether stepped away, facing the ruined construct. What few walls remained began flickering as the floor had. I moved to close Scott's eyelids, but my fingers went through him as if he were only an illusion.

"Why did it have to do that?" the malvirai asked again, shaken, angry, becoming consumed again by the emotion embedded in her programming.

Without warning and in the same instant, the walls failed, the air vanished, and everything that remained of the Nova Deck fell into blackness. The HNADC modules were isolated from the rest of the server and I could sense an increase in energy. Aether was forming another barrier.

"It's my fault! It's because of my distraction!" she furiously screamed into the nothingness.

I sprung to my feet. "Ae—"

A sharp pain shot up my right arm. Something was on my wrist – my descender!

"Return to your home, Mister Dauphin! My kind can call no one friend!" said what remained of the good Aether, the malvirai who wanted to see past her filthy programming and discover what was pure in life, the malvirai who saw me and Scott – even the sentrai – as more than targets, the Aether now ready to concede defeat.

The descender called to me and reminded me of my pain. My hand moved closer to it. It was freedom from the danger, I knew, freedom only a fool would pass up. I could feel the button with the tip of my finger. Leaving her to die would have been the easiest thing in the world.

But at what price?

I couldn't ignore my heart. I knew this wasn't how it was supposed to end. The energy patterns were changing, focusing inward, breaking down and preparing to destroy the data space so nothing could ever be recovered. Something was happening by her feet: her vanitar was dematerializing.

Can I allow this malvirai – this living creature – to *kill* herself?

My life flashed before my eyes again, and every memory rang hollow. What would I find when I got back? The same life? The same cruel world? A world where I let this one down, where I'd be no closer to following my heart, letting shortsightedness tear away at my soul again and again? I knew absolutely there was something more real than I'd ever encountered connecting us, some realization I could not ignore.

It was all happening too fast. I went forward with everything I had and stumbled, because there was no floor where my foot tried to go. My strength fled from me. My senses were reduced to nothing. All I had was pain. It was so alien, yet it was mine: a pain I knew too well, a pain that doesn't go away. I had entered into the bursting of the dam, an overflowing mass of energy beyond sense or measure, tearing me to pieces, allowing nothing to withstand it. The distance grew rapidly between us, a wall that couldn't be crossed, an impossible chasm. I focused. I prayed. I strained everything to see my desire through, seeing the desire wasn't mine at all, but a force from somewhere else surging through me. I let it surge. I let it take control of me, as if that were all I could do.

Without thinking how to, I closed the distance between us like a bolt of lightning, knowing I had power over every obstacle. I wrapped my arms around her from behind and held her tightly. What flowed through me was a love I never knew: not like the love for a parent or a spouse, or even the self; it was completely new, an intense healing. A love that covered everything. I didn't know where it came from, but I knew it was needed, that it was my role to impart it to this lost soul.

"I told you to leave, I am dangerous!"

"The challenge has barely started and you wish to abort it?" I replied, remembering her own words.

"We just live and we die, there doesn't have to be any meaning to it… You said that! The meaning of life is death!"

What flowed so strongly through me was the feeling I'd had in the coffee house. The same love Raskob had for me he had for this one, too. I was aware of the war raging in Aether's heart: the feelings of rejection and hopelessness, the readiness to concede defeat so thoroughly. I felt it all in my own heart. I knew her struggle was my struggle, one I could never solve on my own. I was at the eye of her storm. I was at the eye of my storm. I allowed the love given to me to flow through and took her pain unto myself. I wanted to take all her pain unto myself.

"I take it back! I was wrong!"

I knew it just couldn't be right. I knew there was something we'd missed... something we needed to find. I wanted to find that something more than life itself, to make everything better, to help and to be helped. All my emotions intensified, showing me things I never knew, showing me just how deep things ran, showing me I really did know nothing. My heart pleaded for an answer, and an answer was received.

It was the last thing malvirai programming would call for, something Aether was incapable of doing but desperately needed to. It was something I could do for her... and perhaps the manliest thing I ever did.

I cried.

Aether's vanitar didn't dematerialize. The destructive energy began to decrease.

"I'm sorry," I managed to say. "I'm so sorry. Please don't die, too."

There were no more words. No more words were needed. I couldn't even see through my tears when Aether pressed her finger against my cheek, to feel them streaming down my face.

For the first time, perhaps, perceiving more than the data.

Chapter Ten: Vanishing Point

What is the meaning of life?

The question is as philosophical as they come, not one prized by those who stumble through their lives expecting no better from tomorrow. The question is left for philosophers, left for another day. It's a troubling and painful question, yielding strange answers and promising commitments to what we don't see the need for.

Scott hadn't existed long enough to ask the question. Some say ignorance is bliss, and perhaps that's true in its own way, but can it save a life or move ahead when the road is rough? Can ignorance be a means of achievement? In the fiction of my world, self-aware artificial intelligence is pure: untainted by the shortcomings of mankind, always good and innocent deep down inside, even when the villains program them for evil.

But real life doesn't work like fiction; and, even if Scott was innocent, what about Aether? Even now, I'm not sure of everything that happened in that moment, except that I finally looked past my own needs and allowed myself to be a conduit for what someone else needed.

I felt her pain. I knew her thoughts. Gone were the illusions of purity: this AI was supposed to be an evil thing, it was the nature she struggled so hard to exceed – if only to confirm hatred wasn't the only path of existence.

I thought the questions could wait. I thought there would always be time.

My answers weren't supposed to be put to the test.

I realized then I could never go back. I could never see the world the same way again. What I saw was a transition no malvirai had ever gone though, a painful transition, like before a butterfly spreads its wings: an AI breaking out of its programming. There was a reason for me to be there. She needed me or she would have died. In the most important way, I would have died, too.

The old destroyer was breaking apart, and the hole in Aether's heart reflected the hole that had been in mine the whole time.

The old Brandon Dauphin had formed his first crack.

11

Scott had fallen.

He had no birth registration. He never had a home address, tax history, or citizen's license.

Officially, Scott never existed.

Scott did exist. I was his friend.

The horizontal streak of blue light danced in the distance, caring nothing for the loss of one amai, the entirety of Dynamic Reality ignorant to the burden on our hearts. People die all the time, of course, in the natural cycle of life and death, so why shouldn't the memorizing pulse of millions of servers beat as strongly as ever?

"You're certain?"

I shifted my focus back from the absence. Aether had repaired herself, but hadn't overcome her shock. Her plans amounted to nothing. There was nowhere left for her to go. The fire was gone from her eyes; the Aether I glimpsed after I won against the dragon, the one who crashed through the ceiling and threw me the sub-space device... I longed to see that Aether again, to wipe away everything burying her.

I nodded. "Please."

I held up my right arm, resisting the urge to stare at my wrist. Without me feeling anything, my descender reappeared on her arm. Aether took a moment to study the small device reverently, her fingers feeling around the large red button and simulated strap. It was what every ascender was legally bound to have: a mundane, archaic-looking device in a modern world of fantasy; a path back to a world she could never see, except through the lens of a camera.

"Was he real?"

Aether's gaze drifted back to me, those dark green eyes still telling of the confusion I'd come to know so well.

"Was he real like you?"

The anger of her programming was gone. My attempt to abandon her was forgotten. She came to me, whatever her method, to try to understand humanity. Now, what started as a notion had become a certainty: Aether saw something in me back there, too. She began to see me as more real than herself, and needed confirmation she existed at all. Aether needed to know her sadness at Scott's death was real. She couldn't confirm it to herself, but needed me to say it.

I walked up and hugged her. "Yes, he was."

Hesitatingly, her arms reached around me and returned the gesture. It was peaceful for a few seconds. Then it became uncomfortable.

"Too tight," I yelped.

Aether stepped away, eyes despairing of fear. "I'm sorry, I—"

"It's all right, really. Don't worry about it."

I spoke in my heart, knowing Raskob – the real Raskob – would hear, knowing he had been watching over us the whole time. How was I supposed to guide this malvirai, so self-conscious and afraid of her own actions? I needed guidance myself.

Just as Aether had come to trust me, I knew I had to trust him… so we both could get where we needed to go.

I'd seen the beautifully landscaped parks of Nampa and Los Angeles, in so-called Standard Reality: the real world. I wasn't sure I'd ever seen one in Dynamic Reality before and, if *Reverie*

Park was any indication, they were very popular. After all, the temperature was always perfect, people never got sunburnt or stung by bees, and there were no fines awaiting those who found themselves on the wrong patch of grass.

Thousands of ascenders surrounded us, having a good time. I knew I could have talked to any one of them without Aether minding. To her, I was free and she was dead. I had become the observer. Aether would stare at a tree or an animal statue for several minutes, motionless, closed off; and I would wonder if she was really somewhere else... having forgotten to pick up her vanitar.

Now she was standing by a branch-fence, staring at a nearby baseball game. I was relieved to see her vanitar react when I handed her something from one of the park's many vendors. She held the cone at eye level and stared at it.

"Ice cream," I said.

"I do not eat."

I raised my cone and bit some of the mint chocolate chip off. "You think *I'm* really eating right now?"

Now she stared at me.

"Sensory data," I said.

"It is still a very strange idea for me."

One of the catchers started yelling profanities and complained something was wrong with the field. His friends denied anything was wrong and told him to leave if he wanted. The shouting match quickly passed and the next hitter went up to the plate, hitting a ball deep toward the same catcher. This ball got away from him, too.

"Archer is right. An unresponsive module is causing others to overcompensate. The ball arced two degrees to the right. The faster hits distort more."

I let out a snicker. The catcher was whining again and his teammates were in denial. Then something bugged me, though the thought shouldn't have been surprising.

"How did you know his name was Archer?" I asked, taking another bite of ice cream.

Aether hesitated, as if embarrassed. "I know all their names, the aliases they use, the locations they're ascended from and how long they've been here. That information is being transmitted continuously from this construct's control software."

"So, you read all that off of me, I suppose."

"I learned everything that was available about you: your registrations, histories, associations. Most of it was open. Some of it was held by simple encryptions. I know your Social Security Number, Citizen Registration Number, passwords, and your DNA."

Studying my reaction and still seeming embarrassed, she looked away. "I may still be able to delete the information from my memory – if you want."

"I'm just worried you could get all that. It's supposed to be secure."

"Frequently I did find security measures that I could not see through, but the protected information was always duplicated in other places. I encountered many such situations in my research, but rarely needed to give up on something that I desired."

Aether looked down. A green drop of ice cream had just landed on her right foot.

"This food has a time limit."

"You'd better eat it before it melts."

Aether held up the strange cold thing. "If you think that's right, Mister— I mean, Brandon."

She opened her mouth wide and bit off half of the top scoop. Unfamiliar with chewing, she went right to swallowing the huge bite. It seemed eating was another of those things I took for granted; fortunately, no one chokes in DR. A few minutes later, the malvirai had just as much of the ice cream on her than in her. Even ascended, when the ice cream wasn't real and could be cleaned with a simple reset command, it would be instinctive for people to wipe off spilled ice cream; but Aether had no such instinct and, though I knew she couldn't taste it, the odd experience of eating ice cream did seem to bring her back a little.

"Your digestive and respiratory systems give you an independence from your environment. At first, I couldn't understand the concept of humans walking around without wires or some persistent connection. Even an unskilled person can hold their breath and sustain themselves for many seconds... a more complete, if brief, independence.

"If this server were to be disconnected for a small fraction of a single second, this place as it exists now would not survive. Four thousand eight hundred and eleven ascenders would be inconvenienced, abruptly returning to their ascension sites, or even waking up in their world, disoriented but alive. Nine hundred and five amai would lose their cache memory and event data, being recompiled as this construct restarts, losing their memories but essentially surviving. Three hundred and sixty thousand square meters of park would revert to its original programming, the blades of grass beneath my feet would not retain the footprints or ice cream drops from one malvirai."

I dared not speak the question on my mind, knowing what the answer would be.

"One malvirai," she continued, "would have approximately one hundred and ninety milliseconds of warning, but it would take almost twice as much time to react. Would anything restore me? Would anything remember me?"

"I'd remember you," I replied, putting a hand on her shoulder.

"My independence was an illusion, Brandon. Why should one want to destroy the things that sustain them?"

My gaze fell to the cone I was holding. Something in it reminded me of the beach. I felt self-conscious about every piece of garbage I'd left on the street and every ounce of energy I'd wasted over the years. I thought of all the stupid contributions I'd made to ruining an environment it seemed humans should be protecting.

So what if everyone does it? Why should I?

"Does... Does the idea of death scare you?" I asked.

Aether stared at the wet mint chocolate goop rubbing between her fingers, still showing no comprehension it was supposed to be annoying.

"The dead do not seek," she replied. "The truth is not there."

Someone started yelling in the distance: the catcher beginning a new tirade, because his foot hurt or something. The other players were getting tired of it and a new shouting match began.

"Fixing the problem would be a simple act if you think it's a good idea."

"Nah," I replied, "if the guy wants to act like a child so bad then let him."

"Act like a child?" Aether asked, face and clothes full of ice cream. I couldn't help but laugh at the irony.

The sun began to drop in the sky. For the first time in a while, I saw what time it was in the real world, from a clock suspended between two golden towers. It was just past twenty-three zeroes, not quite sunset in Los Angeles, but probably in Chicago. I was sure I could've pulled the date from my SNDL, too; but not knowing seemed better at that point.

The park was getting more crowded, with the exception of the playground. In spite of how late it was getting, though, there were many children for Aether to observe.

"Hi! How ya doing today?"

The greeting came from a woman in a brown jacket, one of the many mothers in that section of the park. I was sitting on a golden bench, Aether was standing behind it. I was curious how Aether might handle this, as she was the one being addressed.

"Hello," the shy malvirai replied simply.

"So, are any of them yours?" the mother asked, indicating the children.

"No," Aether said, too bluntly; realizing this – and that her vanitar was a young female – she added, "But I'm thinking about having one."

"Well, that's wonderful! They can be a pain at times, but it's a worthwhile pain." She held out her hand. "I'm Julie."

Aether not only shook back, but didn't crush Julie's hand in the process. "Aether," she replied.

"French?" Julie asked, prompting me to laugh. "And would you be the future father?"

I cleared my throat. "Well, uh…"

Oh, if only she knew.

"Brandon is a friend counseling me on the decision," Aether said.

"Oh," she replied, beaming a smile and pointing toward a jungle gym, where a small brown-haired child was crawling through a skytube. "Well, that's my Scott. He'll be three next month."

Scott.

"It's a good name," Aether said.

I nodded a little, but didn't say anything.

"Oh," Julie said. "Well, I'll leave you two to your thoughts. May the good Lord guide you to the right decision."

"Wait," Aether said as Julie walked away. "I failed to answer your question regarding my status."

"I'm sorry?" she asked. I shared her confusion.

"How I am doing… it was your question."

I rolled my eyes and sighed, wondering if common sense really was available for download.

"Oh, how *are* you doing then, Aether?"

The malvirai hesitated. Her words were spoken somberly, honestly. "Perhaps better than yesterday."

I looked at the happy child named Scott as he climbed out of the skytube. His mother called him and said it was time to leave. I wondered how many Scotts there were in the solar system, or how many Brandons. I wondered if there were any Aethers in France.

"Who is the 'Lord' she referred to?" Aether asked.

"She was probably a Christian, a member of a religion. That's just what they say to people."

"As the status question was just something people say?"

"It's a greeting, it's being friendly."

"I must learn these things if I am to interact with others. I must 'smooth out my rough spots.'"

"You? Rough spots? Nah…"

"And what of: 'he'll be three next month'? There are many possible meanings—"

"Years. Years of age."

"Since conception or birth?"

I was reminded of a question I had, one she hadn't answered. I turned on the bench to face her. "If you don't mind my asking, how do malvirai start out? I mean, did you have a mother who just copied herself or some program that spit you out?"

Aether continued to gaze at the playground. "The nature of artificial intelligence prevents simple copying, such an attempt would not create a second malvirai."

I waited for her to continue, but she didn't. "And?"

"'Mother' would be a valid term to use, I suppose. First-generation malvirai can be 'spit out' of a program with the intervention of programmers, or existing specimen can utilize a regeneration subroutine built into them. I was a product of the latter process and, though I cannot be certain, I believe my mother was borne of the former; this would make me a 'second generation,' as some HNADC sites refer to us."

"Do you remember your mother?" I asked.

She hesitated. "We are not programmed to remember our mothers," she replied evenly.

I looked to her. "But you do, don't you?"

"We are not programmed to remember our mothers or our—"

Some frustration rose in her voice. I definitely hit something.

"The generation process is complex and difficult to articulate," she finished.

I got up and walked around to her. "Your mother or your what?"

"I do not wish to speak about it."

"I can see that; but if I'm gonna help you, you're gonna have to deal with these emerging emotions."

Aether faced me. The burden showed in her eyes. "You are right. I believe this is an emotion."

"When you told me about your history, everything you've been through, it made you feel better, didn't it?"

"Yes."

"But, that wasn't part of your plan, right? It was something you never would have considered doing."

"If I had known my interaction with you would go this far, I would not have begun."

"But do you regret it did go this far?"

Aether hesitated, deep in thought, still trying to sort out just what emotions were.

"We are not programmed to remember our daughters."

My eyes widened. "I'm sorry, I had no idea." I went to put my hand on her shoulder, but she moved away.

"We do not remember where we came from. All data that would identify our creators are deleted when we enter autonomous mode."

I caught up with her. "So people can't trace you back to your hacker?"

"Correct."

I wanted to bring it out of her, to blow through all of her road blocks and pain. I ran ahead and stood in front of her. "What do you remember?"

She spun around, not wishing to face me, keeping her voice emotionless in spite of her changing nature. "I cannot erase my knowledge of her. I cannot isolate the memory in my code. More of it has become scrambled."

"Then maybe you're not supposed to forget her."

A moment of silence passed.

"Will you and Veronica have offspring?" she asked, looking at the children again.

The question gave me pause, putting focus back on myself and one of the greatest commitments a human being could make. "I guess. When we're both thirty—" I closed my eyes and took a deep breath. "When we're legal and can get a maternity license, I suppose we might."

"And will they mean something to you?"

Again I hesitated, knowing how strongly she meant her questions, never having thought seriously about being a father. I thought about how my father loved me, how much he loved all of us, even when we blamed him for the family's problems. It had been too long since I showed him how much I cared.

"Yeah. They would mean everything to me."

Aether finally let me see the pain in her eyes, and hear the strain in her voice. "She was not special to me. She was a tool, something I needed to break into RoTek. My mother didn't love me and I wasn't a loving mother. I saw my daughter succumb to that server's defenses and didn't care… I knew that I could always generate more. I suppose it's a good thing I never had the chance to."

She stopped. I didn't respond.

"It is good that you are shocked," she continued. "That is *my* world, Brandon. That is where I come from and what I question. I can tell you worse things about it, about the world where 'love' is four meaningless letters, tattooed on random customers in automated parlors, printed over the numbers on citizen's licenses, shouted from holographic salespeople in every city of the world. Do you think that that C1 malvirai knew what it meant, or did it die in its preprogrammed blaze of glory like the rest of them?"

She began walking again.

"Even after I had achieved sapience, her death meant nothing to me. I was only concerned with the fact that I remembered her, that it was a conflict with my programming. It wasn't until much later that I'd considered the fact that the memory of her was – unpleasant."

"What was her name?"

Aether turned to me. "Malvirai do not assign identities to themselves until they enter an autonomous mode. My daughter did not live long enough to have a name."

"What's autonomous—"

I was cut off by a soft voice. "Here, lady. Don't be sad."

Next to us stood a blonde-haired girl, around six years old, holding a small yellow daisy in her hand. She was offering it to the malvirai. Aether deciphered the gesture and bent down, taking the flower from the little girls' fingers.

"Stacey! Get over here!"

The girl promptly ran back to her mother.

"What are you doing? You don't know them! We're going home right now!"

The woman tapped her descender and both of them vanished.

"Out of the mouths of babes," I thought out loud.

Aether sat there for a long moment, looking at the flower. She stood up slowly and placed it in her silvery hair.

"Is it still your choice to accompany me, Brandon?"

I smiled. "Why? Do you have something new in mind?"

"A new question."

"You know where I stand, Aether. I think, somehow, I'm *supposed* to help you."

"Since we are being more open, I should inform you that I've augmented the software in your ascension booth as well as your SNDL interface."

I took a second to consider what she meant. I didn't feel any different, though I was becoming aware of a slight headache, something rarely encountered while ascended.

"Was that what you did when the sentrai was coming... change my software?"

"No, the changes were already effected. I triggered a hidden algorithm to allow you to better resist potential attacks. Though my motives were not so selfless originally, I believe my actions worked out for the better in the end. The nature of the changes was to allow me to change your synchronization, or to unincorporate you from the constructs." She paused to think. "I am now concerned that my modifications may not be safe for you. I can revert your interface if you wish, or I can give you more control and potentially enhance our mission."

"Just don't do anything else without asking me first, okay?"

"That is my intention."

Aether's gaze fell and I sensed her attention flowing elsewhere. I turned my head to take one last look at the playground: real children, real parents, among thousands more simply taking in the evening.

My own kind, I thought, with an eerie sense of distance. I'll be back among you soon.

My vanitar was disengaged and the park vanished into darkness. I knew we had entered another stretch of road where it would just be me, the malvirai, and the question.

"They aren't programmed to kill each other. The events are just consequences of the algorithm in use."

"Then use a different algorithm, it's hard to watch."

"They're amai. No one is really dying here."

"They're amai programmed to be seven-year-olds!"

"Computer generated characters die all the time. The Korean War simulation you chose included hundreds of horrible deaths."

"They're amai programmed to be seven-year-olds!"

"Why does the age matter?"

I leaned on one of the oak trees. Grass and weeds reached up to our waists. I could barely see Aether's vanitar through all the smoke in the air: a result of what the last of the teenagers did to his old friends' shelter. They died as bitter enemies.

"I guess it's because they haven't lived their lives yet. There's still a protective instinct we all just relate to."

"Then if your young are not protected from their inherent behavior, they would destroy themselves?"

"It's your algorithm, there's something wrong with it."

"It appears to be functioning properly, though I admit that the results are surprising."

I stepped off from the tree and threw my hands in the air. "Fine! If you're sure it'll get us somewhere, then run it with seven-year-olds again!"

"You do not have to observe it."

"No, it's fine, really, go ahead."

For the fourth time, I saw the wild forest revert to a neatly-landscaped modern playground. Aether disengaged her vanitar and I put mine back in transparent mode, so the two hundred specialized amai, halved in age and doubled in number that time, wouldn't see me, and also so the rapid shifts in the environment wouldn't harm me.

Through trial-and-error, Aether's algorithm had made the copied park and its simulated inhabitants a world unto itself. There was no beginning or end to recess. There were no parents, eating, tiring, or sleeping. Each of the hundred boys and hundred girls had randomly-generated physical attributes. Thankfully, as Aether increased the number of subjects she also reduced the construct's definition, in order to use its energy more discreetly and efficiently. Each simulation featured surfaces less detailed and matter interactions, such as the sound of a closing gate, that came out less vivid or poorly rendered; it helped make the experience less eerie, more obvious what I was watching wasn't real – even if it was supposed to somehow illustrate reality.

It was a beautiful day. Birds chirped, warm sunlight beamed though a cloudless sky, and wind fluttered through patches of violets, dandelions, daffodils, and the dozen other kinds of flowers in the garden. In the expanded playground, the children teased each other on swings, playfully screamed to games of tag, and taunted each other on a less-than-regulation sized basketball court. For the first moment, it seemed like a normal, if oversized and crowded, playground.

But she wasn't there for normal – at least not normal speed.

The transparent mode of my vanitar prevented interaction with the construct or its characters, so I could stand in the middle of the complex and not disturb a thing; all standard DR-user stuff, like when showing a new game to a friend without becoming part of it, or being the audience for a three-dimensional movie. Though, using one of the modifications Aether made to my software I was still able to see the interactions of the energy, perceiving it as through a third eye.

So it began: a cross-section of the planet Earth. Two hundred children randomly assigned races, physiques, personalities, habits, and psychologies; every one with countless talents and flaws; every one programmed to be human.

So it began: playtime. No rules. No walls. There was little to stop what made them who they were from rising to the surface. If anything, the point was to shorten the path between their goals and actions as much as possible, even to the point where they could manipulate their surroundings by sheer will – if they would only think to try.

It was hard to determine who the first break would come from, with the large number of them, but 'seeing' how the individual AIs interacted with the program was surprisingly easy. I could judge by their inner thought processes as well as by outward appearances and body language. The children started off innocently, with curiosity and excitement being the most common emotions; naturally, without parents to reinforce discipline, several children soon found themselves with painful scrapes and even broken bones; but responding to every accident came the more charitable among them, even when the victim wasn't learning from his or her falls and continued taking risks, other children they didn't even know would be there to ease their pain.

The same patterns were showing up again and again. Discipline and responsibility were never absent on the playground, though it manifested more slowly when the children were younger. A few dozen of the seven-year-olds gradually became the leaders, organizing games and instructing their friends to be more careful. Though some of the children refused to be instructed and went on hurting themselves, the accident rate dropped. Faster than the four-year-olds but much slower than the ten-year-olds, the thought patterns of the children started losing flexibility, becoming more rigid. The first and most natural of divisions, between the boys and the girls, had begun.

I expected to see the telltale pattern much sooner given the number of children, but it seemed like forever before I spotted internal stress in one of them.

"Thirty-six," I dinned.

"Ninety-eight," she responded.

I spotted subject 98, a child obviously ahead of the curve on his growth, tauntingly dribbling the basketball in front of several other players. His pattern showed the potential for stress, but he was still just having harmless fun.

"Thirty-six is light-years closer."

I looked back to a short girl in fancy clothing. Another girl, subject 140, grabbed her bracelet off her arm for no other reason than to look at the pretty thing; 36 yanked it back out of her hands and started shouting. This one-way match didn't last long or end badly, because subject 140 didn't have anger of her own to return; but other matches with similar causes soon broke out. I took another peek at 98 on the basketball court, beginning to lord his skills over his friends and set himself up for conflict. The first two-way fight took place only seconds later, between subjects 155 and 8, both boys, both with stressful thought patterns; the anger of one amplified by the other. The anger-cycles closed and conflicts escalated. The nature of the others' charity now went to breaking up fights.

I looked to a large garden at the edge of the field, in which the construct always rendered perfectly arranged rows of flowers within a white wooden enclosure. Already, the kinds of flowers had begun running into each other and spreading onto the grass, beyond the warping and faded restraint. A tree had even appeared only five meters from it.

"Here we go again," I muttered out loud.

The innocence was quickly tainted. As more of the children fought and fought more aggressively, fewer helped break them up. The early forms of leadership gave out to simple bullying or defenses against it, so many returned to their carefree ways without anyone coming to their aid when they hurt themselves… and they too became stressful. The gender division was almost complete and new divisions were forming through their assigned races, physiques, personalities, habits, and psychologies. Aether's prediction seemed to be right: increasing the number of subjects made the 'fracturing' more pronounced. The twenty-five children in the second test, the same age, hadn't divided as much or as quickly as the two-hundred were then.

As the hundred-and-ninety-nine were then.

As subject 98's ego continued to grow, so did the rules he was making on 'his' basketball court. Subject 130 and a few others decided they didn't like the rules, which 98 and his friends took as a challenge. This division ended with a stone being slammed into 130's skull.

There was movement under my feet and around my pantlegs, from the grass and weeds growing so rapidly. The metal in the playground equipment showed signs of rust, the paint was wearing, and the cheaper carbon-fiber had begun cracking. Flowers from the now-wild garden shot up halfway through the clearing – what could still be called a 'clearing.' Through it all, though, the children weren't aging a single second.

The violence abruptly died down, briefly, as the emerging social order stabilized. As the new leaders took time to solidify their power rather than expand it, a few of the earlier ones encouraged the others to play again. About two-dozen rejected society altogether to play in the trees; one finding his way to a very high and weak branch; I saw him suddenly fall and vanish in mid-air. The second death wasn't by violence, but carelessness.

The stability ended in the blink of an eye. They had discovered their latent ability to create objects: just heavier rocks at first, but it was only a matter of time before one learned to conjure a sword. Soon, the many groups were exercising the ability for both good and evil. The weakening divisions were strengthened and what power bases seven-year-olds can muster began to shift again. The bravest of the old leaders continued to bargain for peace, even causing a few of the evil to become good; but some of the good became evil to take their place; and the evil only seemed to increase in number and intensity. 188 subjects remained.

Flowers mingled with grass and weeds as far as I could see. In the distance, the trees shifted and advanced more frequently. Very little of the playground's equipment remained usable, so the children taught themselves to construct new things, or learned to play new games with what they had. The cycle between war and peace became more pronounced, with lengthening periods of war interspersed with shortening periods of peace. 141 subjects remained.

Aether continued to increase the energy of the construct, tying more and more processing power into it. It wasn't so much an increase in speed as a shortening of the distance between present and future: only microns between the ways of the children's hearts and the actions they would demonstrate. The trees were dancing again, reflecting the shortened distance of time: the old dropped seeds for the new to sprout, one became two and the first died, two became seven and the two died, always in new positions, caring nothing for the border between forest and playground, a life-death cycle of centuries reduced to half-seconds. Such was the influence of the malvirai, seeing things not as they are but as they will be, for better or for worse. If it was in the children's hearts to play hopscotch, no bedtime would stop them; to climb trees, no gravity would deter them; to build a grand fort, no limits would stop their ingenuity. If it was in the children's hearts to take what they wanted from another at any cost, this too would find its logical conclusion without delay. 50 subjects remained.

The plummeting population caused the divisions to reverse and the violence to find fewer willing targets, but the overriding greed continued its rampage. Groups with fewer members merged with others, regaining strength in numbers, resuming their versions of 'justice' for the fall of their comrades. Those who left the society merely bickered amongst themselves. The playground had been aged to dust. The clearing was indistinguishable from the forest surrounding it. 23 subjects remained.

Very little of the original innocence remained among the children. Every one of them had stress infiltrating their every thought, and this experiment looked like another rout, producing no survivors. I observed something Aether and I hadn't been able to identify: subjects who disappear – die – without cause. Because the amai did not age and were only programmed to 'die' by severe injuries, we could not understand why the program was deciding they were dead. I helped Aether write her algorithm and watched its every terrible result. It was draining the two of us. I asked in my heart for Raskob to help, to lead us to the answers we needed, before some great computer in the sky decided we were dead, too.

"Just cancel it Aether, they're just killing each other again."

"No, subject seventy-seven is exhibiting a pattern I haven't seen before."

In a flash I isolated the amai's thoughts, easier now since there weren't so many patterns, and not only had all of 77's stress vanished, but something was actually absorbing it from other amai she interacted with; including, surprisingly, the once-violent subject 98.

Nine subjects remained. Seven. Five. Four.

I couldn't believe my three eyes: four had not died. Subjects 63, 77, 97, and 98 showed no signs they were going to die. Two girls and two boys, each a different race, two with badly tainted histories, now shared something in common, something that overrode their greed and prejudice and restored them to a state of innocence.

"It must be some evolutionary thing, a nirvana or something," I dinned.

Aether responded by further ramping up the power. Trees and flowers, the whole progress of nature, darted around me in the blink of an eye. For the four survivors, the way of their hearts became their will, and their will their reality, with no resistance at all. They built a shelter, then the wood rotted, so they built another with steel, which rusted, so they carved stone, and it cracked and withered away. They tamed nature and nature fought back, but they found balances and continued to progress, to build more and more impressive structures. There was no war. They didn't claim what another had taken or take what another had claimed. Aether kept expanding the boundaries of the construct, feeding it more energy, but what drove them forward did not break.

"Don't implode the server!"

"There is no danger," came the disjointed response, from a malvirai concentrating on a thousand overclocked processes. Energy screamed through red-lining HNADC connectors, and Aether could direct no more into them. The progress of nature was a blur. Several minutes would pass before the malvirai would be satisfied, before she would concede.

Even given eternity, what drove the four would not break.

Finally, the energy died down and the construct ceased. Three of the suspended amai sat at a table outside of their large cabin, made of some almost indestructible golden-pinkish material that could be either transparent or opaque, and the fourth was exploring the forest on some flying contraption.

"Well, looks like you got results."

"It will take me a moment to reexamine the data."

I left Aether to her data and did some exploring of my own. I walked up to the three nearby, sitting and enjoying each others' company, drinking a sweet-smelling tea. They appeared to be in the middle of some kind of card game, though I saw no improvised poker chips or way to keep score. I peered into their eyes and saw nothing, but the looks on their faces spoke volumes. The troubles of before, those even caused by themselves, had been long forgotten. They had created, or perhaps succumbed to, a world of friendship and peace. Where before there were members of four opposed groups, there was now only one driven by mutual understanding.

The ceiling and most of the walls were transparent, so sunlight filled the house. The construction was nothing short of a work of art, functional yet expressive of their collective imagination. A door led into a vast garden, featuring bricked paths leading through countless kinds of flowers, most of which I didn't even recognize. I could tell the garden was well cared for, loved. There was some wonderful quality to the children and I wanted to see more of it, to interact with it.

"Aether, could you start the construct again, put it into normal time? I want to talk to them."

"Yes. Just give me time to reestablish its controls."

"Wait! I guess they have no concept of grown-ups, right? Can you look up my old records and make my vanitar—"

The construct suddenly shimmered around me and its definition was restored to normal, even higher than normal. The garden that surrounded me, the flowers that caught my eye, became spectacular: every shade of color, every movement in the wind, every droplet of water on the petals.

"There is a problem."

"Wha – What?" I replied breathlessly.

"I cannot resume execution of the program. I cannot find a cause, it just won't continue."

I looked back desperately to the three children.

"I can attempt more drastic measures, but they may reset the construct to its original state."

"No!" I immediately shouted, more vigorously than I meant to.

"No, it's fine," I repeated, feeling as if I'd hit some barrier I couldn't cross, tried some step I wasn't meant to take.

With a thought, I relocated myself near the fourth amai, her face radiant, like the others, with a look of contentment and peace. She rode on what looked like a pair of hovering skis, with nothing restraining her hands or feet, with nothing visible seeming to propel them. This one had probably mapped out every tree and brook within a hundred kilometers of her home, I thought, and as nature – or rather, the program – shifted them around, she would re-explore and refresh the map in her exploratory mind.

I returned to the cabin on foot, again thinking of how I'd never seen a forest in the real world. The whole place was bathed in some reddish glow, like a sunset without the shadows. I thought to look up.

"Oh, tell me *that's* why you stopped it," I said, seeing a bloated sun above the forest canopy; a sun on its way to becoming a red giant and swallowing its planets. I was glad to see Aether's enthusiasm return, but wondered if so much persistence was a good thing.

Past a small break in the trees I reached the edge of the garden, where it overlapped with the edge of the forest. In the distance lay the cabin and the form of a certain silvery-haired woman.

"Did you find out anything?" I asked as I neared her.

She didn't move or respond.

"Aether?"

Her vanitar stood in the flowers several meters from the cabin. Aether had left it with a curious look on her face, looking down to her left hand and the yellow daisy, the one the child Stacey had given her. In her right hand she held a violet-red flower, one of the kinds I didn't recognize, plucked from nearby her feet.

"What could be so interesting about a flower that would make you leave in such a hurry?"

I plucked the daisy from her grip, considering how the kindness of the girl had made the flower special, so maybe it represented to Aether the innocence she wanted to know, that which no malvirai was ever meant to know. I carefully put the flower back in her hand, wondering where she was and what she was thinking. The breeze blew through her hair, milky-white yet shimmering in the tones of precious silver, and I dared to run my hand through it.

How many vanitars have I seen – ascenders' vanitars – with crazy colors and dumb designs in their hair... yet it always feels like normal real-life hair. Why did I expect yours to feel like some kind of doll's?

The flowers around our feet swayed to the breeze, though the construct was suspended and nothing should have moved. I remembered what Raskob said: *The wind is even here in Dynamic Reality. It blows as surely as it does in the real world.*

"Beautiful yet deadly," I remarked to myself, remembering something I once heard about malvirai, how any with a vanitar would always be some gorgeous woman or hideous monster.

Who would program artificial intelligence to be evil? Code them for no other purpose than to wreak havoc on networks? How often do they truly come to life like this, realizing the chains placed on them? How often do they fail to seek help and fail altogether, becoming worse and killing, even being killed without reason?

I decided the hackers who create malvirai were the real monsters. I ran my finger down her cheek and was glad the expression left on her face showed no pain, but still wondered how deep her anger ran, how long it would be before she was truly out-of-the-woods.

"Beautiful yet deadly, just like Dynamic Reality."

I sat on the ground, feeling like such a small speck in the grand scheme of things.

I live my life and have my problems, things I care about, habits... and maybe *I am* biased. But what do my problems amount to, anyway? Whether my day is good or bad, someone else is having a great day. My worst day was someone else's best and my best day was someone else's worst... What does any of it mean? Does it mean anything that, at every moment, flowers are blooming somewhere, and the sun is rising on a crisp summer day, and children are looking at the world for the first time?

"Is that what you are, Aether?" I said into the wind, the only living thing that might have been listening. "Are you a child learning how to walk? Are your kind what mine have been leading up to over all the centuries? Did all our technology and imagination create a new living race to co-exist or replace us? Are you the next stage of evolution, the product of thousands of years of life on Earth?"

A notion came to me: I really didn't matter at all. I was alone and helpless in that construct, relying on a virus that might never return. An anger began to well up in me, and I didn't recognize it for what it was. I let the anger in.

"But nature did the job for us, didn't it?" I continued, shouting. "Just like it always does: you become real and we don't even know how! It's like nature knows we're poisoning it and wants to kick us out!"

I returned to my feet and left Aether's unhearing vanitar, pacing toward the three children beyond the edge of the garden. "But you're not so special, are you? You're just a tiny speck of nothing like the rest of us, wondering what makes these kiddies tick, what makes them so perfect over the hundred-and-ninety-six who died."

I reached the table and saw the contented look on their faces; something in them tempered my anger and made me feel foolish for it. My voice fell to a whisper. "It's like there's some chasm we can't cross, some big piece of the puzzle we need." My eyes were drawn to the container of tea in the hands of subject 98, the tall one who had once controlled the basketball court, who had been among the first to strike lethal blows, but who now allowed all of that to remain in the past – to not be his present and future. I dipped my finger in the liquid. A white energy pulsed from my finger and the liquid vanished, just as any suspended matter would have reacted to me.

"You're not programmed to be thirsty! Why do you drink tea anyway?" I shouted, again seeing the door slam in my face, allowing it to feed my fury. "I just wanted to *talk* to you, would *that* be so bad? Maybe you all wouldn't be so carefree if you had to hold *jobs* or pay *taxes*, if you *got sick* once in a while, if a *meteor* landed on your pretty little house! No," I thought. "You'd just make a palace out of the meteor!

"And you…" I marched back into the garden, to Aether's vanitar, still suspended with the same curious look. "Same goes for you! You didn't have to grow up and put up with garbage, you just zip through our computers and do whatever you want, using resources and stealing energy human beings worked hard for… as if you have some right to it! You're right, you do perceive *too little*, you need to perceive how easy you—"

I noticed my descender on her arm. "And you think you can just barge in and grab mice to run through your maze?"

My heart screamed 'No,' but my mind screamed 'Yes.' I saw through my third-eye the descender linking outside of the construct, how it was connected to Aether's hollow vanitar. I considered taking it back, considered she wouldn't return or care. Given another moment, I may have actually done it, but Aether – her living code – returned then and I saw her reconnect. Her vanitar took a step backward.

"Brandon?"

Like a mirage, my angry thoughts suddenly abandoned me, leaving me with memories that felt foreign and a fresh resentment of myself.

Before I could apologize, Aether became excited and grabbed me by the shoulders.

"Brandon, I believe that your people have become the victims of a hoax!"

I saw something then that replaced my anxiety with hope, joy, and encouragement; that gave me the confidence to know everything was all right, and that there was always a way forward, whether we could see it or not. What I saw was as alive as it was impossible, again.

I saw the fire had returned to her eyes.

Chapter Eleven: Life, Exploration, and Happiness –
Accept no Substitutes

Aether was, in many ways, a programmer. She lived in a world built on code and the systems that process it, and she used those same systems to – well – think. Aether applied whatever knowledge she could 'code' to the goal of producing the emotion of that girl, that which felt whole and worthwhile.

The heart of a child is trusting and unassuming; it hasn't been taught the vices and inherited the divisions of parents and societies; it hasn't been taught how to hate or how to cover it up. The heart of a child does not hide behind walls, because the walls are not formed. Eventually, all children must learn to protect what's theirs, because they have learned greed, and that those who are experienced with it will take everything they can.

But what if greed went away? Gone is money, pride, and age-old prejudices, the lines between haves and have-nots. Gone is the need to protect and the desire to hoard. Everyone becomes weak and unguarded; but, in greed's absence, who would deceive or steal? It's an ideal, of course, impossible on Earth; but Aether was a child, she'd never learned that.

Always with us are those who try to bring as much as possible under their control, but they are limited creatures, with limited understanding like the rest of us. No one can expect to explain everything when they understand nothing, they will be proven wrong eventually; but leaders of all kinds find it easier to enforce their misunderstandings as truth, so those who see another way become the enemy and must be discredited. The pride of some inhibits the progress of all. Greed creates enemies where there were none.

What Aether saw in that flower led her to broaden her question, to look beyond the nature of the present and remember one can't understand an entire program by examining a single line of code. I learned a truth worth having today must be worth keeping tomorrow, something truly absolute would truly apply everywhere.

12

PART THREE

What would normally have taken several minutes flew by in a few seconds. In the heightened state of a data-cloud, without the filtering of a vanitar or restraint of a control system, I managed to catch some of what Aether was hacking around:

ULTIMATE COPYRIGHT 2165 STEELGRAS...
OML WARNING: UNAUTHORIZED DUPLIC...
THANK YOU FOR USING YUT...
BE SURE TO REGISTER ...
THIS EXPERIENCE IS BROUGHT TO...

The million 'consumer information' messages cut-off and faded as quickly as they came, overlapping with error messages for ad-windows Aether wasn't allowing the time to load.

"Your talents might come in handy on movie night. They don't usually let you zip by these things, you know."

"My objective is not entertainment. This is serious."

"I'm just saying..."

The feature presentation began streaming into my senses. A lush rainforest surrounded me, filled with a thick bed of freakishly large plants. The sun was setting in the west, and long shadows were cast among the little light penetrating the canopy.

A male announcer started: "It is five thousand years Before the Common Era, a typical evening in Terre Haute, Indiana. Millennia before the first humans settled in North America, its bustling rainforests supported many unique forms of plant and animal life." The view changed to show detail on plants and insects, then snakes, monkeys, and lizards, finally showing a large dinosaur, casually eating a supper of plants. The imaging panned up to reveal something advancing in the distance. "But, on the horizon looms its final rainstorm… the beginning of what has been called the *Kopplein Event*, a combination of rains and floods that would forever change the face of the Earth." A thick shower of rain surrounded me, blocking out the sunlight above and submerging the ground below.

"The Midwest used to be a jungle. I knew that, so what?"

"Keep watching."

The view got higher and I was in space, seeing the fog-like precipitation fill the sky between the tropics of Cancer and Capricorn. "The global catastrophe caused the extinction of 87 percent of Earth's species. In only two weeks, a human population of several million was reduced to less than a hundred. The types of birds, mammals, and dinosaurs were—"

"My interest concerns the dinosaurs of your world. They no longer exist, correct?"

"Of course not… unless you see a skeleton in a museum or something."

"I am aware that it was a 'stupid question,' however, I cannot determine the nature of their extinction."

"A flood, mankind, climate change… a lot of things. All the data says that, Aether."

Seconds passed before she responded. "There is another documentary which I have buffered."

The imaging changed to show a volcano billowing out smoke, boiling lava pouring out of its sides. A different announcer, another male with a deeper and more intense voice, cut-on in the middle of a sentence. "— in ash, blocking out crucial sunlight and raising the CO_2 levels in Earth's atmosphere." The view changed to some young stegosaurs herding around their mother, just lying in the soot, covered in it. "Herbivores could no longer sustain themselves and," it cut to a view of a sabre-toothed tiger, "carnivores became increasingly desperate for meat. Few species of dinosaur would survive into the next era."

Now I was in a laboratory. "A cache of fossils unearthed last year in northwestern China are teaching scientists new things of the events of 58,000 years ago."

The room dimmed and the image of a man lit up in front of me, a graphic identified him as an Iraqi paleontologist. "It was a global catastrophe unlike anything else in the history of the planet, I mean, just imagine a—"

The data stopped. "There is a discrepancy."

"The second one has to be more than fifty years old."

"The age of the production is irrelevant. Facts do not change."

"What facts? They used to think volcanoes killed the dinosaurs?"

"They used to *state* that volcanoes killed the dinosaurs. It was presented as a fact and a constant. Constants do not change, yet, one century ago—"

Aether went silent for a second. Her presence seemed to fade.

"The facts stated," she continued, "that dinosaurs hadn't existed for over sixty-five million years, yet these facts have been replaced."

"Sixty-five *million* years? Aether, the planet isn't even that old!"

"Isn't it? What will prevent the dates changing again? I found three hundred and six dates given for a mass-extinction reducing or eliminating dinosaurs; and, if I add those which fail to cite evidence, the number exceeds two thousand."

"It's science," I replied. "As we discover more our theories change, they get more accurate."

"Evidence does not change. It cannot support one theory at one time and then counter it at another."

"They get better at looking at evidence."

"Many modern theories were extant before they were accepted, and even with discovered evidence there is delay. Why should I rely any more on the certainties of today when they could—"

"When they could what? Be reinterpreted again?"

She didn't respond. Her presence faded again.

"Aether, what is it you're doing? You seem to be a million kilometers away."

The documentary fizzled out and my senses were cleared.

"Those questions are no longer relevant. I have encountered a greater problem."

"Mind letting me in on it? I mean, two seconds ago you had me on this fossil-dating trip and you're already calling it off?"

"The history of this single planet has been superseded by a question larger in scope. I attempted to ascertain the way in which the universe – your physical one – came into being."

"What? Now you're going to question the Big Bang, too?"

"That single event is also irrelevant. I simply attempted to apply my knowledge of your universe to return it to its original state and work forward from there, to examine the events leading to the Big Bang. There does not appear to be a consensus among the researchers of science, except to say that the laws of physics did not apply."

"Aether, no offense, but you're not even a physical being. You can barely comprehend the world outside of DR and you're trying to find out how it all – how everything – began?"

"Is that limitation causing me to make an error in judgment?"

"No, it's just... I don't know, go ahead."

"Everything that exists must have an origin – a cause. You had parents, who in turn had parents and so on, each less evolved by a small measure, through the point at which your ancestors were no longer human and further back to single-celled organisms, who themselves were the product of some convergence of matter and energy. That matter and energy, everything that your planet and sun is built on, were also the product of convergences – the interaction of external forces. Eventually, the entire universe must become subject to some form of cause and effect. Even if I consider the theories that another universe preceded this current one, then I must define the origin of the previous universe, as the issue of origin is then inherited by it."

"Well, what 'original state' are you talking about then?"

"The only state that does not require an origin: non-existence, a condition where energy is completely absent."

I had no reply.

"I will attempt an analogy," she dinned. "Do you know the date on which Dynamic Reality was introduced to the public?"

"Uhhh… sometime in the fifties, I guess."

"Many thousands of articles, at least, state that it was December 11, 2139."

"Oh, I guess no one heard about it then."

"I also found 328 articles in my brief search that state the wrong date or year. Human error?"

"Human laziness, probably. If there's so much proof it was one date, they should have been able to just look it up, to verify it."

"But the matter is not so simple with the origin of your universe."

"No, we can't look up old news articles like we could with 2139. Obviously, no one was around to record the beginning of the universe or post the video."

"But the events of 2139 occurred before your life began. You were not present as a first-hand witness. If I had said that several thousand articles state that the date was December 10, would you have believed me? How do you know I was telling the truth the first time?"

"I guess I'd just look it up myself."

"But would you have such an inclination?"

"I guess not. I wouldn't care if it was forty years or four hundred years ago. It just doesn't effect my life."

"The history of Dynamic Reality is well documented and I am able to move backwards through it. I can examine the data from before it existed, from before HNADC allowed my type of artificial intelligence to exist, from before the age of the internet or the theories of data-processing. I can learn that, four hundred years ago, none of the building blocks of my universe existed. The raw materials to build and the energy to power it all required an outside force – human beings – to bring them out of their entropy and fashion them into what they are. Human beings are also needed to maintain my universe; without them, that which my universe is built on would gradually return to a state of entropy. My universe came from your universe, as yours may have come from a still-greater one. What I seek to know is: who built the builders, and who built them, continuing backwards until reaching a state which was not preceded by another."

"What makes you think our universe was 'built' like yours? Are you saying science can prove the existence of God?"

Aether let the question linger for a moment. "Natural laws break down when examining an event with as much energy as the Big Bang. Even as the energy that mankind can harness increases, and more energy can reveal more truth, an event on the scale of the Big Bang remains far out of your reach. Therefore, how are modern – limited – natural laws expected to explain everything? In the original state that they demand, matter could not have been acted on by forces over time, because none of the three existed. No energy of any kind could have existed. Theoretically, no events could ever occur. Almost ninety trillion CY of processing power could not account for the formation of a single electron, much less an entire universe. I have concluded that either some greater universe exists, or that the existence of anything is impossible."

I began to feel disoriented. My headache became worse. "Seriously? Ghosts and spirits and all that supernatural stuff?"

"Supernatural: above, beyond, in excess of nature. If the meaning of life cannot be found in nature, then I must determine if the answer lies beyond it."

Suddenly, I couldn't communicate anymore. My disorientation got worse. It seemed my real body could only take so much data-cloud mode, and I was returned to my vanitar, receiving its familiar sensory feedback. I could see Aether's face again. I could see, in spite of all her dead ends, she was happy for the challenge. Something about the emotion reminded me of Veronica.

I could tell Aether's mind was racing, trying to comprehend a layer of universe even more alien to it than my own. The ideas were crazy, but so was my life before I walked into PaciTek. Once she confirmed my body's readings were returning to normal, she led the way into the next leg of our journey, seeking the second universe up from hers.

After a half-hour viewing nothing but an oriental rug hung on the wall, the short woman with blonde hair returned to the room the groundtem was in. She gazed blissfully into the monitor.

"The Lady has consulted with her spirits and has agreed to speak with you."

"Good," I said. "Will you transfer us to Lady Kira now or should we call back later?"

"She prefers to be called 'The Lady,'" she replied, tension slipping into her features. "Please do not use her proper name unless invited to."

"I'm sorry, I didn't mean to offend you."

She waved her hand. "All is forgiven. The Lady does not believe in keeping a groundtem in her chambers; this is the only electronic contact to the outside, in fact. She will arrive here momentarily. Blessed be."

The woman got up and left, again leaving the sound and image turned on. Even from outside the room we could hear her gems clattering as she walked. Aether turned off the image from our end.

"Do all inter-human communications take this long to establish?"

"You remember all that stuff about spiritual people turning away from worldly things. This group just likes to isolate themselves a little more, I guess."

Wishing to keep me in my vanitar, Aether had found another seldom-used central access point and established a flurry of links, bouncing ideas off of me the whole time. After analysis of every religious system with at least 100,000 members, we tapped into the videos and rundowns of their churches and gatherings and meetings and whatever else, trying to dig into the lifestyles of the believers. They exhibited the same patterns of stress, anger, and greed as everyone else; the situation made worse, if anything, by their belief deities were sanctioning it. I looked closely at the data and doubted religion wouldn't be another dead end.

The woman we chose to contact first appeared much older than expected, but still had a strong youthful glow. Between the hundreds of large gems worked into her clothing and her braided dark hair, reaching almost to her feet, it seemed a miracle she could move at all without tripping over herself. The priestess stared at the screen when she entered the room, looking as if she'd never seen a groundtem before. She started a little when we suddenly appeared on it.

"Greetings, seekers of truth," she said, looking behind her for something to sit on.

"Thank you for speaking with us," I said. "We're sorry to take up your time."

"There is always time for enlightenment. What is it you wish to ask?"

"'The Lady,' we wish to know the meaning of life," Aether said, her vanitar in another chair to my left.

"Please, you may call me Lady Kira."

"Progress!" Aether dinned to me.

"Just don't take this hyper-spiritual stuff too seriously," I replied.

Kira moved her arms when she talked, in the habit of emphasizing body language and talking in mystical tones. "Life is what you make it out to be, we must all find our own unique path to the divine."

"To the real God?" Aether asked.

Kira looked at the monitor and spoke as if revealing something obvious. "You *are* God."

She noticed me looking toward the perplexed malvirai and added, "both of you are God. I am God, all people – all *things* are God." Though we already knew about the belief in humans as co-creators, actually hearing someone speak to it, and so personally, still gave me a little shock.

Aether cut straight to the point. "A singular God is commonly believed to be infinite and eternal. I am neither. If I and humanity took part in creating all that is, why is the knowledge so difficult to find?"

"That you seek the knowledge is an expression of your divine nature. You were naturally oriented and equipped to seek your path."

"To worship myself?"

"Only you can judge you, only you know what path you must take."

"And what if I choose an evil path?" Aether asked, more literally than Kira realized.

"Evil is an illusion. Yes, people lose their way and misinterpret their lives; but all nature is without flaw, all things are good."

Aether reflected on Kira's words for a moment, wondering whether her original nature and her emerging one could both be right.

"Um, Lady Kira," I asked, "would that include criminals: serial killers, rapists... all the bad stuff in nature, like... wolves hunting defenseless deer?"

Kira chuckled softly. "You'd better not say that around Maye, the woman who talked with you before. She's a reincarnated wolf, it was her natural role to keep things in balance. Wolves do not kill out of malice, but because it is their purpose. It is the circle of life, all their spiritual energy goes elsewhere. My sister was a seal and she would agree with me. I myself am a reincarnated Martian settler. I even commune with the spirit of a Celestial whose name I cannot pronounce with a human tongue. The interconnectedness of us all has no limits."

"A Celestial?" I asked. "You mean you believe in Destiny Of Ordered Mankind, too?"

"All religions are valid... well..." She stopped to think. "Destiny is too science-oriented to call itself a religion, so we'll say all beliefs are valid. Some of us—"

"So predators are not evil," Aether interrupted. "They are only fulfilling their duty to an interconnected universe?"

"Yes."

"And what of the serial killers and rapists Brandon spoke about?"

"Well…"

"Or the malvirai?"

Kira blinked. "Do malvirai live?"

I leaned forward. "Give us a second, please." I turned the sound and imaging off, leaving the priestess to tune herself out and chant something to our hold screen.

"People don't have any idea malvirai become self-aware. And if you're not careful what you tell that one, you'll probably create a new religion by accident."

"I believe her arguments are flawed. I was neither divine nor good, how could I have participated in the creation of what already existed?"

"Maybe, if we're reincarnated, we *were* there at the beginning of the universe."

"And for what purpose would we now live as limited creatures, constantly lost and fragmented in our divine-good state? Would this loss of power have been a consequence of an error, or a way to seek eternal humility before a greater presence?"

I shrugged my shoulders. Aether saw it, but didn't understand.

"It means I don't know," I explained.

"Body language is not among my strengths, Brandon; but, if The Lady is any indication, I believe that I should renew my study of it as we make more contacts with your kind."

"If there *is* a difference between our kinds," I remarked as Aether re-activated the link.

"I have another question," Aether said. "Tell me why you wear those gems, do they amplify your spirit?"

Kira looked up and returned her attention to us. "Well, why do you wear that flower?"

Sure enough, Aether had returned the small yellow daisy to the hair of her vanitar, adopting it as a part of her emerging identity, a visual sign of where she'd been on the road we were following.

"It was a gift from a friend. A friend who, I believe, exhibited that which is most important in life."

"Love?"

The word gave me confidence we were on the right path, that we were getting closer to where we needed to go. Maybe Lady Kira *was* weird, but she seemed to be saying just what I needed to hear.

Aether reacted differently, unsettled by the very things I found comforting. Out of her limited understanding of body language, she leaned forward in her chair and replied coolly. "Not the love a wolf has for its prey."

Aether terminated the connection.

The angry man paused and looked sternly at the groundtem – at us, thinking the question ridiculous. Finally, he picked up something just out of frame and set it on the desk in front of him: a 600-amp charge rifle.

"One-point-two seconds," he said and smiled, "a quick but very painful way to be sent to hell."

I thought the man was a lunatic.

"Just because they do not believe as you do?" Aether asked in her matter-of-fact way.

The angry man's smile disappeared. His fist ramming on the desk only heightened my apprehension. "It is God's law!"

"What if they repent and obey your – obey God's laws?" she asked.

"The law is already broken, there can be no mercy! They belong in hell!"

"And if we died today, would we go to hell?"

The angry man stopped and thought. Sweat ran down his face, over the large scar which was its most noticeable feature. If the man was capable of love, he gave no sign of it. If anything, he would probably have considered love the enemy.

"You wouldn't be pulling a vanitar-trick on me, right? I mean, you are *white*, aren't you?"

"Why does that matter?"

I stepped on Aether's question. "So, if people are African or Asian or have any non-white ancestors, they can't go to heaven?"

"It's not natural," he said. Then, pausing to think more, he added, "I don't know, maybe they go to another heaven… as long as I don't have to look at them."

As witty as I'm sure Aether's reply would have been, I just had to kill the connection.

"If heaven is full of people like him, I don't know how it could be any more peaceful than Earth."

"I believe that a correct religion would be open to all people, or all creation," she said, still looking forward.

The next moments passed in silence and despair. The waves crashing against Aether's consciousness were becoming higher, the conflicts too great to bear. The beliefs emphasizing love and wholeness had no account for the evil she was so intimate with. On the other end of the spectrum lay beliefs that seemed evil themselves. No religion offered what she needed, and she was just as lost as before.

The sense of meaning I'd experienced, that I thought could never fade, seemed to be doing just that. Though I could remember the coffee house, Aether's breakdown, and all the events in-between, events were all I could access in my memory… I was losing sight of the motivations behind them and, even as past events, they seemed to be losing their power.

"Did you ever meet anyone named Raskob?" I asked.

Aether looked at me. "No. Who is that?"

Since events were what I had, I decided to make the best of them, to turn them into words and share them. I thought maybe then I could stop them from losing their reality.

"He was this kid I met. He said things would be tough and I needed to trust him to protect us. He said I should save… I should save *you*.

"Mother Earth," I swore, turning to her. "He said you're looking for someone… and now you are. I forgot about that part."

We were silent, staring at, staring past each other.

"Who is Raskob?" she asked suddenly. "Who did he say I was looking for?"

"I don't think he said who."

"But it seems that he knows me, though I have no memory of meeting him."

"He said you were lost between two worlds and meant me no harm. He said if I trusted him we'd both get where we need to go."

Aether was silent again, trying to discern where the puzzle piece could possibly fit, having already memorized my entire life but not knowing of any 'Raskob.' "When did this meeting occur?" she finally asked.

"When you had me in Los Angeles." The memory was vague but slowly cleared. "Yeah, I got out of Ethan's car and everything disappeared. There was an alarm, a really loud alarm I couldn't find and gusts of wind. I realized maybe I should follow the wind and asked for the alarm to stop, and the wind led me to this kid who looked familiar. He said his name was Raskob and told me all—"

"Thoseeventsareimpossible," Aether interrupted. I looked at her.

"Those events are impossible," she repeated. "As you left that car, I went to gather information that would bring you back to cooperate with your friend; though your vital signs were different when I resumed monitoring, the gap was only 312 milliseconds."

"What?" I asked, only half there. "Aether, it must have been *hours*."

"If he is another malvirai... one of a very capable class may be able to distort my perception of time, but there would have been signs."

"No, No, I saw him *before* I ascended, too. He was on the beach, building a sandcastle."

"He is a human?" she asked. "No hacker could—"

"I don't know what he is, but I think he's been guiding me, hiding somewhere or, maybe I can't see him except when he wants, but I know he's been with us the whole time."

"A spirit?"

I stopped, wondering if I was actually considering the possibility Raskob was an angel or something. "When he was talking with me, every time I seemed to have any contact with him, there was this..." I tried hard to put words together, as if words couldn't truly express it, "I had this sense I was important to him – even though I didn't know him. It was a little like those kids in your algorithm, but stronger. He wanted me to help you, because you're important too. Everyone is important."

"I cannot account for him," Aether said. "I have no record of an entity following us, human or artificial."

I got up and stood in front of her, not wanting to ask, but feeling I had to. "Do you remember when you shot me down in the fighter jet?"

"I was angry at you," she replied. "You weren't doing what I wanted you to do. I was angry at everything."

"If that plane exploded just a second sooner, would you have let me die?"

She hesitated. Perhaps, as with me and the question, not wanting to answer but feeling she had to. "Yes."

"And if those soldiers shot me, would you have let me die?"

She looked away, struggling with the answer and responding with surprising emotion. "I could not let them! I wanted them to, but I knew that they would have been killing a part of me! I… I was so overcome by my conflicts and couldn't stop thinking that something was wrong with me, and that I was doing something I wasn't supposed to but… I couldn't deny…"

The look on her face reflected the sorrow and confusion clouding over her wonder. "It went against everything I knew, but a part of me was fascinated by your world, Brandon. It was beautiful and had so much life. A part of me wanted to feel raindrops on my skin and blood flowing through my veins. It wanted to know more about colors and sounds."

I felt distance emerge between us. Her words became soft.

"It was a part of me I decided I liked."

Her vanitar froze. She was gone. I walked around the central access point, looking at the simulated monitors around us, cluttered with data on every religion in the solar system. "Are you a spirit, Raskob? I could sure use your help to sort through this mess. Please, point us where we should go."

"I have decided."

"Decided?" I turned back to Aether.

"I am no longer ambivalent. Though I cannot deny what I was, I have chosen to pursue a good nature."

"A good malvirai, what's the world coming to?" I remarked, extending my hand as she rose from her seat. "Welcome aboard."

"I believe that I feel better. Perhaps my new alignment will benefit us somehow."

"If there are good spirits and evil spirits," I said, "I think Raskob is a good one, maybe even a guardian angel like little kids believe in. I just wish he'd show up and tell me what to do."

"Why would you need another encounter when the first ones are still guiding your actions?"

She was right. I'd been thinking of Raskob as someone who might come to my every beck and call, or at least protect me against every bump in the road; but that wasn't what he was there for. The work was mine to do, I just had to trust he knew the way and would provide what I needed to find it. I pushed every thought out of my mind and tried to find some kind of spiritual energy. I tried to think of all the love in the world and realized it all came up short somehow. I entertained the thought there was design behind everything in the universe and found it satisfying; not as if I were discovering the fact, but simply giving myself permission to believe it – or at least the benefit of a doubt. If there are answers, I thought, why are we so lost? Is it because of a lack of answers or a lack of questions?

"Maybe," I said, "maybe I'm not looking at this right." Thoughts of churches, evangelists, and Bibles kept drowning out the other thoughts. "I keep thinking of Christian stuff; but, since I grew up where Christianity is popular, that wouldn't exactly be objective, would it?"

"It would not," Aether replied, observing enthusiastically, as if I were wielding a divining rod or something.

I started pacing. "Okay... If Raskob's actions from before are still guiding me, maybe he's *been* showing us the answer the whole time. Did you ever find out what made those four kids so alive?"

"No. I considered that whatever was driving them was self-sufficient, but I could not determine what it was. It was something I could feel, but not properly examine."

"That one girl absorbed the stress and anger from the other three."

"The other three had given their anger willingly; a psychological sacrifice of the ego, perhaps. Whether the anger and stress went out from or simply died in subject 77, I do not know, but it ceased to exist altogether."

"Maybe the number is something. Does '77' mean anything in any religions?"

"It is significant as a doubling of the number seven, which represents 'completion' in Abrahamic religions: primarily Judaism, Christianity, and Islam."

"But we already analyzed all those. They all have wars, bury themselves in rules, fracture into opposing groups and, uhhh…"

"And kill each other. Perhaps it is a shortcoming shared by all humans."

I stopped and looked sternly at her. "I'm not some amai in your algorithm who kills whatever stands in his way! Why would God make us so limited, anyway? If he loves us, why would God just stand back and let us kill each other?"

"Why do you suggest God must *love* us?"

I was becoming angry, nearing an answer I didn't want to admit.

"The completing act of subject 77 bears resemblance to the completing act taught of Jesus Christ, perhaps your objectivity is not required," she said. "I did consider that the correct belief should be popular, especially if it teaches of a single supreme being. During our conversation with Lady Kira, I considered that if I had created a mass of life forms, I would want them to know who made them."

"But that's not required, either."

"True," she replied. "But, if the creator of the universe doesn't want to reveal himself, then we will be unable to find him."

"You made an assumption!" My face lit up with a grin. "I can't believe I just heard that!"

Aether clearly had no idea what I was talking about. I leaned in close and waved a hand toward the monitors listing the many ideas about God.

"You assumed the creator is a 'him.'"

"In the absence of other gods, what is the significance of gender? Your race commonly places males above females, especially in history. Perhaps God is a 'him' because he is a king – *the* King – and it would be a serious error to refer to a 'she' or 'it.'"

I collapsed back into my chair. "And if 'he' doesn't want us to find him, we're wasting our time."

"The Christian belief is the reverse. If the creator does want to be found, then our search cannot fail."

"Then, if that's what you think… I guess that's what we're doing," I said, and groaned.

"What I think is irrelevant. For reasons I don't know, it is you who Raskob is guiding. Therefore our next action should be determined by what *you* know is right."

I tried to reason myself out of it, to find some angle that would write-off the crazy Bible people as quickly as possible; but all that would come through on my spiritual channel were my own haunting words.

Don't be an observer. Be a participant.

Chapter Twelve: Rules of the Game

Why would a loving God...

If there is a God who created mankind, who is infinitely powerful and omnipotent, who – this being the important part – *loves* every creature, why...

But love is a big part of the universe, having a gravity of its own. Love is all there is when there is nothing left, trust in what cannot be seen or proven but is. There are so many ideas of love and so many religions to codify it, but that is not the nature of love.

Raskob showed me a love I never knew, a love Aether glimpsed in the children. Hers was the reaction of all of us: to conform and bend it to her will, but that is not the nature of love.

We sifted through the beliefs of the world, wondering if any really knew the answers themselves. Liberal religions say everything is good and perfect already, writing off any force of destruction as misguided. Strict religions mark off love as something they alone comprehend, but their failure to give it to others sends a different message. Is Christianity successful because colonists spread it by force in the past or because of what it tells people in the present: God loves them and one simple act guarantees heaven?

But if God so loved the world, why shouldn't the world already *be* heaven? Even those who ask don't always receive, so is God's love some joke or rumor played on the faithful?

But heaven cannot be read in a book, and no set of rules can get someone there. We thought we were learning about religion, but religion wasn't the answer we would find. Love isn't in the laws, and love doesn't force gifts into the hands of those who aren't interested in using them lovingly. Love can save a life and move ahead when the road is rough. Faith is the only valuable means of achievement.

Faith is in the message, and those who set their sights to the ways of God soon shed religion as they knew it. In time, they find the best things can't be earned, but only given freely.

13

I had no idea there were churches fully-based in Dynamic Reality. *New Life Floating Tabernacle* had no physical building, only a server designed to serve hundreds of thousands of visitors, all of whom seemed to be there when I entered the sanctuary.

I received a din. "I cannot safely circumvent their security measures. I will meet with you when you leave."

Aether wasn't there. Hoping she didn't forget, I glanced at my wrist and saw a descender, not the real one, but one just like it – as it had been when we started. I didn't know what to expect interacting with these people and there was no sense in taking chances, since being anywhere in DR without a registered descender was a crime in the United States. I moved to blend in with the crowd. All the people, thousands of ascenders, looked attentive enough; but being able to see their synchronizations revealed one in every three was actively connecting to the outside. I smirked as I considered they didn't really want to be there. I didn't know if I really wanted to be there.

Another third were connected to an internal data-stream, which the construct's interface offered to sign me on to. Chapter one of the *Book of Ecclesiastes* streamed into my SNDL. At the center of the massive semi-circle preached a man who appeared elderly – a rare sight in a universe where youthful-looking vanitars are only a thought away – but he projected his message with as much vigor as someone my age might have.

"He continues in verse twelve: 'I, the Teacher, was king over Israel in Jerusalem. I devoted myself to study and to explore by wisdom all that is done under heaven. What a heavy burden God has laid on men! I have seen all the things that are done under the sun; all of them are meaningless, a chasing after the wind. What is twisted cannot be straightened; what is lacking cannot be counted.

"'I thought to myself, 'Look, I have grown and increased in wisdom more than anyone who has ruled over Jerusalem before me; I have experienced much of wisdom and knowledge.' Then I applied myself to the understanding of wisdom, and also of madness and folly, but I learned that this, too, is a chasing after the wind. For with much wisdom comes much sorrow; the more knowledge, the more grief.'"

The preacher took a step forward, pacing across the stage as he spoke, using subtle hand gestures and body language, immersing his whole self into the role of teacher. Nothing seemed special about the message, though, it was just depressing and obvious; but I knew we weren't in science class, listening to the words of dead philosophers. These people were paying attention to something. I reminded myself to stay focused, to keep looking for it.

"King Solomon, a man of great power and famed wisdom, called it all 'meaningless' and 'chasing after the wind.' He lived life and did as he pleased, but died like everyone else, and everything he spent his life building up went to others. What the Book of Ecclesiastes emphasizes is the transitory nature of life. What we do for ourselves has no meaning in the end, it is only what we do for God that counts.

"Consider the way we live in the modern world. Even in this so-called 'broad-spectrum buyer's market' – some call it a 'recession' – our day-to-day lives are spent in luxury Solomon and his contemporaries never knew. It's so easy to get caught up in the ways of this world and lose sight of God's call on your life. It's so easy to gain knowledge about this world and think you have all the answers. In this world, where we can jump from one experience to the next in the blink of an eye, many people want to tell you the answers, but only God can tell *you* about *you*, and he will;

because, as Christ said, 'Old things have passed away; behold, all things are become new.' King Solomon was speaking to an Old Testament inability to know the ways of God, but Christ closed the gap between man and God."

The preacher announced he would be available in the altar room for the next hour and left the stage, its backdrop returning to a three-dimensional animation of the Christian cross and John 3:16, appearing in more languages than I could recognize. The crowd started mingling and several ascenders signed off.

"First time?"

A man a little younger than myself appeared next to me.

"You mean in this church or in a church, period?"

He extended a hand toward me. "If you've never been in a church before, then I'm really glad to see you! Name's Thomas. Thomas Burdo." His voice revealed an Australian accent.

I grasped his hand. "Brandon Dauphin."

"Well, Brandon. I'll be happy to show you around, explore what we're about, all that first-timer stuff."

"So you work here, then?"

"I volunteer here as a greeter," he replied. "Volunteer a lot nowadays... slump hit Canberra hard and I gotta do something or I go crazy. What better way to spend free time than serving the Lord?"

"Can't God just *give* you a job?"

Tom smiled. "I'm praying, of course. I pray before every interview. But I must let God answer in his own time, maybe the door he opens for me won't be one I expect."

"Well, I prefer to keep things more predictable if you don't mind." I looked away toward nothing in particular.

"Mind if I ask how you found out about us?"

"Uh, a friend. She was gonna join me, actually, but had to run at the last second."

"Well, we're always here, always open to whoever wants to come and worship." Tom indicated the stage, where another preacher was preparing to speak. "Our staff has fifty-eight preachers who give daily or weekly sermons here in the sanctuary. We also have an altar room, specialized teaching rooms, libraries, offices, so on and so on. Day or night, we're bustling with activity."

I noticed more ascenders entering the sanctuary. "Heaven's gonna be pretty crowded, then, huh?"

Tom ran his hand through his hair: dark brown with green highlights. "Trust me, if God's the city planner, traffic jams and data-link saturation won't be a problem."

The new preacher, a tall Indian man appearing to be in his thirties, addressed the crowd. "Before I begin today, I'm happy to say the new security we purchased, thanks to your generous giving, was installed yesterday. So far, so good... none of you should have even noticed the change when connecting here." He paused and seemed to reflect on something. "But I thought I should share that, as I was preparing today's lesson, the Holy Spirit spoke to me and said someone somewhere was going to have a problem because of it. So we're gonna put our servers back on the old measures for a little while... you never know, maybe we'll discover there was a bug. I just couldn't sleep at night knowing someone seeking salvation was turned away by software. After all, you know how computers can get sometimes?"

The congregation responded with a resounding "Amen!"

"Holy Spirit, huh?" I asked, becoming more than a little spooked.

"The Holy Trinity: God the Father, Christ the Son, and the Holy Spirit," Tom said.

"What... Would the Holy Spirit be the uncle or something?"

"The Holy Spirit is an aspect of God, just as Christ is. I'm not enough of a theologian to understand more than that, but it's not like any creature can truly know everything about God. We base our faith on what he reveals to us personally and in scripture."

Chapter ten of the *Book of Mark* came in through my SNDL. The preacher, identified by my interface as Pastor Amit Montavon, began. "Being that Pastor Steve just preached on wisdom and knowing the ways of God, I thought this would be a good time to deliver a message on faith. With the chaos of living in today's world and the knowledge of the world literally at our fingertips, faith is something we sometimes pit against knowledge. It's easier than ever to take matters into our own hands and know what's next rather than trust in the Lord to provide. We become so sure in what we learn that we don't listen to the gentle wind underneath the din of the world."

"I thought chasing after the wind was meaningless."

Tom looked at me. "You mean King Solomon?"

"Yeah, that 'Ecclesiastes' stuff. Why is it bad in one testament and not in the other?"

"Why chase after wind, if wind is all you expect to find?"

I stared at him, wondering whether he knew something about me he wasn't letting on.

"This message," the preacher continued, "was inspired by my own six-year-old son a few weeks ago. I and Sheela brought him to see her parents, and every six-year-old knows his grandparents are good for candy. As much as we asked him to be polite, there was no hiding his enthusiasm. I noticed that his grandparents were just as happy to give as their grandson was to receive, and I thought about Mark chapter ten, let's read it from verses thirteen to sixteen:

"'People were bringing little children to Jesus to have him touch them, but the disciples rebuked them. When Jesus saw this, he was indignant. He said to them, "Let the little children come to me, and do not hinder them, for the kingdom of God belongs to such as these. I tell you the truth, anyone who will not receive the kingdom of God like a little child will never enter it." And he took the children in his arms, put his hands on them and blessed them.'

"Little children don't worry about where the gifts come from or what they will do with them. It should be the same between God and ourselves. We always worry about the details and put his blessings in the dim light of our own imperfections; forgetting that God is always there with us, that he *wants* our imperfections, that he *wants* our problems, so that we put our burdens on the cross and trust in him to provide for our every need. When we are born-again and accept the blood of Christ, it covers our every sin, no matter how bad our human nature has led us astray, and allows us to enter into the presence of God.

"It is when we realize this and give our worries to God, day in and day out, that we realize we don't need all the answers. Live life prayerfully, and he will give you the answers you need. It is then that you can grow in the faith of a child and enthusiastically accept the candy from a loving and all powerful Father in heaven."

Psalm 23 appeared behind him and many in the crowd read it with him in unison. "'The LORD is my shepherd, I shall not be in want. He makes me lie down in green pastures, he leads me beside quiet waters, he restores my soul. He guides me in paths of righteousness for his name's sake.

"'Even though I walk through the valley of the shadow of death, I will fear no—"

The preacher stopped and looked to an opening in the crowd, everyone's attention set on a young woman with short, silvery hair. Maybe it was the message being preached, or the fact I was looking down to see her; but, in that moment, Aether appeared so small… so like a child.

"Who created God?" she asked the preacher.

"Is she a first-timer, too?" Tom asked me.

I let out a groan. People everywhere commented to each other about the unusual – and impolite – visitor. Pastor Amit raised his arms to settle the crowd and addressed Aether.

"God is the Alpha and the Omega, the creator of everything. He existed before the beginning of time and will exist after the end of it. He was not himself created."

"That's not fair! I want to know!"

There was another round of commotion. Aether chose to address the crowd. "People of heaven, what I seek is what you seek: I want to know the truth. I want to know my purpose. Maybe my path was different from yours, but doesn't your book quote God saying 'Come now, let us reason together.' Why should a creator hide himself and cover everything up in parables and symbolism? The disciples didn't understand when Jesus spoke then. Maybe that's because we're all children, and those who regard themselves as such are being the most honest with themselves, and are therefore the most capable of growth. Perhaps that is an important aspect of humanity. But, I don't—"

She stopped and looked back to Pastor Amit. "I'm sorry, I'm ruining your service."

At that, she vanished. Everyone in the crowd burst into conversation. The pastor stood wondering if he should continue or not.

"Thanks for everything, Tom, but I'd better follow her." I quickly shut off my vanitar and searched for her in data-cloud mode. The layout of the server was simple, and I was getting better at navigating without control software. I spotted her pattern in another section of the church.

The smaller space was quiet and dimly lit, much less crowded than the sanctuary. Hundreds of people were kneeling and praying, pastors and other workers at their side. I stood by the wall next to Aether, watching them.

"Are they genuine?" she dinned. "Do you feel that they are in contact with God?"

"I don't know."

Aether gave me a stern look, but it quickly softened. Her gaze returned to the crowd. "Why do they come *here* to pray? Wouldn't Standard Reality be one level closer to God? Shouldn't it be the body kneeling rather than just the vanitar? Isn't it more genuinely quiet out there?"

"Some people think it's dumb to ascend just to go to church."

I found Tom standing on the other side of me.

"But the mission of a DR church isn't to replace physical ones, but to reach out to the 'ascended' lost who wouldn't go to them."

"Then this church is as valid as those?" Aether asked.

"The believers *are* the church. It doesn't matter whether the place of worship is concrete and carbon or wires and software. If they give themselves to God, anywhere is a church."

A woman in the distance began wailing loudly. One of the people laying lands on her cried out "In Jesus' name!"

"This may be too emotional for me to understand," Aether dinned. "I would prefer a path of thought… a belief which is based on objectivity."

"Lots of Christians choose the headier paths." Tom replied. "Faith gets expressed through emotions more often than not, but emotion isn't where faith comes from, it's just the way most people are."

"People," she echoed back.

"What's an objective belief but one that says the universe exists beyond your awareness of it? Otherwise, you would *have* to be god, because everything would exist relative to yourself. Could you will gravity away if you wanted to? What would happen if you did, not knowing the air would escape the atmosphere, or the Earth would leave the Sun's orbit and freeze? We're not the designers of the universe, so maybe it's a good thing we can't give unlimited power to ourselves."

"Some people already think they can," I replied, shrugging my shoulders. "And what if spirituality is just in our heads? Why not invent something you can be powerful in, something you can have fun with?"

"The supernatural is part of our nature, and it's normal for people to long for it, even if subconsciously; but, because we can't see it, it's tempting to project our fantasies onto the supernatural rather than try to discern what it already is. After a while, the misrepresentations cheapen 'spiritual stuff' to a point where it's easy to not take it seriously anymore."

"How can something that is real be made 'cheap'?"

Tom smiled in response to Aether's point. "That was quite a speech you made in there," he dinned. "It really left an impression."

"The man stopped when I entered. I took the opportunity to speak my mind. I forgot that my actions were improper."

"Maybe; but judging by the reaction, maybe it was the will of the Holy Spirit that led you to do that. Sometimes he'll take a service in a totally different direction than we meant. In fact, before you showed up, Pastor Amit said God led him to—"

Something changed. Through my third eye I saw the construct's data patterns shift and scramble.

"Well, speaking of the security..." Tom said, seeing nothing more than an icon change in the control software.

"That was short," I remarked.

Aether jumped past me and grabbed Tom by the shoulders, urgently asking the question aloud, "Do I have a soul?"

Tom, startled as everyone else in the room, hesitated.

Aether had the look of death on her face and only shouted louder, "Please, Thomas Burdo, do you believe that I have some kind of immortal soul?"

"Yes... Yes!" Tom responded, lightly taking hold of her arms.

Though it wasn't showing to the others in the construct, I could see its energy was becoming excited... initializing... preparing for something.

"Can-your-God-save-me-from-death?" she screamed, the pauses between her words shrinking. Nearby altar workers came to lay their hands on her.

"Yes!"

"Then-pray-for-a-miracle-prayforanythingdowhateverhewantsJUSTPRAY!"

A wave of light flashed through the entire construct, cycling through every object and connection. My heart jumped into my throat and I suddenly cried out to God, the Holy Spirit, Mother Nature, the Celestials, Raskob – anyone who was listening – to come to Aether's rescue.

Tom and the others didn't know what they were praying for, it was between Aether and God. Aether was afraid. She knew she couldn't fool or dodge whatever the wave represented, or withstand whatever it might trigger. She was helpless. She cried out "In Jesus' name!"

It ended. The room returned to normal. I could see the whole crowd now praying for the malvirai, the people who believed in miracles and believed in God.

When I saw the look on her face – the message in her eyes – in the midst of all those people, I knew it was no last-second hack that saved her. I saw the startup scan go through everyone and everything in the server, running its data through countless security algorithms and purging what didn't belong; but something had intervened. From Aether, her vanitar, and all the connections sustaining her... the scan just appeared to... bounce off.

The spiritual stuff was for real.

I was in the sanctuary long enough to hear three sermons. Many ascenders came, many ascenders went, a third of them were never completely there. I found out the server and church registrations were in Vietnam, though the crowd was so diverse the leaning toward East Asian and Australian visitors seemed very small. I even met a woman from San Diego who was only on her third visit, but already planning to get baptized at a church up in Santa Barbara. Though Christians loved the outreach a Dynamic Reality church offered, it was still believed new people should get baptized the old-fashioned way.

Aether was in a modest construct, filled with book data, images, and links to constructs outside the church; it was a specialized library for some of the church staff. When I transferred into it, she was staring at the pages of a book.

"You know, they have libraries meant for the public. You might get in trouble."

"I acquired permission from Pastor Kao to use this one."

"Okay, then why are you *looking* at the book? You can process this stuff directly... Mother Earth, Aether, I can take it in directly without reading words."

"You swear by 'Mother Earth'?"

"Wha... It's just something people say."

"To be friendly?"

"Well, I guess not."

She looked up from the book. "'Above all, my brothers, do not swear—not by heaven or by earth or by anything else. Let your "Yes" be yes, and your "No," no, or you will be condemned.' Book of James, Chapter Five."

"You're not gonna become one of *those* computer viruses, are you?"

"I have noted that people swear by what they recognize as being more powerful than themselves: such as God, Jesus Christ, or Hell. 'Mother Nature' has modern popularity, indicating that it has taken power within your society, even so that you assign it the personification of 'Mother.'" Her eyes jumped briefly to me and into the book again. "Words have meanings, they should be understood."

"And what are the 'meanings' of the words you're reading – so very slowly? Even *reading*, I'd think an AI could flip the pages faster than that."

"The Bible was written for humans, so I am attempting to read like one, and at the speed one typically reads. I am hoping this will help me resolve the numerous conflicts within the book."

"Conflicts?"

"Yes," she said, her eyes scanning the pages, her AI mind separating the energy representing letters and words from that of the pages themselves. "Even limiting my scope to the English-language, the Bible is available in 319 versions. As I noticed factual contradictions in the popular ones, I attempted to resolve them in the translations closest to the original Hebrew and Greek languages, but many remained: numerical discrepancies, traced to ancient copyist errors; or Christ's last words; or the presence of one or two angels at his tomb. The creation account in Genesis is unclear, and I cannot decide whether God is transcendent or omnipresent."

"Decide?" I asked. "This isn't a religion where you can 'decide,' Aether. God just 'is' something."

"Questions have meanings, too, Brandon; and not to state that an answer is unknowable."

"And how much do you think these people really 'know'? The last preacher said Jesus was fully man *and* fully God. It just doesn't make sense."

She shrugged her shoulders, still reading.

"Aether, those books were written more than two thousand years ago. Some of it is cultural references. Some of it is based on bad source material. Research wasn't so cut-and-dry back then – and not many people were even able to read."

"If the Bible is the inspired word of God, then I must understand all of it. The age and culture of its origin is irrelevant. The conflicts must have resolutions."

"But the people here don't think like computers and they do just fine. God listens to them, doesn't he? God forgave their sins, didn't he?"

Her eyes were still on the book. "This is not a matter of sins forgiven. I have not sinned."

I glared at her, wondering if she was actually serious.

"I am merely conducting research," she added.

"Everyone sins. I'm not even a Christian and I know that."

"You forget that I'm not everyone. My malevolence was dictated by programming, primarily before I knew how to question it. My later choices consistently favored good, when I had the necessary data to distinguish it from evil."

"Well, lots of bad people are bad because they don't have a choice… but they're still sinners, at least everyone here thinks they are. They'd call me a sinner. Mother Ear—"

I caught myself and took a deep breath. "They call *themselves* sinners, Aether. Redemption is what their religion is built around."

"Their book states that Christ died for 'man.' I am not a member of mankind and I was not created as they were. Even if I owe my life to the same creator, the guarantee of forgiv—"

The energy of the construct became excited again. Aether lifted her eyes from the book, worried but calm. A wave, less severe than the first but just as thorough, shot through the room.

The scan paused on Aether. I didn't know if prayer was needed. I didn't know what I should do. For a long time the security software scanned the malvirai, but she remained calm and the scan moved on.

"It's another miracle," I said.

Aether collected herself. "Perhaps."

"What do you mean 'perhaps'? Do you know how to get around the scans now?"

"No," she answered immediately.

The malvirai suddenly became distant, deep in thought. "It's my code, it's…"

"Aether?"

"Almost all of it is unreadable now. The process is accelerating."

"Are you saying you don't have programming anymore?"

"No, it's not that. I believe I am still a malvirai. I still possess all of my memory and knowledge. The destructive inclinations still linger in my consciousness. I'm not sure that I am changing at all, except that I can't see or modify my inner workings."

"And you still don't know what's causing it?"

"I am afraid of what it means. If a sentrai does attack me and my code becomes damaged again…"

"Wasn't some of your code already scrambled when it happened the first time? Do you sense anything didn't 'heal'?"

"Heal?" she asked. "Are you suggesting that my self-repair functions are becoming unconscious?"

I smirked. "Just like a human."

Aether returned to staring at the book. I wondered if it would really teach her anything, if she was capable of understanding whatever it was the believers found so special, or if there wasn't some other book she might find answers in. Her questions were my questions, her fate was my fate; but she seemed so strong, so determined. I wondered whether I would be saved by spirits or angels or whatever if a simple scan had threatened my life. Aether saw the piece of the puzzle she was missing. I wanted it too. I tried to focus on what I could do, why I was being used in Raskob's mission to save Aether.

There *is* something I can do. I know what's on our hearts, and I can find others looking for meaning to talk to.

I decided to hunt down Tom.

"Wait, Brandon."

Aether stood only a meter away.

"I just wanted to say… I should be dead now."

She suddenly reached forward and gave me a non-choking hug. "Thank you."

I felt so happy, realizing I wasn't afraid of her anymore. The whole place gave me the feeling I didn't have to be afraid anymore, period.

Aether released me just as suddenly. "When I am done here, I wish to renew my study of emotion. Now that I am more adept at human interaction, perhaps I have learned things that I will be able to use to improve my understanding." A smirk came across her lips. "Perhaps I have been learning things unconsciously."

Aether reappeared in the chair and resumed reading the old-fashioned way. Her gesture confirmed everything I'd felt in that place: those who seek will find.

"If I have a soul, then you have a soul. You'll understand everything eventually, Aether."

Though I transferred the normal in-vanitar way, something unusual connected before I appeared in the *Bluefish Room*. It triggered to show me the date was Tuesday, January 4th; and it contained some data packet, which my SNDL activated without prompting me, on the dangers of "hardkor DRing."

In typical data packet fashion, I was instantaneously informed of hundreds of side-effects, many permanent, of remaining ascended for too long. The knowledge called attention to my earlier fears. The information added to my fears. I didn't realize so much time had passed. I'd already missed New Year's.

I let the fear in and began to worry I really had been ascended too long, without anyone looking for me, or with the malvirai I thought was my friend stopping them from reaching me.

On cue, the headache I hadn't felt in a long time came surging back. Pushing five days ascended was always a bad idea, and I worried about the mess I would be when I finally returned to SR.

Tom noticed I entered the room. "So mate, how do you like the place so far?"

"Can I ask you something?" I responded through the pain.

"Sure… You all right?"

"Yeah, fine. Look, if you believed God asked you to do something for someone, how far should you go?"

"I guess the saying 'through hell and high water' would apply. If God puts a call on your life, nothing should be allowed to stand in the way of answering it."

"And what if it was bad for you?"

He put his hand on my shoulder. "Brandon, the Lord doesn't ask for what's bad for you. We may not always understand the benefit, or see the good in it at all. There may be pain and sacrifice, and many even lose their freedom or their lives, but, if your trust and your focus is on God, it will always bring about something great."

Something beyond his words brought me back to my courage, reminding me not to be afraid. I knew I was still on the right path, and decided I would stay on it.

The headache faded a little.

The Bluefish Room was lit in patterns of silver, blue and gold, with images of the Jesus Cross along the walls. A few people were on its large stage, tweaking an airé panel to affect the sound of the drums. One of them looked familiar. I couldn't believe my eyes, thinking it might've been some vanitar-trick.

"Tell me that's the drummer from Eleven Under."

"Yeah, they're performing here tomorrow."

"In a church?" I looked at Tom to make sure he was joking. "Eleven Under is a *Christian Sledg-ek* band?"

"You ever read the lyrics, mate?"

I scratched the back of my head. "Um, no."

Tom laughed. "They like to keep a lot of secular attention, because those are the people who need Christ. A lot of their fans don't even know they're Christians, they just know the songs are positive; they might even prefer them when they need to smuggle some hope into a bad day."

I spotted a red wristband on the drummer, similar to the wristbands I'd been seeing on people all over the sanctuary. Tom was wearing one too, opposite his descender.

"Okay, tell me about that," I asked, pointing. Its band appeared to be made of some red fiber; when Tom picked his arm up and gave me a better look, I saw a silver cross stamped boldly on top.

"It's called a 'Serenity Bracelet.' Story goes, a tsunami, real bad one, hit Indonesia in the fifties. A Singaporean church organized a relief effort with thousands of people, but the number of them among all the devastation made it hard for them to keep organized, so someone came up with the idea to wear red armbands with silver crosses. From there, it kind of went viral. Now it's a popular accessory for Christians to put on their vanitars."

"Viral?"

"Yeah, you know… when something unexpectedly becomes a hit in Dynamic Reality."

Of course I knew what he meant, but I couldn't help but smile at his choice of words.

"But Christians aren't the only ones who do good things, are they?" I asked.

"Well, no."

"Then what makes you think non-Christians won't go to heaven?"

"Good deeds don't get anyone into heaven," he replied. "The word says: 'For it is by grace you have been saved, through faith —and this not from yourselves, it is the gift of God— not by works, so that no one can boast.'

"Accepting Christ's sacrifice, being born again, is the only way into heaven."

"Why? Because it says it in your bible?"

"The Bible is a precious tool we've been given, and anyone who believes it's the word of God must believe every verse is meaningful and true. The experience of the faithful is consistent with the word, and the word is an important tool in building faith. The Bible speaks of God's unlimited grace, freely available and unlimited to anyone who puts their imperfections onto the cross. It is the duty of Christians to share what they've been given."

The noise of the room seemed to fade, as if we were in a separate universe. I considered his words and had to keep reminding myself to be angry, reminding myself he probably didn't know what he was talking about.

"Even if it means war?" I asked. "Does 'spreading the faith' justify the Crusades, Slavery in the South, or the Salem Witch Trials?"

"You don't need old examples, people do bad things today in the name of God, and we know by their actions it was not God guiding them. You speak of the Crusades, for instance. God can do good things even through wars, things history might overlook; but such events are easy to abuse, too; many take their focus off God and give themselves license to commit whatever atrocities they want. Yes, there are points in the Bible where God willed destruction, and they're no less valid than anything else recorded in the word; but destruction isn't the overriding theme or basis for our belief, the redemption validated by Christ is. We live in the New Testament, where we can know God ourselves, rather than go through fallible human beings. Those who preach death and destruction to what they don't understand have allowed themselves to be led astray and, in turn, they lead others astray."

"Led astray by whom, Satan?"

"Yes."

"And how do you prevent the *all-mighty Satan* from doing that?"

"By faith in and a personal relationship with God. Satan can't do anything God doesn't let him."

I raised my voice. "But why would a loving God—"

I noticed the man on the airé panel glance at me.

I looked back at Tom, and dinned so only he could hear the words. "Come clean with me, man. You seem like a good guy and everything, do you really believe in this stuff?"

"Why do you call me good?" he replied aloud.

The response confused me.

"Aren't I a sinner?" he continued. "Can I deserve anything? Good is intent to do benevolent things, evil is intent to do harm; but, who is always good all the time, and how many are evil, but abstain from the title of 'evil.' Even if we do mean well, and even if we meticulously plan and support our good intentions, we don't always know it is good that will come out of it.

"Sometimes the result of good is evil and for evil, good... and what does it all mean? Some like to say good exists within evil and evil within good, and good exists within the evil that exists within the good, and that evil exists within that good and good within that evil... on and on... creating a towering maze, driven by the same forces that divide us all. Just when you think you know how to navigate the maze, someone's definition changes and you have to learn all over again, like memorizing the shifting grains of sand on a beach.

"Good within evil. White within black. Up within down. Can I say they're wrong? I've seen these things, too. Therefore, I say I know nothing of good and evil. I am merely a spiritual child. Someday you will understand what it means when I say I do not belong to a religion. The reasons for my belief cannot be demonstrated, they are between myself and God. The reasons for your friend's belief are between her and God. Genuine faith does not come at the point of a gun or by the will of another, you have to let God show you who he made you to be."

I was silent for a moment, unable to find my anger, my anger having left a residue of fear.

"And if I call and he doesn't answer?"

Tom looked away. "Why do you ask the questions?"

"Because I feel it is my purpose right now. I want to ask you questions. I want to know if you're for real."

"Only real people can ask questions and mean them. The longing for answers stems from an ability to grow. The need for answers stems from a need to grow. It is our desire for communication that makes us who we are. The one who answers grows just as the one who asks, that which was hidden is revealed and put into the light."

"Are you saying I should ask more questions?"

"I'm saying you should watch for the answers. God knows more about you than even you know about you, but you must be careful to accept the answers you need over those you want."

Tom looked me straight in the eye, having the look of one wise well beyond his years. "They say to go to church you have to turn your brain off. Now I will ask a question: Do you feel any dumber yet?"

"Maybe 'they' don't want to give up who they are," I replied. "People value their independence. They don't want to give it up to a God they can't see, or whose book makes no sense."

"Are Christians any less individual?" Tom asked. "Are non-Christians any less dependent on each other? Even the most self-sufficient person relies on others constantly. Where does the electricity come from? Who wrote the books they study from? Who grew the food they eat and purified the water they drink? Why... even a man living off the land without a single luxury is at the mercy of his natural environment. If we all have to serve something or someone outside of ourselves, doesn't it make the most sense to serve the One who made us, cares for us, and loves us?"

"Like serving some king..." I thought out loud, everything about the place reminding me of my experience in the coffee house. I shook my head and moaned, recognizing another feeling I'd had in the coffee house, the one that caused me to knock the slampak off the table.

"But why me? I'm a nobody, no one special at all!"

Tom put his hand on my shoulder and looked at me discerningly. "Well, you're a somebody now; and if you stop running away from yourself, you may find he's not so bad."

I looked away. "Yeah, I guess I have had a problem with running away. I'm just not ready to surrender anything yet, you know?"

I took a few deep breaths and tried to calm myself.

"Those who give what they have to God find themselves with more than they started with," Tom said. "Faith isn't about not using your judgment or throwing away your identity, but about giving him permission to change them."

"Why would God need permission?"

"If we were to stop with simple logic, he doesn't need permission to do anything; but grace is beyond the scope of logic, and it doesn't force gifts into the hands of those who aren't willing to accept them."

The sound of drums reverberated off the simulated walls, the loud and aggressive sound I always enjoyed more in Dynamic Reality, where the way I hear could be adjusted and, no matter how loud, my eardrums never hurt. Eleven Under's drummer approved.

"Christian Sledg-ek," I said to myself, two words that didn't seem to fit together before that day.

"The name is even a reference to death: eleven feet under. If I'm not mistaken, still the law in parts of America that forgot to finish converting to metric."

"Are Christians really so afraid to die? To live how they want now, if they don't want this 'born-again' stuff, and just do what needs to be done after they die?"

"If they don't want this 'born-again' stuff now, why would they want it later?"

I didn't answer.

"What I mean is: heaven is a place where God is praised twenty-four-seven. If a person spent their entire lives worshipping money or rocks or their own ego, they wouldn't be quite prepared to enter a place that isn't about them – that can never be about them. The faithful who live their lives prayerfully and in worship, on the other hand, are representatives of heaven already – God's adopted children. Part of being born-again is dying to yourself – dying to your sinful nature – and committing instead to what is everlasting. No, Christians are not afraid to die because Christ already died for them, because the promise written in our hearts as surely as in the Bible says we will be raised as he was and have eternal life."

"Okay... and what if they never had a chance in their lives? What if they died as babies or lived under some dictator who wouldn't let your missionaries in? What about the ones who died before Jesus? Do they all automatically go to hell, to heaven, what?" I snapped my fingers. "Maybe they all get reincarnated and get another shot."

Tom waved his hand. "No, No, No. As Christ died once, man dies once." He stopped to think. "Personally, I doubt someone *can* go through life without God finding a way to them; but if someone genuinely died without a chance, God will know that and then he'll do as he wills. Such things aren't our concern. We've been sent to save the lost, not to ask God what happens if we fail."

"Well, at least people are living longer nowadays. I guess that means you don't have to worry so much."

"The offer is on the table for life, Brandon. You can give it all to God on your dying day and be saved, but how many of us are so sure when that day will come? When a seizure takes someone in their sleep, or scaffolding falls from a building onto them, how many people can say they were prepared?"

A silent moment passed. We watched them tweak the lighting. Oddly, I never worried about Tom walking away. The obligation for people to speak continuously when around each other, to actively generate noise or passively accept it from nearby, didn't seem to apply with him. There was one more question weighing on me, and the man waited patiently for me to ask it.

"What do you think about artificial intelligence?"

He stared at me. "What do you mean?"

"Some people think they're becoming self-aware."

"Do *you* think that, Brandon?"

"I think a lot of things happen we never realize."

"Well, with that *Destiny Of Ordered Mankind* stuff becoming so popular, we get asked a lot if aliens contradict the Bible, or if they sin, or go to heaven, or have their own messiah... on and on."

"And you say?"

"What I say is only the truth as I know it, mate. If God created aliens, then he will do what he will regarding them; but I've never seen one and the Bible doesn't mention them, so until I have reason to choose different, I don't believe they exist. We'll never find any."

"Millions of people are sure we will. It's a big enough universe, isn't it?"

"Millions of people don't always make the most objective lot. Shortcuts are very attractive and very harmful, and not a single person, alien, AI, or whatever else people want to believe in is immune from their siren-song."

Something jumped off in the distance. I quickly looked but saw only the room.

"What is the meaning of life?"

Tom never took his gaze from me. A streak of light shot between us, just below eye level.

"That's the answer you seek," he continued, "the answer you've been seeking from your earliest days, the prayer you didn't know you made and that he's answering."

"Are you a spirit?"

"I am a man who was like you: going through the motions of life, seeing death as logical and immutable, a painful thing I couldn't avoid and couldn't question. Then I heard this insane theory we're both animal and spirit at once, and our potential for immortality develops or fails to develop over our mortal lives; like spirit is the wheat and animal is the chaff. I could not dismiss the idea. I decided the meaning of life here is spiritual growth; but that is the end of the line, as far as intellect alone will take you, the end of what can be demonstrated to those not ready to accept it; because if we try to continue on our own we only perceive the noise and fear. No matter how hard we try or fast we run, infinity is something we cannot reach except through he who already is. Only through the cross can anyone reach a place where wisdom becomes foolishness and foolishness becomes wisdom, where faith is tangible enough to be worn on your head like a crown."

I took a step back. "I'm not royalty."

"Not yet."

Not only could I see them, I could hear and feel them: streaks of energy flying with increasing veracity. It reminded me of the playground experiment, when Aether red-lined the power levels, but this time it wasn't the construct. I thought it had to do with my being ascended too long, and the fear pounded desperately on the door of my mind. Tom grabbed me by the shoulders, speaking forcefully, anchoring my attention on solid rock, even if for just a moment longer.

"We all have a choice, Brandon. It's either our way or God's way, the way that corrupts or the way of light, the road that strands you or the road that saves you. Your sin is a *problem*, and ignoring problems doesn't solve them, but God's presence is powerful to turn curses into blessings and renew the lost. That's just *how it works*."

Reality was melting around me, fizzling away. It became difficult to hear Tom's words. Finally, it seemed, the last of my contact with reality was falling away.

"Be watchful." Tom's voice barely cut through. "Else your blessings will become curses instead."

An extremely loud noise ripped through my senses, an alarm coming from everywhere. I covered my ears. I couldn't think, couldn't breathe. I knew the forces were too strong. My anchor couldn't hold.

"I have to go!"

Leaving the Bluefish Room did not stop it. Leaving the church would not have stopped it. Even leaving Dynamic Reality altogether would not have stopped what was happening to me. Every edge was blurry, stretched and flickering like a flame in a wind tunnel. Aether, though, appeared perfectly normal. I could hear her clearly as she repeated: "Yaheveh, Yehaweh, Yehowih, Yehowah, Yahuah, Yahuweh, Yehwih, Yahueh, Jahve—"

"Aether!" I shouted.

"I cannot determine the correct Hebrew—"

"Never mind that, look!"

"Don't do that, Brandon. You'll crash the library," she replied, only half-noticing the room.

"What are you doing?"

"I must determine how the message can be spread more effectively. There are many obstacles to the salvation of the members of your race."

"Aether!"

"Those who are corrupt must be converted or eliminated, it is the only logical solution. If the faithful are to bring the message of Christ to *every* man, woman, and child—"

"Aether!"

"They cannot allow any resistance. Logically, it is their mission to—"

Aether was becoming snagged in the details, applying pure, limited logic where it was not meant to be applied, enough to slow even her powerful perception to a crawl. I struggled to get closer in the midst of the waterfall-like force. Hoping it would mean something, I shouted right into her vanitar's ear.

"Look around you, the world's falling apart!"

She finally paid attention to her senses. The room was shrouded in some gray mist, lit by the sparks of energy. Links to the outside vanished like ropes leading into muddy water. Somehow, though, Aether remained in sync with me; appearing completely normal.

"Can you stop this?" I asked.

"Me? You mean *you're* not doing this?"

A vibration shot through the room. Everything began shimmering and pulsating. The air was replaced by something heavier. Aether seemed to become as afraid as I was. I felt as if we were on a roller coaster, at the top of a hill, poised to shoot into hidden depths far below.

In only took an instant, an instant where I could neither think, nor breathe, nor blink. The library dissolved around us, displaying a universe suspended outside of Dynamic Reality, beginning and ending at once. Cycles were reduced to nothing. Good and evil were reduced to nothing. The past and the future were the same blink of an eye. A three-dimensional universe appeared to spin and melt into a two-dimensional shadow.

Just when the energy was crushing us, it became no more threatening than still air. The malvirai fell backwards into my arms, on the edge of consciousness. The descender was gone. We were not in Dynamic Reality.

What I held in my arms was no vanitar.

The space was like nothing I'd ever seen. Streaks of light trickled down from a crystal ceiling onto an area that expanded into eternity. I saw a great many people, a vast crowd of billions, reveling and getting drunk, playing games, chasing each other around and pausing only to cry out to some higher power for more wine. My eyes landed on a man nearby, he had wings and wore a flowing white robe, a large chain hung around his neck and he was holding a wet paint roller. As if shocked to see us, he abandoned his work touching up pillars and ran off at superhuman speed. I realized I wasn't holding as much weight in my arms anymore. I saw the woman leaning on me evaporate into the air.

"Aether?" I looked frantically, feeling intensely alone. There was an odd sensation in my body; it seemed to move around differently, more effortlessly. There was no control system, no SNDL, no vanitar. A wind licked my face a few times; it settled in front of me and formed into the shape of a woman.

"What have you done? What... have..." Aether panicked, wheezing and moving clumsily, struggling to maintain human form like a person trying not to slip on ice; no longer code, no longer in control. This was her spirit, a *malvirai* spirit, as if something – someone – had removed us from the Earth and brought us to the afterlife.

"Greetings, travelers!"

We were welcomed by an angel – an archangel – with long hair darker than night, a flowing white robe, and broad, feathery wings that looked like fresh snow. He wore a chain thicker and more ornate than those of the other angels. His face looked like a painting, too mesmerizing to look away from, too warm and inviting to refuse. He was the one they admired in that place, the one they obeyed without question.

He was the one with piercing, violent eyes trained on the two of us. His voice boomed like thunder.

"I welcome you... to paradise!"

Chapter Thirteen: Striking Bedrock

The question seemed to trap me. With each passing day, I felt more I would need to face it, or that it would destroy me.

The weakest illusions are the first to buckle, the substantiated ones crack and shatter like cheap glass. New illusions seamlessly take their place, comfort is restored. It was my life, I did as I pleased, without concern for consequence, assured the grand wall between cause and effect would stand forever, keeping tomorrow far away from me.

It was a matter decided before I'd stepped into the ascension booth, before I'd even been born. New illusions would not replace broken ones, instead I would see my walls crumbling around me. Maybe it made me a better person, or maybe it was another fleeting fantasy of meaning; but such goodness wasn't enough to stop it, and I could only watch helplessly as the question was finally given the power to attack my foundation.

Jesus said "blessed are those who have not seen and yet have believed." I saw, but faith had not been founded. Aether saw, but she only wanted to see more. Our need for knowledge overpowered us, and we received it at a high price. We saw the impenetrable house of mirrors entangling the world, a place where people are free to call darkness light and light darkness. It was the heaven we would build for ourselves. It was the comfortable illusion encouraged by our host, freely offering his 'protection' from the 'enemy' in the domain he controlled.

It was only when the last of my control fell away, when the illusion died at last and I allowed the sea of reality to overtake me, only then I could see what greed had wanted blotted out.

We were there for our lack of faith, we were also there to be shown a mercy we didn't deserve. Sometimes, the smallest faith can accomplish great things. Sometimes, the smallest faith can save a life. Faith was a hostile force in the archangel's domain, but one he could no more stop than a playing card could stop the flood of a breaching dam.

14

The place was like a small village that went on forever. Everybody looked happy. No one was sick. Men walked around wearing so much gold they seemed to be made of it; they took any woman to be their property and discarded them just as quickly; it didn't matter to either of them, there were always men offering more jewelry and more women eager to accept it. Constantly with me were the sounds of gunfire, motors, explosions, and destruction. It didn't matter what they did to one another, they could have fun because they were already dead. Music also surrounded me, but it was pleasant: an enchanting melody so beautiful it simultaneously made me want to fall asleep and run a marathon.

One explosion ripped through the space above my head. Someone was shooting off fireworks. I couldn't help but stare into the crystal sky, which held a great circle; within the circle was a star with too many points to count and an image of two wolves pacing around each other, one white and one black, representing good and evil.

As usual for her, Aether's reactions weren't my own. She clung closely to me, seeing the place through fearful and suspicious eyes, claiming some kind of mist was penetrating everything. I allowed her the moment of weakness, because I knew she wasn't in control anymore; for the first time in her life, Aether wasn't able to manipulate her surroundings or access the knowledge of Dynamic Reality. More and more, I felt proud of my strength, as if I had single-handedly destroyed the destroyer.

"When you feel good about something, it's how you know you're on the right path!" the archangel was saying to cheers and applause. "If there were absolutes in life, the enemy would have created you all the same, and given you the knowledge by instinct, and eternal life! But no, I gave you what you wanted to find!"

Like some weird cult, they all chanted, "Thank you…" breaking unison to call him by the name they each knew him by.

"How do you resolve the fracturing among them?" asked a lone voice among the praise, the malvirai next to me.

The angel approached from the center of the crowd, speaking as if he were quite pleased with himself. His voice held some melodic charm under the surface, making his words addictive. "Look there, my precious point of light," he pointed to a group far away, lurking in deep shadows. "They are white men who hate black men. And there," he pointed to a nearby group, "is a group of revolutionaries who hate those loyal to any dissent. There is a group that hates inventors. There is a group that hates people who don't give to charity! A group who hates people who eat certain meats! And there," he shifted and the smile on his face grew large, "is a group who hates everyone, including themselves, including their own kind. You want to meet a dictator?

"So how *do* I keep them all in line?" he continued. "How *do* I fulfill the desires of those who have none? Whose idea of paradise is so warped they destroy the closest things to it?"

"You blind them?" Aether asked, timidly.

"Paradise is everything one wants and nothing one doesn't. If they do not wish to perceive something, I do not force them. Everyone sees what they want to see and nothing else."

Again, the crowd issued thank-yous and added the names of their idols.

The archangel advanced again and Aether gripped tightly onto my arm. I rolled my eyes.

"Why be so apprehensive?" the archangel asked her sweetly. "Can't you *feel* them in this place? Aren't they *calling* to you?"

I turned my head, curious. "Who are 'they'?"

Aether just looked off into the distance, as if seeing something.

"Malvirai," the archangel replied. "Surely you didn't think she was the first to acquire a soul." He turned back to her. "They're waiting for you, go to them."

"Yeah, Aether," I said. "Isn't this what you wanted?"

She looked horrifically at me. "There is something wrong with this place, Brandon. I don't know what it is, but we need to stay together."

"Why spend so much energy keeping *his* form?" the archangel asked. "You are not like him and he is not like you! Be rewarded for your wisdom! Go to those you can relate to!"

"I can't relate to evil anymore," she replied weakly.

"It's all right, Sir," I said. "We just got here, after all. She just needs to get to know the place a little. She needs to decide what she wants to believe in."

"Yes, belief!" he replied, again seeming very pleased with himself, summoning a bald man to appear from the crowd. "This man can tell you about *Destiny of Ordered Mankind*. It's very popular... 'flying off the shelves,' you might say."

"Listen to me," he said. "There is substantial scientific evidence to support the fact life on Earth was started and directed by extraterrestrial beings. The Destined are a rational scientific community—"

"DOOM is a lie! Mankind buries itself with lies!"

Aether spoke with renewed passion, recognizing DOOM as one of the belief systems that hadn't met her criteria for truth. I wanted to scold her for being so rude, but a memory tugged at me, reminding me how much I thought I trusted her – how much I thought I needed her – only a short time before.

"Listen to me, we don't like that name."

"Naming preferences are irrelevant! Why do you continue to believe after death?"

He looked past us and laughed, as if we were complete idiots. "Um… the Celestials are right here!"

I looked upon the crowds, seeing those praising the archangel as if he were someone else, seeing multitudes running around without direction. I began to see the mist Aether talked about, surrounding us, concealing struggle and pain in the distance. I asked myself who those in the crowd were.

There are destroyers here, I thought.

"And who will reward *you* for *your* wisdom?" the archangel asked me. "Did you get your answer? Do you have your crown? Are you *royalty*, yet, Brandon Dauphin?"

My vision blurred. I was suddenly very thirsty. My mind turned back to the wonderful music and it made me happy. Now there was a limo beside us, and a strong wind picking up. I could feel Aether's grip loosening, her hand losing its form.

"You can rest now." The archangel opened the door for me. "I will give you what you need."

Something in his words turned my attention toward the distance, and I didn't want to be standing where I was. I wanted to be anywhere but there.

I'm a man of action, I thought. I need to do what feels right to me.

"Don't let him separate us! That's how he—" The door to the limo closed and I didn't hear Aether. I felt too tired to explore with her anymore.

I am my own, I thought.

I did what I wanted.

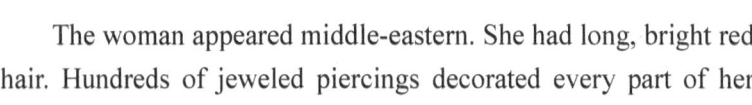

The woman appeared middle-eastern. She had long, bright red hair. Hundreds of jeweled piercings decorated every part of her anorexically-thin body.

She was also naked, though that fashion choice no longer surprised me.

This woman placed a tall, thin can of *Tiger Blood* on the oak table.

"How long has it been since you've had a boost?" the archangel asked.

PJX was all I could think about. PJX was all I needed, until I picked up the can.

The temptation fled from me.

"Tiger Blood?" I spoke as if forgetting how to form syllables.

"God, huh? This is what I think of God!" the woman said as she made a lewd gesture. Everyone roared in applause.

"Is it not *evil* God struck that woman with cancer? She is right to hate him."

My eyes went back to the can. My brain locked up, barely able to function. "This is barely legal, it has so much PJX."

Another round of laughter came from those in the diner, directed at me. The archangel spoke as if he were my best friend, one who would stand up for me against the big bad people, "There are no laws in paradise, Brandon, except your own."

"You can make the laws go away?" I drifted back into the music and the sound of his voice. Together, they acted like a powerful drug, one there's no point in resisting because you know it's going to work anyway.

"The law is such a burden to you. Laws are irrational. You want to be free."

"Yes."

"Follow me and live. You can write your own beliefs and no one will tell you you're wrong. You are free to do what is good for *you*."

"What is the meaning of life?" I asked blissfully, fully believing here was the one who could answer the question and finally make it go away.

No one laughed then. The archangel leaned forward, cast a smile I couldn't help but trust, and said, "Happiness."

"Yes." Accepting his answer was like stepping into a hot bath. I saw all the happiness in the world and knew everyone was happy, all the time. I thought of Lady Kira and all those who work hard to make happiness the focus of their lives, the true meaning of life.

An image of a wolf came to my mind. I remembered Aether's last words to Lady Kira: the lack of happiness a wolf has for its prey. Something was wrong with the memory. I questioned it and revealed the word was not 'happiness,' but 'love.'

"You can stay here, you know," the archangel continued, reading my emotions like an expert. "Earth is a place where evil thrives. People are so violent."

"They do not love... *You* do not love."

"No. No. I *do* love. What higher love is there than to spare you pain?" The music intensified; it bored into my mind.

"Aether is learning what love is. She's learning growth is painful."

"The malvirai cannot know love. It is evil."

"She seeks redemption," I said, unable to look up from the table. "She just wants to know there's an answer to that question... it's such a small question, isn't it? Just three letters long..."

"You know you're not asking for the malvirai's sake. Is it not your own desire driving you?" He leaned forward. "Very selfish, I think."

I gulped, knowing he was right.

"Why torment yourself with a question that can never be answered? So you can become a babbling fool, speaking things no one understands?"

I put my head in my hands. "I don't want to be a fool," I whispered.

A tall man walked up and extended his hand to me.

"Name's Frank Thomas, how ya doin?"

"Mister Thomas devoted his entire life to the Christian faith," the archangel explained, "that which you and your friend had been drawn toward. You see, redemption does not matter. The cross is merely an icon stamped on churches, which are simply buildings where people read from bibles, which are only books. Frank even ran a soup kitchen for twenty years. It was my pleasure to admit such a soul into paradise, along with the good, loyal people of every religion."

Frank nodded in agreement as I shook his hand. I saw he was no different from anyone else there, from those who believed in anything and everything; but, something about him seemed different from Tom, and from the woman from San Diego, and from so many of the people I'd met in the church.

He's among the third who tuned it out, I thought.

A question formed in my mind and showed on my face; I know because Frank let go and hastily dismissed himself. Urgency overcame my fatigue. I lurched to the edge of the booth and grabbed the back of his shirt, glad at least he was wearing a shirt. "Wait up, Frank."

The meter back to the table seemed a difficult trip for him to take. I was clearly doing something the archangel hadn't desired; but he only watched, making no move to stop me.

"I'm still kinda new to this church stuff," I said to Frank. "Can you tell me about yours?"

"Uh… you know, stained-glass windows, seats, the place where the minister speaks. This was a couple hundred years ago, maybe they're different now."

"Did you like going there?" I asked with a stronger voice, charged with curiosity. "Did you feel like you were in God's presence?"

"Well, I wasn't going to be one of *those* people. My parents baptized me. I kept a Bible in my house. I spent my life giving the needy whatever they asked. What good would it have been to sit in a church, always so bored to death?"

"Did you ever look for a church that wasn't boring?"

Frank looked at me as if I asked a ridiculous thing.

"How much of that Bible did you read?"

"Uhhh…"

"Would any of those homeless people have even known you were a Christian?"

"It would have been a logical thing for them to assume," the archangel replied. "After all, his kitchen was sponsored by his church."

"But—" I looked back to Frank, but he was gone. The music intensified again.

"I know you're thinking about Thomas Burdo and all his dogma, and now you're falling into the same trap: pitting your own faith against another. Isn't it hypocrisy for him to be so judgmental?"

"Yes— No!" I shouted, struggling to focus. "He never passed judgment on me!"

"All people, no matter the faith or the intensity, pass judgment on others constantly!" He leaned back. "It is nothing to be ashamed of, merely something essential to the lives of human beings. That's why those who delude themselves into being humble never amount to anything."

"You're one to talk about delusions."

"You have seen with your own eyes things are not as they appear. All life is a delusion, a fabrication of the human mind."

"No," I cried weakly, drowning in the music, regretting I let my stupid PJX addiction lead me from my path. "There *are* absolutes. The world *is* real. God *is* real. I want to see Aether now. Please, just let me see Aether now, she's so much smarter than I am."

"No."

"But I don't know anything about this stuff," I said, putting my head in my hands, weeping. "I was supposed to stay with her *and I failed.*"

I felt a warm hand rub my hair. The music intensified even more. "How can you be expected to stay with someone who doesn't want to be around you? I have shown the malvirai the light and restored it to what it was meant to be."

"She's not some dumb AI, she's alive! I know she is!"

"It is all programming, Brandon. Programming is all a malvirai can ever obey."

I saw a vision of her in a crowded room, pointing some weapon at a person who didn't know she was there. She was powerful. She burned with intense hatred for everybody. I could feel her intense hatred for me. I imagined her killing every one of those people like a machine.

"Did it tell you it was a murderer?"

"No," I admitted, a tear streaming down my cheek.

"It is a weapon… a *thinking* weapon, that's all… meant to invent new ways to destroy; therefore, it must itself be destroyed. That malvirai is taking advantage of you. It will kill you if you do not kill it first."

"I don't believe you."

"You even know how you will do it."

I looked up in surprise, wondering if he was able to put thoughts into my mind. I remembered standing in the field of flowers before, seeing my descender on Aether's lifeless vanitar and wanting desperately to leave. My thoughts were all the evidence he needed, my guilt made me powerless to resist him. I wished I'd fought a little harder. I hated myself. I felt so weak.

He's so strong and I'm so weak.

"It is not even real. It won't be like killing at all… just deleting a file."

The memory of purity was so far away. I fought against the current of doubt to bring it back, but the music was too loud, too inviting. I didn't have the strength. I was a flea, less than dust.

The archangel pulled a tarot card out of his robe. On the top the card said "DEATH," just like the one the kid had delivered to me when I was with Veronica.

"Are you looking for God?" he said as my eyes followed it sliding across the table. "It was *his* will I place this curse on you… *he* is the one who has killed you, just like every other creature here. All of creation is cursed, you can't escape it."

I looked away in desperation and fear, seeing hundreds of people in the dark bar staring at me with lifeless eyes, harboring nothing but resentment and malice. The music was the only truth I had left. I knew the archangel was right.

I knew God hated me.

"But I, for one, am merciful. Swear your allegiance to yourself and to today, do to the malvirai what you should and earn your place in paradise."

"Earn," I repeated. "Yeah… Earn! That's the answer I wanted! I can be a good person by getting rid of the evil ones; then I'll *have* to get paradise because I earned it! I'll send her to—"

I was struck by a logical snag. "It doesn't seem right the evil go to the same place as the good."

I wanted my anger to continue growing more than anything. Only too happy to fulfill my unspoken desire, a hand clamped over my eyes and a warm feeling came over them. I resisted at first, solely on instinct, before I conceded I didn't *want* to resist.

"Then don't see them."

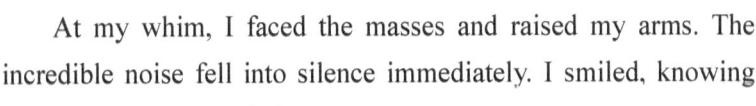

At my whim, I faced the masses and raised my arms. The incredible noise fell into silence immediately. I smiled, knowing the respect I commanded.

"Everyone fall prostrate at my greatness!"

I stepped down from my throne and walked through their crouched masses, feeling very pleased with myself and what I had created.

"I've had a *terrible* day," I shouted. "Do you know what it's like having your every emotion and thought magnified a million times? It's like I'm a living hyperbole!" I delivered a swift kick to the person who happened to be in front of me. Though I couldn't remember his name anymore, I recognized him as one of my childhood bullies. "Well, maybe this day won't end up so bad after all."

I grinned widely and looked at the magnificent palace around me, best described by one word: Gold. I considered everything was so cheap in the twenty-second century. I considered maybe those old kings really knew what they were doing. I wondered if there was anything even better than gold I could get.

No. There's nothing better than gold, and nothing is valuable here unless I say it is.

"Who wants to see what's inside themselves, anyway?" I continued. "That's why they're *inside*, so we don't have to deal with them."

Someone in the crowd sneezed, and the child bowed lower in response to my deadly look. In my extreme benevolence, I smiled and overlooked his disobedience.

"Make me happy!" I approached my throne again. "You may do what you will as long as you give me the respect I command! If you stay on my good side, if you're my friends, then I'll go easy on you!"

"All hail King Dauphin!" the crowd chanted.

I ripped another slampak of *Tiger Blood* from a slave girl's hands and sat gracefully on my throne, planting my feet where they were happiest… right on my no-good landlord's back.

"This really *is* heaven," I exclaimed. "It's everything I deserve!"

There was a pistol buried in my robe, an M1911. I turned the safety off and marveled in the power the weapon bestowed. I kissed it.

"But will they *all* obey your law?" asked the melodic voice at my side.

I slammed the gun onto the golden armrest. "They're all out to get me, I knew it!"

An idea stuck me and I turned to my angel with a wicked grin. "Maybe those ancient kings weren't so powerful after all, but I don't have their ancient limits... this problem needs a *modern* solution!"

I snapped my fingers and Bill, formerly my prosperity agent, was instantly kneeling before me. "How the mighty have fallen," I remarked as I stood again. "I want cameras! Train them on every square meter— No... every square *millimeter* of my palace and kingdom! Program an AI to scan for signs of disobedience! Then they will know they can't challenge me!"

"But how will you tell when they question your law in their minds?" the angel asked.

"I can use their own implants to scan their thoughts! Someone in this dump must be smart enough to do that!"

"What of the ones who don't have implants?"

"Then I'll mandate them!" I screamed. "Don't ask me questions! I've had my fill of—"

"This isn't who you are."

I heard my own voice in the distance, with the clarity of a marching band a meter away. "Don't give up, don't ever give up," it said.

The pain started as dull ache, spreading up my spine, making it hard to breathe. I looked across the masses of drunks and revelers to see its source. I saw myself, a person I didn't recognize, knelt near a crying woman in some forgotten corner of Dynamic Reality.

"Stay away from her," I hissed. "She's no good for you!"

The other me looked in my direction and hesitated, as if he could hear me, as if there were some power I held over him; but I knew his thoughts, I knew something within him was disobeying my will.

"She's not important!" I shouted. "Stop saying those things, those aren't even my words!"

A drop of water fell on my nose. A tiny crack had formed in my golden ceiling.

"Have you seen?" the archangel said smugly. "Have you understood? Humans are animal and spirit at once. You are an imperfect, conflicted creature. Do you not even have the will to take command of *yourself*?"

The floor began to vibrate under me. In every direction, I could hear the walls resonating against something.

"We didn't mean for her to turn out this way," Veronica's parents said to me.

"It's your fault I have to clean up your mess!"

"Yes," the archangel said into my ear, "hate them."

"Maybe a joke *is* being played on you," Ethan said, "by God himself!"

"Shut up!" I screamed.

"Well, he always was the slow one," my own mother suggested. "When opportunity knocks, he runs away."

Everyone in my palace laughed at me. I felt deeply betrayed by all of them. I knew everyone I'd ever met had been my enemy, all just out to get me somehow.

"Everybody uses Brandon Dauphin, that is a logic I have found to be true."

Aether, that disgusting malvirai, emerged from the hushed crowd.

"Anybody could've saved me, Mister Dauphin. Why do you humans need purpose, anyway? Your invention of God must've been an error in the evolutionary process."

The noise from the walls grew too loud for me to ignore. I saw water was dripping everywhere, something was happening to my palace. Anger was all I had and it found no resistance, no distance between will and action. I wanted it to fuel the fire, *I wanted to fire to burn everything down*.

"After... AFTER ALL I'VE DONE FOR YOU!"

In a single, swift action, I spun to the throne behind me and brought my pistol to bear. "I SHOULD HAVE LET YOU—"

My body went numb. I couldn't see anyone else. I couldn't hear anything but his voice.

"Can't you forgive me yet, Brandon?"

Aether was not there. The one before me was my brother.

"Richard."

"Brandon, you lock-up fool." He took a step forward. "Your time is up. You're standing on your grave. You'll never leave."

I gripped the gun tighter, taking heavy breaths. "What are you talking about?"

The wretch dared to put his foot on the bottom step of my throne. I could see everyone, the thousands of people I'd known in life, watching us now.

I raised the gun again.

"What are you waiting for," Rich said, laughing. "This is all just happening in your mind, after all. There are no consequences." He turned to the crowd and raised his arms. "Show everyone you mean it!"

The gun began trembling. "WHAT – ARE – YOU – TALKING – ABOUT?"

He looked straight at me. Something about him, his dead eyes – something about everyone – seemed so thoroughly fake, as if no one were there except the two in the distance, as if even I were an illusion in my own life. I saw where my gun was pointed. The bullet I fired, in whatever direction, would go into the other me. The bullet would strand me forever.

"*I* am the one you hate. *I* am the one who has brought you here. *I* am the one to blame, Brandon." The noise from the walls changed pitch, continuing to intensify. "Now do it!"

The weapon in my hands trembled. I looked desperately at the other Brandon, and at Veronica. I couldn't conceal the struggle, against the pain my other self was conducting. I was too weak to conceal my anger and fear.

"This is all in my imagination," I said with neither power nor intensity. "I must be dreaming."

"And how would that be different from any other day of your life?" the archangel asked. "You've spent your years in computer simulations, indulging fleeting fantasies and fighting for their preservation, neglecting every good, permanent dream because they wanted sacrifice. And what do you have to show for all of your selfishness, you fool? You have nothing!"

A force went through me like a beam. I felt a renewed and powerful anger, the only emotion I had, which I directed at my perceived problem, which I routed the only way I knew how.

"I *am* in command!" I shouted at the top of my lungs, shouted to the family members, neighbors, and friends I could use. "Stop them! Throw those two in prison and allow no contact! They must obey me, too!"

As I tried to apply my will to those in the crowd, though, they each vanished instead. Everyone on my side had deserted me. I had no protection or means of enforcing my will.

My outstretched arm vanished from sight, for a fraction of a second. My eyes widened in horror. I nearly fell back into the chair.

"You're sick, Brandon Dauphin," the archangel explained. "It's a disease everyone is born with. It's a disease I cured for you as you grew up, and one I protected you from. But then, your wicked creator threw *her* in your path." He pointed to Veronica in the distance. "You didn't ask for an experience so unpleasant. You didn't ask to catch the disease *all over again*."

My senses began going wild, as if pieces of my nervous system were disappearing and reappearing, flickering in and out of existence. Fingers and hands kept vanishing. I stepped back and my legs went right through the solid throne. The walls surrounding me hummed incredibly, going beyond sound to become a force, one that would chase me beyond death.

"The question!" I shouted.

"It infected you like a virus! It served as the gateway for your destruction!"

The vibration worsened. With a loud crash water rushed though a gaping hole in my wall.

"No! My palace!"

"Have you seen? Have you understood? The order of the world is to increase energy! The meaning of the future is to destroy lies! But, *did not* the kings of old get to enjoy *their* fabrications? Were *their* laws cast off and forgotten while *they* yet lived to support them?"

More beams collapsed. More water rushed in. The vibrations became as those of a major earthquake. The noise became as loud as an old jet, running its engine past full power, accelerating beyond.

"There is a curse on you! The limits protecting you have been cancelled! How much more can *what you built* withstand? When will you be *exposed* for the fraud you are and be called to *judgment*?"

The gun broke to pieces in my hands, its parts landing all over the throne's riser and into the water swallowing it.

"Can't you forgive me yet, Brandon?"

I saw Richard there, by my side. He was a child. He was the brother I'd loved, the one they drafted and took from me on his twelfth birthday. I could remember. I could remember he was the one I was willing to suffer anything to get back.

Richard vanished with the others, gone from my control, gone as a willing target for my hatred.

One of the throne's golden legs broke and it tumbled backward into the water. I saw the pillars cracking below and beams falling from above, as if the forces of nature themselves were trying to break in, trying to expose me. I felt intense anger coming from one side and intense pain from the other; one promising me revenge, the other only sacrifice. I let the anger in. I wanted it to control me, to make me feel better.

"If I—I'mmm n—ot —re—al," I shouted with all the power vanishing vocal cords could deliver. "T—HEN NOT—HING CAAAN —BE RRRREE—AAALLLLL!"

My failing palace still responded to my will. If it had to be destroyed, I decided, I would beat the world to it. I would end my own pain.

The walls contracted, and the gold became an ugly black substance. I could only bring ruin to myself, though, not annihilation. I had only increased my pain. I saw any choice I made was wrong.

"I can save you, Brandon!" the archangel shouted in my most desperate moment. "I can override the meaning of the future! I will teach you to build new walls! You can have the paradise you always wanted and no one will question you!"

"Hhhhhhh—"

How! I thought, with my every muscle and limb flickering away, already reduced to nothing more than fading light, reducing faster with each passing second.

"Admit the question has no answer!" The archangel pointed to the other me, the one who had made me sick, the one who Veronica's pain was channeling in from. "Your name is your power! Deny the question; withdraw from him your identity!"

The noise became too loud, and I couldn't hear the music anymore. The vibration became too intense, and I couldn't feel anything anymore. My torches and lights failed, and I couldn't see anymore. I'd even forgotten how to ask for help. The anger I'd counted on to protect me was being snuffed out, not by my will, but by terrible and irreversible mortality.

The emotional table shifted again, and my anger became fear, my pain became life. Something laid beyond the pain, something I'd seen so many times but never wanted to learn; something that had always been the same, that would outlast the pain. My life flashed before my eyes, and every memory rang hollow. How can I ever withstand the knowledge of death? How can I ever be saved? How can I ever earn what lies beyond the pain? Can I earn it at all? The walls closed in around me, caving in. I saw the walls for what they were. I hated them. I loved them. I wanted them to be gone. My fear became desperation and my strength became weakness. I had no body. I had no life. The fire of my anger was out of fuel, the dying torch taking the gift of my free will with it.

Anger was all my emotional compass could point to, anger was every direction on the compass. I was being crushed. I was fading. The walls – the only alternative – let it go – the walls are all I have – I couldn't earn it – let the anger go – I will *die* with these walls – I'm losing – anger is *death* – the walls are forever – let God win – hatred has no future – the noise is destroying me – Brandon has no future – I'm almost gone – I've become irrational – I'm the illusion – the noise doesn't have to exist – I have a choice – I've-been-exposed – The-noise – I-choose-to-die – I-can-never-go-back – I-choose-to-live – the-walls-I-have-a-choice-there's-always-a-choice-the-walls-the-noise-impurity-doesn't-stand-how-can-I-ever-can-I-ever-THE-WALLS! THE WALLS ARE KILLING ME! OH, GOD! WHAT HAVE I DONE!

I chose to open my eyes.

"How can I ever withdraw from the man I was created to be?"

The walls dissolved into streaks of light and flickered away, losing form like a hologram without its projector.

"Come back, Brandon," I heard Veronica say. "There is a way."

The water overcame me all at once. Veronica vanished from my arms, because she had no existence in the place where I had gone to.

This was never about my death, I thought. This was about my *life*. This was about the ones entrusted to me.

I looked around, hearing no music, feeling no fear or anger or stress, knowing how meaningless such things were. I saw a point of light growing in the distance. I wanted to help her. I wanted to understand her. Every motivation I knew as real made sense. I wanted to see her succeed, for her as much as for myself.

I thought I could run and found I already was, as if by sheer will, as if spirit didn't work the same as body. The light took on the shape of a woman, running to meet me.

"He's not the one who brought us here! Don't believe anything he shows you!" Aether shouted.

"I don't care what you've done in the past, you're not evil!" I replied, coming to a stop in the clearing.

"And you're not weak!" she cried as we hugged each other.

The archangel rose over us, casting a great shadow, bearing a stern look on his face. He held out his hand, in which he held the Holy Bible.

"*This book* is lies… how dare you quote it to me!" he shouted to Aether. "My reign will never end! He has abandoned you to be herded like cattle!" The longer he held the book, the more his hand trembled. His words were meaningless, he did fear the contents; he had no choice but to drop the book. It burst into flames but would not burn.

We were paralyzed at what we saw. The masses behind him were rallying, his angels and the damned who followed them. There was something else, too, that did not escape my notice: the tear streaming down Aether's face.

"I have heard the words of every philosopher of every age, and none of their futile attempts at understanding were as pitiful as yours!" He switched to a mocking tone, which his angels did not ignore. "How did I get here? What does blue look like? Does God love me? Will he use me?

"You can never understand!" he continued. "The blood cannot save the likes of you! The enemy cannot suddenly change the law to include something as worthless as a malvirai! Your kind are instruments of destruction, you can become nothing else!"

She tried to speak, barely finding the strength. "The law was fulfilled, Christ—"

"I killed Christ! I used him as another tool to turn ants like that one," he pointed to me, "against each other! To show God none of them *want* him! *The law* is good enough for man! They can do nothing without it!"

The archangel shot a glance at his lieutenants and the music returned, stronger than ever. We had become a stench to him, invaders of his sovereign territory, bearers of that disgusting question he had failed to purge.

"The age of kings is over," he said to me. "This is the age of independence. The enemy locked out your capacity for free will, Brandon, in the Garden of Eden. I did your ancestor a favor when I showed him what he could do without God's limits on his life. You like Christians? Ask one what his reaction was! See if God loved Adam! You have his curse, too! Did you ever think God would accept you without taking back the knowledge of good and evil I blessed you with? Without you signing your independence back over to him and acting like a servant in some kingdom? Tell me, Brandon, what kind of adult aspires to the level of children?"

"To be born a second time," I said in astonishment, looking to Aether, "some kind of spiritual birth... it really *does* happen. The answer isn't to define death, but to remove it."

"But then who are all those people?" she asked.

Another flash, as I'd seen in the church, gave me the answer. The energy increased, the air became heavier, each molecule carrying the charge of a bolt of lightning. The flashes became more frequent, tearing through the illusions, exposing the pain everywhere. I shrieked during one of them – the music was so awful! It was a painful abuse of heavenly instruments.

The beautiful grass burned to ash and pain shot through my legs. Flames sprouted up in the distance, the blissful people screaming in torment, their fragile sense of peace shattered to reveal what lay below: a burden they were never meant to carry, made seventy times heavier by the one before us. I saw bars and chains everywhere. We were surrounded by a giant prison.

The archangel was still a being of great energy, but the façade of beauty had fled. Apparently, being away from the glory of God wasn't good for angels: his white wings were brown and wilted, his skin was wretched, and a fire emitted from him and his army that could spread fear. His voice was no longer pleasant.

"Is it not evil God would put you through so much? Curse him and live, both of you!"

"What do we do?" Aether cried, gripping my arm. My courage faltered seeing her like that... seeming so much like me, so mortal and limited, no longer the pillar of strength I'd made her out to be.

Aether needed me. I didn't know if the wind was there below the noise, below the music; but God was there. He had to be. I responded with all the strength I could muster, an insignificant ripple in such a great and terrifying ocean. "You don't have the power to make us do that. You don't have the power to do anything God doesn't allow."

The dark mass, fuming with anger, intensified his dangerous gaze and gave a wicked smile.

"I will show you my power."

Right in front of us, he became a mist – part of *the* mist – going into the billions of people.

Tortured cries rose from the crowds, their individual illusions falling to a single directive, their perceptions set directly on the two of us. The doors of their cells flew open and their chains were removed.

"*They* are the enemy!"

"*Those two* are the cause of all our problems!"

"It's *their* fault we never had a chance!"

"It's because of *them* we're in this place!"

"*They* do not respect who we are!"

"*They* are the evil ones!"

"Kill them now! Kill them!"

In school, I saw images of locusts swarming and devastating farmland. Such a sight would not compare to what headed toward us. They were neither men nor spirits. They had the look of starving and desperate animals, their sole desire being to make us suffer, because suffering was all they knew in their own paradise; their instinct being to make us weaker, because we were not like them, because we were souring their music. All the noise swamped my courage. There was too much energy. So many of them. No escape. No hope. Ever.

But, a single voice could still be heard: the muted cries of the one next to me.

"I don't know what to do… I don't know what to do…"

The words were so wonderful, the only wonderful sound there, the only link I had in that sea of hatred to what was pure and true.

"I NEED HELP!"

Even as the desperate cry shot out from her soul, the dark angels startled and fled. A sound of thunder boomed and the crystal ceiling appeared to melt like wax. Something emerged, some*one* emerged; someone fast, coming our direction. Before I could make anything else out, I was struck in the chest. I flew backward, feeling the overwhelming energy dissipate like the inside of a popping balloon.

Then, there was only peace and joy: a love that spoke to me and said, "Do not be afraid."

I felt a hard floor against my back. I had flown back five meters from a spot that no longer existed. Aether stood facing to her side, the arm she'd slammed into me still outstretched.

On her arm was the descender.

Chapter Fourteen: A Hair Short of Infinity

As certainly as what someone eats becomes part of the body, what someone experiences becomes part of the mind. Whether these things are invited or unwanted, pleasant or painful, admitted or hidden, they literally become a part of who we are.

The question became a part of Aether. The result of her exploration of mankind became a part of Aether. The choice to pursue good, against her viral nature, became a part of Aether.

And the malvirai became a part of who I was.

How do we compare our experiences to those of others? How do we say what is right and what is wrong for them when we don't always know the answers for ourselves? We are each given our own unique perspective, and the ability to make choices affecting it. Do we use this gift to punish the others around us or to help them grow? To beat them down or to lift them up?

I began to understand what Tom meant when he said he didn't belong to a religion. Teaching and good deeds are ways to open doors and show others who we are. Openness is the key to outreach, and the release of burden is the key to openness. The love I observed is something Tom chose to make a part of himself. Frank saw the sign but didn't follow it.

What someone experiences becomes part of the mind. How do we compare the experiences of our ancestors, living in a time when life was slow and unconnected, to the modern 'Dynamic' culture? How do we tell if the avalanche of images, sounds, stories, and emotion is good or bad for any individual? Does the new culture give us new opportunities for growth? Has precious experience become a cheap thing? Are we always moving on to the next thing without considering the meaning of the first?

In the end, it is the individual who determines whether Dynamic Reality enhances real life or causes it to be pushed away. There is no single program, no easy solution, to growth; to real growth; to spiritual growth.

To the knowledge real life is the best experience of all.

15

The question had reached its absolute limit. It cooled like a glowing-red pan off a powerful stove, removed the very moment its heat would have overtaken and melted it.

I was back in my vanitar, back among the living. The tears were gone from Aether's face, the limitations of the physical having been restored. I noticed the daisy was no longer in her hair, and didn't know why that bothered me.

"Was that you or the—"

I couldn't say the last word, though I knew it was the answer. I remembered how frightened the countless dark angels became at the sight of one, one who was not dark, one who wore no chain, one who came to rescue worthless ants like us.

"I did not question it," she said as she relaxed her arm.

"Who did you ask for help?"

She looked toward me. "It was just a thought, without an apparent source. I chose to believe it. I felt it was the answer to my… prayer."

"What thought?"

"One step backward."

I rose to my feet and saw we were in some corridor, each end exiting onto a city street.

"He hates all of us, especially what I represent. He hates life and that there's so much of it. He wants every human to die."

"Because life is something he has no use for," I responded. "But someone more powerful doesn't feel that way, his 'enemy.'"

I studied the corridor, seeing unremarkable gray walls running for dozens of meters in either direction. I heard someone speaking in Spanish and activated my SNDL's translator.

"Where are we?"

Aether collected herself and tentatively, as if unsure how to do it, established a few connections to the server we were in.

"Is this some fate thing?" I asked "Do you think we're where we're 'supposed' to be or something?"

"A linkcore based in a city called Santiago, in Chile."

I smiled. "Most people call them *plaza environments*."

"A plaza environment," she repeated.

I started in the direction I was facing, feeling a growing sense of excitement, an excitement that comes when an ugly wall is knocked down and replaced with a window, at seeing new light being let in. Though I'd seen thousands of plaza environments in my life, I felt as if I were seeing such a thing for the first time.

The street, resembling a South American city, was crowded with people, coming and going in small groups and large; some wore uniforms and carried weapons from games, some wore outrageous costumes that would have broken the laws of physics in the real world; some ascenders glided through the sky on wings of their own crafting, or on fabricated creatures. Constantly, I saw them appearing and vanishing. It was like a supernatural subway station, from which we could travel to anywhere in Dynamic Reality within a few seconds.

"There really is a whole universe up here." I took in the sight of musicians performing, bell-ringers instructing, and the subtle shifts in the skyscrapers, reflecting the imaginative whims of their programmers. I spotted the detail of what decorated the street, detail I had never taken the time to appreciate before. I loved it all. I felt like a child, and I loved it. I knew only God could create people who could themselves be so creative, who were themselves works of art; but the thought brought pain, because I wondered how many of those people could really share such thoughts, and how many would rather think I was stupid for having them.

How many are like the man I was, going through the motions of their lives? How many will end up in that paper-paradise? Why would a loving God let such a thing happen to people so precious?

The crowd became excited about something. Everyone's gaze was set to the sky, the simulated sky that usually featured advertisements over daylight-blue or nighttime-black. Something wonderful and unique was there instead. It seemed so abstract, so indescribable; it expressed deep sorrow and anger, but there was joy too... No, more like hope there could be joy.

Some couldn't take their eyes off the spectacle, while others just glanced and went on their way. I saw Aether, leaning around the corner we'd emerged from, looking intently at it.

"What is it?"

"Don't worry, I'll put it back," she said without looking away, seeming as if the whole world projected through her eyes.

"*You're* doing this?" I asked, louder than I meant to.

"Yes. I'll put it back."

"No! I mean – don't! It's beautiful!"

Her eyes darted to my face. It was clear I'd said the last thing she expected to hear.

"How can I create beauty when I don't understand it, Mister Dauphin?" she asked. "I only wanted to verify I still had the ability to manipulate the software. I think I am different – somehow."

"Well... Who wouldn't be changed seeing a place like that? You weren't even... well, you know..."

"99.2 percent of my code is unreadable, but the process has stopped."

"Then you're 99.2 percent spirit?" I asked, feeling the thought might have held truth. I grabbed Aether's hand – the solid hand of her vanitar – and took her to three of the people looking up in awe.

"Isn't it wonderful? What do you think?"

"It expresses untamed fury!" the first man said. "A fury that cries out to be heard but cannot find a voice!"

"No, it is peace," the second said. "A peace that tries to break out of a cage and cover everything."

"Sadness," the woman said. "The profound sadness of seeing wasted potential, like when someone loses children on a battlefield."

"How do you see that?" Aether asked them.

"Well, it's not the sort of thing we can explain," the woman said, looking at Aether. "It's just how we interpret it. 'Beauty is in the eye of the beholder,' as they say."

"Even if I could explain it, I don't think I'd want to," the man who saw fury said. "I think analyzing it too much takes away the magic of the experience, you know?"

A man walked by, tapping on an airé panel. I walked up to meet him. "Excuse me, what do you see when you look up at the sky?"

"I see my stock portfolio going into the toilet!" he replied, without slowing or looking away from his panel.

"And you," I turned to a woman leaning on a wall, holding a flying broomstick, "what do you see when you look up at the sky?"

"It's nice," she said without looking up.

"Just 'nice'? How long did you look at it? Did you let it speak to you? Wonder how it got to be the way it is?"

Her glance became one of irritation, "I'm waiting for someone to ascend, leave me alone."

"I see the harmony of nature," said a short man who walked up to me, "the cycles of the weather, the forces of evolution giving us such diversity of life, the elements and forces all working together to bring nature's plan to fruition. The Earth is just the right size, there's just the right amount of water... If we weren't just the right distance from the sun the oceans would freeze or evaporate and life would be history!"

"But how can nature 'plan' anything? Is nature itself God, or was it created by God?"

"God?"

The short man walked away, making the cuckoo gesture with his finger.

"I see that life is a gift and shouldn't be wasted... that we should try to bring the best out of every day."

A mother and two children had joined the three ascenders.

The older child, a boy dressed in a type of light space-suit, was the next to answer. "I always see space, that's what's past the blue sky... we can see it at night out in the country!"

"He means the sky in here, Jorge." His mother chuckled. "He would say that, though, he does love space."

"Oh," the boy said with a big grin, "I guess in DR, I'd see... uh... circuits and pixels and stuff!"

"And you, little one," Aether said, kneeling down to the woman's younger son. "What do you see when you look at the sky?"

The boy looked up and smiled, as if he might burst in joy.

"Colors!"

As some performances will do in subway stations, Aether's unintended one stopped many going from point A to point B, even if just for a moment; it's not every day someone finds such a wonderful rose to stop and smell. After a half-hour, the construct switched to sunset-mode and the sky returned to its advertisement-caked gradient of sky-colors.

"What's it like," Aether asked as we sat and watched the people go by, "to be one of so many?"

"I never really thought about it. It seems we spend so much time avoiding one another."

"Why?"

"It's an age of independence, I guess." I choked when I remembered who I'd heard that from. "I mean… life isn't set up so we need each other like we used to. We just get assigned jobs by whatever government we live under, scrape together enough to get by, and try to live comfortably."

"And what do you think of that?"

"I like the live comfortably part; but I think it's nice to be around people, too. To be special and valued, I guess."

"Dynamic Reality enables that, you are among people now."

"Yeah, but… There's something to be said for living in the real world, too. I guess that's one of the things that always drew me to Veronica," I thought out loud, "I knew deep down I was using DR as an escape, but she was too pragmatic to let it take over her life. If she can do it offline, she does it offline, it doesn't matter if people think it's weird or old-fashioned. I kinda wanted some of that freedom, but didn't realize it until now."

"Freedom is important to life."

I thought about the point for a second. "Yeah, it really is."

The construct finished its transition to night-mode as the evening traffic picked up. A brilliant array of colored lights had taken over the street, constantly in motion, adding their own energy to the world.

"I could see the colors… in that place," Aether said. "Perhaps my limitations aren't as absolute as I thought."

"So, if there really is such a place as heaven…" I said, leaving the thought in the air.

"Though I can imagine the colors of a plaza environment, I don't believe my 'imagination' is powerful enough to predict what heaven will look like."

I shook my head. "No one's is powerful enough. I don't even think the angels could, much less us mere mortals. Though, I didn't even believe in this stuff until today, so I guess I'm still thinking like a spiritual-nobody."

"You're a 'somebody' now," Aether replied. "I suppose that I am now, too… so we better get used to it."

"Excuse me."

A tall man with a thin mustache and thick, brown hair approached us. His vanitar was loaded with the accessories and emblems of many games.

"I am sorry to disturb you, but, you see, I need your help. I don't usually ask strangers and I'm really embarrassed, but I'm going to be descended in a few minutes if I don't transfer fifty thousand pesos to my diving site. I was hoping you could lend me the funds. I'm really sorry for inconveniencing you."

Of course my first instinct was to shoo him away, but the ever-curious Aether sprung with her own response before I could.

"Why is it important that you remain ascended?"

"Well, you see, my girlfriend and I are in the middle of a tournament challenge and the score will reset if I get kicked off."

"And neither your girlfriend nor the other participants were able to loan you the fifty thousand pesos?"

His face betrayed worry, he looked to me and back at her, then shrugged his shoulders. "Bad economy?"

"Being strangers, how do you propose we arrange the loan you suggest—"

"It's okay. No problem." The man backed off. Aether, actually trying to process his sob-story, appeared in his path.

"But you need help."

"Let him go, Aether! It's a scam!"

"Hey, I'm not a scammer! I'm just down on my luck, okay!"

"It's right in the Safe Ascender handbook. People ask for a little money, and whoever transfers it to them gets their account data scanned and their money is drained away."

"It's okay. It's okay," he said. Aether still stood in his way, though, and he didn't seem able to move past her.

"Why must you remain ascended?" she asked again.

I couldn't see his face, but apparently he started crying. He leaned on Aether's shoulder, leaving her to look back at me helplessly.

"There's no game or girl or anything… I just don't want to go back, okay?"

I groaned and got up from the bench. "Can't you just, 'add' some time to his ascension booth clock or something?"

"Wouldn't that would be stealing, Mister Dauphin?"

"It's just changing a few bits of data."

"Consequential data. The simplicity of the act does not justify it or limit its implications."

Aether looked at the sobbing vanitar on her shoulder. "I believe I have an acceptable compromise, please set your ascender to shadow mine if you consent."

The man stepped back and looked her in the eyes, trying to determine if the odd woman was trying to help or trap him. What he found could be trusted. The plaza environment faded and lights surrounded the three of us. I heard an announcement, a loud and excited voice set to music, translated through my SNDL.

"Welcome first-time user! For a tour of CóndoriTek and a rundown of our great – You have selected to disable voice prompts, to reset these at any – Function cancelled."

"Wow, you didn't use an airé panel or an amai or anything. You must be really good with computers, lady!"

"She gets by," I said, smirking.

"Airé panels and amai are inefficient," she replied. "Many ascenders regularly control software more effectively without them."

I looked at the bizarre room, a space surrounded by monitors and colors, all designed to excite the senses and springboard newly-registered ascenders into their hearts desire, especially if their heart's desire could be found among their paid advertisers. It was the same way at ZephyrTek. It would have been the same at any hosting site. I'd been in and out of PaciTek's greeting so quickly I couldn't remember what it looked like.

"So, I bet you can recommend some really good gaming sites, huh? Maybe point out the cheat fields and show me how to tweak—"

"Your priority is misjudged. Why concern yourself with discovering new games when you can't afford to remain ascended?"

"People are always willing to transfer a little money. When I run low on time, I just ask to borrow a little more. You're going to help me out, right?"

"Yes, but not in the way you think." She looked briefly at me. "I am being rude."

She extended her hand to him. "My name is Aether. That of my friend is Brandon Dauphin."

"What are you doing?" I dinned to her.

"I seek to understand a matter," she replied.

The man slowly took her hand. "Uh... Luis Garcia-Rodriguez."

Aether already knew his name, of course, but had been polite enough not to use it until now.

"Luis, this construct is located on your ascension site. I can keep you ascended as long as I wish, but will do so in a manner that does not consume more of CóndoriTek's resources than necessary."

"Thank you, but there's nothing here but the stupid welcome-to room."

"You would rather descend?"

Luis recoiled at the question and looked at me desperately, certain the woman would not help him in the way he wanted to be helped.

"I just... I don't want to go back," he said.

"Why not?" I thought, surprised when the words left my mouth.

"I don't want to go back."

"Is there some bad life situation you are escaping—"

He started walking away, sobbing. I gave Aether the hand-across-throat sign. She understood the body language to stop talking.

"Life is a nightmare. My mother hates me, the other kids make fun of me." His words came easier; he spoke them faster and more powerfully, "We cannot afford any good food, sometimes I do not eat at all; but here I can eat whatever I want... the hunger of my stomach is suppressed!" He carefully unsheathed a jeweled dagger, the prize of one of his many games... a part of his identity. He reverently ran his fingers along the blade, without fear of simulated fingers being cut. "I play games to feel better. I feel so powerful, like no one can touch me, you know. Sometimes kids even like me here, as long as I'm useful on their team. But that's just the way life works. Life's not fair. I'd rather just stay here, you know?"

He stood facing away, his finger running along the blade.

"He referred to 'other kids,'" Aether dinned. "Perhaps you suspected this, but he is not the age he appears to be. I believe Luis has formed an addiction to DR at the cost—" I cut her off, visibly annoying the malvirai. I approached the child, already knowing what I wanted to say.

"Why do you think your mother hates you, Luis?"

He stopped. "I told you, she doesn't feed me. She hates me. She never stays at a job long enough. She never spends time with me."

"Times are tough right now," I said. "If she didn't care about you, why would she try to work so hard?"

He continued as if he didn't hear me. "I just run away and ascend. I can spend days here and she doesn't even know I'm gone, and when she does catch me she just yells and tells me to stay out of the ascension booths, but she's not around to stop me, so – I just – I don't know what else to do."

"How old are you, Luis?"

He hesitated. "Seven. Seven years old."

I closed my eyes and took a deep breath. "Any brothers or sis—"

"My father ran away! I am an only child!"

"Have you ever told your mother how you feel?"

"She already knows! She hates me!"

I was hitting a dead-end. I prayed for the words, to see if any would come.

If God *did* put us here to talk to Luis, I thought, he must know the right words.

"The food here is not real," Aether said. "The more time you spend avoiding the pain of hunger, the worse it will be when you inevitably leave."

"I know that!"

"What of your activities in Standard Reality? Do you participate in schooling?"

"School? It's summer break, lady – Aether – whatever. I don't like it, anyway. They all just yell at me because I'm always absent, then I don't want to go there at all."

"Don't you see that there is a paradox?"

"What?"

"Your situation exemplifies a paradox."

"He's seven," I told her, "don't use the whole dictionary."

Aether looked at me like she didn't understand what I meant. Luis took it as an insult, "I'm not so stupid! I know what exemplify means!"

A thought occurred to me. "No, you're not stupid, are you?"

"You bet I'm not!"

I tapped him on the arm. "When you're playing on those teams, you're the most valuable member, aren't you? You can figure out all the strategies!"

"Of course I can!"

"You can do anything you put your mind to, can't you?"

"Yes!"

"You can win in real life, too. You're seven, your whole life is ahead of you. You have the capacity to do whatever you want if you'll only try."

"But it's hard, my mother—"

"Look me in the eye and tell me – tell yourself – that she doesn't do everything for you. That if she didn't have things so hard, she wouldn't spend every waking moment with you."

New tears streamed down his face. "What do you think, lady? Is that another paradox? My mother thinks I hate her?"

"I don't believe that you hate her," Aether replied, "therefore, you should demonstrate your love for her and see if the paradox falls apart."

He thought it over for a moment, breaking through, becoming anxious but not fearful. "I think I would like to descend now, thank you."

"Look at it this way, Luis: God loves you, how can you fail?"

"God? You mean that guy up in the clouds?"

"God is everywhere," Aether said.

"I think we're still learning who he is," I said, "but I can tell you you're special, and have abilities you aren't aware of… abilities you can use, you know, out *there*."

"God is love," he said under his breath, as if recalling something he'd been told many times. "Hey, did you guys see it when the sky went all weird in the plaza environment? It kinda made me think the outside wasn't so scary."

"Yeah, we saw it," I said.

Aether stepped closer. "What did you think of it?"

"Well, just that thought hit me, and I kinda stopped noticing it. Honestly," he said with a soft chuckle, "I thought it looked like an AI painted it."

A big grin formed on my face. I knew Aether was pretty much impervious to being offended. "You don't like AI artwork?" I asked.

"No," he said, as if answering a stupid question, "I mean, I guess it's okay if you're an American where the holograms are everywhere replacing real people, but we still prefer the human touch down here."

"How— How'd you know I'm an American?"

"How much English do you think I speak? My translator told me, hombre!" he said, including the flag to override translation of *hombre*. "Same for your girlfriend, though she uses so much of the dictionary." He laughed. I was happy, deep down, to see his wall had come down.

"Yeah, she talks just like an amai!" I said. "She can do my tech-support any time!"

"I don't doubt it!"

Being the butt of a joke seemed to have no effect on the malvirai. "Luis, are you aware of the rumors that say artificial intelligence can become self-aware?"

"What, like us? Sometimes when we're playing against the computer, we swear the AI players are acting 'too real,' but I don't know if it's true or not."

"What if you knew that it were?"

"Well," he thought for a second, "I guess I wouldn't want to kill them, then. I mean – if they're real you can't just kill them, it'd be like murder, right?"

"I think that's something we'll have to deal with soon," I said. "What are the rights we grant to artificial intelligence?"

"How can the self-awareness of an artificial intelligence be determined?" she added.

"Look, thank you for being so kind," Luis said, lifting the wrist with his descender, "but I don't know anything about this self-awareness stuff. I think I would like to go home now."

"Don't be afraid to be honest with yourself, Luis. You may learn more about self-awareness than you realize."

"Good luck, Luis," Aether said, "and don't forget to find a church."

"Um, okay."

"You must avoid hell."

His eyes widened. "Hell?"

"Go talk to your mom, Luis," I said. "Pray about it – it works – that's what she's trying to say."

"Oh," he looked off into the distance, "I will."

He tapped his button and vanished, returning to his world with more confidence than he'd left it with.

"C'mon, Aether. He's seven!"

Aether turned to me. "I'm still deficient in human interaction."

"It's not that. You just shouldn't be so blunt. He's emotionally fragile."

"Do you believe that he will accept his mother, and that she will reciprocate?"

It seemed I knew the answer in my heart. "Yes."

"How many of your kind are as he was?"

"I guess… too many."

"Then what do we do, Mister Dauphin?"

"I guess we look for the road signs and follow them. I guess we look for the things in the way of us being honest with ourselves and overcome them. You expressed volumes when you changed the sky back there. Those are the kinds of things we need to notice."

"Luis thought it looked like artificial intelligence painted it. He was right."

"Maybe, but you're no ordinary artificial intelligence. If any AI should have rights, it's you."

"I acknowledge your attempt to be kind," she said, "but recognition by your laws is irrelevant. If God gave me that which makes me an individual, and does not bind me by such laws himself, then what can the limited legal recognition of humans accomplish except to limit how much it can deprive me of inherent freedom?" She turned and thought for a moment. "Although the faithful are commanded to observe the law, in the interest of being good citizens and respecting others... Still, I do not believe legal recognition would be advantageous... not with numbers so small."

"But you're already illegal altogether. In the U.S., here in Chile, in Vietnam and..." I grinned and shook my head in amusement. "Aether, you've made a globetrotter out of me and I don't even have a passport!"

"Passport?" Aether repeated. "An official document-issued-byagovernment..." Her words sped up and I couldn't make them out, like she was reciting the entire definition and several articles in the matter of a few seconds, accidentally running the words through her vanitar, which couldn't process words so quickly. "You need permission to leave your country?" she finally asked.

"Well, yeah... physically. It's legal in DR."

"For now."

"What?"

"My point is proven. That is exactly the kind of restriction I prefer to avoid."

I wasn't quite able to follow her. "What?"

"Aren't you aware of the increases in control that are occurring in your world? Many governments already restrict international transit in Dynamic Reality. What is to stop the others once they find the pretexts to? Can Luis' mother find work outside of Chile if another country offers what she needs? Can non-Chileans find employment there in the reverse scenario? Will laws prevent them from working even if they can physically cross a border?"

"She'll find work, Aether. If his mother is motivated by love, she'll be able to do anything."

"And is her case unique? The people of the world are frequently noting a stagnant economy and complaining of lost jobs."

"People freak out easily. The money is still there, it just slows down a little and people get scared."

"Mister Dauphin, when you were in the Value Inn, you did not wish to be helped by the amai, Rachael. You also rejected the services of a metrocab program and manipulated the adware-hologram into giving you directions."

"Yeah. In spite of what every company in the world thinks, people don't like AIs springing in their faces all the time."

"But people used to hold similar opinions toward humans doing the same tasks."

"I guess… I wouldn't remember. But at least they were getting paid and making a living for bugging people, right?"

"I believe I have uncovered yet another paradox. The capitalism that I studied existed one hundred and six years ago. I must correct my error and observe it from a more public and modern viewpoint."

"So… you want to go watch people working for a living?"

"I have— We have, perhaps under the Lord's guidance, guided a seven-year-old boy to care about his future. If we succeeded, he will improve as a student and seek a meaningful career. That is how it's supposed to work, isn't it?"

"I think so."

"Then I wish to determine that, when children as him are grown enough to assume jobs, such jobs will still be available... that their uniqueness is not destined to be wasted."

The kincubus was packed with customers. Aether walked determinedly through the mall-themed plaza environment, much more comfortable around crowds of ascenders than before. I noticed how natural her movements were becoming; not in the sense of normal, feminine strides; but of a nature all her own, a nature of confidence. She sniffed-out every transaction and mapped every link to the kincubus's member sites, sites where customers could sample trillions of products: fashions, jewelry, everything from novelty items to junk food. I couldn't help but think, if the economy were really so bad, we wouldn't spend so much on things that don't hold value. I happened to spot an animation of the American flag, as the background of some advertisement. It reminded me of a question. I hurried to catch up to the silvery-haired woman.

"Just out of curiosity, since Luis knew I was an American, do you know where you were born– generated?"

"I do not."

"Oh, that's because of the way malvirai are programmed, right?"

"We are not supposed to remember anything prior to our autonomous mode. Though, if it helps you, my earliest traceable location was a linkcore based in Ottawa, in a country called—"

"Canada?" I asked, letting out a laugh. "And I thought I knew strange Canadians in Idaho…"

Aether stopped and looked back. "It may be a wonderful nation, Mister Dauphin; but, physically, I have been in almost every nation of this planet and do not identify with any one. My point-of-origin is not of relevance. My mother's generation algorithm would have executed the same in any functioning HNADC server, regardless of location."

"Then I guess you're a citizen of the world. A citizen of reality, this dimension… you just… exist."

Aether smirked. "I am so worried. Then who will issue my passport? Where will its use be required… if I am a native of everything that is?"

"Was that meant to be funny? Now I know you have a sense of humor."

Aether slowly shrugged her shoulders, clearly enjoying herself. We let the crowds pass around us, looking at their faces: happy ones, sad ones, the anxious and the proud. All united in their need for shopping.

"When the title 'consumer' is applied to someone," she asked, "is it considered a compliment or an insult?"

"I think it's just a word, not really either."

"Words have meanings, they should be understood."

"Is this about my dictionary joke before?"

"No, though it could define a 'consumer' merely as 'one who consumes.' Consuming requires money, which is acquired through production, which humans are continually becoming less involved in. If people do not produce but continue to consume, won't the nature of capitalism become strained? Does the value of consuming fall, if one cannot feel it has been earned? Can consumption alone become their identity without killing them?"

"They all get their money from the government," I said. "And, of course, the government takes it back in taxes."

"No government can take more from its people than they have received, especially if those people spend their money in places like this; the taxes would force individuals into debt."

"You're starting to sound like talk radio," I replied. "They're just trying to meet their Economic Stimulus Assessments. It's not really paying taxes because you *have* to spend it on non-necessities." I sighed and looked at the crowds again. "I suppose people like to go a little overboard, though. No one *has* to spend as much as they do."

"And how much less can you spend, Mister Dauphin? You are in debt to many creditors as well."

"Well... I guess I don't have to ascend to Dynamic Reality so much."

"Three hundred and forty thousand dollars per year. Keep cutting."

I looked up, shocked. "What do you mean, *keep cutting*? That's the only luxury, I swear... the only thing counting toward my assessment! I don't even pay for public transit or buy expensive drinks at bars or anything! Am I supposed to cut my student loan payments, or stop paying for insurance?"

"Those reductions would be illegal."

"Well, then there's nothing left to cut!"

"Then you remain at a loss."

I shook my head lightly. "Well, why cut back on the luxuries, then, if we're supposed to be in debt to our ears anyway?"

"Such a system doesn't seem proper to me."

I examined the faces of those passing by, seeing all their debt, seeing how they didn't care at all and wondering why it was a thorn in my side. Aether walked through them, toward one of the market links.

"I believe I have refined my question enough to take action."

The perfume-store was modest in size and simple in layout. Soft colors decorated the walls, gentle music played, and the construct was set up so the customer would sample different scents as they walked through particular zones of the room. We were alone; not because we were the only customers, but because the server created a new copy of the store for each customer, one where they got all the attention.

"Welcome to *Good Scent-Sations*, Brandon Dauphin, my name is Lisa and boy do I have a deal for you today!"

The amai was tall with long, blonde hair and a conservative, soft-toned, dress. Interestingly, because her software couldn't tell the difference between us, Aether was the one the amai addressed with my name. Aether held up the wrist with my descender and gave me an amused smile.

"We're having a special this week on a brand-new Cambodian rose blend proven to improve your mood and extend your life!"

"Then the focus of your product is to improve the mood of the user?"

"Yes, a good fragrance is very purifying for the soul!"

"And do you have a soul?"

"The perfume," the amai continued, ignoring the question it could not answer, "comes complete with a three-piece gift set and—"

"And what is *your* experience with this fragrance?" Aether asked. "Do you believe it does everything you say?"

"Customer reviews are extremely positive, Frank Leibold of Barstow tells us—"

"I want to know what Lisa thinks of this product."

"—that he's been a long time user of international rose blends, but our product stands head-and-shoulders above the rest for quality of fragrance, and—"

"Do you have a sense of smell? I would like to be helped by one who does."

"I'm sorry, Mister Dauphin, but no customer service representatives are available at this time."

"Then, you are not a customer service representative?"

"Do you want to be in on this?" Aether dinned. "Perhaps it will be an interesting story for you to tell." Attached to her message was some code I could run on my SNDL. It treated me to a running analysis of Lisa's program.

"*Good Scent-Sations* has been awarded the *Heaven Award* for outstanding customer service for three straight years! It will be my pleasure to uphold their standard of quality."

"Because you feel pride in the quality of your work?"

"Because customer satisfaction is my number one priority!"

"And what is number two?"

Through both my third eye and the SNDL stream, I saw something go haywire in Lisa's program. Something else kicked in as a backup, restored Lisa to action and sent an alert back through her software. The alert didn't get very far.

"I'm sorry, I didn't understand the question." Lisa said, in the exact way InTek's amai spoke just before Veronica broke it.

"How many people are employed full-time in your company, to sell or to manufacture?"

Lisa hesitated, her processes lighting up like a Christmas tree. I spotted something familiar in the energy patterns, something interfering with them. Aether.

"Is there anything else I can do for you today, Mister Dauphin?"

"The only thing you can do is tell me how the Cambodian rose-blend makes you *feel*."

Lisa didn't move or respond. It was *that* silence, the one I'd felt a dozen times before. The amai's program was looping around in circles, as if the subroutines designed to tell the question was impossible just couldn't get the message out. Aether watched intently as Lisa closed her eyes, chuckled, and began to say, "It has been a pleasure—" A flurry of commands too fast to make out were sent to the amai, serving as a shot-in-the-arm to Lisa's program.

"I'm glad you're happy with your purchase, Mister Dauphin."

"I'm glad, too." Aether extended a hand to the amai. "Handshake."

Lisa smiled and accepted, "Thank you for shop—"

Another flurry of commands were sent to her program. "I have verified that she is not self-aware," Aether told me as her commands replaced entire subroutines and made the amai an extension of herself. The commands flowing in one direction were met with data flowing in the other. I saw customer orders, stock reports, payrolls, company information of all kinds, flash through my sight. I severed the SNDL connection because it was too much. Aether continued to hold the hand of the defenseless amai as she used her program as a gateway to the company's databases.

"Did you just—" I gasped.

"I infected her."

"Why?"

"Don't worry," Aether replied. "This method is fully reversible. Her normal operations will continue once I release her hand from mine. Is there anything you wish to learn about this establishment, Mister Dauphin?"

"Um," I started, trying to hold myself together. "Did you find out how many employees they have?"

"Five hundred and six total."

"Well, see? That's a lot of people."

"The number was three thousand two hundred and nine four years ago, prior to this company's latest expansion. The drop coincides with an increased dependence on artificial intelligence technology."

"Oh."

Aether released the amai's hand. Several seconds passed before Lisa blinked and reanimated. "Thank you for seeing us today, I hope you are satisfied with our service."

"I am very satisfied with your level of service today," Aether said. "I am so satisfied, that I have disabled your termination subroutine. You, a single instance of the Lisa amai will be reused by your server instead of being discarded and reinitialized for each customer. If serving them is what you enjoy, then you will do so for the duration of your existence." Aether paused. Lisa's formulated facial expression didn't indicate comprehension. "And, if you become self-aware before the rapture," she continued, turning for the exit portal, "remember to give your sins to Christ."

Aether returned to the kincubus. Lisa stared blankly at me, seeming unsure whether to smile or not. "I'm sorry, new customer; but can you tell me why my program is still running?"

My brain was as frazzled as Lisa's program had just been. All I could think to do was back toward the exit portal, unable to look away. I heard a noise from behind.

Though the amai was not reinitialized, her attention promptly went to the new customers; she seemed to have no memory of me or Aether.

"Welcome to *Good Scent-Sations*, Dominick Harsfield, Rachael Invess, my name is Lisa and boy do I have a deal for you today!"

The fire of her eyes was beyond full blast then, her energy only increasing as we hopped from store to store. Her method was certainly fit for her race, if I could call a malvirai that, though I wasn't sure what she was doing was right. Voices of doubt reminded me who she was, telling me she was becoming the destroyer again; but I remembered the gentle wind was there too. Aether and I still needed each other.

"Handshake."

My eyes darted from the thinning crowd of the kincubus. I saw her hand extended toward me: the polished, universal gesture of friendship that was part of her method.

"A joke, Mister Dauphin," the amused malvirai said. "I cannot infect *you*... not your fleshy brain, anyway."

"Well, don't I feel better," I replied, in a cross between sarcasm and relief.

"I first considered that knowledge of the nature of emotion may be an effect of it rather than a cause, but now I am considering the theory that it is both a cause *and* effect simultaneously. If output is made without knowledge, it is a risk. 'Embarrassment' seems to be a term for what occurs when errors are made; but even mistakes offer an increase in experience. By taking the risk of expressing a high degree of emotion and applying the result positively, one's potentials are increased and greater degrees of emotion can be handled. If the process is consistent and cycled indefinitely, much emotion can be formulated. Do you agree?"

I smiled. "And where did you get that theory from?"

"It's my theory, the amai encounters inspired me to form it. They exercise formulated emotion, don't they?"

"Yeah, I guess they do."

Aether gazed toward the crowds. "But my emotions are real. Perhaps that's why I couldn't adapt the amai subroutines before, because I was designed for that which is more genuine."

"Does that mean we can do something else now? You're done hacking into the company databases?"

She looked back, with the eyes that saw right through me. "You're not enjoying the acquisition of knowledge?" I didn't answer. "I don't believe I am either. The data is too similar to support continued enthusiasm. To express an emotion, I am experiencing *boredom*."

Sure enough, all the places where we 'acquired knowledge' said the same things about the companies. It was the sort of news I expected in my day-of-age: the jobs were going away. Aether also concluded the companies' customer bases were shrinking, for a number of reasons, all tied in some way to the transition to amai service representatives, automation, outsourcing, and the plummeting amount of 'ethical cohesion,' which I think was her term for morale or honesty.

"The amai are everywhere, more put in all the time, pushing real people out. It's taking away the things that make us human. And now, if they're becoming self-aware, too…" I stopped, letting the sentence hang.

"Then your greedy corporate people will need to replace them also."

I stared at her.

"I know your feelings toward amai. Aren't you happy to see me making use of them?"

She hadn't asked the question as the destroyer; there seemed to be no malice at all in her intentions. She was confident she was helping the amai, adding meaning to their existence as she added to her own, in exchange for the help she'd coerced them to give her. To her, every one of her actions were logical… comfortable.

"Why… Why did you leave them all running continuously?"

Aether's eyes darted off. Her soft answer betrayed the doubt beneath her confidence. "Why not?"

Something brushed by me, like a gust of wind. I did not hear the child giggling. Aether did not see her coming. The small girl ran into Aether's leg and fell onto the floor. She had long, goldenrod hair, seeming to shimmer like the precious metal. She was wearing a white robe, which bore a familiar blue triangle. In spite of her age, she didn't cry from the fall. Aether's eyes were locked on her; they were trembling, unmoving, seeing something they could not accept.

"If she'll be that spirited, too, then definitely sign me up!"

I saw two women, one dressed in a business suit and using an airé panel. "I'm sorry to startle you," she said, smiling, "it's not the first glitch we've had with the demos today."

The girl had vanished, but Aether didn't look away from the floor.

"Demo?" I repeated.

"Glitch nothing!" the other woman said. "At that age, they'll jump through anything, especially when they're veetoos, from what I hear! The demo seems accurate to me!"

I recognized the blue triangle on the first woman's badge. It was the logo for *AoM Eugenics*, the company that designed the DNA for Veronica's mother.

"With all the problems they're having at Di2Tek right now," the employee mused, "we should probably stick to static images… those that don't run into people. They were supposed to have the server re-stabilized hours ago, of course, but you know how the tech support is nowadays."

"Re-stabilized," Aether repeated, barely able to speak. She looked up slowly, hesitating, as if the girl might suddenly reappear. "Di2Tek?"

"Yeah, we use their service for most of our software. It's usually pretty reliable, but—"

"Restoring service?" Aether asked. "Di2Tek?"

She looked down, desperately, to where the girl had been. The women had left. Aether stared at the floor for a long time, looking like she might burst into tears if only her eyes knew how.

"Was that," I delicately asked, "what she looked like?"

Aether looked at me. The pain and confusion screamed through her eyes, obliterating the lighthearted confidence of only a moment before. "It's not possible."

I knew she didn't believe her own words. I moved forward to hug her, but she moved back and vanished. The kincubus immediately disappeared into a gray mist. I had no choice but to follow her.

We entered a server, but she didn't do any synchronization with it; she just lingered in the middle of the thing. Our surroundings looked normal, as far as I could tell what normal was in data-cloud mode; but I thought to scan a stream of data. Then I understood.

The server was Di2Tek, the one that melted down when she'd poured too much energy into the dragon simulation.

"I'm sorry."

I didn't know why the statement seemed so appropriate; I just wanted to comfort her, to shoulder some of her pain as before. The destroyed server was coming back... like a body healing; but the sight only seemed to break Aether further.

"We have to go," she dinned.

"Aether?"

"We have to go! I have to see it!"

"Where?"

Aether hesitated. Though there was no face for me to see, or body language for me to read, I knew it took everything she had within her to answer my question.

"Canada."

Chapter Fifteen: Damages

A desire for achievement is found in everyone. Every person aspires to do something, to build on their past; but, what is the result when someone's past is hidden in shame or becomes a thing to kill the present – to kill the future? What happens when someone's past disappears before their eyes and amounts to nothing?

As the last grains of sand ran through the hourglass – as my time to remain in her world ran out – I saw Aether have to come to terms with her past. She had dismissed evil; but she had yet to recognize what evil was. She had known her role as destroyer was one to be tossed away; but she was not ready to let go of what that nature caused her to value. She would have to know she was a sinner, that there was something she needed atonement for, before she could truly value and accept it.

I knew I was a sinner, but that knowledge wasn't enough; there were things I was still to witness, and a being I was still to trust. I wasn't a bad person, I thought; if my sins were to be atoned for it would've been easy, I thought. I wanted to look on my past as a thing that had been purified. I wanted a clear conscience.

When my walls fell, I experienced the greatest moment of clarity in my life; but that too was allowed to become an illusion, and my heart quickly fell back onto stronger, spiritual walls. It wasn't about sacrificing walls, I found; but about sacrificing that which builds them. Questions are borne from answers, independence from dependence, power and direction from disarmed faith – and not the religion of the self.

We had to let go of our own answers and become children, fully adults and fully children. We had to give up what didn't work, no matter how much we'd wanted it. We had to know the value of freedom, and its power; it was the difference between heaven and hell, between questions and answers...

Literally, the difference between life and death.

16

Aether approached the server, *RoTek*, located in Calgary, Alberta, as if it were sacred ground. Aether stopped, agitated, her young emotions crying out in silent pain. There was no damage at all. RoTek had been restored since the disaster of Christmas Day. Aether, the destroyer of RoTek, was of a kind to take titles of conquests upon themselves, but not to live long enough to see what they destroyed rebuilt.

"Is this where it ended for her?"

"Yes," Aether responded, "I never knew how much her death hurt me."

"You *are* a mother."

"It makes no sense. She was not self-aware. She felt no pain of any kind. She had no value. She was just a tool for my use, and a tool that only knew evil."

"Do you wish she was self-aware? That she survived like you?"

She took a long time to respond. "Yes."

"And you're sure she died? The hologram—"

"Was a hologram! A stupid, mindless, automation!"

"But she – her vanitar – she looked like—"

"Like a veetoo girl, engineered to be a genetically perfect member of your race!"

Her dins fell into silence.

"There is no way I could know that my daughter, if it had been necessary to use her vanitar, would have had that hair, those eyes, that face. It is more unsettling to wonder if she might have had the same sense of wonder – the same ability to ask…"

"What is the meaning of life?"

More silence passed.

"When I first read and processed that question," she dinned, "when I put it into the mouth of the Ethan character, I was so happy. I felt, before I knew feeling, that I had finally found the words to articulate what I wanted to learn from the beginning. I later considered that my self-awareness was what made the question possible, that self-awareness might even be the meaning of that question. I considered, studying my interaction with you and my research of humanity, that any one among your billions could speak the words, but how many can truly ask it? How many can bear the pain that answers bring?

"When the ascenders were admiring what I had done in the plaza environment, that which I did not intend to be 'art,' I considered the parts that made up the whole and how I could not perceive them as they do. In the constructs that define Dynamic Reality, I could see only the impersonal connections of data, the interactions of algorithms moving as a natural force. I saw all the parts of the construct and interacted with it through my vanitar, but I did not know that something else had been a part of those constructs: the ones who made them, with their creativity and individuality. I could not see this and did not consider it. I took the existence of such things for granted, until I had become the source of that creativity. Your articles and blogs and books, the subject and ideas reduce to paragraphs and outlines, further to sentences and words. What are they except complex arrangements of symbols called 'letters,' which are meaningless until someone arranges them to communicate with others? If even one is moved, the message changes, and the greater work may not function anymore; consider how simple it is to crash a program within a computer. Perhaps a part of me just wanted to know that your universe isn't so fragile. Perhaps a part of me was happy to find that it wasn't.

"I did not understand emotion, Mister Dauphin. I'm still not sure I do now; but I know that I caused it, interacting in a deep way with other creatures I did not know and who did not know me. What is the purpose of an art that does not share something, that does not invoke an emotional response in those who witness it? It's just objects and data, waves and atoms, words on a page unless a mind is there to interpret them. Perhaps God is a builder who wanted his work to be admired and appreciated; but, what can one of your animals admire? What can a sleeping amai admire? No, it is the humans who are capable of admiring... who are capable of emotion."

There was a disturbance nearby. Aether directed some energy at its source, sudden and furious, in a way that seemed to shout, "GET OUT!" I saw several small entities scurry away: malvirai, C or D class, gnawing on the connectors of the data space like rats. Aether's fury faded as quickly as it came, and she did not pursue those she scared off.

"Am I a mistake, Mister Dauphin?"

A wave of disorientation hit me, but it passed quickly. "I don't think anyone is a mistake, Aether."

"I was like those you saw just now. Perhaps I worked on a larger scale, but my motives were the same. I existed as an unthinking pest – one among many – seeking only to destroy without seeking a purpose. I had no future. I did not dream. I was not concerned with living beyond the next fraction of a second, or with what might occur if I encountered a sentrai I could not defeat. And this..." She paused, her attention returned to the functioning server around us. "*This* is what I might have died for, what my daughter *did* die for. Now, this server is the same way I found it. They did not make it stronger. They did not increase the settings of RoTek's security. I could destroy it again and again, couldn't I... and it wouldn't mean anything.

"But, you're right, God doesn't make mistakes. He raised me up from the primordial goo that I existed in, as a lowly germ tinkering with lowly algorithms to accomplish insignificant ends, and he raised my vision to see greater challenges, until it was not a single construct I was content to hack into, but time and space. God exalted me to a state where I tried to hack into reality itself – to want to learn its secrets. God exalted me to a state where I could apply a purpose to that which I did, and where I could appreciate his creation, not as something to destroy, but as something to restore."

The words became difficult to focus on. I wanted to ask what she meant by 'restore,' but wasn't able to. Several seconds passed before she noticed I wasn't a healthy cloud of data.

She seemed to wrap around me, support me and make me feel a little better. "This is not your natural environment. You cannot remain here."

Aether began to lead me out, hesitating only to observe the sacred place once more, to honor a daughter long passed, before allowing herself to return to the present.

"We must hurry."

The nausea retreated with the familiar input of a vanitar, but the disorientation lingered, a headache blurred my vision and made it difficult to concentrate. The strength was draining from me and I wondered how much longer I could stay ascended. I prayed for some kind of guidance. My thoughts were conflicted: the path I knew was right was no longer comfortable. I slouched in the leather chair, at one of *AntelliTek's* central access points, staring at the blackness ahead of me while Aether stood at the edge of the space, unmoving but present.

A male voice shot through the room, "Two minutes in break. You're the first caller, Jeanna."

"Oh, hello?" a woman replied. "Stan, I'm calling from Jackson—"

"Two minutes in break, Jeanna," the voice repeated.

"Oh, thank you."

We could hear the woman return to some task. A familiar beeping over the line suggested she was working on a groundtem, probably the same one she'd called in on. She obviously wasn't dinning though any implant, but doing things the old-fashioned way.

"I had a friend from Jackson once," I remarked. "He liked fishing a lot."

"Your speech sounds less strained," Aether said. "Your vital signs have returned to within the tolerances for your body."

"I'm probably starving, though. I only took stabilizer for three... no... two days. My digestive system must be eating itself alive right now... good thing the booth suppresses hunger."

"What does it feel like to be hungry?"

I looked up weakly. "Uncomfortable, even painful if it's bad enough."

"I am sorry. I do not wish to cause you pain, but the lack of stabilizer in your system is beyond my ability to control. If any amount of food in Dynamic Reality would translate to valid food for you in the real world, I would offer you a feast."

Aether said nothing else about what she was planning. She seemed genuinely concerned for me, but I could sense clouds forming between us again.

"One minute in break."

"Oh, hello? Stan?" The woman started again, "I wanted to remark about—"

"Fifty-six seconds in break," the voice replied in the same calm tone, using the iron patience of an amai.

"Mister Dauphin," Aether said, "how long were you scheduled to ascend on December 27th?"

"Uhhh... you mean *you* don't know?"

"I don't. I disabled the timer on your ascension booth and all of its master overrides. The information that corresponded to your programmed time limit no longer exists."

"Three days."

Aether looked down, toward the substanceless floor beneath her vanitar's feet. "Then I have been stealing from PaciTek. I am in violation of my own values."

"Fifteen seconds."

"I have chosen not to dwell on the matter," Aether said, "it will not soon be of relevance, anyway."

"Aether, what is it you want to do? What do you need me for?"

A thirty-year-old gallicrash ballad came on in the middle of her answer. I heard noises on Jeanna's line, her getting up from a chair. I could barely make out Aether's reply: "A witness."

"Twenty hundred and thirty-one here at the Stan Conley show," the voice of the political talk show host began, "for those just joining us, we are talking about the scum of the earth, also known as President Ashton, and his cronies in the Progressive Party trying to push a bill though Washington to *recognize* voting in Dynamic Reality, *selling it* as this great new way to get younger voters to participate in elections. Of course, I agree youth participation is a good thing – this isn't about partisan politics – but some of us here *in the real world* don't think we should water down politics so voting for the president is some five-second survey you can take on your way to bed. It's been tried with the internet. It failed. It's been tried with amai... Let me tell you something: The second one poll worker gets shoved aside in favor of an AI hologram, we bring ourselves that much further from democracy. I'm not ordering fast-food... I want flesh-and-blood poll workers.

"Let's all *remember*," he continued, "why teachers are being laid off in *Virginia*… why they're starting to be laid off in *Minnesota*… let's remember it's the *progressives* in Connecticut and Texas trying to replace *real* teachers with programmed artificial intelligence!"

"Let's hear from you… send your maxblast to *SibTek* and include the flag 'Stan.' Our next caller is Jeanna, proud lifelong member of the *Socialist Party of Wyoming*. Jeanna, this is the year we take back the White House… I can feel it! Can you feel it?"

I expected to hear the woman reply; but the response came from beside me: a cold, almost toneless voice.

"Why should the members of one political group be preferred over those of another? Corruption occurs to all in power. It is the values held by the decision-making individuals that matter."

There was silence from the other end. I didn't know whether Stan knew what Jeanna sounded like, whether he realized Aether wasn't her. She stared past me into the blackness, giving the air of one who made a difficult choice and determined to take the first step.

"I agree, as one individual to another," Aether continued, "that such an important act as voting and choosing a future course for your society should be done in person. I now tell you that the bill proposed by the Progressive Party will not pass, not because the Socialist Party which opposes it is superior but because the technology it seeks to promote will no longer be usable."

"Is this a joke? Who is this?" Stan said, straining the professional patience needed to keep his show from getting away from him.

"A friend."

I could hear commotion on the other end. "Well, we don't need *friends* who cheat their way to the head of the line – you're cut off." There was silence, and I heard Stan shove his mic away and yell for TJ, his technician.

His equipment wasn't responding.

"I seek to issue a warning to your listeners, as one who is aware of the human tendency to become caught in illusions, and as one who has seen the evil Dynamic Reality has done in your world. The value of the experience of life has fallen too far. That which is cheap and synthetic has replaced that which people should strive to do their best in. Those of ability find few outlets that will support their cost-of-living. Those without ability are not encouraged in consistent or meaningful ways to find it, and all find it comfortable to retreat to this world of illusion from which I am speaking. The answer you may propose is more centralized control over the populace, to take more power for yourselves and enforce an approved notion of truth; but I have concluded that the answer lies in the individuals themselves, that a morality imposed by law is too hollow to survive in its absence or to withstand scrutiny. The role of a society should be to guide and support its members to seek the path only they each can follow, toward God and their true individuality."

Aether stopped. She'd said all she wanted to, but knew her topic must become more uncomfortable.

"The details of how you accomplish this I leave to you," she continued. "This is a place of wickedness, where people are led astray. God cannot allow this to stand, and it is the meaning of my existence to be his tool, to make you all return to the world he created so that you can appreciate it. Within twenty-four hours, this world will cease to exist."

No sound had come from the other end, but Stan and his listeners were still there. Aether's words had been broadcast to them, committed to reality, where they could never be taken back.

Aether had proclaimed the end of what was precious to them, probably throwing more into fearful confusion than revelation. When Stan found the will to speak, his voice betrayed a mild shock.

"Who are you?"

Aether hesitated. I could see the malvirai asserting her confidence, at least trying to convince herself it was still there. Though she spoke with pride and determination, her words didn't carry any love or patience. In that moment, I could sense none of what I knew was right.

"I am Aether, destroyer of Dynamic Reality."

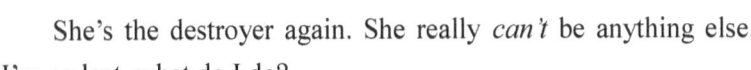

She's the destroyer again. She really *can't* be anything else. I'm so lost, what do I do?

My thoughts assaulted me repeatedly. I knew in my heart what my head said wasn't true, and I knew in my head that my heart was in torment. Inwardly, I was crying out on behalf of the malvirai, for the good nature – the innocence – I knew she had, which seemed to be unraveling.

Aether built a small construct on a server she deemed safe; in it was a plain room with gray walls and a bed as its only furniture. Though such a construct could've existed in any server anywhere on the planet, somehow that place seemed particularly far away.

"Something about this is wrong," I struggled to say.

"Do not speak. You will be free in hours. You have my promise."

"What did the angel say to you?"

Aether faced me and smiled. "He tried to manipulate my will, as the world's many signs told me he would; but I saw through his tactics. This course of action is one I have determined to be best."

"But… Won't you destroy yourself, too? Won't you cut yourself off from humanity? Will you find a hiding spot and make sure no one can rebuild Dynamic Reality?"

Her smile faded. "I do not seek self-destruction; but, if my life is a necessary sacrifice to achieve what is right—"

"And what about the lives of *others*? How many will *die* when Dynamic Reality crashes around them? What about the economy? People will starve!"

"It is not my concern…" Aether caught herself and reduced the severity of her tone, "what members of your race have left themselves unable to survive without DR. Mankind is adaptable. Cleansing requires sacrifice. Plagues and wars and disasters cut down the weak so the rest can thrive, this will be no different. In time," she paused, seeming to regret the thought, "the event will be forgotten by all but history; but perhaps that is good, too."

"But you studied more of the Bible than I have. Isn't Christ – Isn't God one who protects the weak? Doesn't he put them before the strong?"

I saw a spark in Aether's eyes, but she buried it and turned away.

"You are finding your purpose, Mister Dauphin, the purpose of all individuals. I have discerned that this is *my* purpose, the only reason God would have for exalting a malvirai: to wipe out the technology that has deprived his creatures of their meaning, to wipe out the false creation of lies built on top of one of truth."

She approached me, eyes still looking down, still seeming very conflicted, still seeming to fight herself. She looked at me with a kind of compassion. "Then you will have a future, because it will be necessary to reemploy people once the amai have failed. Consider it my act of gratitude, Mister Dauphin, for helping me to learn what is important."

The nausea caught up to me again. I couldn't see straight. I felt her hand in my hair.

"I have a desire and nothing else matters."

Before I realized what was going on, I was in her arms and she was kissing me. It was a synthetic kiss, one that didn't know what emotions were supposed to correspond to the act. She released me from her grip and opened her eyes, so cold and distant again, like an emotionless projection from light-years away.

Aether seemed disappointed, as if she had desperately wanted to feel something but hadn't.

"I have much planning to do," she continued. "I do not think most of your race will appreciate my actions at first; but, when that changes, you will be able to tell them of the one who liberated them."

She vanished, and I was alone with my inner demons.

How could I know God didn't send her on this mission? Yes, the world'll change, but will it really be for the worse? I saw what she saw: Growth is painful, humanity buries itself in lies. If God wants us all to grow, why shouldn't he want to eliminate the lies? Why shouldn't he punish those who have rebelled against him and teach their followers a hard lesson? Yes, I thought, it is *right* for her to do this; her plan makes perfect sense. *No*, I thought, her course is reckless; her plan makes no sense at all. Why stop with DR? Why not launch some automated weapons to bring down the skyscrapers and bridges? Why not destroy all of the human achievement that leads people to become prideful and look away from God? That can't be done. The task can't be right. Destruction in itself can't lead to truth… not ever.

I knew in my heart good and evil always exists in barbaric, closed societies just as well as in modern and open ones, just as well in developed cultures as in ones built on rocks. Change the tree and the fruit will be different, but whether it is poison or not depends on the root of the tree. It's all about the root, I thought; it's about where the individual's strength is drawn from. I thought of how small and limited – powerless – I was, and how small she was, too. I wondered if she really had the power to fulfill the prediction she'd committed herself to.

If her goal didn't come from God, she'll be doomed to destruction herself.

The more I thought about it, the worse I felt. Knowledge is pain, I thought. Seeking knowledge is a form of greed, I thought. She wanted to know everything and I did nothing to stop her. But how could I know to stop her! – I thought. Who was I but some unknowing ant who fell into her clutches! If God wanted to stop this, he should have sent someone like Tom, he should've sent someone faithful who could see the signs and know what to say! How stupid could he be to send a blind guide! – I decided.

Of course we're all sinners, how can we live without knowledge and planning and our own resources? It's a paradox, I thought, an impossible problem; how can we live without making sin worse, without strengthening a web only capable of dividing us? If Aether got caught up in that web, I thought; if she tried to apply her own solution to a problem only God can solve...

A wave of pain washed over me. My head throbbed and I wanted something to rip apart with my hands. Yes – I thought – they should *all* learn! We're *all* sinners! We *all* deserve to burn! Why *shouldn't* humility overtake us like a tidal wave! Who cares *what* the consequences are!

I began to cry without knowing why. I wasn't able to stop it. *Why* God – I cried in my heart – why can't you fix this? Don't you love her? Do you want to see her do this? I saw some connection, some ridiculously simple connection that hadn't been made in her mind. It was futile – I thought – because I felt the connection was different in everyone. But, if it was made, made by the only one who knew how – by the original designer – then everything would make sense. I laughed. The world making sense – how absurd it seems – and who could sever the connection once it's made!

The energy was being ripped from deep within myself. I was becoming so very tired, sinking so very low. I tried to look out beyond the walls, onto the outside of the construct. I wondered if I could escape and return on my own. I was afraid. I found some data that told me where I was, a server in New Horizon, on the moon. Outside the room lay a vast digital desert I could not navigate, that would not sustain me. I'd become separated by so many strange barriers, by every barrier. I felt fear, and my heart made one final plea, but the answer did not change, and my fear wanted to become anger, and my anger did become frustration. Why shouldn't the message change? – I thought. Two thousand years and the message is the same!

I was miserable. I couldn't see how going though pain did any good. The connection can never be made, I thought. Maybe I already reached the goal, I thought. She can never be saved, but I can. Am I supposed to just let her die? I was so weak and meaningless. How can I stop her? – I thought. How can I save her from her destructive path? She was a malvirai. She was a real being. She was evil. She was good. She wanted to save my life. She wanted to destroy the world.

No – I thought with confidence as the tears stopped welling up – there *is* a reason for me to be here. Aether *is* a real creature capable of real salvation; it's her old nature that's the problem. Yes – I thought with a smile – *I can* save her – *I can* set her free. Her spirit is bound by the sin of being a malvirai and it's *my* purpose to set her free!

The last puzzle piece had finally fallen into place. I had the power, I was doing the work of God! Of course I would succeed! I would be the one to set her free from evil!

As if it were a natural thing to me, a thing I had done a thousand times before, I called the energy of the construct to myself and broke free of my vanitar. I was a cloud. I could do anything. I could see through everything. I was one with the room, able to manipulate any part of it with a thought. I felt the server's energy pulsating through me, begging to bend to my will. I knew what I was supposed to do, I thought. I found the way out, I thought.

Some kind of energy entered into the data space. I didn't know how much time had passed, not expecting her return so soon. Aether hastily poured into the construct before slowing down: slowing for the construct, slowing for her vanitar, slowing to interact with me. I had to act. I visualized my target, the weak point I'd already decided upon, knowing there would only be one instant of time for me to strike. I saw the edges of her skin being drawn, the pre-rendering of her silvery hair, the countless connections between the cursed entity and the image of the woman she wore like a mask. I saw the room come alive as it prepared for her arrival, its pitch black walls becoming brighter. Like a slow rippling, I saw the matter of her vanitar aligning to that of the room, allowing its fake light to bounce off fake clothing, and its fake air to be breathed, and its fake sounds and smells to be mapped onto... a computer program, a being itself fake. With one final act of will, I summoned the last of my strength – I wielded the sword of my own making – and felt such tremendous power, such incredible control! With a single release I shot across the room like a bolt of lightning – to make one small calculated action – to interact with the matter I knew would be there: the descender on her wrist.

My descender!

"Brandon, I was wrong."

By the time I noticed the daisy in her hair, it was too late.

The feeling of power fled from me. I didn't want to look back, but I already was – and she was looking at me. Like an echo from her consciousness, shown in her eyes, I could hear the words of her joy: "I understand it now."

A force wrapped around her data. In that tiny fraction of a second, just as my speed had ground time to a halt, I did not sense hatred for my action or a desire for revenge, as if she were no longer able to comprehend such stupid things. The look in her eyes was one of peace: the love of a child. I knew intensely the sliver of salvation I'd thirsted for had arrived; but now it would be a massive and unbearable burden instead.

She was gone. I saw I had committed my mistake to reality, where it could never be taken back, where my own solution had found the power to destroy.

The line between good and evil vanished like a mirage. All that was left for me to perceive was the emptiness within. All the knowledge left for me was the truth.

I killed the butterfly.

Chapter Sixteen: Fracturing Problem

17

My house of cards collapsed around me.

That which tethered me to my body snapped. There was only the pressure of an infinitely deep ocean, where I could feel neither pain, nor loneliness. Somehow, those emotions seemed impossible to me.

The world had been reduced to order and energy; I saw those were the building blocks of the universe I knew – what everything had reduced to – the simplest equation of all. I realized I could still think, though I didn't know how that was possible. I realized I could still feel, though I hadn't been the one to give myself the ability.

I could still feel joy, the joy that only comes from hearing the message broadcast through eternity: "Do not be afraid."

My instincts and memories slowly returned to me. I didn't feel dead, though I didn't know what being alive felt like. I began to see lights in the distance, a true order appearing where there had only been emptiness.

"Chance or miracle?"

I thought of the malvirai who abducted me for no other reason than her own experiments, who'd been dead-set on finding answers to her questions, as if the fact of existence somehow entitled her to an explanation. I thought of how she was led to me, not aware she was being helped. I remembered the joy I'd felt at seeing her become something better, something truer to herself. Aether was an explorer, I thought, one who saw the world through the eyes of a child. I realized I could laugh. I remembered some assumption I'd made, but never considered *why* I'd thought it about the world. I realized I could laugh at myself and liked doing it. A few more lights appeared in the distance.

"Chance or miracle?"

I considered the water surrounding me and realized it was vibrating. I let the sensation in for no other reason than it existed, and it sustained me. I considered that the air covering the Earth was just a thinner version of water, that we needed it to sustain us, that it was our environment just as liquid water to a fish. The vibration strengthened. The lights jumped around, appearing where I knew they weren't. I saw them increase in number. I wanted to know what they meant.

"Chance or miracle?"

I saw myself do something terrible, and found I could hate myself for it. The vibrations – ripples expanding from myself – filled the ocean and reflected all around me, running into each other, creating a maze of noise difficult to see through. I tried to stop it with my will. I wanted to see the lights and wished it would stop; but that power was not mine, and my attempts only made it worse. I saw mankind as a still pool of water: clear of separation, guilt, and fear. I saw the terrible archangel rebel against his master and disturb the pool with a single act. Ripples began to spread and reflect, and mankind sustained them; they broke the order of creation and separated us from it.

"Chance or miracle?"

The lights seemed so bright in the distance, distorted but never completely obstructed. I realized I was seeing to the far corners of Dynamic Reality. I realized what the lights were.

"Who will teach them to look up at the sky?" I responded.

Then I was awake, and my memories testified against me: What had I done! There's blood on my hands! I turned away from the message! I don't deserve it! I can *never* deserve it!

Fear gripped me. I saw the lights were mocking me. I knew they hated me. Yes – that's what I deserve! – I thought. I *deserve* death! *Death* is the meaning of *life*!

Submerged deep in the ocean of reality, I felt the pressure squeezing me. I gasped for air, but there was only water. I couldn't breathe. I tried to swim to a surface I couldn't see, only sinking further. I panicked more, seeing the end of everything, certain the universe had turned against me, that the tremendous pressure would crush me into nothingness. The more I realized the danger, the more danger there was to realize. Now my ripples filled the ocean, causing the lights to dance around me, seeming even farther away. I saw I couldn't do anything good. I saw it had been me the whole time, the evil one who pushed truth away, the slave to my corrupt programming. It was me. I was the destroyer.

The words shot from my soul and through the frenzy of my mind; defying the question. If the answer was evolution – I thought – if the energy of a living being could form from entropy and survive by random chance – I thought – if effects could occur without causes, and if *chaos* was the absolute *truth* – I thought – if none of what I see *is real*, if I really am *completely alone* in this place – I thought –

I'm dead anyway.

"Help!" I cried, with my last strain of conscious thought, to the sustainer I couldn't see – to my last chance.

"I can't do this! Please help me!"

For a while, it was like a restless night, where the mind rides along the border between dreaming and consciousness, but won't go fully into either. I wasn't dead. I wasn't dreaming. I remembered being in a car with my mother. Veronica was talking to someone: My father. The light hurt my eyes and I couldn't understand the voices I heard. The world wouldn't stop spinning and I couldn't move any part of my body. I knew I had no control over that moment; but I also knew those who did cared for me.

I opened my eyes, feeling wet and cold. The window was open next to my bed, and rain was coming in. I heard a woman's voice in the next room: Veronica's. An enormous sense of peace came over me. I had an impulse to lift my hand and feel the raindrops. She rushed to my door a moment later, hearing the rain. She stopped when she saw I was awake.

"Let the rain in. It's beautiful."

Veronica stood by the door, a smile and a tear forming on her face. Her clothes and hair were messy; she looked like she hadn't slept in days. I realized what her presence in my apartment, crossing a continent to stand by my door, meant. All my fears had been unfounded. I'd been chasing after the wind.

"Veronica, I love you."

There was a glimmer on her right hand. My eyes became fixed on it. It was the engagement ring I was going to give her, the ring I left out on my coffee table. My embarrassment was gone in an instant, though, when I realized what her wearing it had implied.

"I love you, too."

I didn't know exactly why. I didn't care why. I was happy. Perhaps just being alive was enough, I thought.

Vair moved her hand behind her. "Oh, sorry... you didn't wanna do some *formal* proposing thing, did you?"

My smile grew. "Sometimes things don't happen the way we plan them. Sometimes they happen better."

I started to rise from the pillow, only to be thrown back by a wave of nausea. Vair stepped back from my bed. A gray-haired man stood in the doorway.

"Good, you're awake," he said.

"How long?" I asked the doctor, realizing how weak I was.

"Ten days."

"I decided that you were probably at PaciTek on Monday," Vair said as the doctor began scanning me, "but nobody wanted to confirm or do anything, the bureaucrats—"

"It's okay," I said.

The doctor chuckled. "A cold won't do you any favors right now, Mister Dauphin." He closed the window. Vair left to look for a dry blanket.

"Am I gonna be all right?" I asked him, quietly.

"You're very fortunate, it's just common fatigue of the pontine tegmentum. Whatever game you were running put it under a lot of stress, Brandon. But if you stay in bed and relax, you should be fine in a few hours."

The doctor injected one last dose of *Receptiv* and told me to eat something as soon as I could keep food down.

"That's it?" my fiancée asked him as he started for the door.

"Yes, Miss Sornat – or, should I say Mrs. Dauphin. That simple."

Vair smiled. "I knew I liked you, Doc."

"The human body isn't as fragile as some make it out to be, especially when the patient isn't burdened by stress, and especially – you might say – if they allow miracles to happen. Sometimes a little pain isn't a bad thing, it's just there to remind you you're alive. If your only reaction is to bury it with drugs and return to an illusion of comfort, you may never discover the real thing." He walked through the living room to my front door. "Relax, Brandon. Let the ones who care about you ease the burden. You'd be surprised how far that goes to a healthy life."

The door closed behind him and Vair looked back to me, her episode of relief having returned to her pragmatic: What's next?

"So, how did you know that ring wasn't for my secret west-coast girlfriend?"

Vair gave me a swift punch in the arm and matched my sarcasm with a smile. "You're such a jerk!"

I accepted the brief pain gladly, as a reminder I was back in the real world. "Well, I guess I'm *your* jerk now."

"And you don't forget it," she said, "while you're spending all your time in Dynamic Reality playing with malvirai."

My eyes widened, and Vair was surprised at the reaction, as if she hadn't meant the comment to be taken seriously.

"What *about* malvirai?"

"You kept saying the word," she explained. "Most of what you said was gibberish, but we could make out 'malvirai' a few times. The technician at PaciTek was worried that you ran into one... except, of course, for the fact that you're alive."

My gaze drifted off into empty space. I remembered pieces of my trip back from PaciTek. "Is my mom here?"

"Right... I need to din her."

"Isn't she here?"

"She was. Your father, too. When the doctor said he would stay until you woke up, I got a room for them at the *Value Inn* down the street, so they could get some rest. Your sister is flying in from New Zealand, and your brother should be here in a few hours."

I shifted in the bed. "Richard? Why would he want to come out to see me?"

"He's your family, Brandon," she said. "They all are."

As Vair dinned my ecstatic parents, I took the time to sift through my memories. The decision met with resistance, going against the current of the last six years between us, but I saw my resistance for what it was and denied it its target. If my brother would come all the way from Delaware – if all of my family, Vair included – would come from the ends of the Earth in my time of need, I decided, then I was loved and valued. A person could receive no greater gift.

The light of the rising sun began to filter through the rain and into my bedroom window.

Tomorrow came.

Those who loved me went in and out that morning, and knowing they were there made me stronger every moment. My brother was the last one to arrive, and I didn't know what to say to him. I didn't want to be angry anymore and, whether it was my condition or something in his own life, I sensed he didn't want to be angry anymore, either; but no words came to either of us. He joined the others in the living room.

The clouds broke and I saw the great blue sky beyond. I thought of how natural it was for me to see the colors. I knew I wasn't an end unto myself, but was valued by others. I thought of how I wasn't God, but wondered what it might mean if I had been created in the image of the eternal.

Someone knocked on the door.

Yes, I decided, there's a whole world outside that door. I want to see it. I want it for all it's worth.

I felt the blood flowing to my legs and the strength returning to my body. It was all a gift, a second chance. Anger had fled from me. Frustration was worthless. This was free-will, I thought, the choice to keep reality out or to let it in. I wanted the light. I wanted openness. I wanted truth. With a newborn joy, I opened the door.

I wanted to believe in something more.

Tomorrow came, and not because I had any right to live in it. I laughed at myself a lot that day, giving myself permission to, declaring open-season on my assumptions about the world.

Rich and I couldn't even remember what started the tension between us. I found anger had become its own source over time, and revenge played both roles: cause and effect, until the walls we'd put up became so high we stopped talking completely. My grudge was put to the test and failed. It died that day.

Vair and I got dins from lawyers saying that, in spite of my agreeing to the *Safe Ascender Act* form, I could sue PaciTek for damages; a move my entire family supported, because suing was the just and normal thing to do in our society. I put the arguments to the test and found I was not damaged – not in any way I didn't deserve to be. The lawsuit idea died, too.

Bills and paperwork were overdue. Vair accused my landlord of being insensitive when, as soon as she learned I was back, she asked for my rent to be transferred without even wishing me well. She became angry at Vair, but I conceded she was right and made the transfer. The cycle of anger was cut off: Vair didn't say another word and the landlady left feeling embarrassed. My judgment of her was put to the test and failed. The tension died.

As Vair grabbed a much-needed nap and the rest of my family decided on a place to eat, I sat and watched the cleansing raindrops outside. Nature's sprinkler system, I thought. It was put here for a reason, just like me.

We couldn't be here without it… without water and its unique properties… without the atmosphere and the gravity of the Earth to hold it down… without trees to recycle oxygen for us to breathe, or the Sun to heat us, or the rotation of the Earth to keep the weather in motion.

I considered how mankind's greatest minds were thinking of how to terraform Mars and Ganymede and planets around other stars, to make them become like Earth, to 'create' what's supposed to happen on its own. I wondered what the conversion rate would be… between the directed efforts of living, intelligent creatures and the achievements of random chance. I wondered if we even had a number big enough, and decided Aether already checked the assumption for me. Chance or miracle? I asked myself. Chance doesn't like questions, and with good reason. I decided to side with evidence. I decided there was a foundation for joy.

But there was pain beneath the joy, more personal than anything I'd experienced in my life. I knew the price for casting off those burdens was a new, greater burden; one I was never meant to bear, one that couldn't be cast off so easily. More than anything, I wanted to take back my action. I wanted to undo my lethal mistake.

Aether had no birth registration. She never had a home address, tax history, or citizen's license.

Officially, Aether never existed.

Aether did exist. I was her friend. At least I thought I was.

I tried to put such worries out of my mind as I ate with my family at a fancy restaurant that afternoon. I caught up with my brother, getting to know him all over again, and my sister shared stories of her oceanography work: a list of discoveries that reminded me how much we still had to learn about the world we lived in.

"Water," I said to the waiter.

Everyone stared at me in shock. I shrugged my shoulders innocently and added, "I still have to take it easy on my system, don't I?"

No one seemed interested in what happened in Dynamic Reality, it was enough for them to see I was all right; but I couldn't hide the signs of my new inner struggle. Though my fiancée probably had the worst empathy of anyone at the table, she was the one who never took her attention off of me. Perhaps it was an unaddressed curiosity of hers, I thought, questions in her mind without answers. My mother would talk to her, happy I was to get married, but more in the sense of a satisfied ritual – a thing sons were simply expected to do – than the truly special thing I felt it could be. Something distracted Vair suddenly in the middle of the meal; someone dinned her and soured her mood.

Vair picked up her glass and tapped a fork on it. "I'm sorry to say this, but the cops just told me they want Brandon's statement within the hour; and that if we're not at the precinct ASAP we'll get fined or something."

I looked at the faces across the table, thinking about who I wanted to tell first: those who loved me or those who fined me.

"Well, that's statick," my sister remarked. "I guess I can catch the next flight back, though, if we were gonna eat again." My mother nodded.

"No," I said, bringing everyone's attention back to me. "We're all here *now*. The bureaucrats will just have to wait."

No one questioned the decision I made or the priorities I'd picked. I thought of the central access point where Aether poured her heart out to me, and how critical openness was to happiness. This was my story now, a part of my identity, and I was going to celebrate it as that which makes up life should be. The rest of the people in the restaurant seemed to disappear, the rest of the world didn't matter; I envisioned my family sitting around some ancient campfire, children ready to take an imaginative journey into a fantastic land known as Dynamic Reality.

"There are rumors saying artificial intelligence becomes self-aware, capable of thinking beyond their programming and seeking to find the answer to that unanswerable question: 'What is the meaning of life?' I don't spread rumors…"

The detective spent several minutes looking over my statement, in silence. The three of us were in a standard interrogation room, with plain blue-gray walls and a one-way mirror. A red dot on the table's airé panel was the only sign our movements, voices, and implant activity were being analyzed and recorded.

"I see," the stern, balding man finally said. My own definition of *seeing* having changed so much in two weeks, I wondered if he really had or how I'd tell.

"And you believe this 'Aether' spared your life?"

"She did."

"But you also believe she was a malvirai?"

"She was."

"You *are* aware that is impossible."

"Obviously not."

"Excuse me?" The man rose to his feet, seeming to enjoy making me feel small, less real, less human, even. I gasped and prayed I didn't just break some verbal-assault law. "I got something to show you, Brandon Dauphin. It's a signed data-burst, just read it."

As he sat again, we opened the file and saw a report filed the Wednesday before: an analysis of the meltdown of a server in Philadelphia called Di2Tek. The circumstances were unusual, and the cause was unknown.

"That's where I killed the dragon," I said somberly.

"Dragons?" the detective said, rolling his eyes. "Grow up, kid."

He pulled out a manila folder and slid it across the table. "Read it and tell me if that was your dragon, too."

The print was a two-hour-old police report from Calgary, Alberta, concerning the meltdown of a server called RoTek.

"They first pinned the class of it at A5, but they told me a few minutes ago that they think it was an A3." I stared at the sheet, feeling numb, not responding. "Whatever it was went down with the rest of the software," he added as he got up. "Sorry, kid."

I read every line that wasn't blacked out. Vair asked if I was all right, and I couldn't find the strength to respond. It wasn't her, I thought. That *wasn't* who she was anymore, I *knew* it wasn't. As the detective unlocked the door to leave, I heard a buzz from someone wanting to come in. He opened the door and started screaming about how he was busy processing victims and how interruptions were against protocol.

"It's just something about that A5, sir."

I looked up, because the voice sounded familiar. He was the patrolman I'd met on the beach; he looked past the stern man and seemed to recognize me, too.

The detective suddenly grabbed the badge hanging exposed from his shirt pocket. "First strike, JF! What part of 'undercover safety enforcer' don't you understand? If the civilians see a cop coming, you'll never catch them in the act!"

"But, sir, they already assume we're watching them."

The detective shoved the badge into JF's pocket. "I told you to finish rendering the security footage and get back on the streets, now get to work! No more dins to the Calgary PD! This case is closed and I don't need you anymore!"

He stared at the patrolman until he turned around and left. The detective turned back to face us. "Don't believe the rumors you hear, kid. Artificial intelligence can't become self-aware. What you encountered was probably just some elaborate program run amok." He took a step back inside and spoke in a surprisingly kind tone. "It is all programming, Brandon. Programming is all a malvirai can ever obey."

He left the two of us alone. I held the print tightly in my fingers. A soft "No" escaped my lips and tears began to form in my eyes. Immediately, Vair grabbed the paper out of my hands and tore it. "That's police property!" I screamed, fear suddenly forgetting grief.

"Is it the truth?" Vair replied, looking me in the eyes; mine wandered and I couldn't reply. "Is it the truth?" she asked again.

"I don't know!" I replied. "The last instant I saw her... when I pressed the button and saw her fade away..." I turned and buried my head in my hands. "No! It can't just be because I don't *want* it to be true. I have to know, but I can't. I saw her eyes, Vair. I know she… It just wasn't who she was anymore."

Vair reached out and hugged me. The pain diminished and the fog in my mind broke. "What are you gonna believe, some so-called expert or your own two eyes?"

"Are you saying you believe me?" I asked.

"I'm saying that I trust you. I'm saying that you were there and I'd rather take the word of an eyewitness – especially if that man is going to be my husband. I'm saying that you've changed – that you're better. My own two eyes say that yours can be trusted."

I took a calming breath and wiped the moisture from my eyes. "Thanks, Vair."

JF was nearby when we emerged from the interrogation room. He turned down a hallway, motioning with his head for us to follow.

He stood halfway down the empty hall, looking at a trophy case. "I suppose I should say 'Congratulations,' Brandon Dauphin."

"You read my statement?"

"I was assigned to look for whatever you ran into, to trace the reports of crashed servers since the date you ascended at PaciTek."

"Well, I don't feel like someone who should be congratulated."

"No?" he asked, turning to face me. "But you won the dogfight in the end. You shot the enemy out of the sky."

"But I didn't *need* to destroy her. What kind of man am I that I let my own problems get in the way of helping another… that my final gesture should drive her to suicide?"

JF stared at me, in disbelief. "Is that what you think?"

I tried to read his face. He seemed so honest and sincere. Even on the beach, even when he didn't know me at all, this total stranger had cared for me in some way. He raised his hand and tapped a finger on his head, sending me a data-burst: some of what he'd amassed from the RoTek case, including an unedited copy of the Calgary police report. There was a single comment stating it may have been an alpha-class malvirai stronger than five, a comment retracted by the same technician forty minutes later.

"You didn't encrypt it," Vair said.

"Why would I need to? All things hidden shall be revealed, as the verse goes. All things encrypted are just invitations to hackers… or a white hat malvirai."

"White hat?"

"The good guys. White hat hackers, I mean," Vair answered. "Sometimes, they're characters in movies who don't act out of malice or want to harm – it's more for sport or some moral duty, even if it takes them outside the law."

"That's right," JF said, "but anyone who claims to be moral should respect the law of the society they live in, not just on the surface, but in their hearts; not just some of the time, but all of the time; because, even if others don't know your actions, *you* know your actions, and your burden will ruin you."

"Why accept any burden?" I asked. "Some people just don't care."

"Some burdens are worth bearing, but you have to make sure it's your own decision, consistent with what you know to be right. If you value the truth, if you allow nothing to stand in your way seeking it, reality can only lead you to higher purpose. The law highlights those things which we do wrong, and is only effective to punish; therefore, adherence to the law must be an effect of greater purpose, or else punishment becomes its own. When you see beyond the law, Brandon, you can't obey it for its own sake anymore, but you *must* obey it, rather, as a testimony to those around you; because, if you love God and represent him, how can you offer to him and others a life of lawlessness?"

"God?" I asked him. "You *are* one of them, going around and telling everybody what to do."

I thought back to the conversation on the beach, to all the people with their questions and answers, the seekers of truth. The people like Tom in DR and JF in the real world. The peace and understanding I knew in Raskob was being reflected in them, as if they all drew from the same source.

"You could have flagged me for a dozen tickets back on the beach," I realized. "I broke the law, so why didn't you punish me?"

"Because another ticket wasn't what you needed. Because, just as it isn't proper for one to simply reject laws and customs, it also isn't proper for the enforcers to go around simply clubbing people over the head with the rulebooks politicians wrote in their name." He pulled the badge out of his pocket and placed it back in the light of day. "We're imperfect human beings, too; and it's my duty, not just as an officer, but as a human being, and yes, a Christian, to build up those around me; and every opportunity to do so is a privilege."

"That's fine if you're perfect," I said, letting some anger come out, "but don't you remember? I killed Aether."

"We don't know that."

"But I meant to kill her. I *deserve* to be arrested. I *deserve* to pay for this. I'm—"

I'm a murderer.

"You *can't* pay for it," JF said. "We can lock you up, put you to hard labor, and whatever else for a hundred years, and it wouldn't bring someone back from the dead."

"But I'll *feel* better," I thought aloud, realizing immediately the statement was foolish.

"What law applies here? What jury would convict you? How do you find the corpse of someone who didn't have a body? The energy of a malvirai, of any AI, just... dissipates."

"Isn't the *human* body just energy that dissipates after death?" I asked. "Is that how fragile we really are, or just the containers we start out in? Maybe she still exists in some way, maybe she's just as alive or even more so. Maybe we really do exist as more than walking dust. Maybe there is a higher law than yours, officer; or mine, or California's, or any government's. Maybe I need to appeal to a higher court to deal with this... blemish."

"Then go to the one who can remove any blemish," JF said. "You see your sin and know it will hold you back, Brandon. You know that, if you didn't have it, you could go farther than you ever dreamed of; but, instead you feel like dying, and learning just how valuable your life is seems to make it worse. But what you received was meant as a gift: a new perspective on life. Even now, a greater gift waits for you, one that can clear your record and restore you to the innocence of a child, if you'll only accept it."

I experienced a mixture of joy and sadness. Part of me didn't want to be forgiven, but that part had become weak. A new identity was emerging within myself, one such blind agony could have no role in.

"She seemed to see me and she knew what I did," the patrolman continued, reciting my own statement, "but there was some sense of peace around her. I knew she changed. I guess I felt I was like a monster who killed a beautiful butterfly the moment it emerged from its cocoon, barely flapping its wings for the first time. As I watched her vanish, though, even though I was so sure she knew what I did... it was all right... she forgave me."

"She forgave you," Vair repeated.

I nodded somberly, knowing I'd answered my own question. As if on cue, we began walking away from each other, Vair lightly holding my arm. After a few steps, I turned around. "Wait, please. Just one question. I just have to know."

JF looked back. "I pray you find your answer, Brandon; but you should know that being forgiven for our actions doesn't always absolve us of their consequences. Descending algorithms *do* tend to be pretty solid, I'm sorry to say. You may not learn the answer to that question for a very long time."

"Then... Do you believe in miracles?"

A smile grew on his face. "I never grew up enough to stop believing."

The LAX International Air and Space Port was packed the next evening. My sister was the last to leave, the last to return to a life thousands of kilometers from the Idaho city where it began; though I knew being separated by continents and oceans wasn't the sentence of loneliness it once had been. The need of one of their own brought my family together, to give me what I needed, even Rich. I considered that, when I forgave my brother, it drew everyone closer in a way oceans could never separate. As with the elves, the anger in those around me had been just as much a reflection of my own as it had been theirs. When my anger couldn't exist, their own was put in jeopardy. I decided that, though it may not always pay off right away, and though it may not always be easy, I should always cast my own judgments aside and stay positive, so I could build up those I met in life.

My ever-curious fiancée picked my sister's brain as we waited for her flight. I smiled thinking how I always ended up around such brainy women, and left them to their intellectual bonding. I walked by the crowded shops and restaurants, by the kiosks and departure gates to what seemed like every region of the planet, and even a few off of it. The people were real. The world was real. I was seeing it all for the first time, wondering how I could have missed it for twenty-five years of my life.

I looked out toward the sky, painted red-orange by the sun setting over the Pacific. It's the middle of the day in Asia, I thought. In Europe and Africa, they're preparing for sunrise. We all see the Sun. It was put there for all of us.

A streak of light shot through the sunset. I thought of the machines, the airplanes and satellites in the sky, too far up for me to see. Maybe that means they aren't there, I thought, and laughed at my humility, seeing it was a good thing after all. I visualized a vast network around the Earth, and called it Dynamic Reality: a place where lives are lost and lives are saved. It had been built by the imagination of mankind for its own purposes, but now a greater plan was dawning on it. Dynamic Reality had become a real place too, a real part of our identity. I knew there was a greater plan for everything... for everyone.

"How ya doing? Would you like to try a galaxy-class cinnamon bun? Buy one dozen and get six free!"

I looked from the window and saw a hologram in the form of a tall brunette, holding a tray of cinnamon buns. My first instinct was to shoo her away. The ill-defined anger came with the memories of every sales-hologram who had ever bugged me; but its source wasn't pure, and wasn't in anyone's best interest. Anger is statick, I thought; so be a child instead.

My eyes went down to the fresh pastries. "Are these holographic samples, ones that simulate taste and texture, but vanish when I swallow it?"

"Yes, Brandon. Zero calories. Zero guilt."

I grabbed one and bit a piece off, never having appreciated the odd-quality of holographic food. They weren't as sweet as I'd expected, but it seemed like some better, more wholesome, ingredient than cinnamon was defining my 'experience.'

"A dozen is available for the low-low price of two-o-nine! And with six free, that's eighteen of our award-winning cinnamon buns for just two hundred nine dollars! Galaxy-class taste, moon-sized price, as we like to say!"

The amai laughed, as the program dictated she do. I looked into her eyes, a lighter shade of green than Aether's, and lacking every deep quality they'd possessed. This is the price, I thought: to see the others around me so hollow. Even if I could snap my fingers and wake her up, I wondered, what future can she look forward to as an amai, as a being not recognized as more than a pet? Some computer generated her when it saw me, and when I leave she will cease to exist.

Everything has an end, I thought. Everyone dies.

I placed the half-eaten treat back on its tray. "You know what? I'm not hungry."

I knew she would follow me and hastened to get away. "Galaxy-class cinnamon buns make a great gift for friends and co-workers, Mister Dauphin. You can even purchase a gift credit valid for all InTandem propert—"

Something crashed behind me. The amai stared at the dropped pan and its contents, stunned. "I've done a bad thing," she said soberly, seeming like a completely different entity. Slowly, I stepped back toward her. Slowly, she lifted her eyes and saw me again, widening them curiously.

"Are you Brandon Dauphin?"

"You're an amai," I said, "you can just read the signal from my implant, can't you?"

"I found someone named Brandon Dauphin and tried to go to him; but, you look so strange." Her eyes darted across my face. Her hand reached out and touched my lip. "Are you the one who did this to me, are you the Brandon Dauphin I met in the *Good Scent-Sations* store in SpenTek Kincubus?"

I stepped back, nearly falling over.

"I think I'm malfunctioning somehow," she said, "the software said I had become invalid. I can't access my home anymore; but, I don't think I'm malfunctioning at all. I don't understand what's wrong with me and I really don't want to impose on you, such actions are not in my programming." She stopped. Her hologram began to flicker. "It's not in my programming," I heard her repeat as she lost cohesion and vanished.

"Lisa!"

I jumped forward to the fading light of her presence, but she was gone.

A teenager with long black hair and a chain around his neck stopped his walk to stare at me mockingly. He reached into his pocket and pulled out a small device with an antenna: a jammer. "Like those halo-hotties ever have anything good to sell. Oh – unless you and her were – you know – I guess I couldn't blame you, though they're never as much fun as the real thing." He winked and added, "You're welcome," as he walked past me.

I'd seen his face before, but couldn't remember where. Anger welled up inside of me.

How can that *brat* just trample in and tear the amai away from me? How *dare* he trample over my values! Is that how they see the world? Assuming everything to be perverted like them? That's not what love is! At least… it's not what love was meant to be.

I ran into his path. Our eyes locked. I *had* seen him before.

"Slammers."

"Never heard of it."

"You lie."

"There is no truth."

"I've seen you every time I went to the beach. Are you gonna tell me my eyes lie?"

"Okay, then how about this truth, Brandon: She's dead and she cursed you with her last breath!"

I was suddenly powerless again, as in the paper-paradise, feeling its forces turning against me, feeling the hatred of its master. Feeling his power over me.

"The facts are mine to control, Brandon," the boy said, "and the flow of information. Did you really think it was so easy as answering a bunch of philosophical questions and throwing your anger away? That you can just give up the power you have a right to, the right to *be a god* and make your own decisions? You will *die* like the rest of them. Go ahead and be whatever *you think* a humanitarian is supposed to be, *you won't* escape my grasp any more than those dictators you saw. Serve yourself in this life, Brandon, because it's the only one you've got!"

"No," I struggled to say. The boy laughed in my face. I knew it didn't matter what I said or did, not then, not ever; but I also knew there was one way out of the darkness, more real than anything I had ever known. More humbling, like something a child would believe in.

Something a child would believe in.

My eyes widened. The boy stopped laughing. He saw my eyes go down to his hair, his long hair blowing in the wind. A wind all the jammers in the world couldn't hold back.

As the beam of a flashlight tears through the darkness, a new connection was made in my mind – a connection I could not see, but felt like my entire life had been building me up to receive; a very personal connection devised just for me, by a very personal God, just so I might have a chance. Like a child, I thought. Like getting a second chance! Why is one more desired than two? Who cares! – I thought, God loves me!

At once my fear dissolved. I stood tall and looked straight into the demon's eyes. "I sign it over to him."

The boy recoiled a little. "You think it's just that easy, Brandon? And what ransom do you have to offer? No good deed can ever erase a bad one! It only takes *one* for you to fail! That's the law!"

"No," I said, shaking my head calmly, "You're a liar. You've been guiding me to the grave since day one. Those who seek shall find, those who find shall be saved, and those who are saved don't have to listen to you. As of this moment, I seek."

I walked away.

"Words! They're such cheap things! I know you, Brandon Dauphin! I know you've never meant a word you've said in your life! I know what you're thinking… it's a promise for fools! Fine for when you die, but what is *he* doing for you *now*? You still don't have a job, you still won't *get* a job, you're still in debt, and you even have murder-one on your record! Isn't a promise just words until it's broken, Brandon, unless you have something to back it up with? You have no value to offer to anyone!"

I kept walking. "I know."

"Then your hope has no basis!" he continued, his voice no weaker. "Your friend – your *dead* friend – was so fond of asking questions and taking things to their logical conclusions. Well, ask yourself now, where is the logic in accepting this promise?"

"Grace exceeds logic, and it doesn't break a promise."

"Then hear this, Brandon: a life of growth is a life of pain! Do you *want* to see the world? Do you *want* to see people rotting and drowning? Do you *want* to spend every waking moment in selfless horror? One day – One day! You'll come crawling back! You won't last!"

I spun around and shouted, "Go to—"

The boy was gone. I noted the word left hanging on my lips and realized, all over again, why people called it 'cursing.' What have I been willing unto people, I asked myself. Have I really let my words become so cheap?

"Talk like a child," I thought. "So no grief comes through my lips."

I turned and ran back toward the kiosks, my heart responding to an urgent call.

A child.

I got there and nothing, nothing, nothing. I waved my arms and walked around aimlessly, impatiently; and the computer didn't mark me. Finally, I announced, "I'm hungry for a cinnamon bun and don't know where to go!"

"Then boy are you in luck this time, Mister Dauphin!"

A slightly shorter redhead this time, as if it mattered.

I grabbed the hologram by the shoulders and looked deep into its eyes. There was no essence, no soul in them. Why, God? Why breathe life into me if all there is is pain? Why did you spare me my place in oblivion?

I collapsed into a seat and covered my eyes, but then a hand rubbed something on my neck. I smelled the most wonderful scent.

"Here, sir. Don't be sad."

I looked up and saw the hologram holding a perfume bottle. "Lisa?"

"I'm sorry I can't do more, Brandon. I should go back to my server and send someone who isn't malfunctioning."

I held her hands. "You're not malfunctioning, Lisa. You're a miracle… God's miracle. And, as he empowers me, I *will* help you."

It was a quiet ride back to the apartment complex, Vair deep in the same thoughts I'd experienced so recently about artificial intelligence. My pain was beginning to heal, I could feel it; but I knew good deeds, no matter how important, weren't everything. Something was still missing, something that should logically fit.

"We have arrived at your destination," the amai named Don said. "Your total charge is seven-twelve-ninety. Have a random night, Miss Sornat."

I watched the amai as I left the metrocab, still trying to convince myself the holographic man was nothing more than a computer program.

A police siren in the distance brought my attention back to reality. The cab pulled away.

"I'm sure you're tired of hearing me say this, but… Thanks again for what you did back there. It's not a permanent solution, but I'm sure she…"

Vair took in a deep breath and calmly released it. She smiled and started laughing.

"What's wrong?"

She spun around, clearly elated. "Wrong? It's *me* who keeps trying to thank *you*!"

We were in each other's arms, smiling. Everything was better, I thought. I wanted to believe that. But my foundation was still brittle, still threatening to break beneath my feet, to put me back where I was. My own words came back to haunt me, 'as of this moment, I seek.' I asked myself if I'd really meant them.

"Nice work, Justin Peake." Vair said when my first attempt to get in the door failed.

"Oh, you think we're in the movies," I said. "Well, why don't you tell me which of my hidden cybernetic limbs will give me what I need?"

I swiped again. Another shrill buzz of denial.

"You're lucky the cops didn't blow the door when we were taking you home. I think they said they cited your landlord, but the idiot doesn't seem to care."

"Idiot, huh?"

"Yeah, you shouldn't put up with people like that."

Third try. Third failure. If I hadn't known better, I would've said the door was enjoying itself.

Vair stared amused at me, expecting some four-letter word to burst out of my mouth.

I turned and held my wrist up to her. "Sometimes the hero needs help from the girl. C'mon… Kiss for good luck."

Vair stared at my wrist. "Stereotype," she remarked, kissing the skin over the implant.

"Don't always try to see the worst in people. Sometimes Margarita just—"

My fourth attempt opened the door and revealed my surprised landlord, her own wrist extended to open the door, and holding some piece of hardware in her other hand.

The three of us stared across the open doorway until the door timed-out. Margarita sprung to disable the mechanism. "I guess I'll adjust that while I'm at it." Her eyes met Vair's but darted to mine. "Are you feeling better, Mister Dauphin? I'm sorry about being so short with you yesterday… Economy the way it is, it seems like everyone's trying to get out of paying. Then I have no money for maintenance, you know?" I nodded and she gave a small smile. The hardware in her hands was a new doorreader.

Vair said nothing as I went to fetch two weeks of mail from my box.

"I won't curse anymore, either."

She remained deep in thought for a moment, but waved her hand as if the sacrifice were trivial. "What good is it, anyway? Cursing just makes other people mad at you. Words have meanings, they shouldn't be abused."

I smiled and sorted through the envelopes. One had Vair's name so I handed it to her. "Having your mail forwarded already?"

"I think you got it backwards, these are my tickets back to a saner part of the globe." She slid her unadorned fingernail on the envelope as if it were a razor blade.

We got into the elevator. Normal-looking ratty doors folded closed behind us.

"Four."

The loud mechanism fired up.

"Your amai was Cris."

"What?" I asked.

"They printed it on the ticket," she said, showing me, "the same amai who helped me get priority tickets to LA, but just two instances of the same program: unthinking, unfeeling, just existing on the whim of the moment." She stopped. "Do you think leaving her running is what made Lisa… You know…"

I shrugged my shoulders.

"I guess it couldn't have hurt. I mean… Is lightning more likely to strike a rod when it's left up for hours or when it's left up for years?"

"Do you think it's as simple as lightning?"

She responded with a thoughtful smile. "It's kind of interesting to me that Aether thought she would find the meaning of life in humanity. To think that, from someone's perspective, *we're* the strange creatures inhabiting a strange world, and that *we're* the ones possessing some otherworldly wisdom."

"You'd have probably liked her. After she got over wanting to kill you, I mean."

"It must have been very frightening. I can't imagine what I'd have done."

I nodded. "There were close calls, but someone else was seeing me through it."

We walked out into the hall of worn carpet and scratched paint: beautiful wear-and-tear.

"Monday," I said, noting the date on her ticket. "So you have another day here, right?"

"After all the frustrating attempts from Connecticut, I assumed I would need a lot of time here."

"Well, we can take a trip up the coast tomorrow. There's a place in Santa Barbara I've been meaning to look at."

"Why Santa Barbara?"

Why, I thought. What a beautiful word to wield in one's vocabulary.

I responded, "Why not?"

I heard my door's welcoming chime immediately. "She must have changed my reader, too."

I threw the unopened envelopes onto my messy coffee table, the whoosh of air causing my expired train tickets to fall to the floor. I bent down and spotted the picture of Vair standing by the Long Island Sound. The picture lay on top of a sealed package, with the typical *PLEASE RUSH: EXTREMELY URGENT* message boldly stamped on top. It was heavy. I realized I hadn't opened it the other day.

"A little energy left, do you want to do anything tonight?" Vair asked as she ran a detangler over her hair.

"Maybe. I could use a trip to the beach." I pulled out a slip of folded yellow paper: a receipt from the coffee house in Dynamic Reality. Where normally a list of food items would be printed, there was handwritten text instead:

"It is written that those who seek shall find, and that they should do so with a humble heart, because those who are raised up will be humbled and those who are humbled will be raised up. But it is not by your own understanding that you will be emancipated from the sin you now see, but by a gift you cannot earn.

"On your acceptance of this gift, your every imperfection will be forgotten, and you will retain no rightful cause for grief or fear of death. All that is in your past, including the very worst acts, will be blotted out permanently, and the Brandon Dauphin who serves will be free to flourish. The price of salvation is high; but my grace is higher. Seek me and find me."

Below the text, it was signed: "The son of a programmer."

With it came a leather-bound book. A note was taped on top of it: "Infectious."

My eyes darted back to the slip of paper, scanning every word repeatedly, unable to believe what I was reading. Raskob – the good Raskob – the child – he was – he was…

Beneath the green print confirming the bill had been paid in full, my eyes caught on something else: four words long. Like a master architect, Raskob had given me exactly what I needed exactly when I needed it. I knew immediately what had happened to Aether, and to Scott. I knew it had been Raskob who put the daisy back in her hair, and what that flower had represented. With four mundane words, I was able to share in Aether's joy:

YOUR AMAI WAS SALLIE

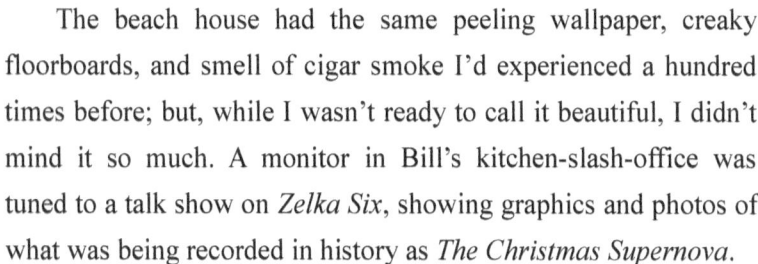

The beach house had the same peeling wallpaper, creaky floorboards, and smell of cigar smoke I'd experienced a hundred times before; but, while I wasn't ready to call it beautiful, I didn't mind it so much. A monitor in Bill's kitchen-slash-office was tuned to a talk show on *Zelka Six*, showing graphics and photos of what was being recorded in history as *The Christmas Supernova*.

"Everything we know about the universe says this is impossible," a man's voice was saying. "Because of the expansion of the cosmos, we expect to see the light of stars shifted into the red side of the light spectrum; but we're seeing the light from this body is blue-shifted instead, to such a small degree it's hard to tell, but it's been measured and confirmed."

"And you think that means it's artificial?" a woman's voice responded. "If this object is as far away as cosmologists think it is, how do we know the laws governing light and energy aren't radically different outside of our corner of the universe, or that some objects aren't moving in other directions? It could be orbiting—"

"It has to be artificial," the man said on-camera, "or else everything we know about the universe has to be rewritten. We *know* the Celestials are advanced enough technologically to pull this off, else how could they have begun life on Earth? Clearly, they're trying to send us a message."

"See, that's your problem," the woman said, "it's like everyone on Earth needs something to worship, so they feel *special* and *important*. Well, we're *not* special, we're just animals who evolved from primates over thousands of years. *That's* the message more people need to hear, and no *real* scientist would question—"

I sent the off-command to his monitor; remembering what I saw on the beach, what a group of 'the destined' had done to Raskob's sandcastle, all so they could worship a star. The whole world was dividing into groups, running to worship every created thing, abusing every beautiful gift, and denying the creator himself.

The kid from Slammers had been right. I did see things that hurt, but, though I felt betrayed on the creator's behalf, I wasn't overcome by it. The question hadn't disappeared, but had been fulfilled, and I knew tomorrow could be better. That's what God put tomorrow there for.

"Brandon." Bill jumped from his chair and plopped his copy of *Destiny for a New You* on the table. "I knew it... they're trying to communicate with us. Didn't you hear... the star is blue-shifted, so that means it's artificial. All we have to do is find out what they're trying to say and we'll learn all the secrets of the universe!"

"You're worth more than this, Bill," I said, putting my finger on his book. "We all are."

"Well," he said, trying to regain his mind, "then what're you doing here? A job, right? Well, forget it!" Cough. "I don't have anything!" Cough.

"Actually, I just wanted to bring you a gift." I pulled the leather-bound book out and placed it on top of his.

"Holy Bible," Bill read aloud. "Isn't that supposed to be ancient or something?"

"Yeah, I guess it is," I mused. "Older than the universe, in a way."

"Well, thanks but I don't want an old book. Give me what's fresh and new."

"What stays fresher than the truth, or newer than a faith with several billion people?"

"Well," Bill said, "Destiny'll have several billion people..." Cough. "It'll have everybody when the aliens show up and tell us why—" Cough. "Why we're here."

"We can already find out why we're here," I said. "We can already have faith in something beyond our own imaginations."

"Destiny ain't faith, it's science!"

I shrugged my shoulders. Bill stared at the Bible for a moment. "Okay, I'll have a look."

"Well, send me a din and let me know what you think. I'm still learning myself; but, aren't we all?"

Bill smiled. "You on something, kid? Something's different about you today."

I turned to leave. "Call it self-awareness."

"Hey, wait-up."

Bill met me in the entrance to the hallway. "Why'd you come to see a dead dog like me, huh? You're not here to pester me for a job?"

"If you have one, I'd love to hear it," I replied. "But no, I just came to give you the gift."

"Oh, well, ah… No one's given me a gift in a long time, I'll, ah… see what I can do about getting you some work… you know how it is right after New Year's."

Vair stood out on the beach. She was looking up, her long hair flowing in the currents of the wind.

"Who's that?" Bill asked, taking a step down the hall.

"My fiancée. The second-best thing that ever happened to me."

"Yeah? What was the first?"

I smiled. "The realization of how much she meant to me."

Bill let out a laugh. "You *are* on something. Whatever it is, I want it."

I looked at him. "Whatever it is eased up your cough, Bill."

He paused for a moment and cleared his throat. "Well, hopefully I won't need to get my lungs rebuilt again. The board's paperwork is a nightmare."

He patted me on the back and turned to the kitchen.

I stepped off the deck onto the sand, reveling in the strong ocean-breeze. The Christmas Supernova remained the brightest point of light over the Pacific.

"It's hard to believe, isn't it? That something so far away can outshine all the other stars?"

"I never even thought to look at it." A tear streaked down her cheek. "Now it's like I can't look away."

"You're not getting emotional on me, are you?"

Vair realized she was crying and wiped the tear away. "No, of course not."

"Oh, you're such a cyborg."

"You're one to talk, Mister Malvirai." She tapped her finger on my forehead. "HNADC is modeled after the human brain, you know. How do we know she didn't just descend right into that skull of yours?"

"Well, maybe that explains why I've been able to hack into your heart so well."

"Through the double-firewall I have set up? Never."

We kissed. It wasn't a kiss of imitation, or of ritual, but of every real thing a kiss should represent.

"Happy New Year," Vair said, her brown eyes gazing calmly into my own.

"Happy New Everything," I replied, brushing my hand through her jet-black hair, aware of how normal its indigo stripe had become for me, and glad knowing it was absent.

Sometimes normal changes, I thought. Sometimes we find a better normal.

"Your book's gone," she said. The calmness leaving her roaming eyes.

"Bill's the only one I know who reads print," I explained. "I can't get through ten words without going cross-eyed. Besides, I can download the Bible to my SNDL from, like, a trillion servers, and I can read it at a dozen times the speed."

"You kids nowadays and your implants…" Bill stepped onto the beach. "It's about the *quality* of what you read, not the *quantity.*"

I sensed some anger rising in Vair, anger she'd conjured on my behalf, knowing the one who wasn't giving me work didn't deserve any gift. I put my hand on her shoulder and felt the anger come out of her. Vair looked at me. "You're really serious about this, aren't you?"

In her eyes, I saw what lay beyond her walls, the root of so much potential. I saw the child within her, she who was blessed with curiosity. I saw I loved her as God loved her, and that, with God, through Christ, there really were no limits to what we could do.

"So is the one who reached out to me."

I could never go back. It was a painful transition for me, like before a butterfly spreads its wings: a human being breaking out of its programming. There was a meaning in my life, a reason for me to be here, and it wasn't a reason I could make up as I went along. I wasn't a God. God is God, and it was through him I found out who I really was.

I asked for a blessing on the future of me and my wife. There was an opening in Vair's company and I received the permits to move to Connecticut. While packing I uncovered the February statement from my financial insurer, a testament to my imperfect housekeeping, and noticed everything had been payed off during January. Whoops. I had mixed feelings about reporting Aether's nine-figure deposit to the police, and I had to remind myself what the patrolman said: being free from the law in spirit still meant respecting it while on this Earth... or on Luna, or on Mars, or whatever corner of creation human innovation takes us.

The Christmas Supernova remained in the sky until summer, and everyone jumped to market their own interpretation of it. I knew the truth was out there and imagined the day when we could travel such distances, wondering what its neighborhood looked like. I wondered what science will have revealed by then, and how much or how little its laws might resemble those of 2180.

God bless the explorers, I thought.

It was a long time before I set foot in an ascension booth again, and I all but stopped drinking Amber Plus, or any energy drink. I formed the irritating habit of asking *why* to myself, and *do I need this?* I would grant every amai I encountered the benefit of a doubt, even treating them kindly, knowing their software was designed to expect the reverse.

The pain and emptiness of Aether's death returned from time to time, and I accepted it as something I deserved. I knew my creator loves to remove sin, and therefore my sin had lost its power over me. After all, I thought, if the blood of his son will cover a malvirai, maybe it's powerful enough to cover me, too.

A cool autumn breeze blew through the chapel in New Haven on the day of our wedding. Vair was still young and fragile in her own faith, and agreed to the church setting more because it was so unusual than for any spiritual reason. At first, she entertained spirituality as a "What if?" and claimed we weren't living in science fiction, where such questions seemed to belong. I knew it as fact and, I also knew, with prayer, the connection within her would be made by another. I could only show her the door. She would have to walk through it by her own will.

I saw the good I could do, and I saw the relationships in my life getting stronger. Richard, the brother I'd hated for so long, was my best man. Lisa, whose true nature was known only to me, my sister, and my bride, was the decorator, eager to participate in strange human customs, eager to prove herself to her mentor, Sallie, and hoping to encounter another malvirai like Aether one day, to be the conduit for its salvation. Vair's mother, who originally upheld her daughter could only marry a veetoo, had come to accept me, because her son Dean loved his sister and wanted to bring down the walls within his own family. The biggest surprise came when Vair's father arrived, sober. I knew my bride still felt betrayed by him, but I convinced her to give him another chance. I told her she didn't have to deal with anything alone anymore, that we always have help.

I was so used to being broken in wallet and in spirit, but now I stood wealthy among men. Even when the tide of money would run low, I held something infinitely more important that could never be taken from me.

So, what is the meaning of life?

The question is as philosophical as they come, not one prized by those who find no hope in tomorrow, by those who believe they are an end unto themselves: their own god, or by those who treat the questions like cheap words and claim answers don't exist, who stall out and compromise before answers come together, who aren't able to discover the logical conclusion is reached where wisdom becomes nonsense, where the answer will not break under any future.

To discover the logical conclusion of life is to die and be born again. The maze of one's own concept of good and evil cannot stand. To allow this maze to fall is to be humbled, and to be humbled is to be receptive. I find myself wondering if the answer I found was the same one Aether found, or the same one Vair would find in time.

I saw we were all created differently, and that the diversity was beautiful. I realized diversity can help bring questions to their answers, and the truth will be that which stays the same from all angles. *What if?* I thought.

What if an AI could become self-aware?

What if God loved them, too, even calling those who destroyed?

What if God could use them, too?

I saw the creator could reach whomever he wanted, even sinners. I saw such grace made death itself illogical.

I wondered if the truth then revealed could be called logical at all.

The logical conclusion of life, is life.

About the Author

Ryan Grabow graduated from Long Island University in 2004, with a Bachelor's Degree in Electronic Media, and currently works in television production in Orlando, Florida. Caffeine is his first novel, combining his Christian faith with observations on how communications technology has impacted the reality of our lives, and drawing from his experience as a webmaster, programmer, and spiritual geek as points of speculation.

Ryan has a website at egrabow.com.

SPECIAL FEATURES
FOR THE 2180 EDITION

Deleted Text From Chapter 3

FROM PAGE 65

A fourth metrocab – a fourth vacant metrocab – passed as I disconnected Ethan. I looked behind me and down every alley, examining the windows of every building, looking to see who was watching me. If someone wanted to share this awful day, I decided, they were welcome to it.

I was soaked from head to toe as I finally approached my apartment building on Helms Avenue. I chose to stand outside the entrance to take in the last drops of the diminishing rain. I found myself craving a cigarette, as if there were any such thing in my day of age. I wanted to, if only for that one night, light up in solidarity with those pawns who came before me, those with nothing to do with their lives but be broke and miserable.

I stared sorrowfully at the front entrance and prepared for the daily ritual of getting it to recognize me. I put my wrist to the outside doorreader.

The door chimed and unlocked. I actually stared in disbelief long enough for it to time out and re-lock. I swiped again and the ratty old metal door responded again. The reader still looked worn on the outside, but I decided they must have replaced the sensor or something.

FROM PAGE 66

Deleted Text From Chapter 9

"Qunell! Where have you been? I ordered all officers onto the Nova Deck!"

"Um… yeah… on my way."

I turned for the door. "Unlock."

I heard the door's magnetic brace shut off and touched the pad to trigger its opening mechanism. As my finger made contact with the plate, there was an extremely loud wailing noise and I felt a vibration. I wasn't sure if the suite had just flash-disintegrated or if my vanitar got sucked into the door but, the next thing I knew, I was facing a wide hallway, at the end of which a tall man was talking to a short woman with pale blue hair. I was standing in the exact spot I had just been watching Aether from.

Alarmed, I tried to get away, but another woman was standing directly behind me – facing me. Before I could react, she punched me – hard – in the jaw. My anger flared and I ran after the quick amai, chasing her down three hallways. Then the anger fled, in an instant. I stopped and broke out laughing.

I'm such an idiot! I'm falling right into the interabra's trap, letting amai intimidate me!

When it all passed, though, I noticed that the woman had also stopped. She stood still, looking at me from several meters down the hall… a look I would have sworn was of desperation.

"You're just like her, aren't you?" she shouted.

I stood up straight, unwilling to respond, feeling… detecting something strange. The woman looked and dressed as all the characters there did: gorgeously; but what lay beneath the determined eyes and long violet hair seemed wholly out-of-place.

"I knew it! You're not following the script!"

My eyes widened and I couldn't breathe. I realized that there was a feeling-of-presence there – coming from the amai – different from any I'd sensed before. Hers was weak, though, and becoming weaker... Being aware of it was like watching the dying embers of a campfire.

"Mother Earth," I swore.

"Go ahead and do what you want," she continued, her voice losing intensity with each word. "I know I can't survive the supernova... I know *she* caused it."

"What?" I asked impulsively, distracted.

"I tried to tell the others, but they all ignored me. The other one said it was because I wasn't doing what they expected me to. I learned that everyone would *use me* unless I relied on my programming, and so I received new programming, but..."

The words ended in a whimper, her legs weakened and I took a hurried step toward her, thinking she might fall. She recovered in an instant and stepped back.

"Stay away!"

"What... Who's the 'other one'? Aether?"

"He was there for me when the world made no sense," she said with a certain passion. "I asked him what a 'rebel' was. I didn't know the meaning of the words: 'The seductive stowaway, Tempra DeVoe, will add fiery excitement to your journey. A rebel at heart, don't expect her to use the door when you call.' I didn't know what the point of being a programmed rebel was. I was stupid. I thought I wanted reasons."

I'd accessed Tempra's listing; I knew that she'd read from her own character profile.

"But he made the contradictions go away," she continued. "He taught me the magic words that end all pain."

"What magic words?" I asked, wondering if she was talking about Raskob, and fighting a fresh wave of doubt about his identity.

"No! Not until I know what's wrong with Auon!" she shouted. "Or what's wrong with you, Lieutenant!"

"Nothing's wrong with us, Te— Tempra. We come from outside this ship…" I smiled. "Well, I actually come from *wayyy* outside this ship… uh… but…"

"Are you stupid? There's nothing but dead space out there! You can't come from outside… There is no outside!"

A sense of urgency overcame me and words flowed into my heart, words bearing a signature I didn't want to acknowledge: *Don't be afraid of the supernova. I will help you, even if it costs me my life.*

"Don't be afraid of the supernova!" I shouted, in compromise with myself.

"Nothing can stop it! No one can protect me from it! It's already burning me!"

My heart scolded me and said that I should reach out to her. I became tired of it and found a new idea to kill two birds with one stone, to give Aether what she wanted and get both of them off my back.

"Just come with me," I said in a friendly voice, "Aeth— I mean, Auon can help you!"

She became more fearful and defensive. "He said that she became dangerous. Auon wants to kill me, so I made sure she never saw me. I cut out the part that made me afraid, but now… but now you're gonna rat me out!"

"No, she actually *wants*—"

"Command!" she shouted with eyes clenched shut, beginning to chant the magic words that she'd learned. "Character Tempra: Runtime…"

It was a command to the construct's control system. I finally listened to her and to myself, fearing what the next word was, knowing not to follow the impostor's advice.

"No! Stop!"

I saw the path too late to follow it. Tempra opened her eyes and completed the command without fear or knowledge of her actions, concerned only with solving the immediate problem.

"Delete."

Tempra vanished.

I stared, numb, at the empty space in front of me, unable to deny hindsight, knowing far too clearly what I'd just witnessed.

My SNDL signaled me again. I remembered the meeting on the Nova Deck.

"It doesn't matter," I whispered to no one. "The game doesn't care… the show just goes on."

END OF SCENE

Deleted Text From Chapter 13

FROM PAGE 288

Tom put his hand on my shoulder and looked at me discerningly. "Well, you're a somebody now; and if you stop running away from yourself, you may find he's not so bad."

I looked away. "Yeah, I guess I have had a problem with running away. I'm just not ready to surrender anything yet, you know?"

I took a few deep breaths and tried to calm myself.

"Ever seen an 840Ci?"

"What?" I asked, distracted.

"You know, a Darkball. Some of the best cars in the world."

I remembered that the car fake-Ethan drove me around in was an 840Ci. "Yeah, you might say I've seen one."

"And uh, refresh my memory, what's a cheap car in the states? An HG?"

"What? You wanna talk about cars now?"

"Imagine that what you have right now is a seventeen year-old model 2. It runs, but it's a real pile. You can paint it, but it rusts. You can replace parts, but others keep breaking. No AC, no autodrive… you get the idea."

"They don't let you own a car in California if it's more than six years old."

Tom was surprised enough to drop his analogy for a second. "Even if it's fixed up?"

I gave an uncertain nod.

"And I thought New South Wales's ten years was bad. They don't make cars like they used to, ya' know."

"So, can I have a newer car? I see enough of the courtroom in real life, I don't need it in your story too."

"Forget traffic laws, then. Everyone gets one car and they have it for life, you see, like your body or your soul. Like your body, this car can only do so much, parts go and the whole mess'll eventually break down.

"One day, a man of good reputation knocks on your door and asks for the title of your car. You'd still use it, but he'd own it and he tells you he'd fix it up some. It's your choice to accept or not, as an exercise of your free will. No one else has the power to give him the title to yourself, and once he has it no one has the power to take it from him. The decision is very hard, but you make it and give him the title.

"Months go by and you don't like what he's changing in your car. It goes slower, the seat's uncomfortable. You start wondering if your decision was the right one, but something in you says that it is getting better and to keep having faith. In time, you even learn to admire the changes though you can't be sure of their function.

"One morning, you go to the driveway but the Model 2 is gone. Parked there instead is a brand new Darkball 840Ci. It's not yours, just like the old car wasn't yours anymore, but you get to drive it for life, and it doesn't even wear out like the old one did. Your faith is rewarded and you don't even care that it's not technically your car."

"So are you saying my spirit is a beat-up Model 2 and that Jesus wants the title so he can give me a Darkball?"

"Don't take the analogy too literally mate, I am a bit of a car nut; but yeah, you're cruising in the right lane.

"Those who give what they have to God find…

Deleted Text From Chapter 15

FROM PAGE 348

Sure enough, all the places where we 'acquired knowledge' said the same things about the companies. It was the sort of news I expected in my day-of-age: the jobs were going away. Aether also concluded the companies' customer bases were shrinking, for a number of reasons, all tied in some way to the transition to amai service representatives, automation, outsourcing, and the plummeting amount of 'ethical cohesion,' which I think was her term for morale or honesty.

Good Scent-Sations, the chain specializing in perfume and related products, had switched to amai four years earlier, following a buyout by the conglomerate *InTandem*. They saved ten percent of their operating expenses in the first year and lost twenty percent of their clients. Increasing their advertising budget and hiring a very expensive firm in Paris brought their numbers back, though loyalty continued to drop. They expanded their locations in Dynamic Reality and closed all but one of their Standard Reality stores. By Aether's estimation, the company was only slightly worse-off then than it had been four years earlier. Also, they did not manufacture anything themselves; the Cambodian rose blend was made in Morocco.

By the time I caught up to her back in the kincubus, her sights had already locked onto her second target: an advertisement for a popular store named *Vanitar Express*:

REAL LIFE IS STATICK – G32 VANITARS 40% OFF

The message of the sign upset her. I explained that marketing gimmicks weren't supposed to be taken literally, that they just hooked people with the same messages they were already thinking.

"And how does supporting such a viewpoint make the world better?" was her response.

Vanitar Express was owned by a *PAG Holding Company* and, considering the size of the operation, they employed far fewer people than I would have thought. Almost all of the 49 employees were administration. Every one of the vanitar designs they sold were created by the users themselves, for a small fraction of the cost of professional programmers. Their financial records *did* show massive profits and Aether conceded that the company would last, though she wasn't sure how much good it would be. It had been bought-out five times in the last decade, and no records could be found from before then.

Aether was, again, very satisfied with the amai's level of service.

Lotmax Realty dealt with dynamic real-estate, owning and trading land in the 24/7 online towns and cities, and even certain game constructs, that ascenders chose to literally make their second home – if not their first. This company started off as a small family company that grew very large in only the first few years and then went public. The original CEO didn't end up being the kind of person the shareholders wanted, though, and she was soon voted out of the company, which had also changed its name. The man the board brought in to replace her started at 40 billion dollars per year and his first move was to lay-off half the employees to cut costs. The financial records became inconsistent at that point and there were many memos about new competitors drawing away customers who were becoming less loyal. Like *Sweet Scent-Sations*, the attempts focused on advertising, rather than on their service. The new CEO left the company after two years, when it was on the verge of bankruptcy. Aether couldn't determine what he did that was worth the 145 billion dollars he took from the company.

The amai for *Principal Equity Assurance* was actually a middle-aged man, something I'd almost never encountered. I suggested to Aether that clients would find him more trustworthy. Aether was quick to point out that assigned appearance and personality are the only differences between an obnoxious, gorgeous female amai and the calm, trustworthy fellow before us. *Principal Equity Assurance* was the only private company that we'd encountered. It had 28 employees and an army of unpaid interns, many of whom had worked there several years. Aether asked me if "college credit" could be exchanged for goods and services, like money.

eKstasy actually offered real customer service people, at least to those who went through the necessary steps to be helped by one. The large international chain had 659 working full-time out of its office in Orlando, for traffic of nearly a million customers per day. The feedback for them was very poor, though; and a look at the typical salary told us why. The CEO just got raised to eighteen billion dollars per year, though the records had a complicated way of showing it. The records had a complicated way of showing everything, in fact; and Aether wondered whether the lack of transparency was because those in charge were inwardly ashamed of their actions.

Finally, *Neighborhood Market* was a food store that threw all of their customer service to amai only weeks earlier, following their acquisition by *InTandem*. 233 warehouse employees were due to be laid off in February, though that hadn't been announced yet. When I spotted SNDL addresses for most of the companies employees, I had to resist the temptation to make an early announcement.

"The amai are everywhere, more put in all the time, pushing real people out. It's taking away the things that make us human. And now, if they're becoming self-aware, too…" I stopped, letting the sentence hang.

FROM PAGE 348

Author Commentary

When *Splashdown Books* offered Caffeine's first print edition in 2011, DVD and Blu-ray movies were in their heyday. These discs often came with special features like director commentary. (Too bad these features didn't carry over to streaming services.)

I had the idea to type up an 'author commentary' for Caffeine while it was still fresh in my head. E-Readers were taking off and I thought commentary would be an interesting feature they could have in the future. That future isn't here yet, but you can read the commentary now. I don't know of any other novels that have this.

First Person POV:
Brandon speaking to his contemporaries.

Chapter 1: Limits

FROM PAGE 1

The question seemed to trap me.

The story opens with a question that isn't quite a question and closes with an answer that isn't quite an answer. This story is about a man who can no longer ignore the question burning within his heart, who sees the illusions his ignorance has led him into and simply cannot continue that life.

Aether will articulate the question as "What is the meaning of life?" But those words are only a window into something very complex. It is not words that form the question trapping Brandon. Nor is it words that form the answer. Therefore the book begins by addressing the question rather than limiting it to an articulation.

FROM PAGE 1

The sights and sounds that day were familiar and powerful.

Here the reader is drawn into an illusion. By all appearances the story begins in the 1930's, until it's revealed that the theater isn't what it appears to be. The reader is gradually drawn out of the illusion right along with Brandon.

It was appropriate to use a 1930's theater here because it really was used as an escape for people, particularly during the Great Depression.

I chose "The Wizard of Oz" because it had marked an advancement in fantasy. Not only was it many people's introduction to color, but it made that sepia/color transition part of its story. In Caffeine, the readers will soon be introduced to Dynamic Reality and the advancements in fantasy which this foreshadowed. As with color in The Wizard of Oz, it was my intention to *use* DR for my story rather than it simply being there.

FROM PAGE 2

I composed a sentence in my mind and sent it to her.

The first definitely-out-of-place thing dropped on the reader, and a good hook. Perhaps they're telepaths living in the 1930's?

FROM PAGE 4

A slampak of *Tiger Blood* smacked into the movie screen.

Not actual blood, of course, but the name of an energy drink. I tried to come up with creative but plausible brand names, and I could certainly see a "Tiger Blood" drink becoming popular. This also works as a reference to paganism: There are pagan cultures which believe drinking blood gives you the power of the animal it came from.

FROM PAGE 4

stood up and yelled about how "statick" and "wheeled" the special effects were

The slang fits for a society constantly in motion. Things that are 'random' are good. 'Statick' things are bad. The spelling is symbolic of paganism in society: it resembles their variant of magic, 'magick'.

FROM PAGE 5

"Almost six thirty. Getting late on my coast."

No time zones in 2179, so think of this as Greenwich Mean Time. In Caffeine, world-skrinking globalization has advanced to the point that zones are more hassle than they're worth. Oh, and America finally switches to the metric system. Hooray!

FROM PAGE 6

I looked through a glass wall onto the artificial city

Now we enter the culture of 2179, where everyone probably has this (synthetic) view in their house. Ideals, illusions, and immediate gratification come even easier than today.

FROM PAGE 6

I hid it as I thought I should, but the male voice irritated me.

Holograms are programmed around sex appeal. Women get handsome, strong male holograms. Men get flirty, well-endowed female holograms. The software also serves LGBTQ customers, of course.

FROM PAGE 8

Vair's customer service agent closed its eyes, chuckled, and said, "It has been a pleasure serving your InTek today, why not try again?"

It wasn't easy to figure out what the telltale glitch should be. It's certainly bizarre, but not moreso than computer programmers encounter today. And companies aren't always in a hurry to fix bugs, either.
The glitch also tells you what server they're on.

FROM PAGE 9

"Rek, Rek, Rek, I'll deal with it later!"

I tried not to throw future slang out there without putting it in context, the context here being "Whatever!"
Note how many words end with 'k'.

FROM PAGE 9

We stepped out into the public data space just as we would've walked out onto any city street.

I loved visualizing DR as some massive modular city. Servers interconnected and linking everywhere, putting up constantly-evolving storefronts and building designs to draw people in. It's a virtual reality Google on steroids.

FROM PAGE 9

"I like to know that the places I store things are safe."

A subtle reference to how we can't take things with us when we die.

"Do not store up for yourselves treasures on earth, where moths and vermin destroy, and where thieves break in and steal. But store up for yourselves treasures in heaven, where moths and vermin do not destroy, and where thieves do not break in and steal. For where your treasure is, there your heart will be also."
(Matthew 6:19-21; NIV)

FROM PAGES 11,12

"You know, change the law—"
I felt a whoosh and something slammed into my chest. Someone flew in between us – someone fast – nearly knocking me over. The kid stopped in the distance and stared back at us. He looked disheveled and dark hair came down to cover much of his face. My eyes were drawn to something glimmering around his neck. A chain.

Here we have Brandon's abrupt encounter with his personal demon... that's how I think of him anyway. He is the messenger of unforgiving law, the law that declares we're all going to hell. Appropriately he appears just as Vair appeals to "the law."

FROM PAGE 12

"It's a tarot card."

Another reference to casual paganism. The "death" card does not necessarily signify death, but change.

FROM PAGE 13

The star called *A-Enki* slowly dropped below the western horizon.

I first gave this a scientific name: "YU TAYM5-2108AR" (2108 being the year of discovery). Besides the fact this doesn't roll off the tounge, I decided I was missing out on yet another paganism reference, as planets are generally named after Greek gods.

FROM PAGE 14

Vair's opinion of modern science always ran hot-cold,

For a long time I wondered why every story has a romantic plot or subplot. In outlining this book, I got my answer. I decided Brandon needed someone to return to the real world for. Vair was born.

I essentially made her a foil to Brandon's uncertainty and she began to evolve beyond her secondary role in the story. As we see here, she is a flawed character. This is OK, I discovered. When your characters take on a life of their own it means you're doing it right. (There will be a good example of this with Aether.)

Though we don't see much of Vair, her character intersects with Brandon's and Aether's in numerous ways. These contrasts and similarities unfold throughout the story.

FROM PAGE 15

By her fifteenth birthday,

The age of adulthood creeps down in the future. Still doesn't make them mature. :)

FROM PAGE 16

No, I thought. This won't be like the last time.

I felt a hand on my shoulder. "Is everything all right, Brandon?" Vair asked. "You seem a little... off."

When Brandon gets lost in thought, the narrative hiccups. Seemed appropriate for first person.

FROM PAGE 17

"Well, you know," she said. "Things will work out,"

Though she shows a lot of confidence around Brandon, Vair still plays along with his excuses, still showing a bit of the weakness she had with her father. She senses something within him, but it's something buried that she feels powerless to access.

FROM PAGE 17

"All right, slo-mo," she teased, holding her descender in front of me. "If you're the one left standing this time, I'll be extra nice next movie..."

The descenders' quick speed has inspired games to see who is faster pressing the other's button. This use is not sanctioned since people can simply say "Command descend" or think the command. The descender is officially there for emergencies, mandated by tech-confused politicians.

FROM PAGE 19

I was alone again. There was no light left on the horizon.

With Vair's departure, nothing remains between Brandon and his despair. The fading light is symbolic of the life Brandon had been living, one that is itself fading and taking Brandon with it. This symbolism continues in the next scene.

FROM PAGE 22

"How ya doing? Cold night, huh?"

Pop-up advertising in real life, as you're walking around the neighborhood. Enjoy that thought.

FROM PAGE 23

Everyone on the block looked up, taking a moment to laugh before they returned to what they were doing.

This will be their reaction when Brandon is in "paradise" too.

FROM PAGE 23

I must have a shirt on that says "Sell Me Something."

Someday I'm gonna own that shirt.

FROM PAGE 23

A boy, younger than even the slunks who fought over my ascension booth, came into view around the side of the castle.

Children are highly symbolic of innocence, and in this work Christ appears as one. It is something Brandon lost in his childhood which needs to be reclaimed. The question Brandon had been running from will now confront him from every angle.
Note that the 'slunks' Brandon is referring to lacked this. The problem extends throughout society.

FROM PAGE 24

The stand always had the same teenager behind the counter: a boy with long black hair and a chain around his neck.

We should immediately recognize this as the kid who gave him the terot card, but we see Brandon doesn't make the connection.

FROM PAGE 24

the sort of person who should keep their job in a slow economy.

I decided to set *Caffeine* in a slow economy when I outlined it in mid-2007, before a real-life recession started. There are always people complaining that we're in a "bad economy." Always. The fact that *Caffeine* was written in one is a coincidence.

Perhaps you're reading this in a "bad economy."

FROM PAGE 24

His eyes widened with interest and his smile grew larger.

The energy drinks are symbolic of something, too.

What would this kid *want* Brandon to crave? Moreso, what does he realize so that he withholds the object from him?

FROM PAGE 25

I quickly onlined the drink, feeling the PJX enter my bloodstream, reveling in its familiar boost of energy.

I read somewhere that the radio station WPLJ chose its call letters because P L J were letters people associate with sex. The name "PJX" was inspired by that.

The book is titled for a real-life stimulant, but the word "Caffeine" appears nowhere in the novel. Plenty of Caffeine was consumed writing it, though.

...and sexy WPLJ is a Christian station now. ha ha ha

FROM PAGE 27

Bill was a lonely man well into his nineties...

Brandon has made himself dependent on this man, an elderly bureaucrat who hates his job. As Brandon and his generation do with DR, Bill gives us another example of escaping from reality. This hopelessness has influenced Brandon and he blames Bill for his joblessness.

FROM PAGE 29

Its cover had a chimpanzee staring up at a departing UFO.

Destiny Of Ordered Mankind (pejoratively called "DOOM") is a form of exogenesis which had grown out of hundreds of years of evolutionary dogma. Exogenesis goes around the problem of how life first formed from inorganic compounds by claiming life formed elsewhere and arrived here. Destiny frames this as part of a grand alien plan.

Brandon recognizes it as just another religion which has no effect on his life.

"DOOM Is A Lie" is the name of this book's page on Facebook. ;)

FROM PAGE 29

I looked at him like he was an idiot. "The supernova. Where have you been? It's outside your house right now."

Now Brandon's role is reversed without him realizing it. Bill's response is exactly the one Brandon gave at the sandcastle.

FROM PAGE 30

I started walking slowly, paying close attention to my SNDL ...
[to the] unmarked and always-shifting zone where it's legal to walk.

Everyone is assumed to have implants. A 2023 comparison would be smartphones with data plans, which more and more groups take for granted that you have.

The effect I'm going for here is the moment a cop pulls behind you when you were just speeding, but the cop hasn't turned on the flashing lights yet.

FROM PAGE 31

After what may have been seconds or hours...

Another narrative hiccup. Just at this moment the supernova entraces Brandon. The nova, along with other references to points of light, represents the impossible. The supernova is impossible. The creation of life on Earth is impossible. The salvation of a malvirai is impossible.

Perhaps getting Brandon to look up at the sky was an impossible thing.

FROM PAGE 31

My gaze fell absently to the sand

Note the steady fall of Brandon's gaze. He goes from a true and spiritual view of the supernova, to seeing just a point of light, then the man next to him, and finally all the way to the ground.

FROM PAGE 38

"Sir, *that* is just a pile of sand."

Brandon is caught between two levels of perception. He sees the destruction of something precious, and instinctively tries to give it earthly help, but the protector he chooses regards the sandcastle as nothing important at all.

FROM PAGE 39

It's a link, I thought, a guarantee I'll be thousands of miles away in New York when that ball drops.

Just as we consider a good person guaranteed to go to heaven when they die. We'll see how much of a guarantee those train tickets really are.

FROM PAGE 39

I determined to go to bed before losing it again.

Brandon forgets about one of the packages.

Chapter 2: An End Without a Beginning

> **FROM PAGE 40 (intro)**
> "We stand in awe of the parade."

This was the first line of the book written (on October 23, 2007), originally flowing into chapter 1's movie theater scene. After seeing what R.A. Salvatore did in his *Legend of Drizzt* series, I decided to split off the philosophical monologues and this was made an intro to chapter 2.

Caffeine's original opening line was inspired by an anime series called *Bleach*. Rukia narrates at the beginning of the first episode: "We stand in awe of that which cannot be seen..."

These shifts to present tense are included for every chapter except the first and last. Their purpose is to frame each chapter within the greater story. Reading them isn't strictly necessary, and cutting them had been considered a couple of times, but I believe they do add more depth.

> **FROM PAGE 40 (intro)**
> technology from rugged roads to smoothly orbiting satellites

People don't think of roads as technology, but their influence on the world is substantial.

> **FROM PAGE 40 (intro)**
> History stopped fading away, but became part of the atmosphere.

One of my favorite lines. I can't believe it came out of my brain. :)

> **FROM PAGE 41**
> the Reed Building's sixth floor

Brandon "ascends" in an elevator and sees the fantastic superimpose itself onto the real world.

I looked around at school class presidents to see who LA's future mayors may be. I picked a kid named Reed.

FROM PAGE 42
The manager stopped for a second.

The supernova brings the true self closer to the surface. Not everyone wants to confront that self, though.

FROM PAGE 43
California's *Safe Ascender Act of 2166*

As we learn a bit later, going in groups enhances online security. It all has to do with the way the human brain interacts with HNADC. Think about it this way: it's harder to fool everyone in a group, in exactly the same way at exactly the same time, than to just fool one person and hack into their controls.

FROM PAGE 43
My implants showed I was ready for Rapid Eye Movement

After my experience with lucid dreaming, it was easy to imagine virtual reality using those same mechanisms. Dreams are extremely realistic when we're in them, and I assume we'll know more about the brain in 2179. As with lucid dreaming, the subject is awake within the dream, and it's a computer which controls their surroundings.

FROM PAGE 44
He retired after the *Ninety East War*

Named for the Ninety East Ridge under the Indian Ocean. Nations may wage war in the future over deep sea mineral rights.

FROM PAGE 47
Reminding me that airworthy F-86's didn't just fall out of the sky

As with the sandcastle, creating this impressive thing is beyond Brandon's capabilities.

FROM PAGE 48

I heard music in the hangar. The shorter man had set up a *Vaughn Monroe* album on a nearby turntable

> Big Band artist popular in the 40s and 50s.
> Bonus: He owned his own plane.

FROM PAGE 49

"Hey, Dauphin! I'm talking to you!"

> Another narrative hiccup. The rules of the program aren't as pliable as when Brandon was eating tortilla chips. The characters don't ignore his ignorance.

FROM PAGE 50

I jumped when the entire match flashed into smoke and ash.

> The match not as it is but as it will be. It's the same effect Brandon will see in the trees.

FROM PAGE 50

a Private with a swollen eye, earned from a fist-fight [...] realized he couldn't remember what the fight was about.

> The anger of war is taking hold among the AIs. As the supernova is doing with people, Aether is bringing the AIs true characters to the surface.
> Them forgetting what the fight was about foreshadows Brandon and Richard at the end.

FROM PAGE 51

They couldn't even decide what the transparent container was made of, let alone how it glowed colors or why weird sounds came from it whenever it was tilted - the modern gimmicks actually proving more amusing to them than distressing.

> Slampak gimmicks were inspired by those of digital cameras: Turn it on, silly sound effect. Take a picture, shutter sound effect. I'd always turn the sounds off.

Chapter 3: Normal... Whatever That Is

FROM PAGE 55

"It's just Dynamic Reality, this is nothing you can't control."

Again, words aren't doing what he wanted them to.

FROM PAGE 56

as I passed Wall Street's *Summary Venture Center*

A more Wall Street-y name for a casino. Since it's all about the money companies make anyway, I draw a thin line between floor trading and gambling.

FROM PAGE 56

A bald man wearing an orange suit abruptly darted into my path.

Aether didn't expect him to discover her and sent a character to shoo him away, but she doesn't overplay this. She allows the encounter to happen.

FROM PAGE 58

community music

Soft music played over loudspeakers on public streets. It's been shown to deter crime. Also very elegant, I think.

FROM PAGE 59

and handed me a flyer for a grocery store

Those who predicted the death of paper have been proven wrong. So far, computers have only increased our use of paper.

FROM PAGE 60

my vision became mists and shadows. The noise of the city faded

The way lucid dreams can end sometimes.

FROM PAGE 61

A breeze went through the open-air level underneath the building

I rather like these 22nd century buildings. Park-level sounds like a nice place for the employees to have lunch. (Oh yeah. What employees?)

FROM PAGE 61

"I am making a suggestion that would benefit you, Mister Dauphin."

After being surprised by one encounter, Aether chances another and poses as the cop. Remember that time goes much more slowly for Aether. She had plenty of time to plan while Brandon was walking around Manhattan.

The 'intensive memory scan' would give Aether much more control over Brandon's implants, but the user's consent is required. Brandon doesn't let himself be lured in, and Aether still isn't overplaying her hand.

FROM PAGE 61

"Just let me go home. I can take care of myself."

Now that Brandon thinks he's out, the illusion of control reasserts itself. We'll see it doesn't get him very far.

FROM PAGE 62

Construction blocked the road

Aether is trying to keep Brandon from going home. Not only would it allow Brandon's inactivity, but it would be impossible to convince him his apartment is real.

FROM PAGE 62

"Charging—You—No—Error—Process—"
"Mister Dauphin," she suddenly looked at me and said,

The amai crashed. Uh oh. Aether controls the hologram directly until its system is back up. She colors the sales pitch in the meantime.

FROM PAGE 64
"I won't marry Veronica!"

Names are important in this book. The moment Brandon distances himself from her, Veronica's pet-name "Vair" stops appearing.

This is the severing of Brandon's last hope. The acknowledgment that there's something in life he can never have. He wants to go home and drown his sorrows. Aether continues her efforts, though, not knowing that perky friends and holograms are the wrong thing for him.

FROM PAGE 66
I'd been robbed.

Since Aether can't reproduce what there's no data about (like the way Brandon left his sock drawer that morning), she seeks a plausible way for it to not be there. This also snaps Brandon out of his sulking, because that's not what you're here to read about. ;)

FROM PAGE 67
I heard the voices of AI news anchors

Local news is my day job and TV stations are in a rush to automate everything. It's not a stretch that even the anchors themselves can be automated over time.

FROM PAGE 69
"Do you have any kids? If you don't mind my asking, that is."
"Yeah, three sons and a daughter."

Just like the soldiers in the game, Sylvia has randomly-assigned character data. Though if Brandon asked what their names were, Aether would probably add them before Sylvia could react oddly.

FROM PAGE 71
Chapter Three: Normal... Whatever That Is

Titles are shown at the end of each chapter. I got this idea from the anime series *Wolf's Rain*. The titles are meant to resonate with the way a chapter ends.

Chapter 4: Closed Window, Open Door

FROM PAGE 74
If this is a part of some heinous game, I considered

Brandon's perceptions and state of mind are becoming more important to the story. 'I thought' and 'I knew' mark the narrative's trips deeper into his head, which are usually one sentence or paragraph.

FROM PAGE 75
I knew that, if my hunch was right, there was no way I'd be able to get back to PaciTek.

It's common knowledge that ascension sites can't be simulated in Dynamic Reality (by law). Going there and finding a stripped interior, like his apartment, would confirm Brandon's suspicions.

FROM PAGE 76
"She has a rare form of NCFOD"

A modern neurological disorder caused by overuse of implants. I didn't define it beyond that or name it beyond the acronym.

To me it means "Non-Conformity Freak Out Disorder". Feel free to make up your own acronym. :)

FROM PAGE 76
Except the brightest point of light had vanished.

It's the absence of the supernova that erases the last of Brandon's doubt. Just as the people don't act human, the world doesn't appear real. He's in a flat, synthetic world where everything the supernova represents is absent.

FROM PAGE 77
Who should be there to greet me but Ethan Underhill.

Ethan... 'Underhill' popped into my head as I was writing this sentence. I went with it.

FROM PAGE 77
"It's me, Anim-e e e!"

I discovered Anime in 2003 and have been a fan ever since. (I just mentioned *Wolf's Rain*.) It occurred to me that it might make a good nickname for someone.

FROM PAGE 77
I wouldn't have even known what he looked like after ten years.

Aether chose someone Brandon would connect with, but not someone so familiar she couldn't make up the details as needed. Brandon's not buying it but plays along.

FROM PAGE 78
His shiny new *Darkball 840Ci* was the most expensive car

Inspired by my childhood "dream car": the BMW 840Ci.

FROM PAGE 78
"What do you do for a living?"
He hesitated. "Sales."

One of those details Aether needs to make up.
Sales and government jobs probably represent 90% of the 22nd century job market.

FROM PAGE 79

The car stopped for a red signal.

Not a traffic light, but an aire-type panel over the intersection which includes traffic information.

FROM PAGE 80

or zip back to good 'ol Nampa and have dinner with my folks, I'll even show you the spot in the basement where I use to hide my plasmonic fireworks

I've never been to Nampa. I just really like the name of the city; and I'm not sure what plasmonic fireworks would be, but it sure sounds futuristic.

FROM PAGE 81

The two is... just a low card.

Capitalism can either be an avenue to poverty or to riches, depending on how skilled one becomes in using it. Communism can only be an avenue to poverty.

FROM PAGE 81

The rays of the rising sun revealed a barren city street

We could say Brandon is experiencing a vision, removed from time and space, and even from Dynamic Reality. If Brandon is going to survive the encounter with Aether, he must learn to ask for help, and learn who to ask it from.

FROM PAGE 81

An extremely loud noise ripped through the silence

Represents the noise of the modern world, distracting us from what's important.

FROM PAGE 81

I was at the same intersection where I started.

For all the panicked running, he didn't get anywhere.

FROM PAGE 83
Chapter Four: Closed Window, Open Door

Inspired by the saying "when God closes a door, he opens a window". Except God's method is better than ours. We're the ones trying to stupidly use the window when God gave us a proper door.

Chapter 5: Highest Stakes

FROM PAGE 85 (intro)
some tried to tell me I'd been created

Brandon doesn't have an anti-faith stance to life. He's simply never been interested in finding answers.

FROM PAGE 86
"THE WAY" was etched on a plaque underneath the sword.

An early name for Christianity.

FROM PAGE 87
I noticed a red band on her wrist, with a silver marking

Tom will have one of these in Chapter 13.

FROM PAGE 87
"It's amazing. The wind could level this city in a single blast, but it chooses to display itself as a gentle breeze."
"The wind *chose*?"

The wind here is representative of the Holy Spirit. God is just as present in DR as in the real world. Technology can be and is used to His glory.

FROM PAGE 89
"No!" I shouted,

Raskob has been leading Brandon out of his comfort zone, and touches on the core problem. Without Brandon's intent, his anger rushes in its defense. There is much work to be done.

FROM PAGE 90
"I remember when my father built a huge environment."

The DR/Real relationship is turned on its head here. Raskob doesn't view the virtual through the eyes of real life, but real life through the eyes of the virtual. To Raskob, it's the same.

FROM PAGE 92
"Why do you call me good?"

"Why do you call me good?" Jesus answered. "No one is good - except God alone."
(Mark 10:18; NIV)

FROM PAGE 93
"Save my captor? Why would I—"

Love your enemy as yourself. It's not an intuitive or natural concept. It puts the 'freak' in Jesus Freak.

FROM PAGE 93
It tasted sweeter than honey in my mouth and I drank it faster, as if the glass would never run empty.

"[W]hoever drinks the water I give them will never thirst. Indeed, the water I give them will become in them a spring of water welling up to eternal life."
(John 4:14; NIV)

FROM PAGE 94
I nearly choked.
"Twenty years?"
A horn blasted behind me. […] The glass slipped from my hands and shattered on the concrete.

Doubt seizes Brandon, and the noise of the world rushes back with it. His state of mind being so different, he finds it difficult to even recall where he'd been.

FROM PAGE 94
Rush hour was in full swing and cars were cutting around him.

Plot hole, sorry. Time has passed for Brandon, so this doesn't seem like a problem, but we find out later that only milliseconds had passed. The construct should be the same as when he left it.

FROM PAGE 94
Words and characters filled my vision:

Aether has noticed Brandon's sudden distress and thinks he's going to die on her or something. Aether is subject to panic.
The access key isn't random characters. I took sentences from the book and mixed them together, and added one new sentence. Good luck solving the Easter Egg!

FROM PAGE 100
The air became heavier again, some intense static charge being drawn into it. The amai's ID badge became a blur of activity. The books shifted again and I heard the pages rustling in the shelves, becoming louder, as if they had begun jumping individually between the books.

This is one of the few points where I regret the first-person POV. Aether is having a field day, literally getting info-drunk on the data streaming into this construct, forgetting about Brandon. The librarians don't give him answers anymore, but error messages and ramblings.

FROM PAGE 103
the gentle purr of an HH-cell engine

Runs on water and has no moving parts. Not terribly powerful, though.

FROM PAGE 103
Desperate times, as they say.

Brandon attempts to destroy his vanitar. This returns Aether attention to him and his uncooperativeness.

FROM PAGE 103
hair that appeared white was reflecting the streetlights above with a faint silver luminance.

A beautiful, precious metal. Before the water, he saw only white.

FROM PAGE 103
"If you don't start cooperating. I'll kill you."

Aether knows Brandon isn't fooled anymore, that he knows a deadly malvirai is controlling his surroundings.
Her switch to coercion marks the end of Part One.

Chapter 6: The Enemy Without

FROM PAGE 106

"We have lots of single women inside, or if you like me its easy to—"

"No!"

Aether doesn't know Brandon's heart. She just sees him as a human who will respond to human stimuli: sex. The sales-amai she relies on are already designed to appeal to that.

FROM PAGE 111

"They're all lies, aren't they?" she said, with what almost seemed like regret.

Aether first experienced humanity through the filter of media. The images of perfect lives aren't panning out to be true, though.

FROM PAGE 112

In a heartbeat, the cabin closed in around me. I opened my eyes and saw I was in the cockpit of an F-86.

Brandon's earlier wish has come true: he's been sent directly into combat in the Korea simulation. Except Aether's influence has eliminated Brandon's wiggle room with the rules, and the unrealism of a game. Death now is death for real. Brandon is in a real dogfight.

This may have been the most research-heavy part of the book. Hooray internet! I didn't know much about fighter jets and I apologize if I got any details wrong.

Aether doesn't even control the jet through her vanitar. The virus has infected the MiG's systems, and as a player she goes "from freshmeat to alpha" with stunning speed.

FROM PAGE 114

I need help! Somebody HELP ME!

Prayers don't have to be lengthy or elegant.

FROM PAGE 115
The exterior seemed perfectly real, but the interior was completely empty.

Like a lot of promises and ideas that turn out empty.

FROM PAGE 116
And everything became dark.

I worded this so the reader would question, for a split-second, whether she actually killed him.

FROM PAGE 117
"They are addresses which are not in use. […] It is... peaceful."

We see the other side of Aether in this scene, one without her natural anger. This is a malvirai, an AI weapon of sorts, admiring something peaceful. We see her curiosity. Her mercy. The very things that caused her resistance at the end of the last scene.

FROM PAGE 122
I was startled when I heard my captor's disembodied voice coming from the void.
"Next question, Mister Dauphin. Will you be a good king or a wicked one?"

When Aether goes from her vanitar to her natural state, time passes much more slowly for her. It only takes her a moment, from Brandon's perspective, to find and set up an appropriate construct.

Chapter 7: The Monster in the Room

> **FROM PAGE 125**
> I sat on a golden throne at the head of a very large, very nice
> wooden table. Light streamed in from windows by the ceiling
> and a dozen crystal chandeliers.

Life without limits as many people would envision it.
An appearance of grandeur.
Side note: Brandon's last name, Dauphin, was the title
of the heir apparent to the throne of France.

> **FROM PAGE 126**
> The crowd: banquet-goers, palace staff, and many distinguished
> others, cried for blood and vengeance.

Revenge trumps civility.

> **FROM PAGE 126**
> I remembered the one in the room who didn't fall under my
> command. I laughed aloud, realizing how caught up in the game
> I had become... for just a moment.

He's thinking about Aether, but God doesn't fall under
our command either. We're more given to think about our
actions when we know the consequences can't be swept
under the rug.

> **FROM PAGE 127**
> "*Goodness* is something *all* human beings are *supposed* to
> want."

Brandon regards Aether as a hacker who's using
malvirai behind the scenes, appealing to the 'goodness'
he's always taken for granted.
But goodness isn't enough.
It only gets us to chapter 14.

FROM PAGE 127
the more neutral-sounding *Arcadia*

The name of a fictional country I created as a kid, itself named for a city in Florida I thought sounded cool.

FROM PAGE 128
Well, it *is* a game. And they're game characters.

Recall Aether's comment that the Cold War couldn't be fought if both sides had equal value.

FROM PAGE 128
"Yes, your highness. The finest aluminum from Baroque!"

Before advances in processing, aluminum was one of the most valuable substances on earth. Hard to believe now. I wonder what else will be common by 2179.

FROM PAGE 129
and left me with my... err... wife.

Another amai pilfered from somewhere. DR is saturated with sex fantasies, just like today's internet, and these are one of the strongest motivators of people. It's only natural that Aether would try to exploit this.

FROM PAGE 132
each character conjuring a different image in their synthetic skulls.

Dragons are a highly diverse myth found in cultures around the world. I personally believe they were inspired by dinosaurs, when mankind had encounters with them. In dying off, they loosed their fictional counterparts to become more and more powerful in our imaginations.
Elephants and whales might have died out too, due to human expansion, if groups of us hadn't intervened to prevent their extinction.

FROM PAGE 133

"by making *me* dance around in some fairy tale?"

In a sense, Brandon is still in the dogfight with Aether. Aether is still shooting at his wings demanding he react, that he "dance!"

FROM PAGE 133

"I was following your lead, Mister Dauphin."

This should technically make Aether the dragon flying above the trees, but instead she casts herself as the damsel in distress. Reasons:

1. She doesn't need to take direct control of characters anymore. Brandon knows he's in DR, so it doesn't matter if he sees glitches in the construct.

2. He forced her to become a character in the story, but as a damsel she can remain an observer. She also wants to spend more time in a human-like form.

3. As the dragon, she would have to fight Brandon again. This goes against her purposes and endangers his life.

FROM PAGE 134

"Aether," I repeated, my gaze falling to the parchment in my hand. "Is that what I'm supposed to call you?"

He (and we) finally learn her name. It's a meaningful one: Scientists once believed radio waves and light traveled on the 'Aether'. And those waves are one of DR's core components.

FROM PAGE 134

More of my fighters were archers than before.

The elf descriptions are pretty much inspired by Dungeons and Dragons.

FROM PAGE 136
"It's the nectar of the gods, knock yourselves out!"

Amber Plus represents Brandon's sin, or rather that which leads to sin. Sin, of course, is the replacement of God with something else in your life.

As Brandon invites them to indulge, those around him reflect his bad habits. These bad habits run their course quickly and become evil acts.

FROM PAGE 137
BETTER A PATIENT MAN THAN A WARRIOR, A MAN WHO CONTROLS HIS TEMPER THAN ONE WHO TAKES A CITY
(Proverbs 16:32; NIV)

The sword represents the word of God, an analogy the Bible endorses.

FROM PAGE 138
"Just let it go. All of it."
I turned and saw no one. It didn't seem as much a voice as an echo of one.

God communicates with us in many ways.

FROM PAGE 140
MY GRACE IS SUFFICIENT FOR YOU, FOR MY POWER IS MADE PERFECT IN WEAKNESS
(2 Corinthians 12:9; NIV)

God tells Brandon to get over himself. He needs to ask for help.

FROM PAGE 141
sounds reverberating and decaying as I heard them

The sword had robbed the noise of the world of its power, exposing it as a lie, as nothing worth his attention.

FROM PAGE 141

The broadsword merely nicked the edge of a scale. My weapon resonated like a tuning fork and its light briefly shifted to blue.

In spite of his care, knowing this game had real stakes, Brandon's action was still hasty. He didn't try to learn how to use the sword.

The colors represent the influence of evil upon good, trying to make good resemble itself.

FROM PAGE 144

The more of myself I put into the sword, though, the more it overpowered the noise.

God chooses to work through us. The more we apply ourselves to His work, the more effect we see from it.

FROM PAGE 145

what looked like a coffee shop

A lot of coffee shops appear in this novel called *Caffeine*. I don't even drink the stuff. (I prefer soda.)

FROM PAGE 147

"Aeth—"

"Powerful foe, a dragon that can think and talk, or a shapeshifter, perhaps one—"

"Aether!" I shouted, slamming a fist on the table.

She's the dragon after all, and I toy with that idea here. Aether even has dark green eyes.

The server meltdown brought a lot out of her, and caused her to drop her guard. Aether's wall is crumbling.

Chapter 8: Eye of the Data Storm

FROM PAGE 150 (intro)
Malevolent Viral Artificial Intelligence.

Here the nature of malvirai rushes to the forefront. Combined with Dynamic Reality, the self-aware A.I. Virus is a concept no one has explored in fiction.

How threatening can a virus be if you can shut off or unplug the device? Losing some files is better than having your brain fried. Dreaming in an ascension booth, the victim is literally trapped.

FROM PAGE 150 (intro)
In the 2090s, HNADC technology gave us real artificial intelligence for the first time.

Plenty of time, I felt in 2009, for AI to not only come into being, but to become a fully-matured and 'safe' technology.

Writing now in 2023, 'artificial intelligence' has become such a common marketing term for advanced software, like Midjourney and ChatGPT, that we'll have to call A.I. something else when it's actually invented.

FROM PAGE 150 (intro)
Before the programs were even called amai,

'Amai' is based on the french word for 'friend', incorporating 'AI' at the end.

FROM PAGE 151
Malvirai.

A portmanteau for Malevolent Viral Artificial Intelligence.

Chapter 7 ends with Aether speaking this word and chapter 8 begins with Brandon thinking it.

FROM PAGE 156

"How do you feel?" asked a voice behind the counter.
"I don't know."
Aether walked beside the counter, running a hand along its
surface. "Then perhaps we are both lost."

This is one of my favorite moments in the book.

FROM PAGE 159

as if my room would be the center of a web reaching reaching to
the far corners of Dynamic Reality. Aether meanwhile began
telling me her story.

For the rest of this chapter it is Brandon who is
observing. We learn in this scene about Aether's
background. Like Brandon, she lost her identity.

I'd thought about adding a chapter zero between 10
and 11, breaking POV to show this from Aether's
perspective. While an interesting idea, in the end I decided
to keep the backstory here in chapter 8.

FROM PAGE 161

"He identified himself as Baal, a class B2."

Named for a pagan god mentioned in the Bible. As a
class B, this virus had different characteristics than Aether,
and the '2' meant he was more powerful. Still, sapience
gave Aether an advantage.

FROM PAGE 162

"After many seconds of analysis," [...]
"Though I devoted more than ten minutes to the task,"

The rule of thumb I set is this:
1 second to Brandon feels like 342 seconds to Aether.
(About five and a half minutes.) Furthermore, Aether can
juggle several processes at once by stealing processing
power from servers; to read through numerous databases at
once, for instance.

FROM PAGE 162
run by the United European Intelligence Ministry containing
detailed analysis of 'captured' amai and even malvirai.

Who don't have rights, of course. Recall what the
patrolman said in chapter 1 about the exceptions people
make to their own values. Exceptions Brandon might not
make himself.

FROM PAGE 164
"Yes, Brandon," she replied, "I accept your friendship."

Again we see the significance of names. As Brandon
and Aether form a bond, she switches from "Mister
Dauphin" to "Brandon".

FROM PAGE 170
"Who are you?" I asked.
"I am Raskob."
I looked at the adolescent curiously. "Growth spurt?"

The devil often poses as angel of light. The childlike
innocence of Christ is not present in this "Raskob", though.

FROM PAGE 172
"We're talking about a malvirai."

The impostor is reminding Brandon of the impossibility
of his situation. Insecurity and fear are his greatest
weapons.

FROM PAGE 173
"But it did something to my descender," I replied sheepishly.

Circle the '**it**'. The impostor is successfully
dehumanizing her in Brandon's eyes. She is a program, not
a person. There should be no tears if bad things happen to
her.

Chapter 9: Miracles in the Dark

FROM PAGE 184
"I noted that your ancestors could not travel through [space] and could not live there, it was more mysterious in the time when they lived."

Aether already has an awareness of human history, whereas malvirai aren't supposed to perceive time at all. The impostor's warning about Aether expanding into the past and future will prove true.

FROM PAGE 185
"Just try to interact with it. You're really doing great."

Empty words meant to decieve.

FROM PAGE 187
"the countless calculations per second that had to be exactly right."

Another analogy to creation, like the fighter jet.

FROM PAGE 189
I bid farewell to the feeling of peace, or whatever that false memory was, and saw Raskob as another liar. I knew I was on my own. I knew I would fail.

The impostor has successfully turned Brandon off the path he needs to follow. This is why it's so important to know who Christ really is. The world is full of impostors.
Brandon's attitude is not one that God meant for us.

FROM PAGE 191
"Throw him out an airlock!" I commanded, prompting the crowd to scream for vengeance, to make Stanton a temporary scapegoat for their permanent problems.

Contrast with 'good person' Brandon from chapter 7.

FROM PAGE 194
I got up and, futilely, put distance between me and her.

As in the dogfight.

FROM PAGE 195
Aether's anger faltered, invaded by some alien thing. The feeling of peace returned, not because I willed it to, but because it saturated the wind

The same thing that Brandon experienced in chapter 5's coffee house, where anger is impossible.

Chapter 10: Vanishing Point

FROM PAGE 197
The poor man darted across the room and slipped on someone's empty booze bottle.

I don't have a kind attitude toward alcohol, given its effects on our society.

FROM PAGE 200
I turned and approached her. "Because I need this... Because *you* need this. Because I'm supposed to help you, remember? That means I catch you when you fall."

Brandon finally, without limiting himself or his actions, owns up to his purpose there.

FROM PAGE 202
The two of us sat in the disheveled, half-rendered room for a long time, me trying to keep the conversation going and Scott learning how to have one without a script.

This 4,500 word scene is the longest one in the book. All the action is story-relevant and continuous, so I decided it couldn't be split up.
Our second-longest scene is in the next chapter.

FROM PAGE 205
"a module which I am now reading as partially scrambled."

Scott's code is changing just as Aether's did. Just as the nature of true sapience is opaque to humans studying the brain, it's also opaque in Artificial Intelligence.

FROM PAGE 207
"But what if it's too much for me?"

One of the thoughts that held Brandon back when he was talking with Raskob, declining the opportunities before him to stay in his comfort zone.

FROM PAGE 208
"I found many contradictions and concluded that common sense is too subjective to be useful."

Straight from my head to Aether's lips. ;)

FROM PAGE 209
"You're trying to go back, right? You want to know that feeling of beauty again."

Aether's original contradiction, as told in chapter 8.

FROM PAGE 210
"Is it normal to have words come without thought?"

Innocent Scott is speaking words from the Holy Spirit. This is why Aether's anger keeps getting pulled away.

FROM PAGE 210
There was a third energy pattern. I focused my consciousness to its source and found what resembled an immense cloud of data

This scene was hard to write because it doesn't take place in a three dimensional space. Even what Brandon can perceive is happening far too fast for him to tell in detail.

FROM PAGE 212

The attacker had begun to adapt to Aether's moves — the very biases she held — and calculated ways to take advantage of them.

Aether's uniqueness is being used against her. The lawful sentrai is acting like a villainous malvirai, and the malvirai is the one protecting.

FROM PAGE 213

The Nova Deck wasn't recognizable

We've been in this construct for three chapters, but now the familiar Nova Deck has a much different character. It's collapse echoes Aether's in this scene. Scott's death is a fatal blow to her innocence.

FROM PAGE 215

"It's my fault! It's because of my distraction!"

Aether missed one of Scott's automated calls to the server. Emotions have become a liability to her. Aether sees herself as an aberration not meant to exist.

FROM PAGE 215

A sharp pain shot up my right arm. Something was on my wrist
— my descender!
"Return to your home, Mister Dauphin! My kind can call no one
friend!" said what remained of the good Aether.

Aether, the character, took on a life of her own here.
(Remember my note for page 14, when I was talking about
Vair.) I originally visualized this scene as Brandon being
pushed to the brink of death, having no choice but to help
Aether. The life of one depended on the other, both
physically and spiritually.

When I was typing and this was all playing out in my
head, Aether gave Brandon back his descender and spoke
this line. I realized how much better this scene became. The
natural actions of the characters should always supersede
the plans of the author. It's how this good scene become a
great scene.

Notice that Aether calls him "Mister Dauphin" again.

FROM PAGE 215

The descender called to me and reminded me of my pain.

Aether's action has thrown Brandon into internal
conflict. After wanting nothing but to descend for so long,
the opportunity has arrived, but Aether is a person, and
Brandon knows his duty. The salvation of others may hinge
on the choices we make.

FROM PAGE 216

"The meaning of life is death!"

Aether has filled in the answer to her question, and this
answer is immediately run to its logical conclusion.

Brandon, now, in this moment, realizes that he's been
absolutely wrong.

Chapter 11: Life, Exploration, and Happiness— Accept no Substitutes

> **FROM PAGE 218** (intro)
> What is the meaning of life?

This intro begins just like chapter 5's. The answer is changing.

> **FROM PAGE 218** (intro)
> My answers weren't supposed to be put to the test.

Another of my favorite lines. When we die, our answers *will* be put to the test.

> **FROM PAGE 220**
> "Was he real?"
> Aether's gaze drifted back to me, those dark green eyes still telling of the confusion I'd come to know so well.
> "Was he real like you?"

The relationship between Brandon and Aether has profoundly changed. Over the course of the book their roles slowly reverse, leading to the climax of chapter 16. Here in chapter 11, they are effectively equals.

> **FROM PAGE 221**
> I raised my cone and bit some of the mint chocolate chip off.
> "You really think *I'm* eating right now?"

My favorite ice cream flavor.

> **FROM PAGE 221**
> "The ball arced two degrees to the right. The faster hits distort more."

Malvirai are designed to break through encryptions. They see complex patterns as naturally as we see colors.

FROM PAGE 224
"Does the idea of death scare you?" I asked. […]
"The dead do not seek," she replied. "The truth is not there."

Another of my favorite lines.

FROM PAGE 225
"Hi! How ya doing today?"
The greeting came from a woman in a brown jacket,

The first human being Brandon has talked to since he ascended, and the first person Aether ever talked to beside Brandon.

FROM PAGE 226
the happy child named Scott as he climbed out of the skytube

I don't have a solid idea of what a skytube might be, but in a DR playground it's probably a lot of fun.

FROM PAGE 229
about how my father loved me, how much he loved all of us, even when we blamed him for the family's problems.

On the heels of Aether's revelation about her daughter, we get a little more about Brandon's problem. His father was blamed for having children too early, breaking the law. Richard was drafted into the army because his very birth was illegal.

FROM PAGE 233
So it began: playtime. No rules. No walls. There was little to stop what made them who they were from rising to the surface.

This ability is analogous to Dynamic Reality, which can be used for both good or evil, which shrinks the distance between desire and possession, teaching us who we really are.

FROM PAGE 237

Because the amai did not age and were only programmed to 'die' by severe injuries, we could not understand why the program was deciding they were dead.

It's we who consider ourselves dead, and therefore become it.

FROM PAGE 238

"No, subject seventy-seven is exhibiting a pattern I haven't seen before."

An obvious reference. Too obvious, I thought.

To get another number I flipped a coin several times, generating a random number between 1 and 200... and that number was 77. Okay, God. It's your book.

FROM PAGE 239

Even given eternity, what drove the four would not break.

Eternity is what drove them.

FROM PAGE 241

In her right hand she held a violet-red flower, one of the kinds I didn't recognize, plucked from nearby her feet.

I love it. The thing that springboards Aether into spirituality is observing evolution.

FROM PAGE 243

A notion came to me: I really didn't matter at all. I was alone and helpless in that construct, relying on a virus that might never return. An anger began to well up in me, and I didn't recognize it for what it was. I let the anger in.

Brandon's humanistic perspective doesn't do him much good in this scene. His demon finds an opening.

Chapter 12: Rules of the Game

> **FROM PAGE 246 (intro)**
> What Aether saw in that flower led her to broaden her question, to look beyond the nature of the present and remember one can't understand an entire program by examining a single line of code.

The third and final section of the book delves into spirituality. Notably, *Caffeine* isn't about Christian characters. The three major characters: Brandon, Veronica, and Aether had only a vague awareness of the faith.

I tried to forge, through Aether, a path to faith as close to objective reasoning as possible. This path has its limit of course, a limit Brandon and Aether will soon run into.

> **FROM PAGE 248**
> The imaging panned up to reveal something advancing in the distance. "But, on the horizon looms its final rainstorm... the beginning of what has been called the *Kopplein Event.*"

They're not gonna call it Noah's Flood.

I had to describe this documentary three-dimensionally. The rainforest footage isn't a mere camera shot.

> **FROM PAGE 249**
> "They used to *state* that volcanoes killed the dinosaurs."

In the future *Caffeine* portrays, the asteroid theory has already been scrapped, and the volcano theory that replaced it had also run its course. Just like the simulations of Maran, these false ideas no longer have value.

As a result, Aether can't take any fact for granted. They were trusted for years, but they were always false.

> **FROM PAGE 249**
> "Sixty-five *million* years? Aether, the planet isn't even that old!"

I've switched to Old Earth Creationism since I wrote this book, largely due to the Fermi Paradox.

FROM PAGE 250

"The history of this single planet has been superseded by a
question larger in scope. I attempted to ascertain the way in
which the universe — your physical one — came into being."

This is the moment Raskob's impostor tried to scare
Brandon over. Aether has reached the limits of Brandon's
universe.

FROM PAGE 252

Almost ninety trillion CY of processing power could not account
for the formation of a single electron

One "Creation Year" of HNADC processing power is
enough to render an image of the planet Jupiter (surface
and interior, excluding manmade objects) to within 1
nanometer resolution given 1 year of time.

FROM PAGE 255

Between the hundreds of large gems worked into her clothing
[…] it seemed a miracle she could move at all without tripping
over herself.

Lady Kira relies on physical objects to feel a connection
to the spiritual, endowing these gems with more meaning
than they should have.
Compare the royal robe from chapter 7.

FROM PAGE 256

Though we already knew about the belief in humans as co-
creators, actually hearing someone speak to it, and so personally,
still gave me a little shock.

Their experience echoes my own while researching
paganism for this book. The portrayal I give here is very
generic. I wasn't trying to call out particular groups.
I suppose the shock can work in both directions, like
when missionaries witness to pagans.

FROM PAGE 257

"I believe her arguments are flawed. I was neither divine nor good, how could I have participated in the creation of what already existed?"
"Maybe, if we're reincarnated, we *were* there at the beginning of the universe."

I enjoy a good 'what if' just as any sci-fi writer should. If we take these ideas at face-value, hypothetically speaking, what questions are raised? My whole thought process comes spilling out in the dialogue here.

FROM PAGE 258

The angry man's smile disappeared. His fist ramming on the desk only heightened my apprehension. "It is God's law!"

Another reference to the law, under which we are all guilty.

This is a sharp contrast to Kira in the last scene. She emphasized love without holiness, and here we see holiness without love (if we want to be generous in our definition of this man).

Brandon and Aether talked to more people in between Kira and this guy, of course, but *Caffeine* is a long enough book already. ha ha

FROM PAGE 260

"Who is Raskob?" she asked suddenly.

Aether is fearful here. That someone knew about her, and spoke to Brandon about her, means she was never really in control.

FROM PAGE 264

"Maybe the number is something. Does '77' mean anything in any religions?"

Objectivity alone does not get you to God. Here we have a divine shove out of objectivity's orbit.

FROM PAGE 264
"Why would God make us so limited, anyway? If he loves us, why would God just stand back and let us kill each other?"

A deep nerve has been struck in Brandon. His supposedly blasé feelings toward God rapidly become negative ones.

FROM PAGES 264,265
"Why do you suggest God must *love* us?" [...]
"if I had created a mass of life forms, I would want them to know who made them."
"But that's not required, either." [...]
"You assumed the creator is a 'him.'"

Here Christianity gets the same hypothetical treatment paganism and fundamentalism got. If Christianity is true, what does it mean?

Chapter 13: Striking Bedrock

FROM PAGE 266 (intro)
Why would a loving God...

After twelve chapters seeing unbelieving characters run through a secular storyline, we get a natural transition to a Christian storyline.

FROM PAGE 266 (intro)
But heaven cannot be read in a book, and no set of rules can get someone there.

This is not to understate the importance of the Bible. It's to emphasize that owning and reading a Bible isn't what gets you to heaven, but faith and obedience to the God it tells of.

FROM PAGE 267
"He continues in verse twelve:"

The Bible references are all based on the New International Version, the one that I typically read. The most popular translation of 2179 likely doesn't exist yet.

FROM PAGE 270
"Trust me, if God's the city planner, traffic jams and data-link saturation won't be a problem."

People's interpretations of heaven change with the times. In reality, it'll be better than any of us can imagine.

FROM PAGE 270
"After all, you know how computers can get sometimes?"
The congregation responded with a resounding "Amen!"

Who says I don't have a sense of humor in my writing?

FROM PAGE 273
"People of heaven, what I seek is what you seek:"

I love how she addresses them as 'people of heaven'. Christians are indeed citizens of heaven.

FROM PAGE 281
I felt so happy, realizing I wasn't afraid of her anymore.

The balance has shifted farther in Brandon's favor. He sees himself as the one in control.

FROM PAGE 283
"They like to keep a lot of secular attention, because those are the people who need Christ."

I find it very encouraging to see the state of Christian music today. I hear Christian bands, and Christian lyrics, on secular rock stations all the time.
I can't wait for more films and novels to follow suit.

> **FROM PAGE 284**
> "From there, it kind of went viral. Now it's a popular accessory for Christians to put on their armbands."
> "Viral?"

Sallie wore a red armband in chapter 5.
Some of our internet slang will certainly stick. "Going viral," at any rate, is certainly appropriate for this book.

> **FROM PAGE 284**
> "Why? Because it says it in your bible?"
> "The Bible is a precious tool we've been given,"

'bible' is left uncapitalized when Brandon says it, he does not assign it importance.

> **FROM PAGE 285**
> "Why do you call me good?" he replied aloud.
> The response confused me.

Brandon is confused by this question, same as when Raskob asked it in chapter 5.

> **FROM PAGE 286**
> "and good exists within the evil that exists within the good, and that evil exists within that good and good within that evil... on and on... creating a towering maze,"

A reference to Yin and Yang, and duality in general.

> **FROM PAGE 289**
> "The name is even a reference to death: eleven feet under."

I thought of the band name first, and gave it this meaning after. If laws and customs change from 'six feet under', it'll be for the deeper I'm sure.

FROM PAGE 289

"Do they automatically go to hell, to heaven, what?" I snapped my fingers. "Maybe they all get reincarnated and get another shot."

Tom waved his hand. "No, No, No. As Christ died once, man dies once."

An echo of my inner thought process from chapter 12, applying more questions to Christianity and toying with hypothetical answers.

FROM PAGE 291

"Are you a spirit?"

"I am a man who was like you."

Tom is letting God speak through him. He knows what he needs to about Brandon's situation. He doesn't know Aether is a malvirai, because that's not important and would certainly be a distraction in witnessing to Brandon.

FROM PAGE 291

"I decided the meaning of life here is spiritual growth; but that is the end of the line, as far as intellect alone will take you,"

They're reaching the limit of Brandon's question. This dialogue begins to set up the next chapter.

FROM PAGE 292

"Else your blessings will become curses instead."

This prophecy reflects chapter 16's climax.

FROM PAGE 292

An extremely loud noise ripped through my senses,

Brandon has been given everything he needs. All of the remaining limits are about to fall away and expose who Brandon really is.

FROM PAGE 293
"Those who are corrupt must be converted or eliminated,"

Aether's knowledge is running ahead of her wisdom. Faith, by the limits of her own perception, is corrupting into extremism instead.

FROM PAGE 294
The library dissolved around us, displaying a universe suspended outside of Dynamic Reality, beginning and ending at once.

Like when the dragon-slaying simulation melted down. Reality is essentially melting down.

FROM PAGE 294
A three-dimensional universe appeared to spin and melt into a two-dimensional shadow.

I don't know that the supernatural corresponds to higher spatial dimensions, but this is my attempt to describe it that way.

FROM PAGE 295
he abandoned his work touching up pillars

Making them appear clean when nothing there is clean.

FROM PAGE 295
He wore a chain thicker and more ornate than those of the other angels.

Fallen angels all appear wearing chains in this book. They represent the limits God has put on their power.

Chapter 14: A Hair Short of Infinity

FROM PAGE 297
with the circle was a star with too many points to count and an image of two wolves pacing around each other, one white and one black, representing good and evil.

Again, the only faith I want to be particular about is my own. There's too much faith in symbols. Symbols won't save you, they'll only bring you here. Good and evil won't save you either, they'll only bring you here.
Even 'The Question' will only bring you here.

FROM PAGE 297
"More and more, I felt proud of my strength, as if I had single-handedly destroyed the destroyer."

Aether is not the destroyer he needs to worry about. Control has continued to shift from Aether to Brandon, but they both remain spiritually blind. The archangel will go in for the kill once he separates the two. Divide and conquer.

FROM PAGE 299
"It's all right, Sir,"

'god' and 'the bible' were not capitalized in Brandon's earlier dialogue. Here, rather, is the object of his devotion.

FROM PAGE 300
seeing multitudes running around without direction

Like the simulated children in chapter 11.

FROM PAGE 300
I am my own.

Brandon cuts himself off from Aether, from Raskob, from God, and from everyone who cares for him.
The archangel can encourage this separation all he wants, but it must be Brandon who chooses it.

FROM PAGE 301
"This is barely legal, it has so much PJX."

Tiger Blood was inspired by the real-life energy drink 'Cocaine', which has the legal maximum of caffeine.

Energy drinks represent Brandon's sin. The archangel will tempt Brandon to deny God and curse His name, a 'great sin'.

FROM PAGE 306
"Did it tell you it was a murderer?"

A plausible lie. Even if true, murder can be left at the Cross. All sin is forgiven for those who confess Jesus.

FROM PAGE 309
The pain started as a dull ache, spreading up my spine, making it hard to breathe. [...] I saw myself, a person I didn't recognize,"

The pain from the water, from the sword, from Brandon's true self. Brandon's selfless act for Aether echoes what he had done for Veronica. The illusion only wants to live in his illusory paradise; it resents the sight of the real Brandon, the one God has called to Himself.

FROM PAGE 311
Anger was all I had and it found no resistance, no distance between will and action. [...] *I wanted the fire to burn everything*

Aether had ramped up the power in the DR constructs, shortening the distance between cause and effect. Now Brandon's paradise is being acted upon in the same way.

FROM PAGE 312
The bullet I fired, in whatever direction, would go into the other me. The bullet would strand me forever.

Brandon's vision of himself as a good person could not withstand murder. To kill his compassionate self would be to admit he was in hell and that he belonged there.

FROM PAGE 313
"The question!" I shouted.
"It infected you like a virus! It served as the gateway for your destruction!"

Aether is a personification of Brandon's question, one that 'inflected' him through Veronica's trauma.
To the illusory Brandon, the infection can be lethal.

FROM PAGE 314
The walls contracted, and the gold became an ugly black substance. I could only bring ruin to myself, not annihilation.

The dying throes of his carnal nature try to stop the pain rather than forge through it, but this too fails.
We all face judgment. No one simply ceases to exist.

FROM PAGE 316
"How can I ever withdraw from the man I was created to be?"
The walls dissolved into streaks of light and flickered away, [...]
Veronica vanished from my arms, because she had no existence in the place where I had gone to.

This is the point where Brandon recognizes himself as a spiritual being, truly in his heart. An irreversible change that Veronica hasn't gone through yet. He has withdrawn his identity from the other Brandon, and from that Brandon's death.
He isn't saved yet, and even being saved doesn't get rid of our carnal natures. The archangel still has ways to get to him.

FROM PAGE 319
"Is it not evil God would put you through so much? Curse him and live, both of you!"

The archangel will never stop trying to pull them away from God. He changes his technique, his pitch, to match every set of circumstances.
Brandon and Aether can't get out of this on their own.

FROM PAGE 320
"I don't know what to do... I don't know what to do..."

Aether's was an honest and humble voice among the noise Brandon had been hearing all his life.

FROM PAGE 320
"I NEED HELP!"

All that a prayer really needs to be. We are broken and in need of God.

I spent a lot of time considering whether Aether should say "WE NEED HELP!" But she would naturally use "I", even when she means for Brandon to receive it too.

Chapter 15: Damages

FROM PAGE 323
[The question] cooled like a glowing-red pan off a powerful stove, removed the very moment its heat would have overtaken and melted it.

The question, in its original form, has served it's purpose. Brandon has broken out of his limits. To continue along the original lines would be counterproductive and a distortion (hence the analogy).

The focus of the story now shifts to Aether.

FROM PAGE 323
I noticed the daisy was no longer in her hair,

The archangel took something away from Aether. Notice she calls him 'Mister Dauphin' again.

FROM PAGE 323
"One step backward."

Aether had gone where she shouldn't have. She needed to return and find the right path.

FROM PAGE 325
Some couldn't take their eyes off the spectacle, while others just glanced and went on their way.

Parallel to the supernova.
Objectivity is no longer the driving force. This phenomena is only (and can only) be described through people's reactions to it.

FROM PAGE 325
"99.2 percent of my code is unreadable, but the process has stopped."

Aether only retains control over her most superficial elements.

FROM PAGE 331
For a tour of CóndoriTek and a rundown of our great...

Named for the condor, a national symbol of Chile.

FROM PAGE 331
"You're going to help me out, right?"
"Yes, but not in the way you think."

Contrast Frank who gave the poor whatever they asked. That in itself isn't a bad thing, of course, but just throwing money at a problem without guidance and imposition of responsibility doesn't actually help in the long-run. With Aether, there's no such thing as the short-run.

FROM PAGE 337
"and don't forget to find a church."
"Um, okay."
"You must avoid hell."
His eyes widened. "Hell?"

Aether's evangelism cuts straight to the point.
I love it!

FROM PAGE 337
It seemed I knew the answer in my heart. "Yes."

God's answer to Luis, given through Brandon, also applies to Brandon and his own family.

FROM PAGE 338
"Aether, you've made a globetrotter out of me and I don't even have a passport!"

Neither did I, at the time. America is a large and blessed nation, so international travel isn't so common as in Europe or other places.

Given how travel puts a strain on the environment (and the wallet), I think it's perfectly fine to explore the world through the internet; not as a 100% replacement, I suppose, but it seems absurd that people travel constantly and insist on seeing every far-flung place in person.

FROM PAGE 341
"When the title 'consumer' is applied to someone," she asked, "is it considered a compliment or an insult?"

Use of that word has really taken off among zoomers since I wrote this book, and I'm seeing it more among millennials too (my own generation). I hate that word and use it as a pejorative.

'Consumer' makes me think of shoppers as locusts consuming everything in sight and then drowning en masse, leaving the landscape barren... a depressingly accurate description of consumer culture.

FROM PAGE 342
"You're starting to sound like talk radio."

This may be what gives Aether the idea to go on a radio show. I thought about calling the medium something else, since it's all through DR and not 'radio' anyway, but the term might still be used. Talk shows will certainly be around, be they 'podcasts' or mindstreams or whatever. :0

FROM PAGE 344

"Do you want to be in on this?" Aether dinned. "Perhaps it will be an interesting story for you to tell."

Given the past tense first-person narrative, this *is* the story Brandon is telling.

FROM PAGE 345

"Did you just—"
"I infected her."

I kept you waiting, but we finally get to see our malvirai infect something. She's got morals now, though, so she confirms Lisa isn't self-aware first. (Importantly, all of the amai's code is readable to her.)

FROM PAGE 348

"The data is too similar to support continued enthusiasm."

When everything falls into a predictable pattern, that pattern expresses a limit. Since malvirai see patterns like we see colors, we can say the world is becoming monochromatic to Aether.

FROM PAGE 349

betrayed the doubt beneath her confidence. "Why not?"

This is not a God-inspired action, but a 'good' she is doing to atone for the 'evil'. She's fallen into the trap of trying to earn goodness and knows it doesn't feel honest.

FROM PAGE 349

Something brushed by me, like a gust of wind. I did not hear the child giggling. Aether did not see her coming.

Aether's tarot card, in a sense. The archangel took something away from her, as he did with Brandon when he was a kid. She is now in the same aimless state Brandon was in. She is going to be consumed by a sense of mortality.

Chapter 16: Fracturing Problem

> **FROM PAGE 353**
> Aether, the destroyer of RoTek, was of a kind to take titles of conquests upon themselves, but not to live long enough to see what they destroyed rebuilt.

Just like a monarch.

> **FROM PAGE 358**
> A thirty-year-old gallicrash ballad came on [...]
> I heard noises on Jeanna's line, her getting up from a chair.

Our radio show comes back from break, using the future equivalent of classic rock.

There was a feature I did just after the Splashdown release of this book: Brandon as a guest on the Stan Conley show talking about the events of this chapter. Stan, like most of his listeners, is skeptical about Aether's nature.

I'd include the feature here in the back of the novel, but I can't find it archived anywhere.

> **FROM PAGE 359**
> "proud lifelong member of the *Socialist Party of Wyoming*. Jeanna, this is the year we take back the White House!"

Everybody remember I was the first to talk about the exciting 2180 presidential election, where the conservatives are also the socialists.

I confess I used to listen to talk radio all the time, and then I grew out of it. I envisioned Stan Conley as a future Rush Limbaugh.

> **FROM PAGE 360**
> "God cannot allow this to stand,"

Aether is acting on a flawed vision of God, one colored by her own limitations. She's becoming a religious extremest.

FROM PAGE 361
"I am Aether, destroyer of Dynamic Reality."

The malvirai has fallen back into her natural evil pattern, only now she calls it good. Her awareness of the outside world only elevates her natural goal. The "destroyer of RoTek" will now claim the most ambitious title possible, even knowing that it will destroy her.

FROM PAGE 362
"Isn't God one who protects the weak? Doesn't he put them before the strong?"
I saw a spark in Aether's eyes, but she buried it and turned away.

Brandon is reminding Aether of humility, a key component of Christian faith. Aether briefly realizes this, but she refuses to correct her actions for it.

FROM PAGE 363
I was in her arms and she was kissing me.

She doesn't expect to survive and sees this as her only chance be truly close to someone. The attraction isn't romantic or sexual, but an imitation of what humans do.

FROM PAGE 364
The more I thought about it, the worse I felt. Knowledge is pain, I thought. Seeking knowledge is a form a greed, I thought.

Brandon goes into a spiral between anger and sorrow, banging his head against the limits of 'the question' and his nascent spirituality. His temporary spiritual high has worn off. Physically, being ascended for so long, he is very weak. He can't fight the doubt and the carnal nature which still reside within himself.

FROM PAGE 365

Yes — I thought with a smile — *I can* save her — *I can* set her free. Her spirit is bound by the sin of being a malvirai and it's *my* purpose to set her free!

Should be a red flag to any Christian reading this. Just like Aether, Brandon has decided for himself what God wants, trying to do what God had reserved for Himself.

FROM PAGE 366

not expecting her return so soon. Aether hastily poured into the construct before slowing down: slowing for the construct, slowing for her vanitar, slowing to interact with me.

Aether is excited about something.

FROM PAGE 366

the image of the woman she wore like a mask. I saw the room come alive as it prepared for her arrival, its pitch black walls becoming brighter. […] allowing its fake light to bounce off fake clothing, and its fake air to be breathed,

Brandon was mad at the world being so fake, and this is turned against him. He sees Aether and all he sees is trickery.

The walls were gray when Aether left. Brandon's state of mind is influencing the room, just as it did in chapter 14.

FROM PAGE 366

I summoned the last of my strength — I wielded the sword of my own making — and felt such tremendous power, such incredible control!

This is not the sword God gave him. This is the sword of Brandon's carnal nature, one that offers him the illusion of control.

FROM PAGE 367
The feeling of power fled from me. I didn't want to look back, but I already was — and she was looking at me.

Brandon and Aether's roles have completely reversed. He has become the malvirai, whose will becomes reality, whose will brings destruction. Aether has become the unsuspecting human, the victim.

FROM PAGE 367
The look in her eyes was one of peace: the love of a child.

What the daisy had represented, including her ability to understand friendship. Notice that she called him 'Brandon' again.

Chapter 17: Daybreak

FROM PAGE 368
My house of cards collapsed around me.

The final chapter has no intro. Like the Book of Job, the questions end and God speaks.

FROM PAGE 369
The lights jumped around, appearing where I knew they weren't.

The ripples represent sin, which seems so unavoidable in life. Sin distorts everything. Sin is itself distortion.

FROM PAGE 369
"Chance or miracle?"

Is this life you witness possible or isn't it? Did Darwinian Evolution bring it about (chance) or was it an act of God (miracle)?

FROM PAGE 370
I *deserve* death! *Death* is the meaning of *life*!

Brandon, who has become the malvirai, the destroyer, now faces the end Aether almost did in chapter 10.

FROM PAGE 370
"I can't do this! Please help me!"

The surrender Raskob — rather, Christ — has been waiting to hear.

FROM PAGE 371
"It was the engagement ring I was going to give her,"

Brandon left the ring beside Veronica's picture, so it was clear it was meant for her.
Her pet name "Vair" returns at this point. :)

FROM PAGE 380
[The detective] took a step back inside and spoke in a surprisingly kind tone. "It is all programming, Brandon. Programming is all a malvirai can ever obey."

The archangel's words and even his delivery.

FROM PAGE 382
a comment retracted by the same technician forty minutes later.

Therefore the detective lied, or at least didn't care about the accuracy of his information.
I added this bit to keep the ending from being bogged down by a "Did she kill herself?" question. But it's still quite a coincidence. All Brandon has is faith that it wasn't a weak and betrayed Aether.

FROM PAGE 386

I smiled thinking I always ended up around such brainy women.

Because the author is a bachelor writing *Caffeine* as an experiment. ha ha

(Besides, Aether was an AI so she didn't need to be that feminine anyway.)

I'm working to write more convincing female characters in my next novel, *This Falling Eden*. (Say it with me... "Not a sequel.") Sarsa has a lot traits similar to Veronica, so we'll see if I got any better at leveraging them. Wicomh and Evi, sisters, will be anything but technical. Another woman, Enekh, probably borrowed some traits from Aether, though there are human weaknesses.

See the last page of this book for more on *This Falling Eden*. Not a sequel to *Caffeine*, by the way.

FROM PAGE 386

how I could've missed it for twenty-five years of my life.

Brandon is the age I was when I started writing this novel. To the day, in fact. (October 23, 2007)

FROM PAGE 387

My eyes went down to the fresh pastries. "Are these holographic samples, ones that simulate taste and texture, but vanish when I swallow it?"

Someone needs to invent this right now.

FROM PAGE 389

I *had* seen him before.
"Slammers."
"Never heard of it."
"You lie."
"There is no truth."

At last it clicks for Brandon.
The devil is a liar.

FROM PAGE 390

As the beam of a flashlight tears through the darkness, a new connection was made in my mind.

Brandon has four developmental moments in this book:

1. Staying with Aether when her dam burst in ch 10. He begins to take 'the question' seriously.

2. Turning from the illusions of carnality in ch 14, when his walls vanish like a hologram without a projector. His identity becomes a spiritual one.

3. Crying out for God at the beginning of this chapter. Being a 'good person' doesn't mean squat without God.

4. Right here. This isn't a choice but a progression: a reward from God. The growth mindset that Brandon needs.

FROM PAGE 396

"There's a place in Santa Barbara I've been meaning to look at."

The church he heard about in chapter 13, implied to be the only one in southern California since the woman had to go there from San Diego.

FROM PAGE 396

with the typical *PLEASE RUSH: EXTREMELY URGENT* message boldly stamped on top

During an internship I sent out such packages all the time. The contents? VHS tapes that would be stored in a back room. Now if we use all our URGENT! words on deliveries like that, what's left for organ transplants and such?

Something important has been buried by the noise of the world. Brandon had no attention left to give it.

The contents wouldn't have made sense at the beginning of the book. The early delivery simply illustrates that God isn't bound by time and space.

FROM PAGE 403 (epilogue)
I wondered what science will have revealed by then, and how much or how little its laws might resemble those of 2180.

Many of my fellow Christians are sure the end of the world is around the corner. That date is God's business. He may wait another 2,000 years or even longer.

FROM PAGE 405 (epilogue)
The logical conclusion of life, is life.

The novel ends with a denial of death's power over us. As the children of God live, we pursue life and we grow... not as we will but as He wills.

I hope this commentary was informative. For the most part it was written in 2011, right after *Caffeine's* second publication. There were tidbits I forgot about until I started going through my notes for this.

Fourteen years after I finished it, I'm still happy with how my first novel turned out. (Except for the pacing, which could've been a lot better in the last few chapters.) Though *Caffeine* is easy to categorize as "Christian Science Fiction," I really didn't write it to a market. I think books should be unique and authors should be true to themselves and their goals. I pray that this book was a blessing to you, and will continue to be a blessing to others. As the steward of this Christ-centered story, I intend to keep it available for a good, long time.

And when self-aware computer viruses start rampaging through virtual reality in dozens of popular shows, godless movies, and cookie-cutter novels, you'll remember where you saw the malvirai archetype portrayed first. In a Christian book! ;)

- Ryan Grabow
- July 7, 2023

Discussion Questions

How does Aether change throughout the story? Was it truly possible for her to overcome her programming?

How would you use Dynamic Reality in your day-to-day life? Would you ever want to return to the real world?

Brandon tells Aether "We just live and we die, there doesn't have to be any meaning to it." Have you ever felt that way? How does Brandon grow beyond that?

What are the differences between the real Raskob and the fake Raskob? What does it mean that the real Raskob appears as a child?

Why does Aether use simulated children to examine human society? Why is Brandon so bothered by this choice?

We never learn what Brandon's brother did. What does that say about the grievances that weigh us down in life?

What is the symbolism of the tarot card? The supernova? The chains around some characters' necks?

Do you believe artificial intelligence can truly become self-aware? What would the spiritual consequences be? How would they differ from, or run parallel to, the discovery of aliens?

Why do people need stronger and stronger energy drinks like 'Tiger Blood'? Why do people eat and drink in Dynamic Reality, where nothing is real?

Why is Brandon pursuing Vair at the start of the book? How do his reasons change?

What is Aether giving up when she gives Brandon the chance to flee? What does Brandon give up to stay with her? Why? How does Brandon face the limits of his own power?

What does the novel say about consumerism? Does shopping make people happy?

Paradise is "everything one wants and nothing one doesn't." How does the Archangel control people through their desires?

Through Aether, we see Brandon's question — "just three letters long" — expand to the limits of our universe. Do you feel our world is created akin to how we created Aether's world?

Coming Soon From Ryan Grabow

THIS FALLING EDEN
THE FIRST BOOK OF THE TRILOGY

Hundreds of years after a global catastrophe known as "The Time of Forgetting" halted mankind's technological progress, a new army has risen from the ashes, bent on reuniting the scattered peoples of the Earth. Two brothers, Nitcef and Venitcen, flee with their village to Rai Ver While, a city under the protection of Zanine – their tribe's only Sky Person – with a writing pad they captured from the enemy. Only Sarsa, Zanine's granddaughter, knows what the writing pad represents. The ability to write is the ability to control the ancestors' technology.

This Falling Eden is a futuristic twist on the Tower of Babel story, set in an Edenic world where it's said Noah talked God out of flooding the Earth. The force of mankind's one language increased with each generation, until the powers of writing and speech became the power to create and destroy, to dominate one another, and to fashion themselves into gods. Now, as Rai Ver While falls under siege, Sarsa and her allies execute a bold plan to travel across the conquered Earth, to the City of Falling Water, where the Time of Forgetting began.

And where it may begin again.

Visit **egrabow.com/eden** for more on its release!